MISTY CREEK

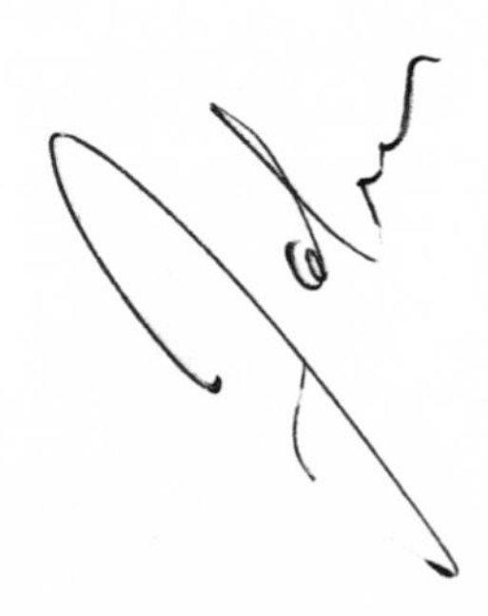

Misty Creek

John W. Vander Velden

Palmetto Publishing Group
Charleston, SC

Misty Creek

ISBN-13: 978-1-64111-065-5
ISBN-10: 1-64111-065-1

Dedication

To Jacqueline, the love of my life. You are my greatest friend…my inspiration.

Also

Glory to God the Father…who gives me life.
The Holy Spirit…who gives me courage.
And Jesus the Son…who gives me purpose!!!

Part 1
The Dusty Road

CHAPTER 1

IT WAS HOT. HOTTER THAN SHE WOULD HAVE ANTICIPATED. FOR the place Elizabeth found herself was far different than the image she had created in her mind's eye, the weeks and months since she had agreed to this adventure. From the seat of the freight wagon, she scanned the gently undulating, nearly table-flat landscape of sun burnt waist-high grass swaying in the breeze. The grass moved like waves across the land, an ocean in various shades of brown that stretched to the distant horizon in every direction. A featureless country broken only by the dust strips they traveled, a land dried up and dead.

What, she thought, *drove those that came to this place?* There was no life it seemed, nothing that held any promise, absolutely nothing. Those thoughts caused her own reasons for coming west to swirl in her mind. She had not been cast off by her parents. On the contrary, Marion and Theodore Beck had begged her to reconsider. It was not her love of teaching and the tremendous need in Kansas that drew her. No, she was driven by other forces. A May weekend, a moment when broken promises, shattered her dreams. How the tears that had flooded down her cheeks and spilled upon her white gown, and washed away all her hopes and plans. Later she wandered Columbus, little more than a ghost, empty and lost, needing a new purpose. And going west to Misty Creek seemed to be that purpose.

She considered the months since she had announced her plans, how defiantly she had stood facing each argument, as everyone pleaded against her going west. Having taught for seven years, Elizabeth felt prepared for anything. No longer a child, she had traveled before, lived on her own, made her way. Was this post so different? But soon found herself furthest from the center of her universe, and had only begun the journey. As time passed and miles fell behind, Elizabeth's confidence shrank like an iceberg drifting into warm seas.

Even before the train rumbled and rattled across the Mississippi, the landscape had changed. Through the dark night they had trr-rumbled on, and the morning revealed an alien world, an open land with widely scattered farms. Elizabeth saw few farmsteads in the distance as they passed, standing lonely with their unpainted barns of weather darkened wood. But even that view could not be compared to the land that now surrounded, an indescribable emptiness that showed no sign of human existence.

Elizabeth did not consider herself adventurous. As little as six months ago, this trek would have been beyond imagining, but her pain and the void within her heart demanded a new environment. The need for a new place drove her, not the label others had used—running away. Elizabeth was no driveling child. Throughout her life she had faced countless challenges and setbacks. Even that May Saturday, when she faced the church filled with tight-lipped faces and accusatory eyes, she did not flee.

Perhaps others had come west out of similar need. How was Elizabeth to know? But would they have come if they knew of the desolation that awaited? Looking across the open land of windblown brown grass, a lifeless place, Elizabeth knew she wouldn't.

Elizabeth drew a breath and grabbed hold of the hand rail, when the wagon struck a particularly large hole or bump or something. Her mind went back to the moment she had stepped from the train. Nothing had prepared her for Thimble. Elizabeth felt the last of her resolve abandon as she stood on the station's landing, at the edge of the place, for she could scarcely call the few clapboard buildings and dirt street a town. When she scanned the leathery faces of those nearby, it took the last of her courage not to turn around, board the train, surrender, and return home. For at that moment her father's words came to mind, "Take care my daughter, there are dangers for a woman traveling alone." Elizabeth had given a silent prayer as she scanned those around her, wondering at the wisdom of her actions.

Returning to the present, she looked to her right, for beside her, with reins in worn dark leather gloved hands, sat Reverend Benjamin Smith. Elizabeth remembered the letter of instruction that she had received from the Misty Creek Board of Education. It had comforted her to learn that the pastor would meet her at the train, the rail's end, for that was what it was, literally the end of the line. Elizabeth was familiar with trains, there were many rail lines where she came from, Ohio, but she had never even considered that a railroad would just end somewhere. Didn't trains go on and on? When Elizabeth arrived, she had looked for the parson, a dark suit perhaps, a collar or tie in the very least, but none were to be found. To be honest she was concerned, coming all that way and alone to a strange place, the very end of civilization, that is if you could consider a rail line a symbol of such things, and no preacher in sight.

How the reverend picked her out, Elizabeth had no certainty, but striding toward her was this cowboy. A tall man much younger than she had expected, dressed in dungarees, a faded light blue shirt, boots, and a wide brimmed hat, which he immediately removed. The man's skin was weathered, tanned from the sun, a sun that was much more intense than she had expected. When he offered his hand, it was hard and rough, very un-preacher like. But Reverend Smith's eyes, bright and deep, a very blue, surprised her as well, for Elizabeth considered those to be the eyes of one of fair skin. She felt certain that anyone of such a rough appearance would likely need serious dental care, teeth missing perhaps, and certainly dark stains on whatever enamel might remain, but Reverend Smith's smile revealed only bright teeth—all of them. The pastor's smile seemed such a contrast to the apparent hooligan whose hand she had shaken.

Elizabeth's expression must have shown her concern, even fear, for the pastor did his best, much more than she might have expected, to verify that he was indeed who he claimed to be. Yet she was certain he was the most un-pastor pastor that ever existed. His voice was strong and very clear his language most un-frontier, if the men she had heard on the train ride were any indication. Yes, by the time he had taken her bag to the hotel, Elizabeth could almost imagine that he was a cowboy preacher, or something to that effect.

Later they had met for supper in the hotel's restaurant. Reverend Smith had changed his clothes, though there was little difference. If one had not taken the time to notice the pattern of his shirt, one would think he simply removed them to put them on again. The meal was good, actually as good as any she had eaten, which surprised her as well. The following day, they met for an early breakfast, again the food was pleasant, for he, the pastor, or whatever he was, needed an early start.

That was this morning, only a few hours ago, shortly before they left any signs of life in this barren wasteland, this "God forsaken" country. Elizabeth felt ashamed for attaching the Lord's name. It was not her way to take it in vain, not even in her thoughts. Though Elizabeth had not spoken but a couple dozen words, the pastor—and with the passing of time it continued to become more likely he actually was one—spoke a great deal. Reverend Smith also broke the noise of the lumbering wagon by whistling, loudly to be sure, and on occasions would burst to song, a hymn, though often not a familiar one.

So the morning had passed, and it grew hot. "You'll find the sun pretty bright," the pastor said, as he removed his hat and wiped his brow with the back of his hand. "It'll be getting hotter."

Hotter! Elizabeth couldn't imagine.

"You have picked such a dark color. This is no place to wear black." It was not black, the dress was blue. "That dress may not have been your wisest choice." The Pastor had mentioned this before they left Thimble, and offered to wait while she changed into something of lighter color and perhaps lighter weight. Elizabeth had instructed him, for that was what she did, being a teacher, that she would be fine. However it was not yet mid-day and Elizabeth was not so certain that fine was the proper description of her condition.

The road—calling it that would in the least be an exaggeration, for it was just two strips of dust stretching, wandering in a general direction, west she thought—seemed to go on and on over the gently rolling land. How many hours they had lumbered on she could not know, when at last they came to a stop. Elizabeth hoped they had neared their destination.

"We will stop," Ben informed her. "The horses will need a bit of rest." Which of course they did, pulling the wagon, loaded to the hearth, with crates and large burlap bags and her trunk and carpet bag as well. Reverend Smith jumped off the wagon, spryer than Elizabeth would have expected, and much more so than she thought she would be, and offered his hand to help her down. He was indeed a gentleman.

The teacher felt stiff and found moving about, though difficult, returned circulation to areas she would not discuss with any man, particularly with a pastor. A wind blew. She had noticed it all morning, a dry wind across a dry land. Elizabeth watched as Ben gave water to the tired beasts. He gently stroked the animals as he spoke to them. And though his voice was louder than need, his tone quieter than the booming hymn singer that had ridden beside her.

"You should let your hair down," Ben said.

"I beg your pardon!" her sharp response.

"Your hair, you have bound it up, so, so, school mar'm. You'll be cooler if you let it fall loose."

"I'll do nothing of the kind. And you know well enough, Pastor Smith, if indeed you are a pastor, I am a school schoolmarm as you so aptly put it!"

"Yes, yes, I know, I meant nothing by it, didn't intend to offend..."

"But you have, and most inappropriately I might add." Yes, Elizabeth was angry, very angry. She had very nearly abandoned this adventure to return to where things were normal, for certainly there was nothing normal here. Yes, after this, pastor had escorted her to the hotel yesterday evening. When Elizabeth had seen things as they were, she returned to the station to book passage home. But while she had waited for the gentleman at the window, she wondered what others might think. She remembered Mitchel Dogerty's words, "You'll be back in a couple of weeks." Mitchel grew up right next door and had been a constant thorn in her side. She had always considered the neighbor more than a bit too outspoken. Perhaps it was pride that caused her to turn away from the thin ticket clerk with the graying moustache and balding head who asked if he could help her. However at this moment, here in the absolute middle of nowhere, the teacher regretted her decision.

In her anger, Elizabeth was about to tell this wagon driver that they would go back, when he spoke again. "I'm sorry Miss Beck. It wasn't my place. It's just, you look so hot. I'm worried, that's all."

The teacher would have thought they were just words but when she looked into his clear blue eyes, she saw true concern. Elizabeth did not respond, but felt her anger soften.

"I know I should not mention it again, but don't you have something else you could wear? The sun's hard on a body," he continued more softly.

Elizabeth had to agree, the day had become intense, and if the pastor was correct it was bound to become hotter. But she was a lady. Elizabeth huffed. "And what do you propose? We are, after all, in the very middle of nowhere!"

"Being in the middle of nowhere offers the potential of a solution," he said from across the wagon.

"Surely, you do not suggest I am able to change garments out here in the open, with no dressing room in sight. I am a lady, sir, and you haven't the slightest knowledge of a woman's wardrobe and the complications thereof."

The pastor, looking downward, just shook his head. "Miss Beck, I do not profess a complete knowledge of such things, but I am a married man. I do understand the slightest, that is, about dresses and the like, perhaps a bit more."

Elizabeth laughed. Truly she had been riding with a man of words. It had never occurred to her, not for one moment, that this freight driving pastor might have a wife. *What type of woman,* she wondered, *would marry such a coarse, weatherworn man.* She had an opinion, but allowed that to remain with her. "So, sir, what do you suggest?"

The smile that her laughter had caused left the pastor's face as he became dead earnest. "Since we are, as you say, miles and miles from anyone, perhaps you could consider this"—he waved his arms indicating the whole outdoors—"as a dressing room provided by God Himself."

"I am not certain I find that completely comforting. You make it sound as if I must change my dress before the eyes of God. And what about you, pastor?"

"I will wander to that hill yonder and not look back. I assure you of that. The walk should take several minutes, and you can observe my progress from across the wagon. When I reach the hill, I will begin my return. I would expect you had finished by then," he said with a twinkle in his eye, a twinkle that made her uncomfortable. "As for God," he continued, "He is everywhere and no less in your private boudoir." With that, he turned and began to walk slowly away.

"Pastor Smith," she called, "I see you are an honorable man, and one that would respect a lady. There is no need for you to go so far. If you turn your back, it would be enough."

He spoke without turning. "The walk will do me good, if you get my meaning?"

She watched him for a moment, wondering just what kind of man Reverend Benjamin Smith truly was. It then occurred to her that she needed to get her bag. Climbing clumsily upon the wagon, moving amongst the crates and large rough burlap bags she found her valise, wedged firmly. Evidently the load had shifted as they had bounced along. It took three good yanks to pull it free, resulting in not only the case leaving the wagon but a teacher tumbling off as well. It was her most good fortune to alight upon the carpetbag rather than the baked, dusty earth at the back end of the wagon.

She was certain that she had shrieked, most at the surprise of it all, and then thumped, loudly, it seemed in her head, as she lighted most ungraciously. Gathering her wits, she rose, and then looking at her traveling companion, was both relieved and upset that he had apparently not noticed. Elizabeth was relieved that he would not think her a clumsy oaf, but though she could not understand why, she found herself concerned that he had not rushed to her aid.

Dusting off her clothing, the teacher realized the parson had very nearly reached his destination, and she had yet to begin the task that had demanded the privacy in the first place.

The catch on her bag seemed particularly stubborn, and it seemed to take an eternity to open. The perspiration she had noticed on her face was, it seemed, not reserved for that portion of her body, as her dress resisted every inch. Tripping in the folds of her dark blue dress, Elizabeth fell once more. This did not improve her mood in the least. Sitting in the tall dry grass she at last pulled the dress over her head and threw it aside. At that moment, of course at that moment, the horses decided to begin the journey, without passenger or driver. Panicked she watched as they moved, relieved that the animals only wandered a couple of steps to find a bit of grass to munch upon. Dizzily she stood once more grabbing the first light colored item of clothing she found and dove into it, just as Reverend Smith turned on the hilltop. Elizabeth was glad it was some distance away. Now she took but a moment to gather herself, slow her breathing, and prepare to repack her bag. The teacher nearly forgot the dark colored torture chamber she had been wearing and had to reopen the bag, which was stubborn once again, and thrashed that dress within.

The pastor looked at her with some alarm upon his return, for she was panting like she had just finished a foot race, rather than one that had simply changed a garment. "Evidently you were correct, Miss Beck. It seems I had no concept of how difficult a process this was to be."

"All is in hand, Reverend Smith," she responded, "all is in hand." Then without waiting for the offer of assistance, she swung her bag forcefully over the wagon's sideboard allowing it to fly very nearly beyond the other side. It settled into place not so very far from where she had found it. The pastor seemed impressed, which, for reasons she couldn't understand, pleased her.

There was a question in the young pastor's eyes, and she wondered what it might be. "Ma'am," he said at last, "perhaps you would like to cover your head?"

Elizabeth looked at him blankly, not because she was confused at the question, but rather she had no idea what had become of the bonnet she had worn only moments before. Without answering she looked down about the grass that was all around her.

Smith perceiving the situation, asked, "Have you by chance placed it in your bag?"

Of course, that was what had become of the elusive item. She moved quickly to the back of the wagon and climbed aboard the loaded vehicle, but the pastor, who was in all truth much closer to the carpet bag, signed for her to allow his assistance. He grabbed the bag and, walking quickly, met her at the back of the wagon. Handing her the bag, he turned, returning to his place, leaning against the wagon and looking across windblown prairie.

Elizabeth struggled once more with the catch; the task seemed to take much longer than it did before. The open bag revealed the crumpled dark blue dress she had wadded at near panic into it. Her bonnet was nowhere to be seen. She dug through her clothes searching, twice. Blinking, Elizabeth began looking about the wagon once more. Then, shaking her head, she prepared to seal her case again, when she noticed the bonnet mixed in the dress she had removed. Relieved, she placed the wrinkled bonnet upon her head with trembling hands.

Smith apparently heard the sound of her closing the stubborn valise, for he was there to take the troublesome luggage and place it once more on the load. The Pastor then helped her back up to the seat, and at last they were on their way again.

"That dress becomes you," Ben said at last.

"This thing," she asked? Elizabeth, in truth, had not taken the time to really notice her selection. It was a soft pale color, a lightweight yellow dress. Her favorite, and certainly not one she had intended to wear while traveling across these wastelands. She worried about what damage hour after hour of bouncing on a wagon seat might do to her newest garment, and the impression it would make upon her arrival. At long last she thanked the parson for his compliment and asked. "What time do you predict we should reach Misty Creek?"

"If things go well," Ben began, "we should get there before dark." Since it was yet morning, the statement alarmed her, but the pastor had yet to finish. "Tomorrow."

Tomorrow! Could the man have said tomorrow? She looked about the desolate land, land she was certain that had no life. The endless expanse of rolling windblown grass beneath the cloudless pale blue sky. It seemed a featureless void going on forever. Elizabeth felt dejected. Ben glanced her way. "It's a good day's wagon ride to Misty Creek, but we have two stops to make on the way."

"You make the journey often?" she asked.

"While the road is passable, every month."

"Passable?" she asked alarmed.

The pastor chuckled. "The road isn't always as fine as it is today."

The road did in no way seem fine, just two strips of dust through miles of dead, brown, tall grass swaying in the wind, looking much like waves. Elizabeth just shook her head.

"When the snows come, well, it's just not safe to go out so far. And when the snow melts the way is just too soft." With a flick of the reins he coaxed the horses on.

"It gets cold in western Kansas as well?"

Ben laughed heartily. She had begun to like his laugh. "Yes, Miss Beck, it does get cold. And when the wind blows across the prairie it can be bitter. It's no place a person chooses."

"You don't go out? I mean outdoors."

The pastor looked over his brow tightened with seriousness in his eyes. "If I have a choice. But often you can't hide from what needs to be done. It'll have to be a real emergency for anyone to go from Misty Creek to the rail head in the winter."

"So all winter you are cut off?"

"Cut off?" the pastor asked, confused.

"Yes," she added, "cut off from civilization." That is if anyone could have called that place, Thimble, an appropriate name as far as she was concerned, civilization. For it was little more than a single dirt street between two saloons, a general store, and the hotel.

The pastor's voice took a sharp edge as he responded. "It may seem that to be separated from the rail road is cut off, as you say, but I can assure you we are not uncivilized." His eyes looked directly ahead as he once more snapped the reins.

Though Elizabeth had not intended, she felt certain by the hard tone in his words, she had offended the man. The teacher prepared to attempt an apology, when Ben pointed upward. Far above, soaring, was a great bird, a hawk he told her. She could hear its shrill voice carried on the breeze.

"He's warning everyone that we're here," he said.

Elizabeth looked all about, shading her eyes, but saw nothing. "Warning whom?" she asked.

"Oh, he isn't intending to, but that scream carries a long way. The rabbits, ground squirrels, prairie hens and all the rest, they hear, and they know." After glancing her way, he continued. "It's not as empty or dead as you might think. With time you'll see."

They rode on and soon the pastor began whistling again, loud and clear. Elizabeth sat steadying herself each time the wagon would jounce while she searched for any sign that life indeed existed in that desolate place. At last they stopped for lunch, a lunch the pastor provided. Smith once more cared for the beasts of burden, which seemed his first priority. Caring for the animals before he took anything for himself. With the horses tended and a few words of grace given, they ate in the shade of the wagon. The midday sun shone so intense in a cloudless pale blue sky.

Miss Elizabeth would never admit to the man that she was grateful she had changed her dress, even if she must be ever watchful not to ruin the fine garment she wore. How foolish she felt choosing the dress her mother had given her. Elizabeth's mind went to the last time she had shopped with her mother and her sister, Catherine. How she loved the dress in the window of Carsen's Dress shop on Maple Street, but knew it was an extravagance. Yet her mother must have seen the wanting look and purchased it. *Pure vanity,* Elizabeth thought, yet she loved her mother's action, which spoke much more than the garment itself.

As she considered those left behind, they seemed so far off. Elizabeth drew a breath. She ran her hands over the yellow fabric with its tiny white flowers. How many times had she and her mother butt heads, and about things much more important that any dress? Yet never had she doubted her mother's love. Elizabeth turned her head as she looked over the brown landscape, so empty and wondered what her mother and father were doing at that moment, oh how she missed them.

She heard her father's words as if floating on the breeze, "Remember, no matter where you find yourself, daughter, we are never beyond your reach. That is the way of love, isn't it? God has bound our hearts together and nothing, especially distance, can break that binding."

Elizabeth bit her lip and hoped it was true. She swallowed as she glanced to the pastor beside her, his eyes looking directly into hers.

"You seem a thousand miles away."

Doing her best to dampen the quiver in her voice as she attempted a smile. "I suppose I was."

Ben turned looking across the land as well. "This is a faraway place. At least far from the place you knew."

Yes, it was far in every way.

They remained there longer than she would have thought necessary. But after Ben had checked his pocket watch for the fourth time, they prepared to be underway.

"You mentioned you have two stops to make," she said as they rumbled along.

The Pastor smiled. "Oh yes, we come to the crossroads soon. Then we veer to the right, a couple hours further we'll reach Hancock's Bluff. We will spend the night there. Mrs. Jenkins, a fine woman, I 'spect she'll have space for you."

"Mrs. Jenkins?"

"Yes, Mrs. Eloise Jenkins. She has the biggest place. It's her home and the closest thing to a store between Thimble and Misty Creek."

"Is there a Mr. Jenkins?"

"Was. But the man died years ago, so I'm told."

"And she didn't leave?" Elizabeth asked.

Benjamin Smith looked at her, blinked twice and asked. "Where would she go? Hancock's her home, been there for years."

"But this . . ." She swept her arm pointing to the seemingly unending emptiness that surrounded them.

"You haven't seen the half of it," he said, cutting her off.

"Then there's better?"

"Yes," he said forcefully, "and worse. But no matter, it's home, where most are born and many have died. For most they are as much a part of this land as the wind or the grass. I'm sure Eloise wouldn't fit in anywhere else."

Elizabeth wondered what kind of woman, a widow at that, belonged to this country. She was certain that it was beyond her imagination, and worse, she was bound to stay under the same roof as this pioneer. What had she gotten herself into?

Her father had begged her not to go out west. Theodore Beck had tried to warn her of hardships he felt certain would await there. But she had not believed, not really. Exaggerations she was sure. Exaggerations he had used to try to keep her closer to home, for Elizabeth had read the newspaper articles and was fascinated by the romance and the excitement of the prairie. And it was the nineteenth century for pity sake, such conditions no longer existed. But now, after so many hours trudging across the open land, she no longer was certain of either her father's exaggerations or her own desires.

CHAPTER 2

ELIZABETH DID NOT SPEAK MUCH AS THEY TRUNDLED ALONG through the hot afternoon. On arriving at the crossroads when they turned to the right, her anxiety began to grow. It was late afternoon, perhaps four, when they approached three children standing along the road. The boy and two girls bounced excitedly as the wagon approached.

Reverend Benjamin Smith took his hat with his right hand and swept it as a greeting, which initiated shrieks of joy, causing the children to dash ahead shouting, "Pastor's here!"

Elizabeth saw the grand smile on the young pastor's face when he coaxed the team onward. "Those would be Joan and Dorothy Ridder and their cousin Jacob Hancock. And yes, his family is why the place has its name."

Elizabeth watched the children run ahead, but saw no town or any settlement, not even a solitary house. As they moved along, they approached what appeared to be random metal pipes protruding out of the land near the hill's edge. The road wound between these blackened pipes which Elizabeth felt must be chimneys. The chimneys protruding out of the hillside made no sense until the wagon rolled down the hill and she saw the fronts of the homes that made up Hancock Bluff.

"The folks here live in sod homes," the pastor explained. "Houses made of the soil cut out of the hillside."

The teacher wondered how people could live so, burrowed beneath the ground like so many gophers. She shook her head at the thought. The pastor glanced her way. "Take care what judgments you make, Ma'm," he said. The comment startled her. Elizabeth found it uncanny, that he seemed to know her inner thoughts.

"Sod houses might appear strange to the unaccustomed, but the homes on the prairie are built out of need. It's impossible, to keep out all the rain when it comes, or the snows melt for that matter, but 'soddies' are both cooler in summer and much warmer in the winter than conventional structures," Smith told her. He paused and wiped his brow again. "There is the other factor, the lack of construction material. You have noticed that we have not passed a single tree since we left Thimble. You see wood for any purpose has to be shipped in, not an easy proposition and very expensive."

The road wound to the left and moved in front of the homes. Elizabeth noticed that the house on the end had been made larger. A more conventional structure built in front, an unpainted wood frame building of two stories that appeared to grow out of the hill itself. The children had gathered in front of that weathered clapboard structure, mulling around in the dusty street. As the creaking wagon approached, Elizabeth saw that Dorothy, Jacob, and Joan were joined by others waiting there—four younger children, two about the same age as their greeters, and a tall girl who appeared older. But the children were not alone. For standing in the hot afternoon sun were men and women, those whose appearance reflected the hard life lived. Men of ages she could not even hope to guess, stood with their wives, women with stern expressions on their sun-weathered faces. As the wagon came to a stop in front of the large house, two men walked up and without a word unhooked the horses and led them to a paddock nearby.

Before the pastor left the wagon, he stood, raised an off-white canvas bag, and shouted, "Who wants mail?" Everyone gathered around as he handed out the six envelopes. The teacher watched as those that received a letter generously shared their documents with any, and all. It was a social event, like nothing she had ever witnessed.

Ben smiled, content just to watch the moment. He climbed down at last, moved to the other side of the wagon to help her off. Elizabeth found herself surrounded by what must have been everyone in that small place. The pastor informed her it was not only those who lived at the bluff that had gathered, but also others that resided on the homesteads thereabouts.

Ben raised a hand. "Hey everyone," he began, "I wish to introduce Miss Beck, the new teacher at Misty Creek." The reaction of the group took Elizabeth by surprise, every eye seemed focused upon her and she did not know how to react to the attention. Then Ben introduced her to the locals. There was Mr. and Mrs. Thomas Lincoln and their three children, Mark, Luke and Joanna. The Lincolns, like many others, had moved to the bluff after Mrs. Lincoln's brother, Abner Holm and his entire family perished their first winter, unprepared and cut off. The influenza she was told. For most of the residents of Hancock's Bluff were farmers that had clustered together in the hope to improve their chances. Smith continued introducing all those that had gathered. So many names, she could not hope to remember them all.

When at last it seemed she had shaken every hand, the crowd parted, allowing an older woman to pass through. The years and their toil apparent upon her, yet she stood straight and tall. The woman approached with a walking stick in hand, a stick Elizabeth felt certain she did not need. She stood nearly as tall as the pastor. Beneath her bonnet was a face weathered by years of sun and wind with dark sharp eyes that focused on the young teacher. Though Elizabeth could not guess what was on the woman's mind, for she did not have the pastor's gift in that regard, the gaze did not make her uncomfortable.

"Who'd ya bring, Pastor?"

Smith smiled. "Why Eloise, this is Miss Beck. She'll be teaching in Misty Creek."

Turning to Elizabeth he added, "This is the lady I spoke of, Mrs. Eloise Jenkins."

The old woman drew an eyebrow. "I ain't been called a lady in more years than I can remember."

There was determination on the old woman's features as they stood face to face. Elizabeth held out her hand. Mrs. Jenkins paused a moment, as if to examine the gesture, stood straight faced, squinting her eyes slightly, tilting her head a bit to the right, glanced then to the preacher, and at last took the outstretched hand. Elizabeth felt that Mrs. Jenkins could crush her hand with her rough leather-like grip. A smile came to the old face. A smile that revealed few teeth. She drew Elizabeth in and wrapped her arm around the young teacher.

"Come with me dear. You must be tired. I'm sure it's been a long day. I 'spect it weren't no picnic. It'd wore out a local." Jenkins' voice came hard and harsh. The old woman led the confused teacher up the steps, across the porch, and into what passed for a store. Eloise stopped a moment at the doorway turned and called out. "Pastor, did that order come?"

With a wave of his hand, Smith indicated it had.

"Joe," Eloise shouted. "Bring it into the store, will ya?"

Elizabeth heard someone callout an affirmative as the door closed. She was led through the front room, a large room that was used as a shop, yet was surprised how little was stocked. Elizabeth scanned the space that contained some canned goods scattered sparsely upon the shelves. She saw a few bolts of fabric, browns, dull blues, and greens draped across a saw horse. A few other things caught her eye. Behind the counter, a carton of cartridges shared a shelf there with a box of cigars. But it was mostly open space. The room beyond was smaller, sparsely furnished with a couple of hard-back chairs and a rocker. A lamp stood on a small round table in one corner next to the rocking chair. The floor lay uncovered made of worn wide-wood planking. The only light entered through the room's single window, passing through threadbare curtains. It was hot. A slight breeze flowed in the open window and out the door to the other room, but seemed unable to relieve them of the afternoon's swelter. Mrs. Jenkins pointed toward the rocker. "Have a seat."

Elizabeth prepared to protest, for she could see the worn rocker was the best chair in the room. She did not wish to impose, depriving her hostess from the chair which obviously was her own, but understood to do so would be rude. She thanked Mrs. Jenkins and settled into the chair, which she found quite comfortable, adding to her feeling of guilt. With brows drawn slightly, Mrs. Eloise Jenkins looked over the teacher once more. Elizabeth considered the words she might share with the woman that was to be her hostess. But before she could assemble a thought, Eloise left her, slipping out a door on the room's opposite end. Clanking sounds came from the direction the old woman had gone, and soon Mrs. Jenkins returned a pair of glasses filled with water. The old woman handed a glass to Elizabeth as she settled into the closest chair.

Taking a sip Eloise asked, "How was the trip, Missy?"

"I must say, much different than I expected."

"Come most of the way by train, I 'spect."

Elizabeth nodded.

Eloise looked across the room toward the window. "Never been on one, weren't no train..." the old woman blinked. "Must make the travelin' easy."

Elizabeth had not considered the rail crossing easy, but compared to the day in the wagon's seat, she had to agree. "Much easier than when you came, I'm sure."

Eloise's eyes rose as she swayed slightly side to side. "You come far?"

"Columbus, Ohio."

"That is a far piece, yes it is." The old woman lifted the glass to her lips once again. "Family there?"

"Yes, ma'am."

"Don't you be call'n me ma'am, or else I might be think'n' the preacher's right by callin' me a lady. I'm Eloise, just plain old Eloise. I'd be pleased if'n you call me so."

Elizabeth smiled. "Yes, ma'am, I mean Eloise. My parents and a brother and sister all live in Columbus. Father is a banker there."

"A banker, you say. Don't that beat all?" she shook her head. "And you come all this way ta teach them young'uns. I 'spect your pa and ma weren't real pleased about that."

Elizabeth knew the truth to that statement.

Eloise tilted her head and asked, "You be the oldest?"

"Yes, but how did you know?"

"Didn't really. You seem ta be in charge, of yourself that is. Your ma and pa didn't stop ya. I 'spect it takes grit to head out on your own."

"And you think only the oldest has, what did you call it, grit?"

Eloise shook her head firmly. "No, that ain't what I meant. Just that, well, I cain't quite explain. But it don't surprise me none, you being the oldest."

"And you, Eloise, were you the oldest?"

"Phs'aw deary, I be as close to the middle as can be. There were fourteen of us born, six before and seven after. Four never made out of diapers…and…" The old woman stopped, drew a breath. "I'm all that's left of that brood, and who knows…"

Elizabeth thought it was wise to change the subject. "Eloise, is it always so hot in September?'

"Tends so. Hot and dry, though it is dry most of the year. Been a bit dryer than usual." The woman's eyes darted left and right.

Finally the conversation turned to Reverend Benjamin Smith.

"What do you think of our pastor?" Eloise asked, tilting her head slightly.

Elizabeth thought a moment, considered what words she should use, wondering if she really knew the man at all. "I'm not sure," she said at last.

A smile crossed the old woman's face. "I guess I'm not either." Eloise leaned back in her chair and looked across the room. "This old body has seen some things," she said softly, "some things better off forgotten. But I have seen more than my fair share of preachers." She said more firmly. "And as far as I'm concerned, most ain't worth a spoonful of spit."

Elizabeth was surprised by the candor and nearly dropped the glass she held. The old woman noticed and quickly, surprisingly so, rose from her seat, took the glass asked Elizabeth if she would like more. She gratefully declined her hostess who set the glasses on a table and then went on. "But Ben's different."

"How so?" Elizabeth asked.

The old woman's eyes gleamed. Smiling, she said, "You'll see. Yes, you'll see."

Elizabeth's mind filled with questions. And by the look in Eloise's eyes, it was apparent that the woman saw them, for with the slightest smile she added. "We'd best get outside, the meetin's probably about ta start, and I ain't been late ta one."

Though Elizabeth had no idea what meeting Eloise spoke of, there seemed an urgency to the words, and so together they made their way to the store's porch. In the shade of the house-store's roof that overhung the dusty boards, they found a pair of chairs. Eloise shooed out two youngsters that had taken residence in them, settled into one and signed that the teacher should take the other.

Elizabeth looked out to the area that lay in front of her, the open land that the road crossed, yet could not be considered a street. Everyone of that place had gathered there, and with the arrival of Mrs. Jenkins, it seemed the meeting could begin. Benjamin Smith walked quickly, Elizabeth had never seen him walk any other way, with a black book in hand and took his place before the people, a place he was evidently familiar with. Then Elizabeth realized that this meeting would be a service.

From her place, a few steps up, she could see not only the reverend, but all the assembly, and observed how those gathered carried a serious earnestness on the faces. Even the children remained silent as they stood at their parents' sides. It was in that place, in that time, at that moment, Elizabeth first observed the freight hauling preacher at work. He had not changed clothing. Ben yet looked very much like a cowboy, though now he wore no hat. She watched the man as he prepared to begin, his sandy hair blowing about in the unceasing wind. His voice came clear and strong. Elizabeth listened as he prayed, as he read from the gospel, and as he preached. Yes, Rev Smith was very different from any preacher she had heard before. There was no angry ranting, no accusations, no warnings of damnation. Rather he spoke words of hope and promises that could be relied upon. There was only love.

As Elizabeth listened to that brief message of God's love for his people. Yes, his people here in this windblown wasteland, the teacher felt a tear come to her eye. Never had she in all her years been so moved by words—the words spoken by a preacher. And Elizabeth knew that it was not only God that loved the people of Hancock's Bluff but also a man. A man with reins in his hand, a team of horses in his control, who came to them with much more than the mail and a few parcels. And she understood exactly what Eloise meant, Benjamin Smith was different.

When the service had ended. When all had greeted their pastor, Elizabeth moved among those that called the bluff their home, and found herself smiling as she spoke to Ben. "It seems Reverend Smith," she began, "that you are a preacher after all."

"Did you have your doubts?" he asked.

"I must admit, I truly did."

He laughed that deep broad laugh she had heard before.

Elizabeth then noticed that a flat wagon had been rolled out. A bed sheet spread across it and almost by magic, foods of many sorts were spread upon it. Breads and meat, of which poor animal she would not guess, cheese and jams, a veritable feast. The pastor asked God for his blessing on the food and all there, and then began, what Elizabeth felt was an organized mayhem, a community dinner.

"Does this happen every time?" she asked Ben above the din of happy voices.

"Yes, yes, the bluff is truly a community," the Pastor said as he held his plate. "They care for each other."

"And you care for them."

The teacher thought she saw the slightest tint of pink on his tanned cheeks. "They have a hard life, but it hasn't made them hard, or at least not too hard," he said thoughtfully.

Elizabeth observed those around her, groups of threes and fours chatting. She heard words of praise over the corn bread and was told to be sure to try the strawberry jam. Standing with the pastor she smiled, as time and again someone came and shared a few words. A child, a very young girl came up to him tugged on the legging of his dungaree. Looking down Elizabeth could see the small pudgy arms reaching skyward. The pastor asked if Elizabeth would hold his plate a moment, which she did. He reached down and lifted the youngster. "Well hello, Jenny. How's my special friend?"

Jenny was beaming, mumbled something, apparently too young to talk in legible tones, giggled, held out a piece of bread. The pastor took a small bite from her offering, and the child giggled once more. "Jenny," he said then, "I would like you to meet Miss Beck. She's to be the new teacher in Misty Creek."

The youngster once more spoke, or rather tried to speak, in happy tones, which seemed to increase the smile on Ben's face as he held her close. A young woman came to them, her face flushed in embarrassment. She relieved the pastor of his burden with many apologies. Smiling, Benjamin told Mrs. Walker that he enjoyed his conversation with the child, that apologies were certainly not necessary.

Looking into the face of her child, Mrs. Walker said, "She can be a handful."

"Jenny's a delightful child," Ben said as he stroked one of Jenny's chubby cheeks.

He returned the wave of the fat little fingers, as Mrs. Walker strode off with Jenny bouncing happily on the woman's hip.

Ben was called away, and Elizabeth moved toward the fringe of the people. She watched the members of the bluff, hearing the friendly banter of farmer to farmer. One spoke of how his horse, Mike, was the strongest in the territory, which only set others to shaking their heads. Children dashed about chasing one another or sneaking under the wagon to reach from beneath the sheet for an extra piece of cornbread.

Elizabeth felt a tug at her dress. "Miss, miss," a child of perhaps eight asked, "are you really a teacher?"

Looking down, she smiled. "Would your pastor lie?"

"No, no, Pastor Ben, he'd never. But it's Dorothy that told me." She said as she pointed toward a group of children gathered at the head of the wagon.

Elizabeth crouched down to the child's eye level. "Now that you have met me, do you think I could be a teacher?'

The child with brilliant blue eyes tilted her head and looked Elizabeth up and down. "I never saw one before.

Elizabeth's grin grew. "Yes, I am a teacher. I'm going to Misty Creek. Have you ever gone to Misty Creek?"

The child shook her head, her blond pigtails swinging wildly. "I've never been anywhere."

Elizabeth wondered about a community so isolated, and having traveled but halfway on the wagon ride to her destination, worried about becoming trapped in some dried up dusty place, as these folks.

"If I lived in Misty Creek," the little girl's words pulled Elizabeth from her thoughts, "I'd go to your school."

A tear came to Elizabeth's eye. "I would be so pleased to have a student like you."

Her new blond friend took hold of Elizabeth's finger and led her to where the other children stood watching. "See, she's not mean at all, Dorothy, ya got no need to be scared, honest." Dorothy looked down and smiled as Elizabeth stretched out her hand to the young lady.

It was some time later, how much she was not certain, that Elizabeth felt the call for walk. Perhaps all the occurrences of the day needed to be digested. So she went, leaving the others behind as she walked up the hill to the top of the bluff. There she turned and looked over the land in the early evening light. The sun hung low on her right and gave long shadows. Far off Elizabeth saw what seemed to be a dark land that she had not noticed earlier. As she stood there with the breeze blowing her yellow dress and tugging at her bonnet, two children came running to join her, Dorothy Rider and Jacob Hancock. She smiled at the approach of two of her new friends.

"Can we walk with you?" Dorothy asked.

Elizabeth nodded and quietly they walked on the ridge together, enjoying the evening.

"You're Dorothy," Elizabeth said at last. The girl smiled delighted that the newcomer had remembered.

"And I'm Jacob," the other said seriously, not waiting for her to continue.

"Yes, you most certainly are," Elizabeth said calmly. "You met us when we came this afternoon." Smiling she looked down at the youngsters. "Do you always meet the pastor when he comes?"

"Not always." Dorothy responded.

"But mostly!" added Jacob.

"It is getting late, soon it will be dark. I guess we should be getting back. Your parents will be looking for you."

"Got no folks," Jacob stated matter of fact.

The comment caught Elizabeth off guard and reached in and tore at her heart. "No?"

"They died two winters ago." Dorothy spoke with a voice that could not quite hide the emotion of one that had lost so much.

"But we have Aunt Elie," the young boy added defiantly, as if he would not allow pity from this newcomer.

"Yes, we have Aunt Elie," Dorothy said, softly.

Bending, Elizabeth threw her arms around her new friends as they walked. "It's fortunate you both had an aunt at the bluff."

"She's not really our aunt," Dorothy corrected. "Everybody calls her Aunt Elie."

"Yeah, everybody."

Elizabeth thought about the woman that had invited her into her home. The woman that offered her the best chair. In a place where survival was tenuous at best; yes, she would open her home to those in real need. "Do you go to school?" she asked.

"Not a school with a teacher, ma'am," Dorothy responded sheepishly. "Aunt Elie teaches us."

Then Jacob added, "Most ma's teach their own."

"We're lucky 'cause Aunt Elie can read. Not everybody can ya know." The young girl finished the thought Elizabeth was contemplating.

"Yes, then you are indeed fortunate," Elizabeth answered thoughtfully.

"Ah, I ain't so lucky!" Jacob answered. "Why, Billy gets to go out and play whilst I got ta work on spellin' and readin'."

Elizabeth had to chuckle. How many boys had she taught that would certainly say precisely the same thing? "Time will tell Jacob, perhaps one day you'll be glad that Aunt Elie took the time to teach you to read."

"No, ma'am, I'll never need no readin' no how."

She pulled the boy in close for an instant.

The western horizon was ablaze in crimson and amber when they reached the steps of the house-store, and Elizabeth stood dumbstruck by its glory. The air had begun to cool. As Elizabeth stood a moment on the porch, many strange sounds came floating on the breeze. Far off, a mournful wail, a strange alien doglike sound she had never heard before. Yelp, yelp, howl came as an answer in the evening air. The howls caused her to shiver. In the dim light she had not noticed that Ben had been sitting within the shadows and waiting. "Have a pleasant walk?" he asked.

Surprised by his voice, Elizabeth gasped. Then she gathered her wits. "Yes, indeed I have and the most pleasant company."

"I'm sure you did," he said with a chuckle. Ben rose from his seat, touched the brim of his hat. "Then I bid you goodnight," he said with a smile as he moved past her.

"And sir," Elizabeth asked, "where will you be spending the night?"

"Beneath the stars, Miss Beck, beneath the stars."

"But, but," she stammered.

"There's nothing quite like it," he said calmly. "Perhaps one day you will have the privilege."

"I suspect that will never happen!" Elizabeth answered as she looked at the man walking, and wondered what kind of woman he thought her to be, for no lady would even consider the possibility of sleeping out of doors.

"It will be your loss. There is no artist greater than God, and nothing can match the prairie night sky."

Ben once again bid her goodnight, and whistling loudly, moved out into the roadway as darkness began to fall. Elizabeth watched him, as he strode off swaying slightly in time to the notes he sent on the wind, and wondered, not the first time, what kind of man Reverend Benjamin Smith was. No preacher she had ever met, or ever imagined, would choose to camp out in the open, especially here in the wilderness.

CHAPTER 3

THE SPACE ELIZABETH HAD BEEN GIVEN, WAS AN UPSTAIRS ROOM – the entire room. Though only a day before such lodgings would have seemed natural, however here surrounded by people that had so little, Elizabeth understood it to be an extravagance. The room was much larger than she had expected, with windows overlooking the prairie. Elizabeth's bag had been brought up. The thought of someone going to the trouble made her feel guilty. She found that Eloise had lit the only lamp in the sparsely furnished room. A room that only contained a small chest of drawers, a hard back chair similar to those downstairs, and a bed. But what truly took her breath away was the quilt. For a magnificent spread of bold colors in bright patterns covered the brass bed. The room the teacher felt certain was a space reserved for guests. A special place where all that was Aunt Elie's best could be found. As she slowly moved about the space, again Elizabeth wondered. What kind of woman was this Mrs. Eloise Jenkins?

Later, much later, she awoke in the dark, in a strange room, in a strange place, deep in a strange land. Elizabeth drew the chair to an open window. There she sat looking out into the night. Even now Elizabeth could feel the slight touch of the breeze against her skin, the wind that seemed never to cease. On that breeze came the sounds of the night. The sounds of creatures near and far, creatures she had never heard before. Odd short hoots, an owl of some sort she felt certain. A distant wolf-like howl similar to what she had heard earlier set the dogs of the community off to barking. Insect's sounds, crickets and katydids, filled her ears. And above it all was the sky, cloudless and simply ablaze with countless points of light. Those lights were more than stars, more than any stars she had ever witnessed. Looking upward took her breath away and caused a tremble deep within. She understood, at least a little, of what the pastor had said. And seeing those stars in that canvas of black, Elizabeth found she could not look away for several minutes.

Elizabeth sat there her mind flooded with so many thoughts. She drew a breath as she considered just how far from home she had wandered. She went back to nights years ago, her mother brushing out the tangles in her hair. A time when many thought she would never become a lady. Those days she could wrestle Mitchel Dogerty to submission. But she had not been a child for a long time, and though she had not lived all those years in her parents' house on Elm Street, having taught for three years in the small Ohio town of London, the ache of homesickness filled her. Closing her eyes a moment she could almost smell breakfast's bacon greeting her with the sun as it slipped through the white curtains of her yellow bedroom. The sight of her father and his paper. The smell of coffee mixed with his aftershave when she greeted him each morning. How far away she felt. But far away was what she had wanted. Something alien to the world that had always been her life.

Now as she opened her eyes to the diamond sparkled sky, she wondered if she had entered a world too different. Elizabeth swallowed as she looked across the open prairie. Sitting there allowing the gentle breeze to pass her cheeks and move an errant strand of hair, the thoughts of home seemed to be pushed aside by the children she had met here on the boundary of humanity. There was something familiar in them, something that all children seemed to have in common. She smiled at the thought and sat by the window until the drowsiness came. Softly it came. It arrived with a calmness she had not felt in a very long time. A smile formed on her tired lips, and in the dark, the weary teacher made her way to the bed and found sleep waiting.

Morning's light found them rolling once again. Elizabeth would have thought that as early as they had begun, few would be up and about. But she was mistaken. Eloise, a most gracious hostess, had breakfast prepared and waiting. The kitchen consisted of a room in the sod portion of the home. Elizabeth found her first experience in a soddy a bit unnerving, being surrounded by walls of earth. Somewhat like a cave she thought, yet different. Elizabeth found Ben seated when she entered. Unlike her, the preacher seemed completely at ease with the surroundings. Mrs. Jenkins made a fine meal, eggs, bacon, bread, butter, cheese and jams. Anything a person might want was available. Elizabeth thought again about Eloise Jenkins, that woman with very few teeth, that woman that had taken a stranger into her home, a remarkable woman.

Now in the early morning light, as they rode the lumbering wagon back down the same road they had taken the afternoon before, Elizabeth had so much on her mind. There had been a great deal of activity about the bluff. When they stepped outside that morning, she saw men and woman hard at the day's work. These and so many other thoughts filled her mind. At last Ben asked. "It was different than you expected?"

Though she didn't really need to think about his question, Elizabeth paused a moment as best to answer. "Yes, but looking back, I am not certain what I truly expected."

"But not what you found?"

"No certainly not! But nothing I have found in this country has been what a person might expect."

They rode a few moments further. Ben straightened his hat. "What has surprised you the most?"

"The openness, the vastness of the countryside. I come from a rural area. I thought I understood the 'great outdoors', but I didn't, not in the least."

Ben remained quiet for a moment. "It takes some time to become accustomed to the sheer volume of this part of God's creation."

"Eloise told me you came from Philadelphia," she stated. "It must have been a shock for you as well?"

"I came from a small farm town just west of Philadelphia, called West Chester. My father was a farmer, a good one, he did well. He always expected me to farm."

"But that's not what you wanted?" she asked.

He laughed. "I could have farmed, perhaps happily, but it wasn't my calling."

Elizabeth had heard that term before. Sometimes it was just a very general explanation, but here it seemed to fit this man she had only met a few days before. She had come to believe that Benjamin Smith belonged here, out in the middle of the wilderness. She had watched him, listened to him, come to believe in him. Strange, she thought, it seemed odd at first, a cowboy preacher, that was her original perception, but that label was not accurate. Ben did not herd cattle, tend fence or do the things Elizabeth would expect of one in that profession. No, he drove a freight wagon, tended to his animals, and he pastured his flock, diverse and scattered. Yes, it was very apparent Reverend Smith had been called to this life he lived.

"So tell me then," she asked with care, "how did you find your calling?"

"I had an uncle, my mother's brother. Uncle Joseph was a Methodist pastor. It was he that inspired me. But I guess I disappointed him as well."

"What makes you say that? You became a pastor."

Ben laughed that loud full spirited laugh. "But certainly not the kind of pastor he envisioned." Snapping the reins he coaxed the horses on. "It was he that got me into seminary, very much against my father's wishes. I believed and still do that you should honor your parents, but…"

"There are things you must do, even if they do not understand," she added thoughtfully as her mind went back to home and what had been expected.

"I never wanted to disappoint my father, I guess I regret doing so," Ben said softly as he scanned the horizon.

Elizabeth looked at Benjamin sitting beside her. She saw another side of the big man she never expected. "And so you went to seminary."

"Yes, and when I was ordained, my father would not come." Ben's face grew grim. It was the first time she had seen anything in his expression other than jovial mischievous love of God and life.

"Certainly he had a good reason for not coming," Elizabeth answered softly.

Ben shrugged his shoulders.

"Surely you have spoken with him?" she asked in alarm.

Swallowing he answered. "I spoke to him, many times, but he has not said one word to me…not one."

"Oh, my goodness." She found herself staring at her traveling companion. "And your mother?"

"She'll not go against Father, which is as it should be," he said without emotion.

The teacher could not find the words to speak. She had no idea of the turmoil Ben had faced. Clearly it was a troubling wound, a wound that might never fully heal. As Elizabeth sat there speechless beneath the blue prairie sky, surrounded by mile after mile of dry grass, a verse came to her. And though she did not know which book, chapter or number, the words came clear, "Because of me, father will turn against son, and son against father…" It seemed to her so very sad. Surely if the man had the chance to see Ben, the Ben she had seen, he would be proud of the man his son had become.

They rode in silence for some time, the longest period Ben had not spoken on the entire journey. She wondered what it was her parents had expected of her. They seemed to understand when she became a teacher. They had not pushed her out of their lives in the way Benjamin's parents apparently had. Yet she knew they had opposed this decision. She tried to place herself in their "shoes" but found it impossible. She may understand what it meant to be a daughter, but here in the openness beneath sun and sky, a place so different than any she had experienced, she realized that only a parent could understand what a parent felt. Only a person that had sacrificed, worried and pained over every little thing their child faced or suffered, only one that prayed each day for their son or daughter, could stand in that place, and she missed her family the more.

At last Elizabeth asked, "Is that why you came west?"

"I didn't think so at the time, but I would suppose it might have had something to do with it." Ben pulled the horses to a stop. They had reached the crossroads once again, and the pastor felt it time to give the beasts a drink and some rest. They climbed off the wagon. He tended his task as Elizabeth stretched her limbs. Ben spoke as he did his work with his strong clear voice. "When I was ordained, I began my calling in a small church in Pennsylvania. It was there I met Leah. Oh, my Leah." The love in his voice evident, a love that caused her to smile. "But when I heard of the need, the terrible need out here," he swung his arm to indicate the big country all about them, "something started a yearning in my heart."

"Were you married then?" Elizabeth asked.

"Yes, and our first on the way," he said as he took water to the second horse. He stroked the velvet nose of the animal as he stood beside him. "I tried to put it out of my mind. I mean, I just couldn't pick up and leave. I couldn't drag my dear Leah halfway across the country."

Elizabeth held her tongue, for he had done just that. Uprooted his family and left what must have been a secure position, for this. It seemed so different than the man she was coming to know.

"But the strange thing was," Ben began again, "Leah felt the same way, even stronger. It was she that forced me to come here." He looked over the hot animals patting them gently. As he walked a bit, his eyes it seemed continually roaming over the land. "Sometimes God calls you to something very different." He turned to look at Elizabeth. "God called me to this place. I'm as certain of that as I am the sun is over head now." A weak smile at last returned to his trembling lips and he moved to help her back up to the wagon's seat. "And what brings you to the prairie?"

It was a question she had expected. In truth Elizabeth was amazed it had taken the pastor so long to reach it. The teacher answered with a very well-rehearsed response, "I was in need of a change." It was the truth, well part of the truth, and as much as she was yet willing to share with anyone. Even her family would be unable to understand, and she had not shared the real reasons even with them.

The pastor turned to look at her. She observed the questions in his eyes. Retaining her stern expression, the pastor turned away as if realizing she would say no more. He did not pursue the matter, for which she was grateful, for the very root of what had driven her lay in places she did not wish to return, not now in any case. Places filled with pain and disappointment. Again they went on for a time in what felt to her a tense silence. When at long last the preacher began to whistle, Elizabeth began to relax a bit.

It seemed the horses pulled the load more easily, that the road must be descending. Elizabeth asked Ben if it were so, and he, surprised by her perception, told her they had entered a wide though shallow valley. They were bound for a settlement called Paradise at the valley's center.

Soon she noticed squares of what seemed bare earth in the distance, much like the areas she had seen from the bluff. Ben informed her that these were fields, laying prepared for planting. Soon winter wheat would be sown on half of them. The others would lie fallow with the hopes the land would gather a little moisture for the next year's crop. They rumbled on, a few buildings came into view standing, grouped near each other and among some pitiful looking trees, the houses and barns of the farmers. Drawing closer, it seemed that the place was anything but paradise—name or not.

Chapter 4

When they came to houses made of sod as those of the bluff, but standing out in the open, the earth walls could be seen on all four sides, she asked, "Yesterday when you spoke about Eloise you said there were places worse. Is this?"

Ben nodded solemnly.

No children ran up to the wagon as they approached. Rather the small ones stood clinging to their mothers, watching wide-eyed as the wagon slowly rumbled past. Paradise was made up of three houses. These soddies stood along a dry creek bed, two on the north bank and the other on the south. Each home stood near what appeared to be a sod barn, and a paddock fenced by gnarled and twisted limbs. The only other sight in Paradise were the six or seven trees, if the poor desecrated vegetation could be called trees that lined the dry waterway.

The wagon came to a stop. "Well ma'am, welcome to Paradise."

Elizabeth couldn't help but shake her head at the thought, and once more considered this collection of houses was anything but….

It was so different from the bluff. Here everyone remained at their door, watching, wondering, with fear in their eyes. The pastor climbed down gingerly, helped Elizabeth down, and moved to the rear of the wagon. "I have a parcel for Holden," he shouted. "And there's a bit of mail."

"Who's the mail fer," came a harsh raspy voice very near that startled Elizabeth. Turning, she saw a young man, dirty head to toe, barefoot, and desperately in need of a shave, though his facial hair certainly could not be considered a beard. The man's face was grim. The brim of his hat cast a shadow making his eyes difficult to see. He was not a person Elizabeth would wish to deal with.

"Why Josiah," the pastor responded cheerfully, "there's two letters this month, and one's for your wife." He reached into the canvas bag and sorted out the envelope and handed it to the grungy farmer.

She watched intently as the man handled the letter as if it was the rarest of treasures, gingerly rolling it over in his hands. "Where's it from?" he asked.

Benjamin looking over the man's shoulder pointed to the return address. "From a Mrs. Agnes Timmans, Marshalltown, Missouri."

"Maggie's Aunt Agnes," the man said in awe. "She wrote all the way from Marshalltown." He walked away almost in a trance, staring at the envelope as he made his way to an equally dirty woman standing with two dirty children, one clinging to her skirt the other in her arms.

Holding up another letter Ben shouted, "Got mail for Martin M. Allen."

A man, standing in the shade of the doorway of a barn, if the sod structure could be called a barn, waved his hand and began walking toward them. The man, though not clean by any means, seemed practically sanitary by comparison to Josiah. He took the letter forcefully, looked at the address, and stuffed it in his pocket. "I'll take that parcel too," he said with a hard tone. Mr. Allen stood shorter than Josiah, but was broader. He had a determined skeptical look about him, with dark eyes. "I'll see Jeremiah gets his stuff."

The pastor looked the man over. "Where is Mr. Holden this morning?

Allen shrugged his shoulders. "Can't say. Ain't seen him all week."

"None of us have," said a woman from the nearest house.

"Good morning, Mrs. Taylor," the pastor said, removing his hat.

Then turning toward Mr. Allen he smiled as he said, "it's a mighty fine offer you made about getting Mr. Holden's parcel to him, Martin, but I'm afraid I have to have his signature."

"Signature?"

"Jeremiah has to sign for it."

"But I told ya, he ain't here!" Allen said, forcefully in sharp tones.

"Yes, you did. I'll have to hold it till next time."

"But that's crazy!" the broad man said, standing with his feet apart, determined.

"Maybe, but it's the rules," Ben said as he began to return to the front of the wagon.

"But what if'n he needs it?" Martin asked.

"I'll ride through week after next. That's the best I can do. If he needs it sooner he'll have to come to the creek."

"Hell, he ain't gonna ride clear out there."

All this took Elizabeth by surprise. Not only the language the man used when talking to the preacher but also the determined resistance Ben showed. "Can't be helped," the pastor said at last, looking downward, clearly weary of the discussion.

Allen Martin's eyebrows stood out showing his intention to debate the point further. It appeared Ben considered the situation settled, for he turned his back on Martin and began speaking to a rather tall man with sharp eyes, and what Elizabeth would describe as a neatly trimmed beard. Ben introduced Mr. Isaiah Levendowski to her. With his clean clothing and combed hair, the man seemed so out of place. But his appearance was not the only thing that she found unusual. For though he spoke with a strong accent, his voice seemed soft and not nearly as deep as she had anticipated a large man to have. "The wife asked," she heard Isaiah say, "if you were going to have a meeting today?"

The pastor slapped the big man on the back. "Of course Isaiah, of course! Tell that dear wife of yours, as soon as I have watered the horses."

"We got no water for those nags of yours!" shouted one agitated Martin Allen rocking on his feet.

Everyone grew still, not a murmur or whisper, only the sound of the wind through the nearly leafless scrub trees could be heard. Elizabeth felt the tension build. Ben stood frozen, his hands clenched. Allen continued to rock from side to side, lips turned downward his face drawn tight with a furrowed brow, standing his ground with arms folded across his chest. The teacher watched, worried how the situation would play out. She seemed certain that Ben would turn and face the man, perhaps even tell the farmer off. But though she could see a flush growing on the pastor's face he remained calm. Ben moved to the barrel which was bound to the wagon and began to fill the green canvas buckets he had used over and over again as they had traveled. Ben said not a word, to the small brash, dusty, angry man.

While Ben worked, Mr. Allen stood squinting, as if he was meant to enforce the rules, rules he apparently made. Elizabeth had not noticed Mr. Levendowski's departure, but observed the man returning with a wooden pail full of water. Allen dashed up in an attempt to take the water from the big man, but Isaiah, drawing his eyebrows down with a look of determination, brushed the small man aside. Allen quickly turned and tried to jump Levendowski from behind. Ben's powerful voice shouted, "Enough!" Everyone in the dusty settlement stood frozen. Ben moved between the two men. For a moment it seemed he was not certain what he should do. He looked first at Allen then at Isaiah then at Allen once more. "I know the difficulties you folks have faced this year…"

"You don't know squat!" Allen shouted.

Now Ben glared at the little man. "Perhaps I don't, Martin, perhaps I don't. But I have brought all the water my animals would need." He moved over and took the handle of the pail Mr. Levendowski held, handing it to Allen. A look of glee grew on the dusty farmer's face. "Isaiah I appreciate the kindness," Ben continued, "the generosity…"

"It's not his water he's givin' away!" the yet angry little man screamed.

"See'n it was me that dug the well whose water would it be?" the big man asked, turning to stand toe to toe with Mr. Allen. Elizabeth could see the defiance on Martin's face crumble beneath Isaiah's glare. She watched his anger replaced by fear. Allen tried desperately to gather his courage, but as the big broad farmer looked down upon him, it was plain he was failing. It seemed to Elizabeth that things were quickly getting out of hand. Glancing from one to the other, she wondered what kind of place she found herself. It seemed such a lawless land where neighbors stood in anger against neighbor, a place where violence reigned. As she watched two men came to stand behind Isaiah and another man stood with Mr. Allen. It was obvious that this was not the first point of contention among the people of Paradise, and she feared for her own and Ben's safety.

Just at the moment she was certain things were about to come to blows, Benjamin pressed himself between them. Throwing his arms over the shoulders of the two men. "The water is God's, you men know that. It's a gift to us all," Ben said cheerfully, looking back and forth between the two angry men.

"Ya," Isaiah said, "pastor's right. We don't own the water, dug down to it but it was there all along."

Allen's face stiffened. "Bah, a gift. Hell if it were, then why don't God give us more?"

"Have you asked him?" Ben questioned.

Martin Allen tore himself free, spit to the dust and in a cold heartless voice said. "Ask God? Hell, God don't care. He don't care about us. He don't care about anything! If you ask me there ain't no God, no how!"

"I'm sorry you feel that way Martin," the pastor said as Allen and the other man walked away.

Allen turned. "Oh, you think you're something special. Come here every now and again, preach at us. Maybe it eases your conscious but it don't do no good. All ya got is words nutin' more. And words don't do nobody no good!!!" Fire had returned to his eyes. The man spat once again as if the words he spoke soiled his tongue, or perhaps at the mere presence of the pastor.

Once more Ben said, "I'm sorry you feel that way…"

"Is that all you got ta say…sorry!" screamed Allen. The small, angry man turned and began quickly to walk away.

"Don't turn you back on God, Martin," Ben said firmly.

"Cain't," the angry man said without turning. "He don't exist!"

Elizabeth saw Ben begin to speak, but the pastor stopped before any words left his mouth. He stood there with deep sadness in his eyes watching Allen as he walked away.

As Mr. Allen walked across the dry creek bed, he threw the bucket and its contents. The wood skidded on the pebbles, spilling the precious water it contained, then slammed into a rock, splitting and becoming nothing more than kindling.

"There was no call for that!" shouted Isaiah. Elizabeth felt certain that Levendowski would go after the other, but Ben's strong hand on the big man's shoulder caused him to stand firm.

"Let it go, Isaiah," Smith said softly.

"But it was a good bucket!"

"I know, my friend."

Mr. Levendowski turned to face the sad eyes of his pastor, and as he glanced into those eyes the anger in his own appeared to fade. Then, looking down, the big man said softly, "I'm sorry."

All this seemed to leave Elizabeth bewildered. Why would Isaiah need to apologize? It was not he that had done wrong. Wasn't it he that offered water to the horses? Wasn't it his bucket that now lay scattered on the dust dry streambed? Didn't Allen, out of spite, refuse the sharing of that single pale of water, only to throw it away?

Elizabeth watched as a smile returned to Ben's weathered face. "You're a good man Isaiah; there'll be another bucket."

The big man nodded meekly.

"Tell your dear wife," Ben added, "the meeting will begin directly."

The bearded man nodded once more and walked from them toward one of the homes made of earth. Ben returned to the task at hand, seeing to the care of the horses. Once more Elizabeth wondered what type of man this cowboy preacher was. Over and over again Reverend Benjamin Smith showed different facets of what she now realized was a very complex man.

When the task was completed, Benjamin gathered his worn black book, and, smiling, he offered his arm to escort the teacher the short distance to where a few stood waiting in the shadows of the scrawny twisted nearly dead trees that lined the dried creek bed. He introduced Elizabeth to those there. She met Opal and Thomas Weck. She kneeled to greet the little girl, their daughter, only to have the child hide fearfully behind her mother's dress. Next was Amos and Laura Markley with their three sons, Jacob, James, and little baby John. Then came the last, the Levendoski's, Isaiah, his wife Rachael and four small children, David, Isaac, Mary and Deborah.

Rachael became the focus of her attention, tall like her husband, with clear blue eyes, and slightly mischievous smile. She carried a delightful accent which Miss Elizabeth could not place. European to be sure, but different than any she had heard. The Levendoskis seemed so different from the others and this desolate place.

They had gathered in the shade of the healthiest of the sickly trees on the creek bank. It was cooler there as the wind, the wind that always blew, made standing nearly comfortable. Elizabeth expected the same sermon she had heard yesterday, but after a prayer, the singing of a hymn she did not know, Reverend Benjamin Smith began a very different message.

He spoke of forgiveness, of compassion, of caring for one another. She heard his words. She watched those around her. Elizabeth noticed out of the corner of her eye the others watching them at a distance. Mr. Allen and the man that had stood behind the angry, soiled, bitter man. Ben's voice was clear and strong. Strong enough, Elizabeth was sure, to be heard all through the valley. Certainly strong enough to be heard by Allen and his friend.

As she heard Ben's heartfelt words, Elizabeth considered the untamed country around them and the tenuous life the people of Kansas lived. But more here, in this small place named Paradise. She had seen how a few words could divide those that relied upon each other for their survival. How this community stood at the flashpoint, and at any moment people could be injured or slain. That though the presence of Ben might be a buffer, she feared those that did not respect him. Men like Martin Allen seemed beyond the words Ben shared, perhaps rejecting God's purpose of love. And if that was so, and Elizabeth feared it was, then who would pay the price of their frustration? Would that price fall on Isaiah Levendoski, his wife, their children or others of the community? Even now while her friend preached, the words seemed unable to touch all. She wondered. Perhaps violence would strike Ben and any that traveled with him. She shuddered as she glanced over to the men standing at the distance with clenched fists.

The sermon was not long. Ben it seemed said what he intended and repetition was not necessary. They sang a hymn, one she knew, the pastor prayed and closed with a blessing. Strangely all people simply dispersed. Only the Levendowski's remained, it did not surprise her they would.

They made small talk about the weather, if there had been enough rain, and if the crops would bring a fair price, Deborah's first steps, and, of course, the new teacher. "You'll come to the house," Rachael said at last.

Ben smiled. "But of course Mrs. Levendoski, we would be most pleased to accept your kind invitation."

Chapter 5

The house, the furthest to the west, looked little different than the others. But there was a small box of raised earth in front with of all things—flowers. A bit of color in a world devoid of it. Petunias of red and purple, surrounded by a shorter plant with white, red and yellow blossoms Elizabeth did not recognize. Elizabeth stared at the beautiful flowers, a display she felt so out of place.

"You like Rachael's flowers?" the big man asked with a twinkle in his eye. "Some say they are nothing but a waste of water, but I know better. She has more blooming in her garden out back. Go, Rachael, she show you."

Rachael and the children led the way around the house, through a gate for the backyard was fenced, to a sight so amazing. For there behind that simplest of homes, there in a land so devoid of life, was a veritable Eden. A beautifully tended garden with rows and rows of vegetables, potatoes, carrots, lettuce, cabbages and so much more. But not only carefully tended food stuffs, but also several rows of flowers.

Elizabeth stood speechless. She had seen few finer patches, but more, here was a place where the dusty prairie surrendered its dead grass for something more alive than she could imagine since first setting eyes on this broad land. Rachael showed each variety carefully explaining how with a bit of water, the land could produce. Elizabeth smiled as she watched Mrs. Levenedoski and her brood, for though the farm wife did her best to maintain her modesty Elizabeth could see a well-deserved pride in her eyes.

Later they entered the small sod house. Elizabeth had no idea what to expect, but whatever she had imagined was quickly swept away. The space was dark and cool, reminding her of her parents' cellar. The only light within that home came through the open door and a single small window. The window had no glass, rather a strange fabric covered the opening allowing light but offered no view, not out, and she felt certain, not in as well. Yet even so, that opening was framed by white curtains. The greatest surprise was the floor covered with row upon row of smooth flat stones. Not the dirt she had expected. Isaiah had made and baked the clay stones. The farmer was also making brick, stone by stone, to build a proper house one day.

Elizabeth and Ben were offered tea; its aroma filled the space. A space she could believe was truly a home. For though the room was simply furnished, it contained enough things special to those that found shelter there. The table and chairs were made of fine hardwood, brought from a place very far away. A free standing cupboard stood along one wall, displaying small porcelain figurines, a pair of bone china cups and a small brass bowl.

They spoke, for the conversation came easy. Elizabeth asked from where they had come. The Levenedoski's seemed embarrassed to tell her they had come across the sea, from Poland. But just as she wanted to learn a bit about these new friends, they too hungered for knowledge about her, of Ohio, of her trip, the train.

"Few stop here from away," Isaiah said softly.

Rachel nodded, "Out of the way we are."

Elizabeth thought about the long ride bouncing about on the wagon, out of the way seemed to fit. "Surely others come from time to time?" she asked.

Rachel and Isaiah looked toward each other. "One, maybe two, since we come. Only the pastor, the good man."

Ben looked down at the table top. "I'm not that good," he responded softly.

Rachel placed a hand on the pastor's shoulder. "You show us that someone outside this place thinks about us. You bring da Bible and God's word here."

"Ya," Isaiah added. "You come bring news and sometimes mail." The big man nodded. "But not everyone happy when pastor come."

"Like Mr. Allen?"

"Ya, like Martin. But he worse now. Mrs., she die last year, maybe the year before, hard to remember." Isaiah said as he looked toward the window.

Rachel continued at her work and added softly, "Mary, sweet woman that one. This country too hard for one so sweet." The farm wife paused a moment and seemed to look far off. She shook her head. "Sometimes, I think she just give up."

For an instant Elizabeth felt sorry for Mr. Allen. Then, remembering the fire in the man's eyes and how he had cursed even God, she drew a breath and returned to her earlier opinion, that he was an angry dangerous man.

"Mama, we do not speak so, not today. Today we have Miss Teacher. Time I think for happier things." Isaiah turned to look at Elizabeth. "We come across the country, Rachel and me, across this place Ohio where you come. This place different, I think."

Elizabeth's mind went back to the time she lived in rural Ohio. For when she stated teaching seven years ago, the only position she could find was just outside a small town called London. It seemed so far from Columbus, so far from home, then. A simple brick building along the road, a structure with a single classroom, nestled between gently rolling fields. Here surrounded in a land covered by dried up grass, a dusty place where even the houses were made of earth, seemed such a contrast to the green farmland that had stretched to Ohio's horizon. She had felt cut off from her family that term. How had she chosen a post in the wilds of Kansas? Had she really thought it through? Had merely mentioning the opportunity and all the conversations it drew, pushed her into coming? Everyone said it was folly. Her family and friends were firm in the belief she would never go "pioneering" as they called it. Was she sitting in the house of sod out of stubbornness, or to prove she had no fear?

"Yes, very different," she finally responded with a smile. She looked over to Ben, who seemed to sit quietly absorbing the words that flowed around him. "The land is open and…" she did not know how to describe it correctly. "There are so few trees. At home we have trees everywhere." Elizabeth hoped the words she had chosen would satisfy.

"And the people?" Benjamin asked.

She tightened her lip and drew her brows down slightly as she glared at Ben across the table.

"You come from the east Pastor, further than I, you know the answer to that question." She left it at that, displeased that the man had put her on the spot.

All the while they had sat there in that dim room, Rachael at work while Isaiah held their youngest. Soon other scents began to flow about the room. Elizabeth became upset with herself for being so engaged in the conversation she had not noticed Rachael hard at work preparing a meal. Elizabeth certainly would have helped had she known, but so enthralled by the conversation she simply had failed to observe the woman at her tasks.

They shared a simple, wonderful meal. A feast of beef, potatoes, some boiled cabbage and a bit of bread, freshly baked for the occasion. It would be a time Elizabeth would always remember. How those that had little, so gratefully shared what they had.

When they had finished the meal Isaiah said, "My Racheal, she cook good, no?"

"Yes, indeed, but…"

Ben cut her off. "Isaiah, you are a fortunate man."

Elizabeth looked at Ben, considered the words on the tip of her tongue, *you have so little*, she felt grateful he had interrupted, for they were words best unsaid.

Rising from the table they began to move toward the door. Racheal touched Elizabeth's hand and bid her stay a moment as the others moved into the sunshine.

There in the room, surrounded by sod carefully stacked, Elizabeth looked at the tall strong woman that spoke. "I hope you do not think this words of a simple woman. I see sadness, Elizabeth, in your eyes, I see."

Elizabeth began to speak.

"Please let me." Rachael said as she tapped Elizabeth's hand. "When we come to this country, when I say good bye to my mama and papa, I cry, I cry much. Isaiah is a good man, but he no understand how I feel. There was no future for us in Poland. I loved Isaiah and would go where he go, even to the moon I go. But that day when I looked at my mama, I know. No more I would see my mama or my papa, no more that day no more ever.

"Now you go far from your mama, your papa, not so far as me but far. Sad maybe too."

Elizabeth lips trembled as she tried to smile.

Rachael wrapped her arms around Elizabeth and held her firm. "Yes, Racheal, she sees, she knows. Maybe it helps a little, maybe?" The farm wife pushed her away just enough to see into Elizabeth's eyes. "You see your mamma, your papa again, yes, Elizabeth you see dem. But not to hold sadness so deep. Not good. I know. Not good to hold sadness where no one can see all the time." She hugged Elizabeth and led her out.

So the time came to leave, and for the first time since she had left Ohio, Elizabeth regretted that the moment came so soon. Elizabeth shook Isaiah's hand, a good strong hand. Then bent to say her farewells to the children, and finally, perhaps because she really didn't want to part, she embraced her new friend Rachael Levendowski.

The teacher couldn't help but look back as they slowly rolled out of Paradise. Glancing one last time, when they had travel a goodly distance. She saw Rachael standing surrounded by all the dried up lifeless grass that seemed to make up this place, standing there with her family and waving her dishcloth, waving one last farewell. A tear came to Elizabeth's eye. A tear at the sight of the farm wife slowly drifting far behind. In this open land, Elizabeth had come a stranger, unaware of what life on the frontier demanded. But in a world that seemed filled with desolation she had experienced, in an instant, a bond, a friendship. How could such a thing happen in a few brief hours? Now parting, they were no longer strangers, and Elizabeth feared for the Levendowskis, and wondered if they would ever meet again.

Ben and Elizabeth bounced along for a time in silence. When the pastor began to whistle again, she dared to ask him why the place was called Paradise.

"The Levendowskis, Allens and Baxters were the first to arrive that's what they thought they had found," Ben said in all earnestness. He snapped the reins to coax the animals onward.

"Paradise?"

"Yes, Paradise," he answered firmly. "You have to understand. It was a hard journey they had made. No railroad, just a Conestoga and miles and miles of land that had to be crossed. They left nearly everything behind, if they had anything to start with. But they came with a dream. When in the spring of the year, they arrived in this valley, it was very different from what you have just seen. The creek flowed and just as you saw what a little water could do to a garden, imagine what it did to the entire valley. Yes, when they arrived, they thought they had found paradise." Again he snapped the reins. They took the same route that had brought them, but now it slowly, almost unnoticeably, went upward, and the horses trudged against the load.

Elizabeth looked about the land, seeing the sea of tall brown grass swaying beneath the constant wind. Though she tried, the young teacher just couldn't imagine the land as anything but the lifeless place she had observed. "Poor Isaiah, will he be able to fix that pail? I expect he'll need it," she said in a soft voice. Soft enough she was not certain Ben heard.

But Ben heard. "I'm sure he'll try." Smith scanned the horizon to the left. She had no idea what he was hoping, or perhaps not hoping, to see. "But I 'spect it's no more than fire wood."

Elizabeth was alarmed. "What will he do?"

She couldn't help but notice the smile that grew on her traveling companion's face. "Well, I hope he finds another."

Her eyes opened wide. "And where would he find one?"

"The lord provides."

Elizabeth stared at the young pastor, wondering why he was positively beaming. "And what would the lord provide here in the absolute middle of nowhere?"

Ben snapped the reins. "Why, a leather bucket. Well at least until I come through next month."

"Pastor Smith what have you done?" She smiled.

"Well, it so happens," he said with his booming voice, "that I forgot to throw that bucket back on the wagon. I must have left it just beside the Levendowski's front gate. Imagine how foolish I feel."

Elizabeth knew the man did not feel foolish in the least, and was about to tell him so when together they laughed long and hard. As Elizabeth gathered her breath, she wondered who, in a land where survival hung in a tenuous balance, would pay for Ben's impulsive act of kindness. They had far to go and the horses would need to be watered. "But what will we do?" she asked at last.

"Oh, we'll get by. I'll just have to think about it a bit."

She heard a confidence in Ben's voice. Perhaps the pastor would come up with a solution. It had grown hot and the animals once more were worn long before they reached the cross roads. Ben stopped to rest the horses and with his hat carried water to the beasts. The task took several trips but Elizabeth was impressed with his ingenuity.

As Ben worked, Elizabeth wandered a short distance, looking over the land that seemed no different than any of the country they had crossed. Just mile after mile of softly rolling, open, barren land covered with tall, brown grass that showed only the slightest trace of green. In every direction, the country all around her seemed nothing more than a desolate empty wasteland. She felt melancholy. What had she gotten herself into? Surely her father was right. Elizabeth thought of the place called Paradise. How those that had originally come could even imagine they had found something so special. It was nothing—absolutely nothing. And those that lived there and at the bluff could barely scratching out a living. How they survived she had no clue. Nothing she had seen, nothing since she had left the train offered any promise. Elizabeth had not asked Ben any details about Misty Creek. The name, it was the name that had until this morning given her hope. But if the place they had visited could be named Paradise, then what on earth would she find at a place called Misty Creek?

CHAPTER 6

THE YOUNG TEACHER REMAINED EVEN MORE QUIET THAN USUAL, when they started out once more. Ben noticed. Oh, he had been whistling all along, had sung two hymns—loudly. From time to time, Elizabeth had noticed him looking over toward her, and yet she did not speak.

They at last reached the crossroads. Turning left, they continued on the road they had taken the day before. "How much further?" she asked at last.

"Oh, it's not too far," he said with a gleam in his eyes, "maybe three hours." He looked toward her. "We'll arrive a bit later than usual. Spent more time than I had expected in Paradise."

"Will we get there before dark?"

"Yes, we should. It's been a long day."

It certainly had. If Elizabeth wasn't so close to exhaustion, she was certain she would demand to be returned to Thimble. It was all too much. Nothing had prepared her for what she had seen. Never had she imagined the life that people here on the prairie were forced to live. She couldn't think of as single reason any of them would remain. At that moment Elizabeth couldn't think of a single legitimate reason why she had come. Drawing a breath her weary mind filled with swirling thoughts of home and hopes dashed to pieces. When she had left Columbus, what seemed an eternity ago, she felt confident she would find freedom from painful memories. A new life, new possibilities but this emptiness, a world devoid of hope could not be the answer she sought.

While her mind nearly overflowed with these thoughts, Ben calmly stated. "There seems to be something troubling you."

Something troubling her, troubling her, she must have been stark raving mad to even consider coming to this God forsaken place. There she had done it again. It was not her way to use God's name so, not her nature at all. Elizabeth wanted to scream out of frustration. She wanted to beg they return to Thimble and the end of the rail line. To go back, so she could leave this land of desolation forever. Elizabeth bit her lip, steadied her breathing, and slowly, carefully, clearly, asked the question she had been too afraid to ask, but now she could wait no longer. "Is Misty Creek like this?" she asked with a sweep of her arm.

Elizabeth feared his answer. Certainly the point was moot. Had she seen anything different since day they had left the railhead? Out here among the dried windblown land, even further from civilization, she could not hope that Misty Creek be anything but another Hancock's Bluff or a place like Paradise—no paradise at all. She thought all these things and so much more in the instant it took Ben to look over toward her and speak. "Misty Creek? No, Misty Creek isn't quite the same. Why it's a pearl."

A pearl, a pearl, what did the man mean? Elizabeth expected him to say more. The man, after all, had spoken a great deal on this trek, much more than she, but he did not elaborate. Yet something in her felt different. Somewhere within her, a small seed of optimism seemed to sprout. Misty Creek was different, different than Paradise, different than the bluff. A pearl! It must be better! But what did Ben mean? And who was to decide what better meant? Her small sprout of optimism quickly began to whither.

"I suppose I should tell you a bit more," Smith said at last. "I don't know what they told you before you came."

They had told her practically nothing. They had told her that they needed a teacher. A progressive school she had been told. A small community, she had been told. Our pastor will meet you at the station. She had been told. These things Elizabeth shared with Reverend Benjamin Smith.

"Well that's not very much," he responded.

No it wasn't. It wasn't much indeed. In truth, it shouldn't have been enough for anyone to consider uprooting oneself to come here. But it was her desperation, and so she took things for granted. Things like what the prairie would look like. Things like how the people would live. She had allowed her imagination to create a world not so terribly different than rural Ohio. But now she knew it was different. It had more in common with the surface of the moon than Ohio.

The pastor cleared his throat. "First off…"

Did he say first off? They had been bounding the wilderness on this wagon for nearly two days, first off!

"…this wagon belongs to Mr. Matthew Sonnefelt. He owns the mill."

Mill he said mill. Mills need water don't they. Wait, the name Sunnefield. Elizabeth had known a Sunnefield, a Dutchman. Didn't Dutchman use wind to power their mills? Elizabeth knew they did. She felt certain that there was sufficient wind on the prairie to drive one. The wind had not stopped since she had arrived. The teacher thought about this and wondered. "Then this load belongs to him, this miller?"

"No, most is an order made by Mr. Peabody. He owns the store."

"A store?" Elizabeth asked, the small seed of optimism growing once again.

"Yeah, Peabody's General Store, a Mercantile. It's the only store in town."

Town, he had used the word town.

"If you need something, he'd be the man to see, Mr. Howard Peabody. Mind you it takes a while to get things. It's not like we're right on the railhead you know." Ben snapped the reins once more. The land now was table-top flat, flatter than she had seen, flatter than she could imagine, just going on and on.

At last, two large hills came into view ahead. When they drew closer, Elizabeth could tell the road wound upward and ran between the crests of those hills. They stopped to rest before they began the long arduous climb. The pastor helped her from her seat, then began reaching and stretching as he limbered stiff limbs, and he soon began to care for the horses once again. Elizabeth stood just a short way off, shielding her eyes to better see the hills in the distance. She heard him say, "It's called the Saddle, that soft valley between the hill tops."

It indeed looked very much like a saddle, that soft grass covered sweep that connected the hills that ran left and right as far as the eye could see. Elizabeth saw how the road wound back and forth across the hillsides, before it at last crossed over in the lowest part of what she would call a pass.

But these certainly were not mountains, Elizabeth had seen mountains. Well, at least pictures of the great mountains of Tennessee and Kentucky. No, these were not mountains. Just large hills, made larger by the fact they had crossed nothing but flat land for nearly an hour.

Elizabeth walked a bit on legs that felt weak and rubbery. Weariness seemed to wash over her, a weariness not from physical exertion, for she had done little, but rather a weariness from the very conscious desire that this trek could be over. "Much further?" she asked weakly, fearing her fatigue showed in her voice, though she had tried her best to hide it.

Ben didn't seem to notice. "No, not far," he answered. "You'll be able to see Misty Creek from the Saddle."

See Misty Creek from the Saddle? Her emotions began to well. Emotions of anticipation, of curiosity, of relief that the long journey was nearly completed. She drew in a deep breath. There was another emotion, one she understood clearly—impatience. Though she stood on legs weary from too many hours bouncing along, she felt the undeniable urge to march onward. Elizabeth wanted to go to the top of this Saddle and see for herself the place she had destined to travel halfway across the continent to reach. And she would not follow that winding road either. No, she would not be deterred. A straight line was the shortest distance, and she had traveled far enough.

Elizabeth prepared to tell Ben how she intended to go on, to walk at least for a bit. However she remembered talk of snakes and other creatures hiding among the tall grass. So gathering another deep breath, Elizabeth turned and watched the man at work. It would not be long now, soon they would be moving, slowly. And though the road's snake-like path was longer than the route she would have taken, it would at last reach the top of the Saddle. She bit her lip as she looked once more toward the road they intended to take.

Ben, sensing her desire said, "It looks farther than it is, we should reach the top in about an hour."

"And then?" Elizabeth asked.

"Another hour and a half, maybe a bit longer. I'm afraid it will be nearly dark by the time we get there."

"Will I be able to see the school?"

"From the Saddle? No. I don't think you can quite see the school, but soon," he said as he finished watering the second horse. "We should be off in a minute."

Elizabeth drew yet another breath and then climbed on the wagon unassisted, preparing for what she hoped would be the last leg of an exceptionally long journey. The pastor hoisted himself and soon they were moving along once more at what seemed even a slower pace than ever. Elizabeth understood it wasn't so, but it seemed that not only were those poor horses dragging the loaded wagon but also a plow.

The road up from Paradise had been a gradual slope, one that went nearly unnoticed. But this road was clearly climbing. The road wound to the left and then to the right, making the climb much more gradual though longer, but true to the pastor's word they came to the crest in just over an hour.

The sun hung low in the west, yet high enough to reveal the land that lay before them. Here on the Saddle, high above the valley that was before them, Elizabeth saw the very last thing she had expected. For what lay before them had nothing in common with the land that for two days they had crossed. The pastor had said that Misty Creek was a pearl. Now she understood. He stopped the wagon, while in awe she beheld a land full of life, so green in the late afternoon light. Elizabeth could see fields of corn, straight rows and orchards. Houses, Elizabeth couldn't believe her eyes when she saw houses made of wood and painted. There were great barns and cattle grazing in pastures. She stared certain they had somehow returned to Ohio. No, it was greener than the Ohio she remembered.

In the distance, Elizabeth saw a lake. Water, real water, the first she had seen in days. The silvery lake sparkled so bright, she had to shade her eyes. And trees, real trees, not the dried up scruff she had seen in Paradise, stood all about the lake and continued far beyond, surely following the stream as it entered the lake and left again.

At the end of the lake, a bridge crossed its narrow end. There she saw buildings. It was a place called Misty Creek, Ben told her. At the far end of the lake, stood a large red wooden building, the mill. And somewhere among the trees, hidden from her view stood a white schoolhouse.

Elizabeth couldn't explain how she felt, freed from all the anxiety that had been building. She had been concerned even before she had left home, bound for places unknown. But since she had reached Thimble, the name of that place still caused her to shake her head, fear gripped her, with a clutch that tightened hour after passing hour. But at the sight of this valley, a place alive, an environment she could understand, Elizabeth found she could breathe again.

As they rode downward, downward toward the green land of the valley, her mood changed, and with that change all the questions came out in a rush, questions Elizabeth had not asked for fear of answers to frightening to hear.

"Tell me about the school?"

"Well, the building is just two years old," Smith said as he glanced her way. "We also use it for our church."

"The church?"

"It serves double duty," he said with a smile. "We built it on the other end of the lake so it wouldn't be too far from the farm families downstream."

Elizabeth nodded. "A one room school then?"

"Yes. There'll probably be thirty some students, all sizes and ages." He looked her way again. "You'll be the only teacher."

"I have taught in similar situations."

"Good. I don't expect you to have too much trouble. They're good kids. Known them since I arrived."

They rumbled on as Elizabeth digested what she had learned. "And Misty Creek, the town?"

"I don't know if you would call the place a town, just a few houses and the general store."

"Peabody's."

Ben nodded as he eased the horses' pace. Going downhill with their destination in sight the beasts seemed impatient as well.

"And your family's home?"

"The parsonage is just east of Peabody's. It's supplied by the community, not large but big enough."

"And there are other houses?"

"Only two. The Peabody's have the biggest house in town, and next to theirs is Eleanor Lewis's. That pretty much makes up the place."

Elizabeth smiled at the thought of a living vibrant community.

"I'll not speak about anyone's personality or character. You should have an open mind. You'll learn soon enough of each person's strengths and weakness," he said as he pulled back on the reins. "But I should tell you a bit about the Baughmans." He glanced her way. "They're the folks that will be boarding you."

"So I will not be provided with my own house?"

"I hope that won't be a problem?'

In the past Elizabeth had been provided a small house. It was considered part of her compensation. Though she did not enjoy the additional work of keeping her own home, she did savor the privacy. "I have not boarded before."

"Hmmm..." Ben looked forward and tilted his head slightly. "I don't think there is anything else available."

"Tell me about the Baghmans?"

"Abner is a retired farmer, well mostly retired. He and Alberta live near the school, so it's handy."

"They have children?"

"Yes, but they're grown and moved away."

Elizabeth thought a moment. "So they have no relations in the school?"

"That's why the school board chose them."

Elizabeth considered that an acceptable reason for selecting the couple. "Have they boarded teachers before?"

"They have. I haven't heard any complaints." Smith paused a moment, his eyes moved about. Elizabeth wondered what other thoughts were on his mind.

Elizabeth then became bold enough to ask, "Pastor Smith why would a pastor like yourself need to be moonlighting?"

The boldness seemed to surprise her more than the pastor who laughed loudly with that strong voice she enjoyed. "It allows me to reach out to the outlying communities on a fairly regular basis, but it's a matter of economics." He looked her way once again. "The truth is the community can't afford a pastor with a family, and I certainly have a family," he chuckled.

"I noticed that no collection had been taken at the bluff or Paradise for that matter."

The man became very serious, for the smile left his face as he said softly, "They live hand to mouth." Ben drew a breath as he shook the reins to coax the animals onward. "There's a box at the bluff. Eloise cares for it. When anyone can spare a penny or two it finds its way there. Come a time when there's a need, there's a bit of cash."

"I noticed," she began again, "a difference between Paradise and the bluff, the people I mean."

"There's a dramatic difference," Ben responded thoughtfully. "It's not that life is easier at the bluff than in Paradise, but the people feel differently. I mean about each other. They all settled about the same time, so that's not the cause."

They bounced a bit in silence, then she said, "If they were all like the Levendoski's…"

"Then things would be different," Ben finished her exact thought.

Elizabeth rode a bit, thinking about Paradise and the gracious family she had met, and how she would be forever changed by those special people. Softly she spoke to herself, "If everyone was like the Levendowski's then not only would Paradise be a better place, but the whole world as well."

She was surprised she had allowed the words to pass her lips, and more surprised that Ben nodded in agreement evidently hearing her words over the creaking and rumbling of the wagon.

After a moment of thought. Elizabeth returned to original question about a pastor hauling freight. "But you don't own the wagon. I mean the team and wagon their not yours."

"No, no, they belong to Mr. Sonnefelt."

"The miller."

"Yes, that's right Mr. Matthew Sonnefelt."

"Then he also operates a freight company?"

The pastor blinked and looked thoughtfully for a moment, as if he had to consider how best he could answer. "No, he doesn't really operate a freight for hire business, if that's what you mean. He has this team and tack, and two others with four wagons besides." Smith snapped the reins reminding the horses they had yet a distance to go. "He needs the wagons to haul out the meal and flour and sometimes grain as well."

"But you said most of this load was to go to the store. Surely he charges that man for hauling?" she asked.

The pastor looked toward her and with an earnest voice replied. "I don't believe he does."

"He doesn't charge the storekeeper for hauling all this?" she asked as she waved her hand over the bundles and crates behind them.

"Nor will he charge for your passage, Miss Beck," the man said firmly.

She blinked. It had never occurred to her that someone would need to pay for her ride from Thimble.

Then Ben added, "The wagon has to come back doesn't it."

Elizabeth thought about that a moment. It was true that the wagon would need to return. "But," she said at last, "an empty wagon…"

Smith cut her off, "…does no one any good."

"Well, it seems to me that this Mr. Sunnefield…"

"Sonnefelt…"

"That this Mr. Sonnefelt," she went on, "is not a very good businessman. It seems to me he is allowing Mr. Peacock…"

"Peabody…"

"Yes, yes, Peabody to take advantage of him."

The pastor stiffened, he seemed a bit ruffled when he answered. "I don't believe that to be the case."

Elizabeth felt she had offended the man, though could not understand how. She quickly went over the conversation in her mind. In the end the teacher still couldn't understand what she had said so wrong. For a time they rode on silently, or at least they didn't speak, for the wagon lumbered along as it had creaking and groaning.

Then, without warning, Ben said. "I must apologize Miss Elizabeth. I had no right to be cross."

"Were you cross? I hadn't noticed," she said, which was a lie.

"Whether you noticed it or not, I was," he said with a gasp, apparently noting the sarcasm. "You are new," he said calmly, "things are different out here." He drew a breath. "There doesn't need to be a profit in everything," Ben answered. He seemed exasperated once more.

Elizabeth felt it best to leave the subject as it was, though she was certain she was right. This man, this miller was certainly a fool, and she might be bold enough to tell him so when she met him. For Elizabeth was certain they would meet.

As they rode this last part of the long journey, things felt different. Elizabeth couldn't explain it, but it seemed tension had joined them. The man at the reins, the pastor, Reverend Benjamin Smith remained silent. He didn't even whistle. Slowly ever so slowly they moved on. The tension made each minute seem longer than the one that preceded it. Elizabeth had come to the point of asking the man to stop the wagon, so she could walk the distance that remained. However she noticed that it was growing dark much more quickly than she could have expected.

Ahead she could see lights of Misty Creek. It was not far. To her right, she could see the last of the sky's light reflected off the water of the lake. Even in the weak light, Elizabeth could see the expanse of water. Far across were other lights as well. The road followed the lake's edge, winding first to the left and then back. A short time later they came to a wooden bridge that crossed a stream of water, which Elizabeth felt certain was Misty Creek. Beyond that bridge, they came upon what must be a town, though the few buildings, three houses and a general store, could scarcely be called a town. A place known as Misty Creek.

PART 2
THE ARRIVAL

Chapter 7

Elizabeth did not know what to expect when she rumbled into the community that called itself Misty Creek, for it seemed that the west—every aspect—surprised her; not being anything like the newspaper articles she had devoured. But whatever she might have anticipated would certainly be different than what happened next. Ben brought the wagon to a stop in front of a wood frame building, which in many ways resembled Eloise's home. Though light spilled out the front windows, and little more than a basic outline could be determined in the darkness.

"Welcome to Misty Creek," Ben boomed. His strong voice seemed especially loud now that the wagon and tired horses stood silent. "Peabody's Mercantile," he added with a flourish of his left hand. The doors of the store burst open and several people poured out into the darkness to meet them. Ben spent his time introducing Elizabeth, as he had done on each of their stops, to one and all. When a man, a person she would describe as large, not especially tall, but broad, forced his way through.

"Miss Beck," the large man said in a commanding voice. "I'm William Clark, president of the school board. We're so glad that you have come." The others moved aside to give the man room. Whether it was out of respect or fear Elizabeth could not determine. "Let me help you down," he said as he offered his hand. From that moment on, Mr. Clark did the most talking. It was apparent the man was not only the head of the school board but also someone of influence.

Mr. Clark led Elizabeth through the crowd toward Peabody's General Store. "Make way," he shouted, "no need to stand out here gawking in the dark."

Elizabeth felt uncomfortable surrounded by a sea of strangers, and finding herself the center of everyone's attention. She looked back for Ben, the only person she knew, and saw him standing beside the team, talking to a tall slender man. Stopping at the doorway, she watched the pastor and the tall man that held a lantern dressed in work clothes, a laborer of some sort it seemed. She gasp at the sight of the man in the darkness. It just couldn't be. He stood tall and straight and moved with confident direct steps. Elizabeth watched the silhouette of the man as he moved. His walk the movement of his arms seemed familiar. Surely it couldn't be, Alexander. Elizabeth had heard the man had gone west but she could speak to the fact that west was a large place and of all the places it contained surely that man had not come to this location. Oh how, she loathed Alexander, such an arrogant buffoon that continuously belittled his younger brother Jameson.

"A man is measured by the sweat on his brow and the calluses on his hands," he had continually boasted. But his studious younger brother had other plans. Alexander continually showed his disdain for the younger Elders aspirations. "The workers of this land carry you book worms on our backs. You are no more than unwanted cargo." Alexander never noticed the downward glances his brother gave. Those words had cut into Elizabeth as well. She had loved Jameson, and even now after all that had happened, she still did. She just couldn't help it. She loved Jameson Elders. And it angered her that Alexander, big strong Alexander, never noticed the hours of work invested and the greatness his brother achieved. Becoming a doctor took more than ox-like thoughtless repletion of lifting, digging or any other of the menial tasks of which Alexander bragged.

She watched as Ben slapped the tall man upon the back. Elizabeth could not make out the man's features in the darkness, but the man stood like Alexander, walked like Alexander, and deep within her an anger grew, a white hot rage fueled by words not forgotten. The man grasped the bridle and began to lead the horses away. Where, she had no idea, but her trunk and carpet bag yet aboard as the wagon moved off into the darkness. Tightening her brow she intended to march back down the steps and to the roadside to speak with this man.

Ben quickly turned, and passing through the wake she and Mr. Clark had made, reached her with just a few quick steps. "I'm sorry," he said, soft enough that only she heard. "I certainly did not intend to abandon you."

"My things?" she asked

"Not to worry, Miss Beck, not to worry."

Elizabeth did not wish to acknowledge her discomfort or concern, so she nodded slightly. Ben held out his arm, but Mr. Clark, still at her side, nearly dragged her into the store itself. Peabody's Mercantile had been rearranged, she was sure, to make room for what was a reception. A long table was set up with refreshments. A pitcher of lemonade and trays with cookies and cakes set on clean tablecloth with a red checkered pattern. Ben began to properly introduce her to the town's folk, but was once more interrupted by Mr. William Clark, who began of all things a speech.

"Miss Beck," he began, "as President of the School Board I would like to officially welcome you to our fair town. We had decided to put together this little reception for your honor. I hope you will find us to be the warm and friendly folks we are. I know you will find the school to your satisfaction." He then swept a glass off the table and held it high above his head. "Here's to Miss Elizabeth Beck, our new teacher." Cheers rose all around and Elizabeth was certain she was blushing.

The speech was not entirely over, though later she would not remember precisely what was said. Elizabeth's head seemed filled with a fog as she remained surrounded by people she really had not yet met. Finally when Mr. Clark had finished, he began to introduce the town's folk. First came William Jr., Mr. Clark's eldest, a young man perhaps twenty-three or there abouts. Then came Jennifer, William's daughter, a young lady of perhaps ten. Elizabeth wondered about the age difference but said nothing. She was introduced to Josephine, Mr. Clark's wife. A handsome woman that Elizabeth was certain was much younger than her husband. Again she did not mention the fact. Elizabeth then met Mr. Howard Peabody and his wife Martha and their five children. She thanked the Peabody's for hosting the gathering. The comment seemed to make Clark a bit huffy. Then Mr. Clark ended the introductions as he escorted the new school teacher to the table, all the while talking about the modern school they had and the simply delightful place Misty Creek was, and not allowing her the space to force a word in edgewise.

Perhaps an half hour had elapsed when the man left her, for whatever reason, and Elizabeth found herself standing next to a woman she had yet to meet. Ben arrived at her side—this other woman's side. The pastor kissed the unknown woman on the cheek and smiling, introduced Elizabeth to his very attractive wife, Leah. Though Mrs. Smith was not what Elizabeth had expected, she felt a connection and knew they could be friends. The woman with fair hair and skin stood a bit taller than Elizabeth. Dressed in a blue dress with a pattern that resembled the shirt Ben had worn at their meeting, she carried a broad smile, which set off her sparkling blue eyes. When the pastor completed the introduction, Leah threw her arms around the new teacher, pulling Elizabeth tight in her embrace. Yes, Leah was much like her husband, open, warm, and honestly friendly. An older woman reached them, handed Mrs. Smith a small child—James, the Smith's youngest. She had two other young Smith's in tow. Micah the oldest, a lad of seven and Rachael every bit of five. The older woman was Mrs. Alberta Baughman, a cheerful, though plump woman, in her sixties, Elizabeth would guess. Her husband had not come. He wasn't beholding to such things, whatever that meant.

When the chaos died down and Elizabeth had found a seat; she was quickly joined on the right by Leah and by Mrs. Baughman on the left, which pleased her greatly, for they were the only two, other than Ben, she had come to know. From her seat Elizabeth watched how the people of the community all around her responded to one another. She was particularly interested in Mr. Clark, as he moved about shaking hands and speaking to nearly everyone. One would have thought him a politician seeking an office of some sort. Then there was Ben talking to the Peabody's, laughing at one thing or another. Elizabeth could hear his now familiar voice over the din. Mr. Clark repeatedly glanced the pastor's direction, and did not seem amused by Ben's boisterous voice. She wondered what the big man thought of his pastor.

Elizabeth looked about the store. The shelves seemed well stocked and the floor swept spotless, though that may have been for her arrival, yet she thought not. As the teacher scanned the interior she noticed someone working in the back room. The tall man she had seen with Ben before. Now as he moved about, passing the doorway from time to time, she saw him clearly. Elizabeth took a breath for it was not Alexander after all, and found herself relieved. The man was tall and could be described as thin, in a dusty work shirt and dungarees. His hair was dark and his mustache was covered with a white dust. Later she observed Ben leave the party, going to the back room. She watched as Ben spoke to the tall thin laborer. This did not seem unusual, for certainly the man was another of his flock. They spoke for some time when suddenly Ben laughed, slapped the other on the back, causing a small cloud of dust to rise, and returned to the group. At that moment Mrs. Baughman told her she must leave, for Alice and Leo Tomkins, the neighbors that had brought her were homeward bound. "I'll see you later," the older woman said with a smile.

Elizabeth returned the smile and nodded.

While Mr. Clark continued moving around the room, speaking to any and all it seemed, many of the mothers came to her as she sat, each politely reintroducing themselves and their children—if they had brought them. Elizabeth smiled as she tried to remember all the names. On other occasions she would have remembered the names and faces, but being so very tired and overwhelmed, the teacher found it beyond her present capabilities.

Ben took the chair vacated by Mrs. Baughman and asked, "Ladies how are you doing?"

Elizabeth lied and told him she was fine. She could tell by the look in his eye that Ben knew better. "I believe," he said then, "it is time you go."

"Perhaps it is," she said softly but not so softly he was unable to hear over the sound of other voices, "but it would be rude for me to do so. After all the trouble these fine people have gone through for my arrival."

"Nonsense, the party's over," the pastor said loud enough to be noticed by most there.

"Ben's right dear," Leah agreed, "there will be time enough for all to become acquainted."

Ben continued, "I'll see if Matthew is nearly ready." He strode out of the room through the door to the back, which left the young teacher confused. He soon returned but was called aside by Mrs. Peabody. Elizabeth watched the man in the back once again. She must have been staring, for she started when Leah told her that the man was Mr. Sonnefelt, the miller.

Shocked she asked, "Matthew Sonnefelt?"

Leah nodded.

How could that be? How could the dusty man, the laborer in the back of the store, the man that in so many ways reminded her of

Alexander Elders be Mr. Sonnefelt? She looked at him once again in disbelief.

In all the noise and bustle, Elizabeth noticed a change in Mr. William Clark the moment the tall dusty form of Mr. Sonnefelt entered the room. She observed Clark's hands tighten into fists, open only to be drawn tightly once more. Clark stared at the miller, his eyes beneath tightened brows with the skin of face drawn and straight lips. It even stopped his conversation with Mr. Peabody and she was certain others noticed as well. Clark swayed slightly, the moment passed, and he turned his attention to the storekeeper who had continued speaking though Clark's attention was clearly elsewhere.

She looked at Sonnefelt, the man in a faded flannel shirt which at one time must have been a red plaid, now grayed as his dungarees by dirt of one kind or another. His eyes moved quickly about the room not staying in any one direction but an instant. He stood at the end of the counter remaining at the fringe of all that filled the store. He seemed out of place, not only in his dress but by his behavior, and Elizabeth wondered about the man, and what about the miller that troubled Mr. Clark.

The teacher's thoughts were shattered by a loud voice, the familiar sound of Mr. William Clark. "Well, folks, it's getting late and I know most of you have got chores to do and supper to get to. If the pastor had gotten here when we had expected him it wouldn't be so late."

Ben was about to speak, Elizabeth could see fire in his eyes, a fire not so unlike she had seen in Paradise that morning, but another voice, a clear strong voice, a voice she had not heard before, came from the end of the counter. For there stood a tall man, a slender man, a dusty man, and he said. "The fault is mine. I'm sure Ben came as quickly as he could, considering..." He paused just the briefest of moments as if to allow the words to find their home. "The wagon was heavy and we should be grateful that he and the cargo including Miss Beck arrived safely."

Cargo, she thought indignantly, *cargo!*

How dare he? Elizabeth wanted to stride right up to, this, this man and ask, no, demand an apology. Cargo what kind of vermin! Oooh, how dare he? She rose to her feet to do just that, but surrounded once more by the townspeople all biding her goodnight, which formed a barrier between Elizabeth and the object of her wrath.

CHAPTER 8

WHEN THE ROOM HAD CLEARED, FOR IT CLEARED QUICKLY, LEAVing only the Smith's and the Peabody's, the dusty man had left. Elizabeth thought it was a good thing he had. Still angry she shook her head.

Leah leaned close and with a voice soft enough only Elizabeth could hear whispered, "He meant nothing. Just a poor choice of words."

Elizabeth looked toward her new friend certain that now the fire was in her eyes, when Leah tilted her head slightly and added, "Honestly."

"The least I deserve is an apology!" Elizabeth said, coldly. "Cargo!"

"Did Ben tell you," Leah spoke calmly, "that you would be staying with the Baughman's?"

"Yes," Elizabeth said, trying to get her temper under control. "How will I get to their home?"

"Well," the pastor's wife said carefully, "it was intended that you be taken there by wagon."

"By wagon?" she asked. After riding two long days on the seat of a freight wagon, the idea was not welcome.

"It is some distance, and quite dark."

"By Mr. Sonnefelt's wagon?"

"I'm afraid so."

"And would your husband be driving that wagon?"

"It really wasn't what we had planned."

"Then I will walk, thank you very much!" Everyone that remained turned to look Elizabeth's way, including a dusty tall thin man standing at the doorway.

Ben rushed to them. "Is there a problem?"

Leah whispered into her husband's ear and then said, "Perhaps you should take our teacher to her new home."

"That won't be necessary." Elizabeth stated firmly. "I am sure I can walk. Have the man load up my luggage, if it is not too much trouble. I will not burden his wagon with unnecessary cargo!"

"Elizabeth…" Leah began, "I'm sure we can straighten this whole misunderstanding."

"Misunderstanding. Misunderstanding. No, I believe I understood quite clearly!" She glared at the miller who looked downward. Catching her breath she stormed toward the front door. Mr. Sonnefelt stepped aside without a word. Elizabeth marched across the porch and down the three steps. She saw her trunk and other things loaded, and she bound into the darkness. Elizabeth took to the road going the way the horses were pointed. It seemed logical that it would be the right direction. Misty Creek was a small place, surely anyone would find their way. It was dark, very dark. Her eyes had not become accustomed to the night. She tripped. She fell. Fortunately it was dark. No one could have seen her there lying face down in the middle of the road. No one. Scarcely had she felt the road against her face when she sensed a hand, a strong hand, a gentle hand. Turning her head she saw an outline of someone crouched beside her, offering help. What could she do? Elizabeth rolled a bit, tucked her feet beneath her and with his aid stood upright. Elizabeth began to slap the dirt off her clothing, her favorite yellow dress. Ruined she was sure.

"It would be best if you rode the wagon," said a soft voice, a very calm and considerate voice, but it was a voice she knew, the voice of one Matthew Sonnefelt.

She jerked her hand free. Glaring at him in the dark, not that she could clearly see the man, but she would not let his condescending words fool her. Elizabeth felt certain the man looked at her with the same critical, judgmental eyes Alexander had always shown. Which only increased her anger and determination. "I said I would walk, and I shall." And Elizabeth strode off once again. This time she made nearly twenty steps before she found herself face down once again.

Elizabeth was not really surprised that the man was there the very moment she tripped, beside her to lift her back to her feet once again, which only increased her rage.

"Ma'am," he said, "if you are so set on walking, slow down a bit."

"Slow down! Slow down! Now sir, are you implying I need your instruction on how to walk? I'll walk at whatever pace I choose, thank you very much." And once again she stormed off.

"You'll fall again."

"Perhaps I will, but I don't need your help. I have been picking myself up all my life. I am sure I can do so tonight."

"I'm certain you can, Miss Beck, but where are you going?"

"To the Baughman's farm of course!"

"Then perhaps you should go the other way."

The other way! It had never occurred to her that she was bound in the wrong direction. She had stormed off in a rage. Gone the direction she felt had to be right. Now standing in the middle of the road, standing in the darkness her anger seemed tempered by her embarrassment. She had, after all, tripped twice and was not certain how many had noticed. And though she was yet angry, very angry at Mr. Matthew Sonnefelt, Elizabeth understood that her rage had gotten the best of her. Looking down she slowly said. "Perhaps you are correct Mr. Sonnefelt. If you could show me the way." She paused as she turned to face the man in the dark road. She saw that he held out a hand but refused take it. Then he pointed the way they had come.

Elizabeth had not realized how far she had walked. It seemed with her mind racing, driven by anger, she had gone quite some distance, nearly reaching the bridge. She decided against mentioning the distance covered, and hoped that man, that Mr. Sonnefelt would not mention it either. So they walked the dark road side by side without a word shared. From time to time she could not resist the urge to glance to her left and see the tall slender man walking next to her, so close yet a world away.

Several minutes passed as they walked in silence before they returned to Peabody's Store. The team and wagon waited for them. Mr. Sonnefelt offered a hand to aid her climb to the seat. "I think I'll walk," she said calmly, actually surprised at how serenely the words flowed from her lips, "if you will direct the way."

"It's some distance, most of a mile."

"And you think I'm incapable. I'll have you know…"

"No ma'am," he interrupted. "I'm sure you more than fit enough."

Fit enough. What was that supposed to mean?

"To walk," he went on, "but seein' I'm bound that way anyway."

"No, Mr. Sonnefelt, I have ridden on your wagon long enough. I'll not burden it further."

"It'll be no burden, Ma'am." The man paused as if wondering what he would say next. He began to speak, then stopped, tilted his head slightly, and at last said softly, "I would appreciate the opportunity to take you."

The words caught her by surprise. Elizabeth stood there a moment beside him in the dark road. She considered that other eyes might be watching from store and the houses nearby. Though the night surrounded them, Elizabeth wondered what observers might notice. What impression was she giving? These thoughts mixed with the anger that flowed around in her mind.

Sonnefelt waited. Elizabeth did not answer. He waited a moment longer. At long last Mr. Sonnefelt spoke. "I'd like the company." And again he offered his hand.

He'd like the company. What did that mean? She was about to reject his outstretched hand once again, but wondering how walking behind the wagon would appear to any that happened to notice, and the wagging tongues it would certainly fuel, caused Elizabeth at last to put her hand in his—his strong hand—a hand yet gentle.

Once seated, he hurried, untying the team and with one quick step bounded up and beside her. A snap of the reins and they were off. Elizabeth did not speak as she sat beside him, and he said nothing. The miller turned the wagon about and they left Misty Creek behind. And leaving that small place, they left any light that spilled from the windows. Though her eyes were now accustomed to the night, it was incredibly dark. But as the night before, the sky above seemed filled with bright diamonds, so many standing out against the night sky, that for a moment it took her very breath away. They moved on among trees, oh, how she had missed them. The trees lined both sides of the road as they rumbled onward into the night.

To her right she could, from time to time, see glimpses of the lake and the stars reflected on the smooth dark water. The wagon moved slowly, a pace she had become accustomed to. At times, the trees on both sides would reach high above, their branches meeting and tangling together, creating what seemed like a tunnel. Then even the stars above were hidden, as they lumbered on through a deep pitch. Elizabeth had never feared the night. Never in her entire life, but for an instant, a very brief instant, panic swept over her. The woman's mind considered all the things that had happened, all that she faced here on a strange dark road, riding with a man she didn't know, in a place she had never been, bound for a destination uncertain.

Elizabeth stole a glance at the man beside her, only a dim silhouette, a darker shape in the darkness. She saw his hands firm grip upon the reins, and just the slightest gleam of his eyes as they focused intently on the road before them. And for no reason she could determine, the sight of him brought her comfort, the fear left. Elizabeth drew a deep breath, apparently loud enough to be noticed, for Mr. Sonnefelt looked her way. Though the teacher could not be certain, she imagined he smiled.

"It'll not be long now ma'am," he said as he snapped the reins once more urging on the tired beasts.

They rode past a farm on their left. Bits of light spilled out of curtained windows, a dog barked—the only signs of life. Then once more moved into the pitch, beneath the spreading branches that hid the stars. But this time instead of fear, Elizabeth opened herself to everything around her. For though the noise of the wagon hid all but the loudest of the night's sounds. She heard another dog barking far away. She could feel the gentle breeze that moved the branches with their yet green leaves. The world that was all around her felt alive. It was so different than the country she had just crossed. Here there was life. It was then, there in the dark, sitting, feeling the world around her as she sat on a freight wagon, that Elizabeth, for the first time since stepping off the train in Thimble, did not regret coming. Her mind quickly grasped the thoughts of new friends, Leah and Alberta. She thought of the children. Those she had been fortunate enough to have met, and those she was certain were scattered all across the countryside. No, Elizabeth felt the arrival made the trek worthwhile. And even though so much unknown yet lay ahead, she felt an excitement growing deep inside.

Mr. Sonnefelt turned the team onto a lane and out from beneath the canopy of the great trees. It was yet dark, but in the brilliance of the stars reaching from horizon to horizon made it less dark. Soon they saw the lights of a house, a large house, it seemed. In the starlight she saw a grand barn as well. They had reached the Baughman's farm.

Mr. Sonnefelt brought the wagon to a stop beside a gate in a fence that ran about the house. The door opened and standing there waving, illuminated by the light that flowed out onto the porch was Alberta Baughman. "We're here," the miller said, hopping down. He strode around the wagon so swiftly that it surprised Elizabeth to see him with hand outstretched.

"Why thank you, Mr. Sonnefelt," Elizabeth said as he helped her from the wagon's seat.

Soon Mrs. Baughman reached them, and gave Elizabeth a hug as if they were long parted friends. "Come in child," she said, "you've had a long day." Turning she asked, "Matthew will you help with her things? I'll send Abner."

"Thanks I can manage," was all he said as he grabbed her trunk and began after them. "Where would like this?"

"Oh, Matthew just bring it in. It would be too much to ask that you cart it upstairs."

"No ma'am. If it needs to go upstairs then lead the way."

Alberta began to protest, but saw there was little point and directed him toward the stairs. "First room on the right, the big one."

The miller smiled and went on his way, quickly. It seemed to Elizabeth that everything the man did, he did quickly. Then Elizabeth met Mr. Abner Baughman. The farmer was a large man, big in every way. Tall and broad, dressed in coveralls with snow white hair and a warm smile. He greeted Matthew on his return from delivering the trunk to the upstairs room. Mr. Sonnefelt shook his hand. They spoke a bit about the weather, could use a bit of rain, and then Sonnefelt left quickly. A moment later the miller returned with her bag and was about to hurry it upstairs when Elizabeth stopped him. "There's no need, Mr. Sonnefelt," she said, "thank you for all your help."

He stood there in the parlor awkwardly for a moment, before handing the carpetbag to her outstretched arms. Alberta invited the Matthew to join them for supper, but the dusty man declined, saying something about the horses, their needing to be cared for, or something of that matter, and he was gone. Alberta waving as she closed the door. "Now there's a fine man," she said softly as she turned.

The comment took Elizabeth by surprise. It was more than just Alberta's words, for she saw agreement in Mr. Baughman's eyes. Elizabeth wondered what the Baughmans saw in the man. He seemed no more than laborer. So much about him reminded her of Alexander, and that infuriated her. She would have given it further thought, but the conversation changed. Things said like, "Would you like to see your room?" and "Supper's nearly done." And many other statements and questions that she would not remember come morning, but each one sensitive and kind. That was how she began to think of the Baughman's—sensitive and kind. Caring people, that opened their home, but more, opened their hearts to this new comer from Ohio.

The room, the first door on the right at the top of the stairs, a large room, larger than her bedroom at home. It had two grand windows facing the house's front and two smaller ones on the left as she entered. Light from the lamp that Alberta carried showed a nicely furnished room. The bed with a brightly patterned quilt, a wash stand in the corner, a standing wardrobe in another corner, the third corner had a large overstuffed chair of brown fabric. There was what she would describe as a full sized dresser, with a mirror no less, a chest of drawers and a desk. Elizabeth couldn't believe her eyes. It was truly a place she could live, but more, a comfortable place to work, if the need called. Typically Elizabeth had done her work at the school. For she had taught for seven years and had long ago developed a system, or at least the framework of a system, that seemed to function best for her and her students. Elizabeth stood a moment speechless, which was for her a bit unusual. Mrs. Baughman looked at her with a concern that the young teacher's silence was a sign of displeasure. But at last Elizabeth smiled, wrapped her arms about her new hostess, and said, "Oh Alberta, what a wonderful room."

Alberta smiled in return. "Take a few minutes to look about dear. Supper'll be on the table soon." With that Alberta set the lamp upon the chest of drawers and left Elizabeth alone in her new room.

Elizabeth felt the bed, bounced upon it, judged it as the rest of the room—wonderful. She rushed down the stairs grabbed her bag and brought it up.

While she unpacked Abner's voice came from below, calling for the meal. And what a meal it was. Elizabeth could not remember a time she had eaten better, though perhaps her appetite affected that opinion, for she had not eaten, for all points and purposes, since they had left Paradise, that is except for a cookie and a piece of cake at Peabody's Store.

During the meal Elizabeth learned a great deal. How the Baughman's had boarded teachers before. The community considered them the perfect people for the job. The Baughman farm was near the school. A good point to be sure. But more important, they did not have children, or grandchildren attending. Elizabeth considered the arrangement wise. There could be no tongues suggesting favoritism in that regard.

Elizabeth was told that the school was built on a small piece of ground that had been donated. That it stood on the edge of the lake, down the road a piece. The location chosen to make the school accessible to the whole valley. That the building was also used as the church. An idea Elizabeth had never considered but thought clever. There had been thirty-four students the year before, though the Baughman's did not know the exact number that would make up this term. It seemed reasonable to assume the number to be similar.

When Elizabeth asked if she might see the school, Alberta suggested she wait until morning. "It's dark dear. Don't you think it best to wait until you can see it properly?"

But she felt an irresistible need to see the school. Yet when Abner offered to walk with her, she felt she was imposing and declined. "You have been both so kind. I'll not put you out so." She said all the while planning a night excursion on her own.

After the meal, she helped Alberta with the dishes. Elizabeth couldn't explain it, but she found a comfort in that house and among those kind people. When the dishes had been cleaned and put away, they sat on the porch getting to know one another better, enjoying the night. Later the Baughman's told her they would turn in. "Best not to stay up too late, dear, "Alberta said with a gentle hand upon the teacher's shoulder, "tomorrow will be another day."

Elizabeth smiled as she told them that she would remain for a time, for her mind was racing far too fast to sleep. That perhaps she would stretch her legs.

"Now don't go too far." Alberta warned.

Abner looked about into the darkness and added, "The night is not a safe time to be about."

Elizabeth thanked them for their concern, and told them she would not venture far.

She sat there in the warm night air, listening to the katydid's call that filled the night. Elizabeth waited, waited for some time, waited until she was certain that her new friends had gone to bed. Then she got up, moved down the steps quietly, and walked out of the gate and down the lane, calmly, so not to fall in the dark.

CHAPTER 9

THE ROAD BENEATH THE TREES SEEMED DARK AS HER AUNT JOAN'S root cellar the time long ago when her brother had playfully closed the door above her. That darkness drove her to panic and tears, but she was only a child then. Tightening her jaw, Elizabeth stood there looking into the pitch, the incredible blackness, and reconsidered her plan. Perhaps she should have brought a lantern. Well, it was too late for that now. Elizabeth wanted to see the school. She had traveled all this way, come to teach school, here, in the absolute middle of nowhere. It was curiosity but more. It was a need.

So she drew in a deep breath and began, and found it was not as dark as she had imagined. No, Elizabeth could make out the road. There was no need to fear, or at least that was what she told herself. Surely Mr. Baughman had exaggerated. She could not consider that the man had purposely lied. Elizabeth convinced herself, that there was nothing to fear as she went along. The road continued to follow the edge of the lake. On occasions she would catch a glimpse of the water. The trees on her left thinned, and she could look across farmland with its tall rows of corn and open pastures. The moon had broken the horizon, the last quarter. Now as the golden half-round moon rose, its light played on the land, the trees casting shadows across the road.

With the moon's light she could see more, and her mood improved as her courage grew.

Elizabeth came to a fork in the road, or rather the road continued on and had a branch to her right. She stood there a moment and wondered which way. Remembering that the school was on the lake's edge, she took the right fork. It proved to be a wise selection for very soon she came to a place where she could see the small white frame building, standing on well cared grounds. When at last, she stood at the gate of the fence that bordered the school grounds, though her attention focused upon the building she had come to see; she also notice that the mill lay just across the water and in plain sight. Elizabeth allowed her eyes to roam in that direction for a moment examining the only structure that lay within view. No light came from the great building, a sleeping hulk it seemed across the water.

Elizabeth stood a moment and wondered about the mill and the man that operated it. She thought of the conversations years before she had with other teachers, sharing difficult experiences they had at their schools. Every community had a vast mix of people each with their own idea what the school should teach. Most quietly sat at home with their opinion as they approved or disapproved of one aspect or another. But at times there were those that just made the task of teaching difficult, at least more difficult than it need be. Elizabeth's own run-in with Cecily Sawyer came to mind at that moment. Her first year behind the desk, just seventeen and green behind the ears. She was not prepared for Cecily. Elizabeth drew a breath and thought of the woman, a spinster that lived with her widowed father, their house not two hundred yards from the rural school outside of London, Ohio. The lanky scarecrow of a lady, always dressed in shapeless dark colored dresses, moved like as a stick figure beneath a tent. Elizabeth shook her head at the thought. Cecily passed rumors about like they were pies at a bake sale. And if there were none, she could create gossip better than anyone Elizabeth had ever met.

Often she told the neighbors of Elizabeth's failing in discipline. Too harsh or too lenient, it did not matter, one spread as toxic as another. Elizabeth suspected the woman sat in her father's parlor with her knitting forever looking out the window to the school so close by. Twice she had caught Cecily on the school grounds peeking into the windows while Elizabeth had taught.

The inexperienced Elizabeth was at a loss of how she might deal with the busybody. An evening's conversation with the woman only resulted in fueled mistrust on both sides. Mr. Amos Johnson a member of the school board defused the situation to some degree. He had spoken to Jonah Sawyer, Cecily's father, the man seemed disconnected to the whole affair, but put the brakes on his daughter's meddling. It did not stop the woman entirely but with time Cecily became little more than an annoyance.

The years had taught Elizabeth many things, and among them she had learned lessons in how to deal with those that lived near a school. Though she did her best to be friendly, there were always those that kindness seemed wasted. The unreachable, Elizabeth sometime called them. Those that required a little outside intervention, a pastor perhaps or some other respected community member. But the best defense had always been to do your best, treat students fairly, care about each one of them, sometimes that part was hard, and to above all remain open and above board. She had no use for secrets in the classroom—no use at all.

Now she wondered, with the mill nearest, would Mr. Sonnefelt become her new Cecily Sawyer? And if he did, how would she handle the man? Elizabeth shook her head, this was not the time to dwell on what might or might not be a problem.

She returned her attention to the dirt road that she had taken. Seeing that it led on, going across the top of the dam that held the water that made the lake. In the dim light Elizabeth could see two small bridges, much like the one at Misty Creek. One stood near the dam's center the other nearer the mill. The sound of water flowing over rocks floated on the still night air. Elizabeth tilted her head, and if she would have let her curiosity take its leave, she would have walked further to see the water flowing through the spillway. But the teacher had come to see the school, and that was what she would do.

As Elizabeth approached the schoolhouse, a new concern gripped her. What if the door was locked? She stood at the base of the stairs and wondered, perhaps she had walked for naught. Well if that be the case, she could at least tell herself she had seen the school and knew the way. She moved on carefully, stealthily, feeling like a burglar. She reached the door, drew in a breath, turned the knob, opened the heavy oak door and walked in.

The interior was dark. Of course it was dark, it was after all the middle of the night, or sufficiently close in any case, but a bit of moonlight spilled in through the windows. Elizabeth moved among the pews. For a moment she felt mistaken, that the white building was not the school at all. Then she remembered the school building also served as Misty Creek's Church.

She moved to the windows, gazing out across the ground that stretched toward the lake with its water reflecting the stars. Unable to help herself, she stared out into the night, the trees and the water, and the star-filled sky. Standing there totally engrossed, Elizabeth was startled by a gentle rap on wood.

Someone stood in the doorway. For a moment she felt a fear, no, terror. But the someone in the doorway spoke with a calm, almost gentle voice, a familiar voice— the voice of Mr. Sonnefelt. Though her fear diminished it blended with the anger that yet remained and the disdain she felt for the miller. Why was it he was everywhere she turned?

"I would think it would be late for you Mr. Sonnefelt," she said coolly.

"It is ma'am."

Elizabeth had expected some other comment. Something like… "What are you doing here? Don't you know it's dangerous being out at night, especially this late…?" But the man said no more. Instead he moved quickly, once again she thought how he always seemed to move quickly, to a lamp. Striking a match he lifted the glass and soon had its golden light filling the dark space. Though one small lamp could not make the room a place of brilliance, it revealed the interior hidden in the blackness. He strode across the room to another lamp, one much closer to her, and following the precise procedure had that one glowing as well. Now she could see the room better.

The room filled with orderly rows of pews, while the desks were neatly lined along the back wall and stacked, one desk placed top down on the other, with chairs placed upside down on the stacked desks. The large desk stood in its place, or so she imagined, a bit to the right of the doorway she had entered. Elizabeth turned to face the front of the room. There she noticed a raised area on which stood the altar as well as a podium for the pastor. Strange, her mind suddenly filled with an image of Ben, tall and tan standing there preaching to his flock. A cowboy preacher, dressed in dungarees and a flower patterned shirt and his worn Bible in his left hand, while he flourished the other as he spoke of love and forgiveness and such things that preachers say. She shook her head swiftly and then everything was as it was, an empty church—school, empty except for her and Mr. Sonnefelt.

Mr. Sonnefelt. What would people think? Alone in the school in the middle of the night with a man and Mr. Sonnefelt at that.

"I'd best be going," she blurted.

"I'll walk you home," he said graciously.

"Thank you Mr. Sonnefelt," she said in clipped tones, so harshly it surprised even her. Then added a bit more softly, though only the slightest bit, "I have managed to find my way here, I am perfectly able to find my way home."

"I'm certain you can, ma'am. But seein' you're new here…" he began, "it would be unfortunate if'n something drug you off in the night. This be'n your first night an all."

His words startled her, and though she had no intension, Elizabeth felt her eyes open at the suggestion of danger. She caught her breath waiting a moment to respond. Finally she answered, "Surely you exaggerate. I'm certain I'll be perfectly fine."

The man nodded. Elizabeth began for the door and for a moment wondered if he would step in her way. Why that thought had come she could not discern, for strangely she felt no fear of the man, only disdain. "You'll put out the lights, Mr. Sonnefelt."

"Ma'am," he said in a bit louder tone than he had used before. "I would not consider myself a gentleman, if I did not accompany you."

A gentleman. He would think himself a gentleman. How could he? This man, this dusty man, though now he did not seem as dusty for he had changed his clothes, was no gentleman though he might be dressed such. Well, Elizabeth knew better.

"I can assure you…" she began.

But he raised his hand. "I'll walk you back to Baughman's, whether you accept my company or require I walk in the shadows behind. But I will see you safely home one way or the other."

Who did this man think she was? It seemed that every step she had taken since she had taken left Peabody's Mercantile had been controlled by this man. Was she some wayward child that needed his continuous attention? Elizabeth felt certain that this common laborer considered her no more than a burden or worse, a fool. Most men were so full of themselves, Alexander had been, and this man was just like Alexander. Jameson was among the few that recognized the fact that women need not be coddled, and even he, dear Jameson, had cut her to the quick. But this man was nothing like Jameson. No, he was just another self-important man like Alexander that could not see beyond their own puffed chest.

Squinting her eyes she drew a breath and stormed out. Elizabeth nearly tripped on the steps before she slowed her pace to one her feet could keep in time with. When Elizabeth reached the road, she was relieved that he had not followed. But less than a minute later she saw a lamp moving quickly up the road behind her. She began to pick up her pace. But remembering how swiftly the man seemed to move felt it fruitless. Soon he was perhaps three strides behind. Elizabeth believed he would soon come along side, but he came no closer, always some three strides behind.

Her shadow danced lively in front of her, set to motion by the swing of the lamp caused by the man's step. And since her shadow did not change, at least not dramatically, Elizabeth felt no need to look over her shoulder. Now the road did not seem so dark, or she did not notice, for though he carried a lamp, it gave little reprieve from the darkness. Her anger, which grew with each step, hid the darkness from her mind. Surely the man acted as if she was a total incompetent, that she could not do anything without his assistance. Had she not traveled on her own without his or any man's aid?

Sonnefelt followed as she left the road onto the lane that led to the farm. The act stirred her anger further. Elizabeth had not spoken a word, not one, since she had walked out of the schoolhouse, until she reached the gate that led to the Baughman's yard. There she stopped. Glaring at the tall man that came up behind her. "Are you satisfied now," she hissed, "I told you I could find my way!"

"It was not about finding your way." The man said softly, with a calm voice, which only upset her further.

"Well, Mr. Sonnefelt, I am home. You have done your duty. Or do you intend to remain until I am undressed and in my bed." She was shocked at the words she had used.

Elizabeth prepared to apologize, when the miller, shook his head slightly, touching the brim of his hat said, "Good night Ma'am," turned and was gone.

She stood there and watched the man. He walked swiftly, which was no surprise. Soon she could not make out his form, only the lamp as it swayed to and fro in time with his steps. Elizabeth didn't know why she continued to watch until he had reached the road and was hidden by the trees. Even then she remained at the gate for several minutes. When Elizabeth at last reached the door she looked back and caught a glimpse of the lantern far down the road as its light slipped past the trees, which stood as guardians at the roadside.

Later as Elizabeth lay in the dark, with so much on her mind, she thought about the things that had brought her here to this place, leaving her family behind. At that moment, those she loved seemed so very far away. She pushed the reasons out of her head. No, she would not dwell on that— not now. But her mother and father, her sister and friends, and everything she knew, these things Elizabeth saw clearly in her mind. The sad look in her mother's eyes. Was it truly sadness, or was it fear—fear for a daughter venturing out so far afield.

She shook her head there in the dark, in an unfamiliar room, of a stranger's house. But they were not just strangers, they were the Baughman's. They were new friends, and this was their home, and this was to be her room. Soon she would be teaching in her school. Teaching her students. It was a grand adventure, so much lay ahead. As Elizabeth focused on these things, the excitement she had felt the months since she had received the letter came rushing back.

There had been an advertisement in the paper.... *"Wanted: a school teacher willing to relocate. The community of Misty Creek,.... offers good pay and housing to qualified teacher.....contact Mr. William Clark...."* That had been the beginning. How Elizabeth had stumbled upon the ad remained a mystery. Perhaps it was fate, or more likely just chance. That was her feeling, just mere chance. She had written Mr. Clark. Not right away, no, she had considered it for some time. Elizabeth hadn't discussed the opportunity with her parents. She was, after all, a grown woman, twenty-four and certainly no child. Seven years she had taught, and most of that time she had lived on her own. Was this so different? Yes, it was different—different in every way.

Elizabeth had written Mr. Clark and expected nothing in reply. So why bother her parents about nothing, but there was something. Oh, it took nearly six weeks, but a reply did arrive. She had been accepted, just like that. No interview, just come and teach our children. That was late July. There was a great deal of preparation needed. A week nearly passed before she told her mother and father she would be leaving, going west. They did not take the news well. Only her kid sister seemed excited. In truth more excited than she.

Elizabeth thought about Catherine, two years younger, already a mother of two. Catherine dear sister Catherine, how different their lives were. Catherine was the pretty one. But Elizabeth didn't envy her sister's beauty. Though different in so many ways they had always been close—so very close. It was in Catherine she confided. It was Catherine that had convinced her to write Mr. Clark. Perhaps she wanted Elizabeth to find what she had, that is a husband. Mark was a good man and provided well. He had worked at the bank right out of school. Diligent and enthusiastic, Mark did not go unnoticed. He now managed one of the smaller branches. Even so Elizabeth was certain his upward spiral had not reached its zenith.

Marriage. Elizabeth would not think of that word, not tonight. She had not come for marriage, far from it. She had a need, an unbelievable need to leave Columbus—Ohio for that matter. Now as she lie in the dark, she could not be certain she had left all she knew behind.

Her thoughts then turned to that very night, the town's reception, new friends, the schoolhouse, and of course her night's trek. Elizabeth thought of that man, that tall dusty man, that miller. How different he was, most unusual and quite irritating. But perhaps the most troubling thing about the miller was how he reminded her of Alexander, the man was so typical of his gender, self-important, over confident, and certain of, well of everything. Perhaps it was the words she had overheard that painted the picture of the man she disdained. Words she was never meant to hear, at the Elder's family gathering last Thanksgiving, most of a year ago. As she sought Jameson she overheard Alexander's voice, "I tell you that man I work with is lacking."

"Lacking," Jameson had responded.

"Yes, old man, he's been married all these years."

"He seems happy enough."

"You know what the Bible says; sons are arrows in a man's quiver."

"That's not exactly what it says."

"Close enough. Well, Ronald's quiver is empty." Alexander laughed.

"That' cruel."

"But true."

There was a moment's pause as Elizabeth stood gasping in the hallway.

"And you, Jimmy."

"What about me?"

"You know very well. How will that banker's daughter reward you?"

"Careful Alexander, you speak of my fiancé!"

"Fiancé, she's not your wife…yet."

"None of this is any concern to you!" Jameson's voice rose.

"No need to get worked up, Jimmy."

"Why do you always call me Jimmy?"

"It fits you."

"You know I hate it."

Alexander did not seem put off. "Whatever. Maybe it doesn't matter to you, but what of mother and father."

"Mother and father?"

"Don't you think they want grandchildren?"

"If you are so concerned about whether our parents receive grandchildren, then why not tend to the situation yourself?"

"I will, Jimmy, I will."

With that the conversation ended. Elizabeth was hard pressed to move away so she would not need to face Alexander's smug face. She convinced Jameson to take her home a short time later, feigning a headache. Though she had not purposely eavesdropped, she never mentioned what she had heard to anyone, not even Jameson.

And this Mr. Sonnefelt seemed so like Alexander, and all men that measured themselves by grunt and growl. Yes, she was sure this Mr. Sonnefelt would be a problem. Elizabeth would deal with him as she had that very night, ignore him if she could. That might not be so simple. The mill, after all, was the closest building to the school. Oh, it wasn't right next door, well it was the next door, but nearly a quarter of a mile of water separated the two structures. But she felt certain he would be a problem. If the situation became out of hand, she would ask for Mr. Clark's help. Elizabeth felt certain Clark would remedy the situation. Yes, Mr. Clark and with that thought, she drifted off to sleep.

CHAPTER 10

THE NEXT MORNING, AFTER A GOOD BREAKFAST, ABNER TOOK Elizabeth to the schoolhouse. She gave no indication that she had visited the structure the night before. Though this troubled her, for she did not want deceit to find its way into their relationship. Yet all the same she did not mention her night's walk, nor her encounter with Mr. Matthew Sonnefelt.

The building looked quite different in the sparkling morning air. When they rounded the corner and she saw the freshly painted church-school standing near the lake shore, the water gleaming, it very nearly took her breath away. She asked Mr. Baughman to stop the team a moment to take in the view. Oh, how different it looked. Abner smiled when later he drew the wagon to a stop in front of the school. The farmer gave a quick tour of the grounds and structure then told how he would press on to the mill. The comment caused Elizabeth concern, for she felt certain the miller would mention their meeting of the night before.

As Abner began to leave, she swallowed hard and said, "Mr. Baughman." He turned to face her. "I feel I have a confession to make."

The man drew his brows a bit. "Confession?"

"Yes, I must tell you this is not the first time I have been here."

The old man tilted his head.

"Last night, late actually, I walked here. Please forgive me for not telling you, but I just couldn't wait."

"Miss Beck," the farmer said sternly, "this is not Ohio. It is not wise to wander the road alone in the dark. You don't know this country." His brows drawn, he gave her a look not so unlike her father might.

She took his hand in hers. "Perhaps it was not wise, but I'm not afraid of the dark."

"You should be, and being out alone." he shook his head.

"If comforts you, Mr. Sonnefelt walked me home."

A smile came to his lips, though she noticed he tried to look stern. "Matthew?"

"Yes, Mr. Sonnefelt."

"And what do you think of our miller?"

What did she think of Mr. Matthew Sonnefelt? There was a great deal she thought of Mr. Sonnefelt—very little of it positive. All she had seen and learned of the man had left her repulsed. But she remembered what Alberta had said the night before and so she tempered her response. "I would admit that I do not know the man sufficiently to say one way or the other."

"I 'spect that's true." the farmer responded. "But I'm sure once you get to know him…."

Elizabeth felt she knew him, and all men like him, well enough.

"…well, when you get to know him you'll understand."

Understand? she thought.

"Well, I've my business to do," he said then. "'Spect to be done in an hour at the most. I'll stop on my way back. Take you to the farm if you like."

"Thank you, Abner. I am not certain how long I will be. But it's a fine morning, I think I would enjoy the walk."

"Yes, it is a fine day, isn't it? You know your way," he said as he looked back the way they came. "It's full light, so you should be fine."

He turned to look at her once more. "But I'll stop all the same, in case you change your mind."

With that Abner Baughman touched his hat and left her alone in school house, yet set up for church services. Elizabeth tried to visualize how the room would appear, filled with desks and noisy children. She pulled out the chair at her desk, sat a moment looking over the space now filled with pews.

Elizabeth sat there when a rap, rap, rap brought her out of her day-dreaming. On his departure Abner had left the door open. Startled by the sound Elizabeth turned to see Mr. Clark standing in the doorway. "Well, good morning, Mr. Clark."

Removing his hat, now here was a gentleman. "I hope I'm not interrupting."

"By no means, sir."

"I thought you might be here this morning. Thought I would stop by and see if there is anything you might need."

"It is hard for me to be certain, Mr. Clark."

"Please, Miss Beck, call me William."

"I am not certain that would be proper, for you are the head of the school board," she answered carefully. Shrugging his shoulders, he waved that she should continue. "Where was I? Oh yes, it is hard to tell, that is until the room is properly prepared."

"Of course, of course," he answered. "But seeing tomorrow's Sunday, surely you can understand the need."

"I do, I most certainly do," she answered patiently. "When will the room be, shall we say, rearranged?"

"Right after services tomorrow," he answered, emphatically.

"Well, then, Mr. Clark, I will know more at that time."

"Certainly, certainly," he answered. "Oh, by the way, Mrs. Clark asked if you would join us for dinner tomorrow. That is right after church."

Elizabeth considered the invitation but a moment. "Why, I would be honored."

He moved toward the door as he said, "Till tomorrow."

"Yes, tomorrow."

"Good day, Miss Beck."

"Good day to you, sir."

And Elizabeth was alone once more. She rose from her seat, glancing about the room again she imagined bright smiling faces sitting at their desks in neat rows. Things were going nicely, that is except for the miller next door. She understood the need to be on good grounds with the president of the school board, if there were to be problems of any kind. The invitation to dinner made that seem likely. A gesture made of courtesy, she was sure. Elizabeth stood before a map of the United States fastened to the wall. She placed a finger on Columbus, Ohio and felt a small ache in her chest at the thought of those she had left behind. Slowly she allowed her finger to trace across that map, a journey, a long journey, her journey to the place she now found herself or an approximation. For Misty Creek or Thimble, for that matter, would certainly not be on this map or any other she was certain.

As Elizabeth stared at the map, looking at the open large unmarked areas, for a moment she felt lost. For a moment the feeling of grand adventure she had undertook, well, it got displaced by fear. What had she done? Why she couldn't even explain to the folks back home precisely where she was. Just two days wagon ride from Thimble, the very end of the rail line. Two days wagon ride beyond the very end of civilization, if Thimble could even be considered civilized.

She was surprised again, this time by a child. A girl, perhaps ten, standing just inside the doorway. Elizabeth smiled at the youngster. "And who might you be?"

The young lady looked about carefully then said, "I'm Josie Tomkins."

"And what brings you here this morning Josie?"

"I heard that the new teacher come."

"Had come," she corrected.

"Yes, ma'am. The new teacher had come."

"And you wanted to meet her."

"Yes ma'am," the child said with a smile. "But it can't be you."

Surprised, Elizabeth asked, "Why would you say that?"

"'Cause you're too pretty."

Too pretty—the sweet child. No one had called her too pretty. Why she never considered herself anything but plain. She walked over, bending down, and looked Josie in the eyes. "What a sweet thing to say, but dear, I am your new teacher." Elizabeth smiled at the young student. "And are you looking forward to school? It begins Monday."

"Yes, ma'am."

Crouching down to see the young lady more easily she then said, "I'm certain you are a good student."

The smile left the girl's face as she swayed a bit from one foot to the next. "Better than some, I'd 'spect and not as good as, well not as good as Lilly Atwood. She's smart, real smart."

"But you do your best, don't you?"

The girl nodded.

"Then you are a good student. I cannot expect someone to do more than their best."

Josie smiled, gave Elizabeth a hug, then turned and shouted out the doorway. "Told ya was the new teacher, and she's nice, too."

"Who's out there, Josie?"

"Only my brother John. And Mary. She's my friend."

"And they sent you in to meet me?"

Again the child nodded.

"Shall we go out and visit with them?"

Josie smiled and, offering her hand, led Elizabeth down the steps to the frightened children waiting, or rather hiding behind a large oak tree.

Elizabeth sat at the base of the tree while Josie coaxed her brother and Mary, whose last name was Simns, out to meet their new teacher.

"I'm so happy to meet you," Elizabeth said when at last they stood before her. "Are you two ready for school?"

"Mary don't come 'ta school," Josie stated, softly.

"Doesn't come to school," Elizabeth corrected. The young Simns girl looked down. Gently Elizabeth, placing a finger beneath the child's chin, raised it just enough to look into Mary's eyes. "Why don't you come to school, Mary?"

The girl remained silent, looking with sad eyes directly into Elizabeth's.

"She just can't," Josie whispered in the teacher's ear.

Elizabeth wanted to ask why a child, a beautiful young child, just couldn't come to school. She stroked Mary's cheek. The teacher knew better than to ask the children. She would wait, but she would not wait long. Her emotions ran from sadness, for a child unable to attend school, to a confusion on what on earth reasons might be preventing her attendance, to anger at whoever or whatever that reason was. Elizabeth drew in a deep breath tried her best to smile and then told her new young friends it might be best if they returned home.

Elizabeth watched them as they walked to the road and turned right. The three began slowly moving down the dusty trail on what was becoming a warm morning. When they had nearly reached the first bridge, they turned. Elizabeth, embraced in her thoughts, saw Josie looking back and waving. The teacher stood, returned the greeting and observed them as they continued homeward.

Now that the children were away, she allowed the rage that had been brewing to release a scream—a loud scream. The very sound of her voice caught her off guard. "Who would dare keep that child out of school?" she shouted. Elizabeth drew a breath allowing the air to slip out of clenched teeth. She stared across the water at the mill and considered the miller. How much he reminded her of Alexander Elders, they seemed men cut from the same cloth. She took another breath and strode up the steps in her rage. Closed schoolhouse door with a firm clunk. She had no answers, but somehow, somewhere down deep inside, Elizabeth felt that it must certainly have something to do with Mr. Matthew Sonnefelt.

CHAPTER 11

STOMPING DOWN THE STEPS, SHE TOYED WITH THE IDEA OF GOING directly to the mill and telling that fool man, just what she thought. Elizabeth had taken several strides in that direction when it occurred to her that it would accomplish nothing, absolutely nothing. No, tomorrow she was to have dinner with the Clark's. She would deal with it then and there. She would have her answers, and Elizabeth felt certain that Mr. Clark, president of the school board, had the power to do something about it.

"Yes, that is what I will do," she told herself. "I will take it directly to Mr. Clark." Certainly that man was a man of action. If anyone could, he would set things right.

Elizabeth stood a moment in the road, looking the direction Josie and the others had gone. She walked a bit further and came to the first bridge. The rocks that made up the spillway were dry. No water crossed there. Moving onto the bridge itself she could see the water was nearly three feet below the spillway. This confused her. From here she could clearly see the mill wheel. It stood stationary. *Well, mills don't run all the time,* she thought. Perhaps Mr. Sonnefelt has no work at this moment. Or perhaps he is making repairs. But she noticed that the water level was below the sluice. There was no possibility of operating the mill unless the water was raised.

This seemed all the stranger since she remembered seeing water entering the lake the night before, while they had crossed the bridge at Misty Creek. Yes, water was entering the lake, she knew that. Elizabeth walked further, crossed another bridge, and another dry spillway.

The teacher followed the road as it ran along the top of the main dam. As she approached the mill on her left with the lake to her right, Elizabeth came to the large wheel. It seemed larger than most of the millwheels she had seen back home. Not that she had taken much interest in such things. There she observed something very strange. For water was flowing around the bottom of the wheel, and flowing swiftly. The sound of the water filled her ears. *Something must be wrong,* she thought. That water was leaving the lake going downstream seemed wrong.

From where Elizabeth stood she could see the sluice gate far above the water, as well as other gates. Gates she thought might be the flood gates. These three gates were open, allowing the water to flow out a channel and around the base of the wheel on to the creek bed below. As she stood there on a very short bridge, the third bridge, the one she hadn't noticed until that morning, looking down at the water flowing noisily along, a voice, a voice she certainly knew, a voice she had hoped not to hear again, or at least not this day, the voice of Matthew Sonnefelt, say, "Good day ma'am."

Surprised, Elizabeth looked up. She was not certain it was a good day. It had been a good day, an especially good day, but, but for the injustice she was certain the man whose voice now called out to her must be responsible.

Her emotion must have been revealed in her face, for the man stepped back a half step as she glared at him. Sonnefelt appeared much the same as he had at the store the night before, wearing the same clothes perhaps, a tall dusty man, though less dusty perhaps, and maybe a bit taller, not quite as thin as she remembered. Though she was angry, and became more so, for she reproached herself for noticing, the man was, dare she think it, handsome, very nearly dashing. Elizabeth blinked at the thought, then regaining her earlier feelings, answered, "Perhaps it is a good day Mr. Sonnefelt…but if it is, you certainly had nothing to do with it!"

She watched as the miller blinked twice, tilted his head slightly, and looked at her with a very confused expression, all the while the teacher glared, as if willing him to make some other fool comment. Mr. Sonnefelt's mouth opened slightly, as if he were about to speak, then it closed. He shook his head, a slight shake, the movement barely noticeable. Then frowning his brow ever so slightly said at last, "I hope you enjoy your day," touched the brim of his hat turned and was gone.

"How rude," she muttered to herself. The man was totally uncouth. Not that it surprised her. Elizabeth began to walk with determination back the way she had come, but by the time she had reached the furthest bridge she realized something. The rudeness was not on Mr. Sonnefelt's part, but her own. She stood there for some time looking first across the lake to Misty Creek, the town, if it was indeed a town, far off. Once more she considered how much like Ohio this country seemed, and how different than the country she had crossed. Elizabeth swallowed as she looked the other way. The spillway was dry, yet visible, it led under the trees back to the creek she was certain. But before her eyes was a stand of trees, of willows and hardwoods as well a few pines. Everything was green. She looked back toward the mill. She saw a wagon coming her way; Abner she was sure.

While she watched the wagon moving in her direction, she wondered, what had led her to believe that Mr. Sonnefelt had anything to do with young Mary Simms. What had driven her to that totally irrational conclusion? Though she did not care for the man, there was nothing she had seen or heard that would indicate he was opposed to any of the children attending school. Then while looking across the lake once more, Elizabeth noticed that there was something calming, something that seemed to reach deep within her and soothe her heart. She had always loved the water. There was a time she would have thought a house on the sea shore would be the closest thing to heaven she could imagine. Not that she had ever seen the ocean mind you. But she could see the water and waves in her mind, feel the cool breeze, and hear the calls of gulls. Elizabeth drew in another breath and found the rage that had held her, only a short time before, had left her entirely.

The old farmer smiled when he drew near. "Climb on and I'll take you home."

"I think I shall walk," she said returning his smile.

"If you must," he said. "But don't be long. Alberta will have dinner on the table at twelve. She's never late."

Elizabeth thanked him and sent him along. Her fingers gently felt the locket she wore. A gift from her father, oh how she feared it had been lost. How many times had its disappearance filled her mind? Absent the whole crossing, only revealing itself when she unpacked the trunk the night before, from the sock she had tucked it in. A safe place to protect the treasure from the expected rough handling of her luggage. Opening it revealed a watch and a small photograph of her parents. Elizabeth swallowed. Closing her eyes, she could still see the concern on her father's face as he slipped the small package into her trembling hand.

He had drawn a breath. "I wondered what I might give you, my daughter, something to remind you of us, and home, and our love for you." His lip trembled as he failed at the attempt of a smile. "But you know me, it needed to be something practical."

"Will you put it on me, father?"

The smile came as he moved behind her and fastened the clasp. "I hope you are not just running away."

"You know me better."

"Yes, I do," She heard him sigh. "But..." he sighed again. "It's a terrible thing that has befallen you."

Elizabeth had turned to face him with damp eyes.

"Jameson..." he began, but she placed her finger on his lips.

"There is no need father, what was was, and what is is. That is all there is to it."

He nodded and looked down. "You are our oldest. Perhaps your going so far away was to be expected. But..." She saw tears in her father's eyes. "I'm not ready my Beth. What will we do without you?"

Elizabeth threw her arms around him, doing her best to hold her own tears in check. "It will not be forever, father. Before you and mother miss me, I shall return."

He nodded. "But tomorrow you leave us, and I fear for you."

She smiled. "There is no need, I take your and mother's love," she said as she held the new gift. "And you have taught me, wherever I travel God goes with me."

He blinked and swallowed. Drawing a breath he looked toward the west, as if he could see the distant place she was bound for. He kissed her on the cheek. "Goodnight my child, your mother will be along soon."

She held the precious timepiece within her hand. It meant so much more than the apparent value of the jewelry. It was a link between her and those she loved. Elizabeth drew a breath as she checked the time, and estimated how long it might take to return to the Baughman farm, for she did not want to disappoint her new friend. But before she would begin that journey, Elizabeth had something she knew needed to be done. So drawing a deep breath she walked back toward the mill. The mill itself stood some yards from the road and the dam on the far bank of the valley. When she came to the broad heavy door, which stood open, she peaked inside.

Elizabeth realized she had never seen the inside of any mill. So what she saw surprised her. The air was filled with dust which seemed odd, considering the stationary wheel meant the mill was not operating. She observed two men working with brooms, holding them inverted and, of all things, sweeping between the great beams that held up the ceiling, or rather the floor above. And as they worked, they were continually knocking down dirt and grain dust. A short stocky man cursed when a particular wad of the dust fell in his face. A tall man laughed then told him to watch his language. The stocky man shook his head violently and began to curse once more. "There's no need for that talk!" the tall man said firmly.

"But…"

"There's no need, Eldon," he said more softly.

"I'll try…but I cain't promise," Eldon answered as he drew his handkerchief across his eyes.

The tall man slapped him upon his back and, as a cloud of dust lifted to add itself to the already thick air, said, "I know, Eldon, I know."

The miller was smiling as he turned and faced her, but as he saw her, that smile vanished. "Ma'am," he said loud enough that the other could hear. "Is there something we could do for you?"

Elizabeth couldn't help but smile at the ridiculous way he appeared. His eyebrows, hair even his mustache completely covered with the dust. His skin itself seemed pale, nearly white, covered with it, and she had no idea what color his shirt and trousers had been in the day's beginning. She stared a moment, the briefest of moments. Elizabeth noticed his eyes beneath those dust covered brows, deep brown eyes. Eyes with a depth she had not noticed before. Eyes that showed something she had not seen before. What it was, and what it meant, she could not know. But as the teacher looked into those deep brown eyes, she found she was unable to speak. Elizabeth swallowed, trying to look at something other than those eyes, but found she could not. So she stood there mute for what she felt must have been a very long time. Appearing, she was certain, the fool and yet she could not speak.

The trance was broken by the tall man, the miller, as he said, "Eldon and I are cleaning the mill. You see the water is down."

"So I noticed."

"Yes," he continued, "the water is down, and so we are doing our best to clean all the cobwebs and dust, to tidy things up. I'm sorry things must appear a mess."

She smiled. Elizabeth couldn't believe that she smiled. "No, I understand."

Again there was a moment of silence, but this time she forced herself to look about and get to the point. "Mr. Sonnefelt, I have come to apologize. I fear I have acted most rudely this morning."

The miller did not answer immediately. She watched him, and she could see in his eyes, for she stared at them again, a faraway gaze. He seemed to evaluate what he had heard, perhaps wondering what he should say. It was clear to her, as clear as crystal, that the man had limited social abilities.

"There's no need to apologize, Miss Beck," he said at last.

"But my attitude was uncalled for."

"I'm sure you were upset by something...and...I...well...I was there."

Yes, he was there. Yes, perhaps that was it. Perhaps she was looking for someone or something to attack, and feeling about the man as she did, made it easy, wrong perhaps, but easy. Then she blinked, blinked again and paused once more, had Mr. Sonnefelt noticed she was upset. Perhaps he was just giving her an excuse—a little wiggle room. But...

"You are correct sir, I was upset, and for no reason I can fathom I blamed you," she said softly.

A smile slowly came to his dusty lips. "And you have determined that I am not at fault?"

The miller didn't speak like a laborer, which put her off balance. It seemed that everything about the man was, well, it was wrong. And Elizabeth felt a deep need to leave. It was not fear. For though she could not understand, she had never felt fear in his presence, rather the opposite. That drove her need. She found herself too comfortable. Unnaturally comfortable and Elizabeth felt certain it was wrong. She swallowed and drew a breath saying at last, "You will have to excuse me, Mr. Sonnefelt, but I must be going." Turning, she felt she had handled things poorly. Yet could not comprehend how she could have managed things differently. She hurried out away from the dust, away from that man.

Elizabeth felt confused by the feeling that came upon her in the presence of that man. She would not allow subtle feelings to take charge of her life no matter where their roots began. Becoming angry with herself for the uninvited sensations that seemed beyond her control, she gritted her teeth as she walked hurriedly away. The few strides of separation from Sonnefelt offered an escape from the strange feelings of comfort she had felt. No, she would not allow illogical feelings into her life again. For didn't emotion lead her to the heartbreak that destroyed her hopes and dreams. Her heart no longer had room for absurd emotions, and she would take the steps necessary to prevent such nonsense.

Elizabeth had gone only a few steps when she heard a voice behind her. "Miss Beck, if there is anything I can do to help, I mean at the school or for the children…"

Turning briefly, she cut him off. "Thank you, Mr. Sonnefelt, but I am certain I will be able to manage."

He closed his eyes, tightened his lips. "I have no doubt of your capabilities, ma'am." And with that turned away.

Elizabeth continued toward the road. Checking her watch again, she felt the need to hurry. Oh, there would be plenty of time, but she would rush onward, get away from that man. Yes, she would hurry. As Elizabeth walked, she tried not to think about that man, not to think about those eyes, but most of all not to think of how she had felt. No, she would not think of those things not now—not ever!

Elizabeth was still walking at a brisk pace when she first saw the opening to Baughman's lane. She stopped then, waited, and caught her breath. She was perspiring, most unladylike to be sure. She wanted her breathing to calm. Why had she hurried so? What was she fleeing? Of what was she afraid? Shaking her head, clearing her thoughts, gathering her wits, Elizabeth began again, now very leisurely. There was no need to hurry, there was plenty of time. She continued very nonchalantly, but thoughts of her past came crashing, crashing into her consciousness, filling her mind. Thoughts she did not want. Thoughts she had held so carefully locked away.

Elizabeth stopped. She looked about the countryside. She tried to drive the memories away, the reasons away—the reasons she had really come to Kansas. Everything reminded her that she had come west to escape. She couldn't. No matter how hard she tried, she couldn't stop the past, and the pain it had inflected then, the pain it inflected now. A tear came to her eye, there were many ready to follow, but Elizabeth was stronger, stronger than the pain, stronger than the memories. She stood there in the late morning sun, at the gate to the Baughman's lane. Yes, she remembered. She would always remember a Saturday in late May—remember Jameson. Her jaw became tight. An anger grew deep inside, an anger that overshadowed the pain. Yes, Elizabeth would always remember, but she would not allow it to control her, and she would not allow anyone to hurt her that way again.

The teacher stood there for several minutes. She saw it all again. Elizabeth had thought that she had left it behind. Left all those pains and disappointments behind. She had wept then, blubbered for days inconsolable. But that was then—that was there. She was here now. She had much to do now. Much more to worry about than one weekend last spring. Elizabeth shook her head, drew a breath, dried her eye, and strode on, head high. She was Miss Elizabeth Beck, school teacher who had come to Misty Creek to teach the children. Yes, she had come, and yes, she would teach.

Elizabeth became determined, or rather she became re-determined, for it was determination that had brought her here, a determination that she would not be bounded by her past. No, it would not limit what she would do, or who she was for that matter. With that determination once more in place, in the place where she felt it must be, Elizabeth walked confidently toward the farm house that was to be her home, at least for the term in any case. Elizabeth had been hurt -- wounded deeply then. She would not allow anyone to cut her in that way again. She believed that a person needed to learn from their past. She had learned. Oh yes, she had learned, and she would never forget.

These were the things she thought as she walked those last yards to the Baughman's. Though so many things had passed through her mind that last part of her walk, she pushed those thoughts aside as she forced a smile and entered the large white farmhouse, the house of Abner and Alberta Baughman.

Chapter 12

Sitting in the church, in a pew three up from the back, the pew in which Baughman's typically sat, Elizabeth could not help herself, as she looked over her shoulder at the desk that would be hers. The space, for it was difficult for her to think of it as a sanctuary, was nearly filled. The pastor, Reverend Benjamin Smith, stood straight and tall on a platform at the front. Elizabeth had expected the cowboy preacher, of course, but she was surprised, though she shouldn't have been, to see him in a dark suit, with his stiff starched collar. It was the first time he truly looked the part. It was difficult for her not to stare at the man. He seemed so different.

As he spoke, though she did her best to pay proper attention, her mind drifted. Drifted to a man standing on a dust road, his voice clear and strong, as it was now, speaking of hope to farmers that had very little hope. Here his message was more traditional, but in it, she heard much of the same themes—love—forgiveness—compassion. The entire Smith brood, Leah and their children, sat in the front pew. And though all eyes should have been forward, many glanced from time to time at the new teacher. Elizabeth tried not to notice, but did. She also noticed that Mr. Sonnefelt shared their pew, sitting next to Abner. She did not look his way not once, well maybe once, during the entire service.

At the service's end, all greeted the pastor and his family as they left. Mr. Clark stood waiting just outside, at the base of the steps. Elizabeth had not forgotten his invitation, though now regretted accepting. Josephine and their daughter Jennifer were presently seated in a fine looking carriage as she and Mr. Clark approached. Climbing into the coach, she realized that not all the men had yet left the church, or at least not Mr. Sonnefelt. The teacher glanced toward the open doorway and saw motion within the building. Though the opening offered little view, it was evident that there was activity within the schoolhouse-church. Elizabeth was about to ask the Clarks what it might be when she remembered what the miller had told her that night, about the changing pews for desks. No one had mentioned it during the service. Evidently there was no need. Elizabeth wondered, only briefly, why Mr. Clark or his eldest were not assisting, but the jolt of the carriage as it moved away set her mind on other things.

The ride was pleasant enough. The road soon moved away from the stream and out into open farmland. She watched as they moved past farms and orchards, and soon were out in more open country. A land not so different than the grassland she had traversed on the wagon ride from Thimble. Only here the grass stood green beneath the sun. On they moved, across the rolling land covered with rich looking green grass blowing in waves driven by the wind. A large number of cattle spread about the rolling landscape, far too many for her to count.

Elizabeth sat quietly looking about, absorbing the contrasting sights. Mr. Clark did the most speaking, asked about her accommodations. Did she find them satisfactory? There were other questions he asked. Questions about her preparedness for the term about to begin. The teacher smile politely and answered, often in very vague terms, for she was certainly prepared, at least prepared if school here was anything like where she had taught before. If it were not, how would she know what preparations would be needed.

The road wound up a gentle grade, and as it reached the crest, Mr. William Clark hauled the reins to bring the carriage to a stop. From this vantage point they could see The Sweetwater Ranch. Though they had been riding for some time across lands the Clark family controlled, here, she saw for the first time the house and outbuildings. The house was a large single story structure, built primarily of field stone. Not just rocks but rather stones that had been broken forming a nearly smooth wall of many colors and patterns. The whole of it was very impressive. It very much fit the man, big, strong, and something else, what is was Elizabeth could not quite put a finger on. Something bold. Yes bold, but something else as well. As they moved on, it troubled her that she couldn't put that missing thing into a concept her mind could grasp, a concept that better described Sweetwater.

As they drew closer, the house only seemed to grow more magnificent. Elizabeth couldn't say she had seen anything quite like it. As large as it was, and it was very large, it had a porch that ran the full length and wrapped around one end. A ranch hand stood waiting when they came to a stop. Without a single word or even an acknowledgement to the man's presence, Mr. Clark stepped out, aided Elizabeth and then his wife, and then with a sweep of his arm toward the house, indicated for her to proceed. He continued speaking as they went. Clark walked at her side while Josephine and Jennifer followed at their heels. William Clark spoke continuously about the house, the number of rooms—sixteen—how many wagonloads of stones that had been required—more than one hundred eleven—and such things. Elizabeth knew she would not remember the details of that conversation, for she was overwhelmed by what she saw.

They entered the edifice by crossing that great porch and passing through large French doors made of thick Oak, coming into a vast space, a grand room. It would be hard for her to describe exactly what she saw. It was mostly open with a divan and matching chairs of deep brown leather. There was other furniture, a table and such, but if she would have but one word to label it that word would be masculine, very masculine. Yes, that was it. From the bear skin on the floor to the elk's head mounted over the great stone fireplace, from the varnished floor to the coarse wood mantel, the room was definitely masculine.

They swept through the room, passing to the left of the fireplace into an equally large space, the dining hall. It contained a long rectangular table, prepared for a banquet. Quality was apparent, as was quantity. Elizabeth escorted to her seat by Mr. Clark, who was speaking the entire time. There were servants, moving about like a well-oiled machine. As they performed their duties, Elizabeth observed that William Clark paid them no acknowledgement, scarcely recognizing their existence. It was Josephine that spoke to them, giving them instructions. Elizabeth smiled and thanked a young woman who carefully removed her plate when she had finished the main course. The waitress, for whether or not that was her station, smiled in return, blushed as if unaccustomed to any comment.

The whole effect made Elizabeth very uncomfortable. During dessert her mind began to wander. She wondered if Mr. Clark, being head of the school board, would treat her similarly one day. And as she looked about politely, listened halfheartedly, Elizabeth thought to herself how she had been invited to this grand meal. No, she was respected by the man. Of that she felt certain. All the same there was a discomfort she could not completely explain. Yes, the teacher was out of her element. Yes, the house was grand. The meal was grand. She had never experienced anything remotely equivalent. Surely that was it—off balance—out of place—but was it? She couldn't help feeling there was something more. But what?

After they had eaten, they returned to the great room, the entry hall as she thought of it, for coffee and conversation. Elizabeth watched as Mr. Clark poured himself and William Junior a brandy. It would have been awkward had he offered the drink to the ladies, so Elizabeth was grateful he did not. Then sitting in a large leather chair, his chair, lighting a cigar, he droned on and on about the school, about family, his family, the ranch, and the future of Misty Creek. That dirt farming was in the past, a fact that farmers just hadn't realized—yet.

Elizabeth smiled politely. Did her best to listen, politely. Yet the discomfort she felt remained. It grew more stifling as the conversation dragged on and on. Rarely did anyone other than the house's head speak. Of the others that dared, young William spoke most, not that he was young being, she guessed, very nearly her age. He did not give his opinions rather responded to questions and comments. All the while, Josephine sat quietly sipping her coffee, appearing disconnected to the goings on, and Miss Jennifer, who had asked to be excused, left the room what seemed hours ago.

At last Mrs. Clark rose. "Miss Beck would you like to see the house?"

Elizabeth nodded.

"William, you will excuse us?"

"But of course, dear."

Elizabeth was grateful and would have told Josephine so when her hostess spoke. "You must forgive William. He does not go on so, well not normally. He is trying to impress you."

Why on earth would Mr. Clark wish to impress her?

Josephine gave an understanding smile. "He is the head of the school board. It is not a duty he takes lightly. You are the new teacher, you have come highly recommended. Perhaps you did not know. He, I mean the school board, looked into your background."

The alarm must have shown in her eyes as Mrs. Clark continued. "Nothing so devious my dear. Only your work record and transcripts. It's just so, how can I say it, you are so much more than the teachers we have had before."

"And you would like me to stay?"

"We are hoping you will want to stay."

"But I haven't even taught one day."

Josephine turned to face her as they stood in the hallway. "That's the rub dear. It is not so much whether the board will keep you…is it?"

Now Elizabeth understood the discomfort, or at least part of the discomfort. Yes, she had found herself out of her element, but in the back of her mind she felt she was being measured. That her invitation to Sweetwater was some sort of a test. Yet with Josephine's words Elizabeth understood that Mr. Clark did his best to impress her, to nudge her along in the direction that would lead her to remain teacher of Misty Creek School. The concept seemed alien. What expectations did the school board hold? She swallowed, drew a breath and followed her hostess through the vast house. The rest was as what she had seen before—grand. Large bedrooms, the whole of Blankenship's soddy could be contained in each one, a sitting room, library that contained more books than she had seen since leaving the university, and at last the kitchen.

After they had roamed the entire house, Mr. Clark met them at the broad front doors. "What do you think of our humble abode?"

"Sir, your house is a grand place, grander than any I have had the fortune to see. I wish to thank you for your invitation."

The man smiled, obviously pleased. "It was our pleasure."

"I would hope you not find it rude," she began, "that I might take my leave. I have a thing or two I wish to do before classes begin on the morrow."

"But of course. I'll have William bring the carriage. He will see you safely home."

She prepared to suggest that transportation would not be necessary, that she could walk, when she realized he would consider such a comment ludicrous, so Elizabeth thanked him. All the same, she did not consider the arrangement comforting. Though she had not felt at ease all afternoon, the idea of being alone in the open country with the young man she did not know was disconcerting. Josephine, dear Josephine, must have noticed for she called out for Jennifer. "Jenny dear," she said, "Miss Beck is leaving I thought perhaps you might like say goodbye."

The girl dashed into the room, clearly to the dismay of her father, whose face could not hide his mood as the child slid to a stop pushing the bearskin into a heap. Elizabeth defused the situation by crouching down to the child's level.

"Your brother is taking Miss Beck home," Josephine said calmly.

"Can I go, can I?" the child said, bouncing. The behavior continued to affect Mr. Clark, though the teacher saw nothing unusual.

"Why, Jennifer, I think that is an excellent idea. It will give the two of you an opportunity to become better acquainted," Josephine said with a smile as she winked at Elizabeth.

"There'll be no need," the rancher boomed. "School starts tomorrow, there'll be plenty time for that."

"But William," his wife said coyly, "let the child go, I'm certain Miss Beck will not mind."

"Oh, it will help me." Elizabeth chimed.

"Help?" the big man asked.

"Certainly, Jenny can tell me what the children have learned, so I might better know what to expect."

"Well, if you're certain you don't mind," Clark boomed.

"I don't, no, I most certainly don't." The idea of having Jenny share the ride relieved Elizabeth.

They heard the horse and carriage come to a stop. Jenny led the teacher out the door across the porch down the steps by the hand. Elizabeth said her goodbyes and climbed aboard. She then noticed young William. His eyes glancing back and forth between his sister and the new teacher revealed that he was not at all pleased about the turn of events. She also heard it in his words as he tried to convince Jennifer to remain behind, practically ordering his younger sister to get out of the buggy.

Again Josephine smoothed things somewhat, though Elizabeth feared there might be repercussions on the young man's return.

"It was so good that you have come," Mrs. Clark said as they were about to depart. "I hope you will join us again, soon."

"Thank you for your graciousness," Elizabeth answered. Then more softly, soft enough that only Josephine could hear, "Thank you for everything. You have been most kind. I'm sure we will be friends."

Josephine smiled, nodded slightly, and the three aboard the carriage were off.

CHAPTER 13

AS THEY MOVED ALONG, A BIT FASTER THAN THEY HAD EARLIER, Jenny chattered. The child, it seemed, had inherited the desire to speak from her father. Though the prattle tired Elizabeth, she found her future student delightful. During the journey Jenny informed Elizabeth four times that she was nine. William ordered her three times to be still. And three times Jenny remained silent, but only for a moment. Twice the young lady had the teacher laughing so hard that Elizabeth found it difficult to breathe.

Finally Elizabeth asked, "Do you know Josie Tomkin?"

"Of course. And her dumb brother too," Jenny answered in a rush. "I know everybody."

"Then you know Mary…" Elizabeth couldn't place the last name.

"Mary Simms or Mary Swartz?"

"Yes, that was her name, Simms."

"Well, I don't know her very well. She's Josie's friend. She doesn't come to school."

"Why not?" the teacher asked.

The girl just shrugged her shoulders.

"None of the Simms go to school," William added. It was nearly the first thing he had said other than his attempts to stop the continuous rattling of his sister.

"There are other Simms?"

"Oh yes," the young driver exclaimed. "Must be seven of them."

"And Mary, she's the oldest?"

William shook his head. She watched as he seemed to mouth names. "She'd be the middle. Or nearly."

The teacher had to digest that fact a moment. Then there were other Simms that ought to be in school, perhaps several others. "William, why are the Simms children not in school?"

"No one knows," he answered. "At least not for sure." Snapping the reins he went on. "Some say it's against their religion."

"Their religion?" she asked. "I didn't see them in church today."

"They never come to church, Miss Beck." Jenny was obviously delighted she could add to the conversation.

Elizabeth thought about the situation and though it troubled her, she believed she would learn nothing more, at least not from the Clarks that day, so she shifted the conversation. "William, you work with your father?"

"Yes, ma'am."

"Is that what you want?"

"Is there something else?" he asked with a laugh. He then swept his hand and added. "One day this will be mine. That's say'n something."

Yes, indeed it was saying something. And yet, considering the young man was nearing the mid of his twenties, she found herself wondering about the young man.

Then Jenny interrupted her thoughts. "Willie's not married."

"Hush, Jenny!" Young William's face flushed as he glared back at his sister.

With a devilish twinkle in her eyes, unaffected by her brothers words or stare, she went on. "But he's had girlfriends." The girl giggled. "Lots of girlfriends."

"Shush, Jenny."

"Well you have. And pretty ones."

"Jenny now stop!"

"But none as pretty as you, teacher."

William pulled the wagon to a stop and turned, squinting his eyes at his sister.

"Well, they weren't."

"Enough," he shouted, "that'll be enough! One more word and I pull you out and you'll just walk home!"

Evidently the child took her brother's warning to heart, for she remained silent for several minutes. Elizabeth thought about the girl's words. It was the second time in just two days she had been called pretty. She had never thought she was. She understood beauty. Her friend Marsha was beautiful, everyone said so. But no one had told her that she was pretty until yesterday. That is, no one had said it in earnest, Elizabeth was certain of that. Yes, there had been those that had, using empty compliments, told her she was pretty, but she knew they were not sincere. Yes, she knew beauty and even now hearing it said by this child, repeating what Josie had said yesterday; the words seemed hollow, no more than strange ridiculous sounds.

When Jenny's courage returned, or perhaps she had forgotten her brother's threat, she asked, "Miss Beck, did you always want to be a teacher?"

Elizabeth smiled at the young girl sitting beside her. "Yes, I suppose I did."

"Just a teacher?"

"What do you mean?"

Jenny cocked her head a bit. "I mean didn't you want to be something more?"

More, more, Elizabeth wondered. She could have easily taken offence by the question, but she saw the young girl's eyes contained no malice. She thought a moment, and then thought another moment.

More, more than a teacher—or more than just a teacher. At last Elizabeth asked, "Is there something wrong with being a teacher?"

"No ma'am," came the quick reply.

"Then what more would I wish to be?" she asked at last.

"A mommy," Jenny blurted.

The directness took Elizabeth by surprise. By the look in young William's eyes Elizabeth saw that the comment had taken him by surprise as well.

He turned with brows drawn, "Jenny mind your own business.

Elizabeth drew a breath. She was not offended by the question even though it caught her off guard. She was not angry at the asker, though the subject was not something ordinarily approached so bluntly. For a time, she did not know how to respond. And though Elizabeth felt a chill, as if a cold winter wind had suddenly blown off the prairie, she knew she was blushing.

Sometimes children notice things others are unable. "I'm sorry, Miss Beck…I…I…"

Elizabeth took the child's hands in her own, smiled weakly. "There is no need to apologize, Jenny. You have done nothing wrong." She drew in another deep breath, then looking into the eyes of her new student she said. "When I was a little girl, about your age I think, I knew I wanted to be a teacher. I worked very hard at my studies. I went to school, to college, and at last I became a teacher. But you are right. Perhaps you did not ask the question quite as well as you might have. Each of us are more than just one thing or another. I am a teacher, but I am also my parent's daughter, a Christian, a citizen of this great country, and I hope I am also your friend. As for other things, we will see what the future holds, shall we not?" She pulled the girl in close with a hug, and they rode in silence for a time.

They had come to the trees, leaving the open land behind. "William," she asked, "might we stop at the school for a few moments?"

"I'm to take you home."

"Yes, yes, it will not take long. Or if you like you can drop me off at the school, and I will walk home."

"No, ma'am. Like I said I'm to take you home, to the Baughman's.'

"I suppose I can walk back to the school later," she said at last.

"Why do you want to go to the school?" William asked. "You were there this morning."

"That is true," she answered. "But then it was a church. I would like to see it as a school"

William snapped the reins. "Seems ridiculous to me."

It didn't seem ridiculous, at least not to her. Elizabeth was about to embark on a new endeavor, the excitement was building, a new school filled with new students. She just had a strong urge to see it—to walk it—to feel it.

William did not respond one way or the other, but when they reached the crossroad he veered to the left and headed toward the school.

CHAPTER 14

SHE STEPPED OUT THE INSTANT THE BUGGY CAME TO A STOP. Thanking William, Elizabeth assured him that she would not be long.

Jenny leaped out as well. "Can I come too, teacher?"

Elizabeth smiled and nodded. She invited William to join them, but the young rancher declined with tight lips and a sour expression. It surprised the teacher to find the door propped open by a chair. As she approached, holding Jenny's hand, she noticed, a familiar scent, a schoolhouse aroma. Elizabeth could not immediately place the fragrance that flowed out through the door. Oh, it wasn't chalk dust, that smell was burned into her mind. No, it was different, yet, very, very…

Elizabeth entered the building. She paused just inside. Though she had expected it, she felt astounded by the transformation. It was a school, a real school. The fact that the space was shared with the church was almost invisible. Yes, the pews were carefully placed out of the way. Stacked cleverly to take a surprisingly small space, and the pulpit yet stood at the far end of the building. But it was a school. Oh yes, it was a school!

She didn't notice him at first, the workman. The man worked, rubbing a desktop, waxing it actually. That was the smell that had greeted them, the scent of furniture wax. Elizabeth nearly jumped when she saw him, the man laboring, the man in work clothes, his shirt drenched with sweat. The man looked up from what he was doing. "Good afternoon ma'am," he said, cheerfully.

It was him, that miller, Mr. Sonnefelt. Elizabeth was shocked to see him. Yes, she had been surprised to find someone at work in the school that was true, but she was stunned it was that man. Elizabeth found she couldn't speak, not a word.

"I see you have a new friend," he said at last.

"Did you think I would remain friendless?" she asked coolly, with just a touch of sarcasm.

"By no means, I was certain you would make several and quickly."

Now what was that supposed to mean? Elizabeth wondered about those words, squinting as she looked his way.

But before she could answer, he spoke again. "And Miss Clark, how are you this fine afternoon? Are you escorting your new teacher home?"

Jenny smiled. "Yes."

"Yes you are fine, or yes, you are escorting Miss Beck home?" he said with a twinkle in his eye.

Elizabeth noticed how he spoke to the child. He actually spoke to the child. Many adults speak at children, especially if they are not their own. Though she had known more than a few parents that had that problem as well. But this man spoke to Jenny.

"Both," Jenny answered.

With that the man straightened, having been hunched over the desk, and laughed. "Miss Clark, you are a wonder, yes indeed, a wonder."

"Yes, Mr. Sonnefelt, Jennifer and her brother have been so gracious to carry me home." Elizabeth said at last having regained her composure. "I have burdened William to bring me here on the way, so I might see the school. He was kind enough to do so and is now waiting patiently outside. I cannot tarry long."

The miller nodded. Sweeping his arm he asked, "Does it suit you ma'am?"

"I believe it does, Mr. Sonnefelt, yes, I believe it does." She moved to her desk pulled back the chair and sat. Looking about once more she asked, "Have you nothing else to do, sir, or is janitor just another of your duties." Elizabeth turned away quickly, for the moment the words left her lips she knew, oh how she knew, she had spoken poorly.

The miller grabbed the cloth and went back to polishing the desk. "I wax the desks form time to time, if that's what you mean. And I am not so bored out of my wits to spend the afternoon here." He rubbed a bit more then moved to the next one. "The desks are stacked through the summer; they need a good cleaning when they are taken out. Certainly that does not seem so unusual?"

No, it did not. And now she regretted what she had said all the more. She got up and walked closer, but no closer than the next desk. "They look wonderful, Mr. Sonnefelt. You have done a fine job."

He smiled weakly as he shrugged his shoulders.

She ran her hand over the top of a finished desk. "These are fine desks. I have not seen any quite like these. Where did the school acquire them?" she asked as she watched him at work once again.

"We made them," he said softly.

"Here in Misty Creek?"

"That surprises you? We have to be as self-sufficient as we can. It's just the way of things. Do it yourself or do without." He had finished one desk and now moved to the one beside the new teacher. She moved over one as well, telling herself she needed to give him space to work. He seemed not to notice. "We're fortunate. We have the wood."

"That is why the houses here are wood frame," she said mostly to herself.

"Yes. The folks out on the prairie aren't so lucky. Have to work with what you have."

"But surely the valley here could provide wood for their homes," she said with a hint of indignation.

"Maybe, maybe not. The valley's not such a big place. Yes, we have trees, several trees but lumber trees not so many. It takes a long time to grow trees."

"But everyone here has a proper home, and out there…"

"Who's to say what's proper?" he asked looking up only an instant.

Flustered she said in a strong voice, "You know what I mean!"

"This is not Ohio," he said firmly.

"Now sir, you take me for a fool. That perhaps I have forgotten where I am!" raising her voice slightly.

"Though none of us is as wise as we would hope to be, you are certainly no fool. I was simply stating a fact."

"But…" she began to cut him off, only to have him continue.

"Things are different here, out here in the west. This is a new land, only settled for a short time. In time things will change, you'll see."

"But it is not fair!"

"No, it's not fair," he agreed calmly.

The agreement took her by surprise. It calmed her just a bit. Though still angry, she didn't know how to respond. When she disagreed with him it was easy. She knew her point, knew she was correct and he wasn't. But for him to agree with even the smallest of points well it left her speechless.

"Life is not fair, Miss Beck. Never has been."

What was it about this man that upset her so? Why did he always get her dander up? He was finishing another desk and they went through the motions of moving to the next. For a moment she looked at him, really looked at him. Sweat pouring into his eyes, it had soaked his shirt through and through. The man was not as she had thought at first, thin. No, he was tall, oh yes, he was tall, and that "tallness" had hidden his broad shoulders and strong arms. She remembered that night, that night on the road. The hand in the darkness, that strong hand that helped her to her feet. Now seeing him, perhaps for the first time, she saw the strength, and that strength did not frighten her. Strange, it was so strange this man she loathed did not frighten her. Rather the opposite. It was this un-fear that once again caused her concern, and she moved further away, forcing herself toward the door. Sonnefelt noticed, glancing her way but said nothing, for he continued waxing, hunched over a desk.

Elizabeth watched a moment longer. Then looking about the room once again, she said, "I cannot believe the transformation. Just this morning I had my concerns but now…" the words drifted off. She expected some kind of response but nothing came, even Jenny stood silent. "The men of the church have worked wonders."

"They are happy to do what's needed, ma'am."

"Will you convey my gratitude?"

The man stopped, straightened himself, looked her in the eyes, and nodded.

"William is waiting. I fear I have been longer than I had anticipated," she said at last. "I bid you good day. Jenny, let us leave Mr. Sonnefelt to his work."

The young girl ran to her side and, taking her hand, they began out the door. "You don't like him much do you?" the child asked in a voice loud enough that Elizabeth felt certain the Sonnefelt had heard.

She did not answer until they had gone down the steps and even then bending down and with a voice scarcely more than a whisper told her new friend. "My feelings about the man are totally irrelevant."

"But you don't like him?"

"I don't like him."

"You could be wrong you know," the child said as she burst away, running to the carriage and climbing quickly aboard. William stood at the wheel, giving Elizabeth a hand, easing her up and in the carriage. William was a gentleman, a fine gentleman. He smiled as she climbed aboard. A moment later he was at the reins and they were off.

It was only a few minutes before they turned into the Baughman lane. She thought about the words exchanged as they had left the school, words between Jenny and herself. She remained quiet as she thought—perhaps too quiet. But her mind raced as she thought of that question, and all the reasons she felt the way she did. Mr. Sonnefelt was just a man. A man she scarcely knew. Yes, he had driven her home that night, and found her face down in the dust earlier. And yes, he had surprised her at the school today, and that night. Surely it had to be more than just two days ago—but it wasn't. It seemed she was always bumping into him. A man she did not like. For events of her recent past had an ill effect on her opinion of the male gender. There were exceptions but by and large she did not place much value on men, particularly single men, in general. She didn't trust many, and the more masculine the specimen the more bitter her estimation of the individual. And Matthew Sonnefelt was very male.

He hadn't done anything especially rude, well except for that comment about cargo. He had, it seemed, been respectful. The Baughman's liked him. They had invited him to Sunday dinner, another reason she was pleased to be away. Fact was, she just didn't like the man, though he never made her feel afraid or uncomfortable. Elizabeth really didn't understand it. But it was the other comment that seemed to place her the most off balance… "You could be wrong you know…" Was she wrong? Had she judged the man in unfair ways that had shaped her opinion?

William junior must have heard the conversation just outside the schoolhouse. He must have guessed at the thoughts she was having for when he held her hand to ease her climbing out of the carriage he said softly, "Dad doesn't like him either."

It surprised her that the young man had heard or was even paying attention for that matter. She nodded in response, though she didn't know what she might say, at least about Mr. Sonnefelt. She smiled and thanked the younger William Clark, for seeing her home, and though she did not mention the other matter, she mentally thanked him for that as well.

"Perhaps," he began smoothly, "you will allow me to see you."

"To see me, Mr. Clark?"

"Yes, in a most proper social way," he answered with a smile. He had a most delightful smile. "I would very much like to get to know you better."

"Your father is on the school board. Would it be wise?"

"I don't see a problem," he responded. "Perhaps next Sunday, after dinner we could go ridding. You do ride?"

"I'm afraid I haven't ridden in years."

"The buggy then."

"Mr. Clark, you are indeed persistent. I will give it some thought. I am not certain I will have the time. I have no idea how school will proceed for my primary duty will be to my students. But I will think about your kind offer, and if not this Sunday then perhaps another time," she answered carefully.

They said their good byes and Jenny gave her a big hug, which pleased Elizabeth greatly, and the Clark's were off. As she watched them drive slowly away, Jenny turned in her seat waving. Smiling she returned the greeting not knowing if her new young friend saw. Standing at the Baughman's gate in the late afternoon heat, she thought for a time. She thought about the Clark's and the grand way they lived. Grander than even any she had known in Ohio. She thought about Mrs. Clark, Josephine. How much younger she was than her husband, scarcely older than she. Surely she was the man's second wife, for William Junior would not be eight years younger. Then she thought about the young man that had driven her home. A full-grown man but a few short years younger than she. Elizabeth pursed her lips, surprised he was yet unmarried. Heir to what she was certain was an empire, she knew William junior would be a very desirable suitor, and that, not taking into account the man was very handsome.

For the briefest of moments her mind ran wild. She saw herself on William's arm, imagining that they belonged together. Elizabeth shook her head as if she could dislodge the notion from her memory. She swallowed, drew a breath. Jenny had said he'd had many girlfriends. A lady's man perhaps. He had made an invitation. It seemed he was interested or perhaps if he was indeed a rouge, seeking another conquest. Elizabeth doubted he was a rouge, but she was most certain she would not be anyone's conquest. No, she had not come here in search of that kind of relationship. In truth, it was the furthest from her mind. No, she would have no attachments—not while she remained in Misty Creek—perhaps never. She would do her best to put him off, politely to be sure, but she knew she had to be careful. He was, after all, the son of the head of the school board.

No, Elizabeth thought, as she turned and smiled, seeing Alberta waiting at the door, she had no intention of marrying, and certainly no plans of spending her life here. Perhaps it was, as Pastor Smith had said, "a pearl," but she knew she belonged in Ohio; that was home and always would be. Elizabeth would teach this term, the next at most and then return to the world she had left. That was the plan, and she had always been one that knew what she wanted and how to achieve it.

Soon the day would be ending and she was certain Alberta would want to hear about her afternoon, and she would be glad to share it. But with the day's closing, when the stars would fill the night sky, then, oh yes, then the excitement of the anticipation would be replaced by the anxiety of what lies ahead—a new school—new students. Elizabeth knew she was ready, but all the same she doubted herself. And though she was far from home, the beginning of each school year was not so different. Certainly she had been surrounded, by those who knew her best. Yet even then, she put on the brave face, a false courage to hide the frightened child living deep inside. For it was at those times she felt more like one of her young pupils than a teacher. Yet each year when she faced the first day, she put on a confident face. She had always fooled them all.

Tomorrow would not be so different. She smiled as she was greeted by Mrs. Alberta Baughman. Yes, she could do this. Somehow she would do this, and no one would know—no one.

Part 3
School Daze

CHAPTER 15

ACTUALLY THE WEEK OPENED BETTER THAN SHE COULD HAVE expected, for sleep had abandoned in the earliest hours of Monday's morning. Her head swirled with a mix of self-doubt, anticipation, blended with the sensory overload of Sunday afternoon. Each time she closed her eyes as she lay in the dark room, images of Sweetwater Ranch, the Clark's grand home, and the life they lived there seemed to push what was expected of their teacher beyond the abilities she possessed. At those moments her breathing became rapid, how would she please the school board in general and Mr. William Clark, its president, in particular? Elizabeth knew her limitations. She could not move mountains or work miracles for that matter she was just a teacher.

Her sleep-preventing thoughts included the ride home from Sweetwater. How would she respond to young William? A complication she had not sought. It was enough to set her head pounding.

The only comfort that came to her in the dark was the vision of the classroom, set up and ready. But even as she considered the neat rows of desks, the memory of the workman laboring over each desk confused her. Matthew Sonnefelt was the last person she had expected in the school. The man hard at work seemed such a quagmire. Though he made the room seem fresh to do so on the Sabbath when work was prohibited surely meant something. The building was more than just a school, but God's sanctuary as well. The commandment "Remember the Sabbath day and keep it holy" kept returning to her mind. Now, in the dark, she felt that Sonnefelt's actions violated God's law, and wondered if the man considered himself above that law…man's as well.

At last when she felt she had tossed and turned enough, Elizabeth lit a lamp and wrote her first letter to the family she had left behind.

Dear Mother and Father,

I have no idea when these words will reach you, or when for that matter this letter will even be able to leave Misty Creek. But I have at last found a bit of time to send you word that I have arrived and am well. When I return to you at term's end I will share my travel adventure stories. For now I will tell you my first impressions of this place. Pastor Smith called Misty Creek a pearl. From what I have seen, it is no exaggeration. The valley known as Misty Creek is much like the Central Ohio countryside, with its lake and rich farm ground. The folks I have met have been warm and open.

I have been given a fine room in the home of Abner and Alberta Baughman, an older couple that live near the school. Dear, salt of the earth people that I am certain you would love. I am yet trying to find my place in their home, which is to be expected, but they welcome me as family, and more, as family they love. My room upstairs is much larger than I could have expected, nearly as large as the entire house I had been allotted in London. A cheery space where I am able to read or work, if I choose. But being new, I have so much to see and have spent these first days looking all about this new country. The Clark's invited me to Sunday dinner yesterday. Mr. Clark is head of the school board and is the largest rancher in the area. It would be impossible for me to convey how broad the expanse of their property. Surely there is nothing comparable in the whole state of Ohio! We shared a fine meal while I was completely overwhelmed, finding myself in a world beyond my imagining.

Today is the first day of the term. I feel prepared and yet not. I should weep if I thought of how far I find myself from all those I love most, and have supported me each year I have taught. Even when I, little more than a girl, began teaching in London and felt cut off, I knew you were only a few hours away. But the journey west has taught me that the space that separates us is more than miles. So now as I begin this term with new faces, in a new school, in a far off place, I think of you both, and of sister Catherine and her family, of brother Albert on his own, and take to heart the love you have always given, love that has been the cornerstone of my life. I find myself to have been given such a grand gift…your love, but also the faith you have taught me. I know that God will see me through this year. That he will provide the strength I need to teach the children of the valley.

I must stop now, for time runs short. Know that I love you all, that you are in each day's prayers. I will write again soon.

Love,
Elizabeth

CHAPTER 16

THE FIRST DAYS WERE BEHIND HER NOW, AND THEY HAD GONE well. It really shouldn't have surprised her. For though she had, these last years, taught in a larger school, fifth grade to be exact. Elizabeth had begun her career in a one room schoolhouse. That school in a small town called London, Ohio was not so different than what she found in Misty Creek. The younger children sat at the front, the oldest toward the back. She kept the girls on her left and the boys on the right. It just simplified things.

She had done her best to learn as much as teach. To learn about those that were her students, and through them more about the community that was to be her home. One strange fact surfaced the first day. Jenny Clark informed her that they had not finished a school term in five years. Carefully, she gleaned further into the matter, for it concerned her greatly. It seemed that no teacher remained through the year. No wonder Mr. Clark and the others behaved as they did when she had arrived. Elizabeth also wondered if it had anything to do with her being so quickly accepted to the position. She felt it probably was so. But when she asked Jenny and a few others, those she knew best, why the teacher had left, none knew. Elizabeth had also approached the subject with the Baughman's and was amazed they knew no more. A new teacher came each fall, and most left by Christmas. It had a woeful effect on the student's progress, though many of the mothers had done their best to fill in the gaps. She would delve into the matter further. Perhaps Mr. Clark, if anyone, could shed some light on the subject.

Elizabeth had agreed to dine with the Clarks on Sunday again. That decision came easily. Jenny had brought an invitation, a proper formal invite, but that was not the main factor, nor was young William. Rather the fact that Mr. Sonnefelt was coming to the Baughman's. That was another thing Elizabeth had learned. Most Sundays, the miller was their guest, and Elizabeth wished to maintain as much distance from him as she was able.

Though this arrangement could be complicated by young William. Somehow she felt more able to deal with that man than the other. At present, her feelings for William were…well neutral. She could not say the same for Mr. Sonnefelt. However she was relieved that she had not seen him at the school these first days. No trace of him since that Sunday afternoon when he waxed the desks. She had to admit, he had done an outstanding job and everything was set and proper when she arrived early Monday morning. That had been a fine morning for a walk, for though clouds had built during the night, it had not yet rained. Elizabeth wondered if it ever did. The early morning air still carried with it the freshness of the night. It was almost cool. The new day energized her and had an effect of calming her nervous stomach and made things manageable.

Now that she had been in the valley a week, things seemed a bit more familiar. She had begun to make a schedule—order her life. Yes, things were progressing quite favorably. That was until near the end of the school day, Friday. Elizabeth caught a glimpse of someone outside the schoolhouse among the trees. What troubled her wasn't so much that the man was there, but rather where he stood. For he stood in a place she and she alone could see him. It seemed he stood there waiting for her to notice, and then darted out of sight. The surprise of it affected her most of all. The teacher saw him, too far to be certain who it might be, but as soon as the man seemed to know she had seen, he moved deliberately out of her line of sight, most peculiar. As she finished the day, the first school week, thoughts of the incident filled her mind. Elizabeth came to two possible conclusions. One it was simply an innocent situation that didn't merit any further thought, or two, it was that man again—Sonnefelt. By the time she had dismissed the children she had come to the second conclusion, and would deal with it forthwith.

So, on that Friday afternoon in September, though she had papers to grade, Elizabeth postponed that work. She gathered her things and walked out with determined steps. Down the stairs to the pathway that led to the road that led across the bridges, along the top of the dam and to the mill. All the while she thought about what she had seen. It might seem to another of no meaning, but not so to her. Elizabeth thought of the other teachers, the ones that had come and gone before her. Perhaps, just perhaps, there was some sort of connection. Well, she would see. Yes, indeed, she would see!

That was the state of mind she bore as she entered the mill. Standing just inside the large door, a rage brewing within her, Elizabeth saw Sonnefelt sweeping the broad wooden planks which made up the floor. She was uncertain if he had heard her. Perhaps a shadow passed him as she entered, but the man looked up from his work. His face carried no expression. Tilting his head slightly, squinting his eyes just a bit, the miller began to speak. But Elizabeth did not allow it. No, she had come for her say and she was to have it. "How dare you?" she said in strong even tones.

The miller's eyes widened, shock clearly evident on his face.

After a moment had passed he began to speak, and again she cut him off. "You know exactly what I am talking about. Do not be coy."

This time Sonnefelt blinked, turned, and set the broom aside, leaning it against the counter. Then there came a silence, such a silence. Had Elizabeth taken the effort to notice, all she would have heard was the breeze in the treetops, the chattering of the birds, the only sounds that drifted into the mill through the doorway. She stared at the man. It had gone long enough. It would end now.

He looked at her hard, though not as hard as she might have expected and certainly not as hard as she bore at him. "Ma'am, what have I done now?"

The calmness in his voice, the matter-of-fact way of his words, only fed her rage. "You know very well, Mr. Sonnefelt!"

"Miss Beck," he had said her name. Strange she thought, he had never used her name before. But the using of her name did nothing to calm her. She felt it only a distraction. "It is plain to see that you are angry…"

Of course she was angry.

"And I can only believe you have justification for your feelings."

Certainly she was justified. Wasn't it obvious?

"So if you can tell me exactly what I have now done that was so very wrong."

Her eyes opened wider. How dare this man—how dare he?

She drew a breath. If this was the game he intended to play, so be it. She drew in another breath and slowly allowed the words to slither out from her clenched jaw. "I saw you…"

"You saw me…" he repeated with furrowed brow and questioning eyes.

"I saw you watching me. No, spying on me…"

"Ma'am?"

"Don't you ma'am me. Don't you ever ma'am me! You were outside the school and spying, you, you, animal."

The man's face changed. The questions that seemed to fill his eyes were now replaced with something she could not place, but that what she saw surprised her, and those deep brown eyes took much heat out of her anger.

"Show me where," he said, grasping her hand as if she was but a child. Dragging her, he walked with a speed that forced Elizabeth to run. Yet his grip was not more than firm, and certainly not cruel. After only a few strides Sonnefelt noticed her difficulty to keep step. The miller apologized, released her hand and bid her lead the way.

This only confused her, but Elizabeth went on at her own pace. Soon they reached the schoolhouse. Sonnefelt asked her to show him where she had seen him. His request seemed most odd, for surely the man knew. However she would do so to amuse the man, and doing so she would see his undoing. Elizabeth moved among the trees on the lakeside of the school. In truth she could not be certain which tree it had been.

"You saw the man from the school?" he asked.

Of course she had, wasn't that the point, but she only agreed.

"And where were you when you saw?"

"You know very well. I was at my desk."

"And no others saw him?"

"No, you were careful."

"Careful. How?" he asked.

"You stood where only I could see you."

He nodded his head and looked about a moment. "Perhaps," he said softly, "if you were to go to your desk look out the window we might determine which tree."

That was enough. She had gone along with this charade long enough, but as Elizabeth looked at him she saw something in his eyes, something earnest, yet something more or perhaps less than she had anticipated. She saw no sign of deceit, no telltale signs of someone taking delight in her situation. She did as he asked.

It turned out to be an excellent idea, though she would never admit it. When seated Elizabeth realized Mr. Sonnefelt yet stood too close. She used her hands to direct him to a more likely spot. Then she realized that the man that had stood there or very near that spot was someone other than Mr. Sonnefelt. It was more than the clothes he wore, for when she had directed the miller to the place, closing her eyes, she could bring up the image. And though it was too far to recognize whoever it had been, the man was shorter than Mr. Sonnefelt. She drew her hands to her mouth at the realization. Quickly she rose from her desk and going to the open window and shouted, "Mr. Sonnefelt, it was that tree, I am sure of it."

Elizabeth ran from the schoolhouse to join the miller among the trees. On arriving, she found the man searching the area on his hands and knees. Elizabeth remained still as he looked at the grass closely.

"I am certain it was that tree," she said softly.

"Yes," he said, "but I find no signs." He looked as she glared at him. "I didn't say this was not the spot, only I can't find any trace."

"Then you don't doubt me?"

"Why would I doubt you?" he asked as he rose to his feet, slapping any trace of soil from his knees.

"Mr. Sonnefelt, I feel I owe you an apology," she began softly. "From my desk, I could see that you were not the man. It was very wrong of me to…to assume."

For the first moment he did nothing. He did not even look her in the eyes. Rather he looked toward the school, then, moving away and to their left, he looked ever at the ground and spoke at last. "You were upset ma'am, and had every right to be."

Yes, she was upset, and yes, she had the right to be upset, but she did not have the right to make accusations – cruel accusations. And yet this man, this miller did not acknowledge her apology, an apology that was extremely difficult to make. Why did the man always exasperate her so?

"Whoever it was knew what he was doing. He came and went without leaving a trace."

"Like a ghost."

"I 'spect he wasn't," Sonnefelt said, calmly. "Was there anything you noticed?"

"I only saw him an instant."

Once more he looked at her, and once more that something was in his eyes. Elizabeth realized what she saw was an earnest concern. "Sir," she said, "I am certain it was nothing."

"Perhaps," the miller said as he forced a weak smile.

She returned the smile and then added, "I have taken you from your work too long, sir. I wish to thank you once again for your assistance."

Then looking about the wood a bit he said, "Miss Beck, if you will gather your things, I will escort you home."

"I don't think that is necessary," she said, as deep within once more an anger began to grow. Did this man think she was helpless? She certainly was capable to care for herself.

"I 'spect it isn't, but I would be honored for the privilege."

Elizabeth now felt trapped, it was not a feeling she enjoyed. How could she refuse, having been asked in that way? After all she had just wrongfully accused him of stalking. "As a favor to you?" she finally asked.

"Yes, ma'am."

"Not because you feel I am in dire need of your protection?"

"Heaven help anyone that dared to do you wrong!" he said with a smile – with a nice smile.

A few minutes later they were walking the road, beneath the trees, along the lake, on what would seem a hot summer afternoon. The air too warm for the season, being mid-September, but even so, there were signs that the weather would soon change. The mornings broke cool, or cooler. Elizabeth had been there only a week and she noticed the difference. And she had noticed spider webs, clinging to the bushes and branches, sparkling with dew early in the day. These are the things she had seen since she was young—signs that the summer was passing into autumn.

They walked at a leisurely pace. The teacher noticed the man forcing himself to slow. Neither spoke for a long time. When Elizabeth glanced over to her escort it seemed the miller had other things on his mind. Finally she spoke, in an attempt to make conversation. "Is the weather always like this?"

Sonnefelt blinked, drawn out of his thoughts with a start. "Been a bit hotter than usual lately," he said. "'Spect the rains will be coming soon."

"I am afraid I am keeping you from your work."

"I won't say that I don't have things to do, but it can wait," he responded with a smile.

"But you can return to your duties, sir, I will be fine," Elizabeth said carefully. "I mean I see you have other things demanding your attention."

"I am sorry, ma'am, I was just thinking about, well about what you saw. Try'n' to put it all together."

"I am sure it really wasn't anything. I fear I have overreacted."

"I 'spect so. But it just don't jive right in my mind." He stopped now, looking about as if trying to see something. For what the man searched, she could not tell. "I'll keep my ears open. Most stop by the mill sooner or later. Some on business, some just to chat. Yes, I'll keep my ears open and my eyes too."

"Please don't go to extra trouble, Mr. Sonnefelt," she genuinely implored.

He smiled as he signed they should proceed. "It won't be any trouble ma'am. I'll just pay a little closer attention, that's all."

"I'm sure I was over reacting."

He just nodded. They walked a few steps further when he asked. "What do you think of our community?"

"I will admit that when I left Thimble, I was concerned."

"Concerned?"

"Yes, by all means, things were not what I had expected."

"What did you expect?" he asked.

"I am not quite sure. But certainly not that open dry wasteland we crossed. Why it's practically a desert."

"No, ma'am. I've seen the desert."

"You have been to the desert?"

"It's been a while, but yes. I've been to south Texas and the open territories west."

This surprised her greatly. The man was only slightly older than she. She had never assumed he had traveled. "Then you were not born here."

He chuckled. "No, ma'am. Few have. Mostly the young."

"Then where do you call home?"

With a wave of his arm he said, "Here, ma'am, here. But if you're asking where I was born, well that would be Dakota Territory."

"Then you're as far from home as I."

"Like I said, this is my home. I 'spect it always will be. But yes, I've come a piece to get here, though not as far as Ohio."

"And you traveled?" she asked as they walked slowly along.

"Wandered's more like it."

Elizabeth wondered about the man with whom she now walked. How little she knew of him. She thought about her judgment—a rushed judgment. Throughout her life she had relied on first impressions, and they had usually been very accurate. As she considered this, she remembered a time – a terrible time when her instinct was very wrong. But by and large, her intuitions had not failed her.

Elizabeth thought a moment, about conversations on the wagon, conversations with Ben. It was then she began to draw conclusions about the man that owned the wagon, the miller of Misty Creek. Elizabeth thought about the first sight of the man, a tall dusty man, a man of labor. When the whole town seemed to gather to meet her, he was working, dutifully perhaps, but working. And she thought about the first words she heard him speak, and among those words was a term cargo—a word she took exception. Even now, on this quiet afternoon, the thought of that word brought a flush to her face. She thought about a question asked, by a dear child, Jenny, "You don't like him much do you?" Her answer then was very clear. Elizabeth was certain of her feelings. But the child had said something very profound, something one does not often hear from children, "You could be wrong you know…." Perhaps, just perhaps, she wondered. But if she had rushed to judgment before, she would not rush to a very different opinion now. No, she would rely on her first impression and her instincts, but with an open mind. So as she walked with a man she really didn't like, she wondered what kind of man he truly was, and with an open mind Elizabeth felt certain, with time, she would know.

Presently they arrived at the end of Baughman's lane. "I'll be fine now, Mr. Sonnefelt. I want to thank you for your company."

He touched the brim of his hat and with a smile, a very nice smile, and answered, "The pleasure was mine." Then turning, he left. Elizabeth watched him for a short while. Watched the man she realized she did not know. A few steps down the road she heard him begin to whistle – whistle an unfamiliar tune. *Perhaps he made up the melody as he went along,* she thought. She shook her head as she began the last part of her walk home.

CHAPTER 17

THE SUNDAY THAT FOLLOWED WAS VERY MUCH LIKE THE SUNDAY before. Elizabeth would have liked to remain after the service to assist in the rearranging of the room. However, Mr. Clark, who was to be her host, had no intention of waiting. He implied that the meal would be spoiled if they delayed. Even so, she watched a moment as the men of the community moved with practiced grace, quickly setting the pews aside. And among them was the miller. As always, he moved swiftly, perhaps the swiftest of all, as he grasped one end of a heavy wood bench, and he and another man carried it carefully and set it in its place. Mr. Clark called out to her the third time. Elizabeth could not keep him waiting any longer. As she turned, the teacher saw Mr. Sonnefelt, who with a smile, gave a wave so slight that no one else would notice. Elizabeth couldn't help but return his smile and a slight nod in recognition.

The meal was, as it had been the week before, extravagant. The servants had done their very best, and she was indeed impressed. Once again after dinner, they went to the great room for coffee and conversation. Mr. Clark did not drone on as he had the week prior, but rather sat thoughtfully with a brandy as Josephine asked about Ohio and Elizabeth's home. Josephine, too, had come from the east—New Jersey. She told how William, that is William Senior, had written a friend about the loss of his wife—a dreadful thing. Rosemary, the first Mrs. Clark, had died of a fever. The friend, a Mr. Andrew Holt, told William of Josephine, and that perhaps he should correspond with the young lady, which he did. She spoke warmly of the letters, the man that would become her husband wrote, and found she could not refuse him. Josephine smiled as she looked over to the man, and said, "And I have been here ever since."

Then young William strode in. The man had not joined them for either dinner or church. Dressed quite dashing, hair neatly combed, with his hat in his hand, he did not look anything the cowboy rancher, but rather a fine gentleman. Not so unlike a young man Elizabeth might have met in Ohio, a doctor perhaps, or businessman.

Josephine smiled at the arrival of her stepson, and Mr. Clark looked up only a moment then returned his gaze to the brandy glass in his hands deep in thought he seemed. William asked his parents if they would excuse their guest, which they gladly did for they knew he had promised to show her around.

Jenny immediately attempted to join them, however this time her mother indicated that she would not be allowed. Though the child looked downward, her face filled with disappointment, a look of relief could be seen on young William's face.

Soon Elizabeth found herself seated with the gentleman in the buggy hitched to a very fine looking animal, a gleaming pure black horse. With a snap of the reins they were off, moving at a pace much faster than the week before. The route they took led them through the valley parallel to a small stream of water on their right. On they went among the green grassy land and then their path wound up some hills on their left. From the hilltop they could see the vast open country. Wind blew through Elizabeth's hair as she examined land very different than what she had been accustomed to seeing back home. The land similar to the expanse she had crossed with Ben, except down near the water the land was much greener. But here on the hills and beyond it was the same as the miles she had crossed, the dry nearly brown grass swaying in the incessant wind. William pointed to the herds of cattle. A large number, how many she could only guess.

"All this land, everything you can see belongs to us," William said proudly.

The statement astounded her. Never had she imagined that any one family could control so much. She brought her hand to shade her eyes in order to better see. Elizabeth wondered how the Clarks had accumulated such a vast domain. Though the curiosity gnawed, she did not feel it her place to ask. Onward they rode. On along the hill tops, observing other groups of cattle grazing. Elizabeth found herself a bit confused by the lack of fences. The country was just so open, vast beyond imagining. On the ride from Thimble with Ben, the country seemed a wasteland, vacant space they must cross. Just inhospitable land a few dared to try to eek out a living. But here it seemed so grand, and it left her speechless.

Finally, pointing to the stream of water far below, she asked, "Is that Misty Creek?"

He nodded and added, "What little water Sonnefelt allows to flow. The man hoards the water."

"Don't you think that a bit harsh?"

"Harsh? Harsh?" he shouted, which made Elizabeth feel ill at ease. "Look at that lake, all that water. Who do you think that benefits?"

"But the lake is down, and it has fallen a foot since I have arrived." Elizabeth surprised she was actually defending the miller.

"Only because he can't hold the water back that is seeping through the dam!"

Elizabeth had walked the dam on more than one occasion. She knew that William's words were not entirely true. Yes, the lake had water, a great deal of water, but even from her schoolhouse she could see it shrinking day by day. More water was leaving the lake than flowed into it from the south. All the same, observing young Clark's temperament, Elizabeth thought it unwise to correct the rancher.

She told him she was impressed with the property his family controlled. The smile that grew showed the comment pleased him. She asked if he could begin the journey back.

The return route he chose was very different than the way they had come. William Jr. drove the carriage down the hill, across the stream, and up the hill beyond. From that point they looked upon a farm some distance away. The land reminded Elizabeth of the land she had seen at the bluff or paradise. Though the house was made of wood and it had a simple barn, the crops looked in much need of water. Here the land had fences, for an area was closed off for a few sorrowful looking animals, three cows and a pair of draft horses.

"See," William said, "this is what happens when you don't get water." The image indeed looked grim. It reminded her of the stop in Paradise. In just the short time she had been at Misty Creek she had forgotten. In the valley everything seemed to prosper, but here just a hill away, lay desolation. "At least the Donnellson's have enough sense to get out. They're leaving," Young William said smugly. "We made them a fair offer."

"Have they accepted it?" she asked. Emily Donnellson was one of her prize students; it troubled Elizabeth to consider losing her.

"Oh, they will," he said as he snapped the reins, and they moved on briskly again.

Turning down the hill they once more crossed Misty Creek and continued along the stream, a route that led back toward the ranch. He then turned right, taking a trail upland away from the water. From the top of that hill, Elizabeth could see the house corral and buildings of Sweetwater Ranch, laid out in its grandeur. But they did not go back toward the road but rather crossed open country as they continued south. At last they came to the hill that lined the west edge of the valley. From here the farms and orchards that lay on the west side of the lake were in plain view. William did not stop there, though the sight was beautiful. When Elizabeth glanced over to the young man, she saw his jaw clenched, which only confused her further.

"Farmers," she heard him mutter, but he said no more as he continued to drive across the hill. The rancher seemed more at ease viewing the wide open country. Heading south once more across open grassland, they traveled a goodly distance before coming to the remnants of a road. The dust path ran south a bit, then turned east back over the hills and led into the valley. In that way they came to Misty Creek from the other side.

"I have never come into the valley from the west side, William."

He smiled as he snapped the reins once again. "I'm happy I have been able to show you a bit of this grand country."

Soon the carriage reached the side road that split off to the north. The road that skirted the lake and led back to the Baughman's farm.

The day had nearly ended when they at last reached the Baughman's, and Elizabeth felt exhausted from the hours riding around the countryside. Yet Elizabeth smiled as she thanked the young man for the tour.

"I wonder, Miss Beck, if I might be able to call on you, say next week?"

The young woman from Ohio now found herself in a most difficult situation, though it was something she had expected.

Elizabeth looked up at the man yet seated at the reins. "I am honored William, but I have only just arrived here, and there is the fact that we have only just met. Perhaps we should allow some time to pass?"

She could see by his expression as he glanced away that this answer did not please the man. "Then maybe in a few weeks," he responded with his words coming in clipped tones through straight lips.

"Perhaps."

Fortunately, the young man did not press the point. He bid his farewell and with another snap of the reins the visibly weary horse drew the buggy off.

Elizabeth felt strange when he left her there at the Baughman's gate. She didn't take time to watch him leave. She just turned and moved toward the house, up the steps and into the kitchen, but she felt relieved somehow. Elizabeth realized she had been tense – very tense, and with William's leaving, that tension left as well. She found herself confused by this realization. There was nothing specific that William had done. Well, he had shown a bit of temper, spirit perhaps. That was not so unusual. Then she realized, yes, she understood, or at least thought she understood. The man's intensions had fueled her discomfort.

She had no desire to make any attachments, not here, not now, perhaps not ever. At least not that type of attachment. And it was plain to see that young William Clark, a most eligible suitor, seemed to be interested—too interested to suit her. Now Elizabeth had a problem and wondered how she would deal with it. She would give it some thought. He was a handsome young man, heir to a sizable enterprise. Any young woman, that is young woman of the area, would consider the man a prize. She would think on the matter further, keep some space, and consider things carefully. Yes, that was what she would do.

CHAPTER 18

THE NEXT WEEKS WERE RELATIVELY UNEVENTFUL. ELIZABETH found her students a delight, well most of them in any case. Becoming more acquainted with their past progress, she had begun to plot a course of action that would help many of them gain ground lost in the years past. She had taken to visiting Leah Smith, her new dearest friend, walking over to the parsonage twice a week. On those excursions she usually stopped at Peabody's. The mercantile was much more than just a store where one might attempt to purchase things needed. It also seemed one of the centers of social activity in the valley.

Everyone came to Peabody's, well almost everyone. The store held the closest thing to a post office. Mr. Peabody held the mail until someone went to Thimble or even better a bigger town called Baxter, though that was rare considering just how much further Baxter was from the valley. Whenever a wagon returned from its monthly journey to the rail head, Howard Peabody sorted and held the mail until its owner came in to fetch it. Which wasn't long, for everyone knew the system and came by soon after Ben's return in anticipation of any word from beyond the valley.

Most times as Elizabeth entered she was met with warm smiles pleasant conversation. Often as she moved about the clean store, gossip seemed to ooze out of every corner. She did her best not to pay close attention to the words spread about, but it was impossible not to pick up bits and pieces. It brought a smile to her lips as she thought of how people were not so different even here on the frontier.

There was nothing unusual about her stops at Peabody's, and the first few gave her an excuse to go next door to the Smiths. Now that those visits had become a regular occurrence, Elizabeth didn't need a stopover at the store as a reason to spend time with Leah and her brood. She enjoyed her visits with her new friend, but they also made her feel useful the weeks Ben was away, hauling freight, while Leah had to deal with her household in his absence.

So after a brief stop at the store to drop off letters she had written to her mother and father, a longer one to sister Catherine, and even a brief note to Albert her brother, Elizabeth crossed over to the parsonage. Leah greeted her with an embrace at the moment Elizabeth gave her gentle knock. She noticed Ben scurrying Micah, Rachel, and James out of the room. "Your mother has company," his booming voice began, "let's go outside and play."

Micah and James dashed out, but the curly haired Rachel rushed to Elizabeth. The teacher, yet in the doorway, lowered herself and hugged the dear child. Smiling the girl asked, "Don't you want to come out and play too? Daddy's always fun."

Leah tousled the child's hair. "Not today, Rachael. Miss Beck has come for tea." The words seemed enough, for the child dashed after the others.

The preacher's wife led by what had become a familiar way to the kitchen. The scent of fresh bread met them as they entered, the room bright and clean. It always surprised Elizabeth that the mother of three boisterous children could keep things so perfect.

"You've been baking again."

A slight color came to Leah's cheeks. "One must be prepared for company."

Elizabeth smiled. "It does seem that you were expecting me." She looked around the room as she sat. "But what if I had not come today?"

Leah patted her hand. "I would have understood…really."

Leah poured the tea and slid a plate of cookies fresh from the oven a bit closer to Elizabeth. It did not seem odd when on this visit Leah spoke to her about young William Clark. The whole valley was aware that she had gone to the Clark's for Sunday dinner and of the extended buggy ride.

"Take care," Leah said with a smile, "he really is quite dashing."

Elizabeth prepared to tell her friend she had no intention of leading the man on, when Leah said softly. "I am not one to spread gossip, and I would not tell words heard as such if you were not new to our community and had no opportunity to witness for yourself."

"I know he has had several sweethearts. Jenny told me."

"That is indeed true. But there is a more serious matter," Leah said choosing her words carefully. "Some time ago, William Clark Junior was seeing Miss Abigail Walker. She is the daughter of Thomas and Evangeline, they have a fine farm at that, north of the lake. They were, everyone thought, soon to be wed. But suddenly Miss Walker left the valley. Of course tongues wagged for months. I will not discuss what was implied. However I found with my visits with Evangeline that the young lady went to visit her aunt in Missouri. She returned most of a year later, different somehow.

"I am certain you know what I am implying. And there is only one who knows the truth. I trust you will understand that I would not even mention this whole affair if we were not friends. It may be nothing. I expect it is. I believe you are a woman of character. Yet all the same there are times even the strongest of us might, shall we say, lose our good sense. Take care."

Elizabeth was touched by the concern her friend showed. She held the china cup between her hands. Her eyes focused on the crisp white curtain that framed the window above the sink. Swallowing she drew a breath. "Young Mr. Clark is dashing. He will be a man of great wealth. But I have not come to Misty Creek in search of a husband. I know most would find that difficult to believe, but in truth…" She paused as the hot tears began to form. Elizabeth looked across the table to her friend.

Leah blinked and reaching took Elizabeth's hands.

Elizabeth looked down at the unfinished cup of tea before her. Blinking she shook he head slightly. "I am certain you know how fortunate you are." She looked up into Leah's concerned eyes. "Men of Ben's caliber are indeed rare."

"No man is perfect Elizabeth, especially not Ben."

The faint sound of the children at play, laughing, came from just outside the door. Elizabeth blinked back a tear. "That is not my meaning. Ben is someone you can depend upon." She swallowed. "He loves you Leah, it is plain to see. He is someone you can trust with your heart. You have no idea how few are worthy of that trust." A tear flowed down her cheek as she held back the sobs that threatened to shake her to her core.

Leah's thumbs rubbed Elizabeth's hands, yet she said nothing as she looked deep into her damp eyes. Elizabeth saw the questions in Leah's eyes, deep loving questions, those questions unspoken caused the dam to burst. The dam Elizabeth had built. The dam she had used to protect a heart so badly broken.

Then Elizabeth spoke the name that had not left her lips since the past June. "His name is Jameson Elders." She swallowed, blinked, and drew a deep breath. "He is a doctor now, Dr. Jameson Elders," she said as she raised her chin. "I was in love, am in love with him. I expect I always will be." The sounds that drifted into the room distracted her a moment, reaching deep inside her. She looked away from her friend, gasped and trembled. "Jameson was the one, the one and only. A man like no other…and." She paused took a breath and continued. "I had always known Jameson. His parents and my parents were friends. I believe my feelings began before his. It was a wonderful day when he asked Father if he might court me." Elizabeth gave a shaky smile. "That was the summer before I left for teacher's college. Jameson was bound for school, as well. We fell in love, oh so in love." She swallowed. "Together we made the plans that lovers do. Of home of fami…" Elizabeth closed her eye as the tears flowed in earnest.

Elizabeth blinked, drew another breath, and used her handkerchief to wipe her eyes. "Jameson was so handsome. He was the one, you know the one." She paused to wipe her eyes again. "That day he presented me with his grandmother's ring, I thought my life complete. But I had a secret and it was unfair to accept that ring before he knew." She looked into Leah's understanding eyes. "It was so difficult. I remember the night we sat on my parents' porch swing and I held his hands. I wept when I told him. I cannot ever have children."

"Oh my," came Leah's soft voice as Elizabeth crumbled to her tears and sobs, gasping for each breath. The preacher's wife left her seat across the table to take the chair next to Elizabeth, and wrapped her arm around the quaking teacher.

"I had been ill as a child. Mother told how I had remained on death's threshold for more than two days." Elizabeth turned to look toward her new friend. Tears flowed down Leah's cheeks as the woman squeezed her shoulder. "I survived that sickness, but it left its mark."

"Poor, poor dear."

Elizabeth raised her chin slightly. "I mean I am grateful God spared me…but…"

"And when you told your man?"

"He asked if I was certain, that perhaps I was mistaken. That with time we might have children." Elizabeth shook her head. "I told him not to cling to false hopes, I had no doubts of my abilities in that regard."

She swallowed closed her eyes as she began once again. "Jameson said it did not matter. He told me that he loved me. That we would marry and live our lives together forever." Elizabeth calmed herself a bit and dried her eyes again. "I accepted that beautiful ring and felt certain I was the happiest woman in Columbus to be loved by such a man." She stared at the small red rose that decorated the saucer beneath her cup of her now cold tea. She looked toward Leah and tried to smile but felt a tremble move through her lips.

As they sat in silence, she could feel the warm touch of Leah's hands. In that touch she felt something solid she could trust. "What happened Elizabeth? Did Jameson die?"

She shook her head. "No," her voice trembled. She took a gulp of air and began again. "We were to marry when he finished his education. Those years seemed long." She looked up into her friend's eyes once more. "I taught school and sent him every penny I could spare. Together we made it. Together side by side, we struggled for his dream." Elizabeth blinked, drew another breath used her handkerchief to wipe her eyes.

The stillness that followed allowed the happy shouts from the backyard to filter in. "Do you want to tell me what happed?"

Elizabeth shook her head firmly, but then went on. "When Jameson neared completion of his studies we began planning our wedding. All our friends and family looked forward to the day long put off, nearly as much as I. We would wed in late May, following Jameson's graduation, when my term teaching at Brandtworth Elementary had finished." Elizabeth looked upward as she drew a breath. "I would no longer be a teacher," she said doing her best to hold the sob in her throat. "I was ready to become a doctor's wife." She looked toward Leah surprised that her weeping had ceased. "It was a glorious day, Saturday, May 25th. The sun shone, not a cloud in the sky. The church, I had never seen it so full. Everyone seemed to be there. And I waited."

"Waited?'

"Yes, I waited. I had been given a small room in which to prepare, you know any final touches while being hidden from the groom." She tried to smile. "I was so excited, all the years we had waited, soon it would be behind us, a new life…Jameson's wife. I scarcely noticed the time pass, but it did pass."

Leah rubbed Elizabeth's shoulder, but said nothing.

"I began to hear rumblings outside the door. I would have gone to investigate but my bridesmaids held me back. Rachel Henderson, my maid of honor had left earlier to discover the delay, but she had not returned. I sent Mary Baxiter to find Rachel." Now the tears came in earnest. Flooding like rain as they flowed down her cheeks.

Elizabeth sobbed as Leah held her. "Perhaps, dear, this is a place you should not go…not yet."

It was some moments before Elizabeth continued. "Poor Mary, she trembled so when she returned." Even now Elizabeth could see her dear friend, the color drained from her face, hear the words from her lips. "They're gone, Rachael and James…they're gone…" Mary had nearly fainted as she spoke the words.

"I couldn't believe that Jameson…" Elizabeth began again, her eyes closed, the pain yet fresh. "There had to be another explanation." she looked into Leah's eyes. "But there wasn't. I don't know how I did it. How I went into the church," she said as Leah blinked back her own tears. "When I understood the truth at last, I knew I must."

There in Leah's kitchen, Elizabeth relived the moment she entered the sanctuary. Smiling faces turned at the sound of her entering. The scent of Aunt Pauline's excessive perfume blended with spring air that flowed in through open windows. The candles had burned down, the wax drips formed clumps along their stubby remains. Moving up the aisle in a daze, she remembered how the church grew so still—deathly silent, and there before them all she stood a moment carefully thinking about what she would say, as all eyes focused upon her. "I thanked my family. I thanked my dear friends, and I thanked Jameson's family and friends and then told them all that there would be no wedding." Again the tears flowed as she did her best to control the sobs. She had broken down a moment, but closing her eyes she drew a breath. Elizabeth had not been crushed then. She would not crumble now.

She had stood there at the front of that church afraid to move, in a room filled with people scarcely able to breathe, in a space more silent than a tomb. "I stood frozen not knowing what I should do." Elizabeth blinked and shook her head slightly. "Catherine, dear Catherine, my sister, ran up the aisle to gather me." The image of her sister's tear stained face filled her mind. Catherine had taken her arm, looped in her own, and led her away.

There Elizabeth's story ended, there was no need to go further. As she wept in Leah's arms, she felt the warm embrace of someone that truly cared. The wound had reopened, and yet she felt relieved she had someone to share her pain. Leah held her, whispering, "My poor, poor dear," over and over in her ear and wept with her, wept in her pain, wept for her.

At long last when Elizabeth had calmed herself, or at least calmed herself sufficiently to get a few words out between her sobs, she said, "I'll never marry. And I will never trust a man with my heart again."

"Now, dear, you have had an awful experience, but you cannot allow the actions of one man to poison all," Leah said at last.

"But surely," Elizabeth said, "does not a man deserve a wife that can give him children?"

"My dear Elizabeth, what each person needs…well, it is different than any other. Jameson wronged you. He wronged you by not being honest, and for that I am truly sorry, but do not close your heart to all possibilities." Leah held her friend tightly a moment and then went on, "Time passing, that is what you need. You may think that you can never heal. You may feel that already much time has passed, but it has not.

But for now weep, let that pain flow, I feel it has been pent within for far too long."

Elizabeth did cry. And though she would not realize for many days, it was the time healing finally began. Even so, she continued to harbor a bitterness against the male gender, though there were exceptions, Mr. Baughman for one and Ben another.

Yes, Leah had become a dear friend, but now they had bonded in a way that only two that shared a secret, a deep secret, could. Elizabeth felt grateful to have made such an acquaintance, for she needed , a dear friend, a friend very near to her age, someone she knew she could ever count upon. So that when she had left the parsonage that day she felt lighter, as if a great burden she carried was no longer borne alone. But Elizabeth also knew that she had received a great treasure—Leah's friendship.

Chapter 19

October had begun and Elizabeth was quite pleased with how school was proceeding. She had remained at the school grading papers, and as with most Fridays, scrubbed down the chalkboard. Tomorrow the men would arrive to convert the space for Sunday's service. She didn't want to add to their work, so Elizabeth made certain that all was in place and out of their way.

The door stood open. The last days seemed more like summer than the middle of autumn, and she enjoyed the scent of the changing leaves that flowed around her. Busy at her work she did not hear the man that came in, and started when she looked up and saw William Clark Junior near. "Mr. Clark, you gave me a fright."

He smiled. Once again she noticed the handsome features of the young man that stood so straight and tall in her school. His dark hair and chestnut eyes set off a face with just the slightest dimples. He seemed so out of place, dressed with a tan leather jacket and dungarees. A three piece suit, she was certain would fit him better. The effect caused her to catch her breath. Elizabeth pushed such frivolous thoughts aside, blinked, and returned to the moment just as he began speaking.

"I saw the door open and I thought I might stop by a moment."

Elizabeth straightened. Surrounded by her cleaning supplies she pushed a stray strand of hair behind her ear, certain her appearance left much to be desired. "I don't believe you have seen the inside of the school. I know you have come to church, but it looks far different, wouldn't you say Mr. Clark?"

"What is this Mr. Clark business? I thought we were friends." He moved closer.

"I'm not certain that friends is really the right word. Perhaps acquaintances?" She moved a quarter step back, placing her hand upon Jenny's desk.

He moved closer placing his hand upon hers. "I would have thought we were more than acquaintances."

She slid her hand from beneath his. "Perhaps not." She said with even tones as her eyes glanced about the room. Elizabeth drew a breath, "I am sorry if I gave the wrong impression."

He looked away, but remained near, too near, his shoulder touching hers.

She moved a bit to her left, and away from him. "I have not come seeking attachments." She forced some air into her lungs. "There is someone back home." He didn't need to know that Jameson had married another.

"In Ohio?"

"Yes. In Columbus. My home town."

Drawing his brows, he asked, "And he allowed you to go west?"

"I will be no man's slave!"

William cocked his head. "Not even when you marry?"

She looked away as the tears threatened to come. Drawing a breath, she said, "If I choose to marry, not even to him."

"I'm not certain I believe you."

She raised her chin. "That I will not surrender my independence?"

"No, that there is a man waiting." He took her hand in his. "You don't have a ring."

Elizabeth pulled her hand free and involuntarily hid it within her other. Her mind quickly went to the memory of the wedding ring meant for her finger, and that the man she loved had placed that ring on another's hand. The tears were coming and she grew angry at this man that dared to push her to those places she wished to avoid. "I really don't care what you think!" She looked away, "I have told you that I am not interested in advancing our relationship further and that should be enough."

As she turned to leave the man took hold of her arm. "There's no one in Ohio."

With a quick yank she pulled free. "And now you call me a liar." Squinting she added, "Perhaps others might be overcome by your charm, Mr. Clark, but I am not!" Elizabeth felt certain her face showed a flush of her rage. "If you will excuse me, I must finish and be on my way."

The day had grown late. The sky had faded from blue to the milky white of dusk, yet full light...almost. Elizabeth walked with determination, her case swinging in time with each step. Her confrontation with young Mr. Clark reinforced her opinion of men, that is men in general. What really got her dander was the arrogance of the man. As William left, he spoke over his shoulder, "You'll come around. In a week or two you will come to your senses. I'll still be here."

"Men," she huffed as she felt her face grow warm.

Someone approached, it was not surprising for many walked the road that led north from Misty Creek. When the man drew near, she saw it was the miller. She paid the man no heed, but as he came closer he spoke. "Good evening, Miss Beck."

"Good evening, Mr. Sonnefelt."

"It is late, Miss Beck. I hope there has not been a problem?"

"A problem?"

"At school."

What was the matter with the man? She did not consider her conversation with William a problem…really. But did Sonnefelt think that any time her schedule did not fit with his expectations that there had to be a problem? "No problem, Mr. Sonnefelt, no problems at all." Elizabeth answered coolly.

He just nodded and stood there silently. Watching the man she couldn't help but wonder what he was thinking. "I was grading papers and the time slipped away." Which was the truth. Well, mostly.

Again Sonnefelt did not speak.

"I must be on my way, it is, as you have mentioned, growing late. Alberta will soon send a party to seek me."

He swung his arm, a gesture so she might pass. Did he think she needed his permission to walk the road?

"Shall I escort you?"

"That will not be necessary." The words slithered from her lips. "You need not fear. It is yet daylight."

The man looked downward and shook his head.

She stared at the man that shared this piece of an otherwise deserted road. Elizabeth noticed the tightened jaw and the faint tremble of his cheek. She never considered the reason she remained there. With her brows drawn it seemed at that moment she waited to see who would flinch. Sonnefelt opened his eyes, glanced her way. Then looking down the road the direction Elizabeth intended, he said, "Have a good evening."

She was having a good evening that was until... "I shall, you can be certain of that, Mr. Sonnefelt. An evening without any problems." She formed the words with tight lips in clipped tones.

Facing her in the now fading light, lowering his left eyelid the slightest, his face grew flushed. "What?"

"Why, was it not you that implied I had problems?" Her voice was hard.

Drawing a deep breath while shaking his head, he said, "I was only trying..."

"I know very well what you intended, Mr. Sonnefelt."

He blinked, his mouth moved but said nothing. Turning he left her there striding swiftly on his way.

Elizabeth watched him, mentally daring the man to look back. He didn't.

She charged on her way, angry that the encounter with those two men had spoiled a good day. When Elizabeth had gone a hundred yards or so, when her anger subsided a bit, she stopped. Looking back, the man no longer in view, she wondered. What had made her so angry with Sonnefelt? "It was that man's attitude," she muttered to herself. "He was just like Alexander."

She felt her cheeks flush. For the coals of justified anger, at least she considered her anger justified, piled up, fueled her indignation. Elizabeth continued her journey once more with quick steps. Some paces further, her mood had tempered and she halted again. How had she recognized the man's arrogance? His words. That's what it was. Sonnefelt made it plain that the only reason she could possibly have for walking the road at this hour was her inadequacy. "Problems at school" he had so clearly put it.

Once again she stormed onward, the fire of the injustice white hot.

Elizabeth was panting when she reached Baughman's lane, the last light of this autumn day soon to be a memory. As she drew a breath, her mind went back to the man and his words. Swallowing, she blinked twice. With the next deep breath she recognized that the man was only being cordial.

She frowned at the thought. Why did Sonnefelt upset her so? Could it be that he reminded her of Alexander? Had she viewed every action, every word as though they had come from that man? She looked back down the road in the growing gloom and felt ashamed.

If only the man had spoken differently, perhaps had asked, "How was your day, Miss Beck?" Well then, he didn't, but would it have made a difference, really? She would like to think it would, but feared no matter what Sonnefelt might say she would find fault.

The tumultuous end of what had been a productive week made sleep impossible. The thoughts of William's stop at the school and his arrogance seemed mixed with the reasons she had come to Misty Creek in the first place. Her heart remained torn apart by the man she loved. Elizabeth did not know when or if she would ever recover.

As she lay in the dark with thoughts swirling she found herself troubled by the meeting on the road. She bit her lip as now she realized that Sonnefelt had stumbled into her pain and anger. She had handled things so badly. Several times in the dark hours she had chided herself for allowing her temper to lash out at others. Elizabeth felt certain she owed the miller an apology. What made the whole event worse was the man had just finished helping Abner hang the storm windows of this very house. She shivered at the thought of Matthew on a ladder hanging the heavy wood framed glass on her windows as well. Had he peered into her private space? After supper when she had learned of the task completed, she had rushed to her room to determine if she had left it proper, not that it was her way to leave things strewn about. All the same, perhaps, she had left one thing or another out by oversight. Why it troubled her that Sonnefelt might have seen something while he worked, she had no idea.

She was pleased that the man helped the Baughmans, but it would be the kind of thing Alexander would do. But unlike Alexander, this man did not flaunt the act of kindness. Maybe that was what prevented sleep. Sonnefelt moved about like Alexander Elders, he made his way with strong arms and back, like Alexander. Tall and straight like the man she had known, but yet she began to notice differences.

Elizabeth would have sat by the window, opened it to smell the musty scent of autumn, but the storm windows now sealed night breeze out. It was ridiculous, but for an instant she blamed Sonnefelt for that as well. "Stop that, Elizabeth," she whispered to herself. "Winter will come and you will find yourself grateful."

After she had mulled over all these things and so much more, for the fourth time, somehow the thoughts released her and she drifted into troubled sleep, filled with dreams of abandonment. She found herself reaching toward Jameson while he drifted further and further away… and she was all alone.

CHAPTER 20

It was a Tuesday in mid-October. Late in the day that had a gray sky burdened with heavy dark clouds that hid the sun and painted the world in drab tones. He was back. The man Elizabeth had seen before returned. However, this time he stood calmly, staring directly at her. Once again he stood in a place where only she could see, but now much closer than before. When the man captured her attention, she saw or heard nothing else. As he stared at her, she watched him, looking carefully to notice each detail. He was not especially tall, but thin. His face had hollow cheeks sporting stubble of some day's growth. He wore a soiled, heavy, woolen coat buttoned tightly against the brisk autumn wind that blew across the lake. Without shifting her glance, she called Homer Reynolds to her desk, but the instant the young man came, the stranger slipped from view.

"Mind the class a moment Homer," Elizabeth said as she quickly rose, dashed to the door and ran outside. She had no idea what she intended to do, but felt that this was no coincidence, that this man constituted a threat to her class. Her students were her responsibility, a responsibility Elizabeth took seriously. These thoughts filled her mind as she rushed out the door and around the side of the schoolhouse. She would speak with this man, drive him away if necessary.

But he had gone, vanished it seemed. Fueled by her anger, Elizabeth looked about for the stranger that had leered at her. Drawing a breath she walked the grounds peering behind the trees and even the schoolhouse itself. As she searched, another thought came. What if that strange looking man intended to do her or her students harm? In her anger she had not considered that possibility. Taking another breath to cool her temper, she turned and saw her entire class with their faces pressed against the windows. Elizabeth shook her head and returned inside.

Everyone seemed very studious on her return, sitting quietly at their work. Though most, she noticed, glanced over their books, slates, or up from their papers, to look her way as she returned to her desk. Elizabeth thanked Homer for managing the class, though she knew he had not done the task as effectively as she might have hoped. The young man returned to his seat.

Jenny Clark raised her hand, but spoke before Elizabeth had the chance to call her name, "Did you see the ghost, Miss Beck?"

Elizabeth blinked. "Ghost?" She glanced around the room.

"Our last teacher, Miss Hagelbock, said that there is a ghost in these woods."

"She was just funnin' us," Joe Tyler injected.

Jenny and several others shook their heads firmly. "You remember the day she was white as a sheet. She said she saw him right out there." The girl pointed toward the trees in the general direction of where Elizabeth had seen the man minutes before.

"I am certain she was mistaken."

"Are you sayin' she lied to us, Miss Beck?"

Now Elizabeth found herself in a dilemma. "I do not know what your teacher saw, but I did not see a ghost, I simply saw a man."

"But can't a ghost look like anything it wants?"

"There are no ghosts," Elizabeth responded firmly.

Sam rubbed a finger along his chin. "I don't know. Everybody's heard about Colton Snit."

"Yeah," came a chorus of voices.

Elizabeth couldn't prevent the slight smile that came to her lips. "Colton Snit?"

"Yeah, he died in these woods long ago, so everybody sez."

Elizabeth knew that the area had not been settled all that long, yet to her students ten years might be next to forever. "Long ago, Sam."

"Before the mill and everything."

"Nobody knows where the man was buried, but when they built the new dam it must have flooded over him, and he's been mad ever since."

Elizabeth had heard enough. "We will have no further discussion on ghosts. I saw a man standing among the trees. A flesh and blood man, certainly no ghost."

Elizabeth could not remain focused on her work after seeing the man spying and all this talk of Colton Snit. Though she did not believe in ghosts wandering the wood about the school, all the same the events of the day unnerved her, so she decided to dismiss the class early.

Most days Elizabeth remained after class, grading papers or preparing the next day's work, and that had been her plan. However the teacher felt strange sitting alone in the empty building. That strangeness grew with each moment and made her very uncomfortable, and once more she found herself so distracted she could not function.

Elizabeth had just decided to gather her things and go home when there came a rap, rap, rap on the door, and it opened a bit, revealing the face of one Mr. Sonnefelt.

"Yes, Mr. Sonnefelt?" she asked.

"I noticed you let the children leave early."

"And you had a problem?" she said coolly, being in no mood to be questioned about her methods.

He opened the door a bit more until he stood in the doorway. "By no means ma'am. I…I mean…well I…," he stammered. "I wondered if there was a problem."

There was that word, problem, again. Elizabeth supposed that this time there was a concern, but she certainly would not discuss it with him, and was just about to tell him so, when two things occurred to her. One, she expected he would find out the stranger had returned anyway. It was a small community. And two, the seriousness he had given the matter the first time. "I am not certain it is a problem, Mr. Sonnefelt, and I am unsure, since you are not on the school board that I should discuss with you.

"I'm just offering my assistance, if you have a need, ma'am."

Elizabeth couldn't help but smile, though she tried her hardest to suppress it. "I know you are, Mr. Sonnefelt, and I appreciate that… but…"

Standing in the doorway, he just looked at her. She glanced away a moment wondering what she would say, but when she looked once more toward the doorway, the miller yet had that look about him, a look she could not fully describe. His dusty brows pulled down slightly. Finally she sighed and said, "The peeker was back today." There she had told him.His look changed. He drew his eyes partially closed and tightened his lips straight. Mr. Sonnefelt looked intently serious. "The same place?" he asked.

"Closer, much closer," she answered. "I was able to see him quite clearly. He did not seem the least bit concerned that I might."

The miller stepped inside, closing the door. "Did any of the children see him?"

"No, none did. I called Homer Reynolds up, hoping he could see the man, but the stranger slipped out of view before Homer had a chance." It took effort for the teacher to remain calm. Discussing the event had begun to raise her temper once again. "Mr. Sonnefelt, I am, concerned for the children's safety."

"Certainly, ma'am." Matthew then asked her to describe the man she had seen. When she had finished he said, "I know of a couple of men that fit that description. It would not be proper for me to assume it is one or the other. I will ask around, perhaps in a day or two I might know more." The miller glanced about the room, drew a breath, looked her way, and then stared out the window. It was plain on his face that the situation bothered him.

"Thank you, Mr. Sonnefelt, but that will not be necessary. I have sent a note home with Jenny Clark, and am certain Mr. Clark will see the situation is remedied."

"That was a very good idea, ma'am, but all the same…"

"Well, Mr. Sonnefelt, if there is nothing else," she said as she cut him off, "I have finished here and would wish to go home."

"I would walk you if you allow me."

"That will not be necessary. I am certain you are a very busy man," she answered firmly.

For a moment, Elizabeth felt certain he would press the point. For a moment, though she could not understand why, she wished he would.

"You are certain, ma'am?"

How Elizabeth hated being called ma'am. That was a term to describe old women. And though she no longer considered herself young, being every bit of twenty-four, she certainly was not old! "Yes," she said though she was not certain her voice conveyed confidence. "I am."

His face changed again. It carried a look of concern. Elizabeth nearly changed her mind, but inside, deep inside, she had a need to prove herself even to that man, though why she had no idea. So Elizabeth got up from her desk, put on her coat, grabbed her things, and moved toward the door. Mr. Sonnefelt held the door and she went out.

She walked boldly down the length of the lane, turning left, going right down the center of the road. Elizabeth told herself not to look back, but after only a few steps she did. Sonnefelt stood there, at the door of the school, watching her. She wasn't certain if that gave her comfort or just contributed to her aggravation, but onward she strode.

Elizabeth did not need any man's protection. She could take care of herself, and told herself so repeatedly. The leather valise she carried, the weight of it usually a nuisance, gave her confidence. *I dare someone to come,* she thought to herself as she swung it up and around. *I'll give them what to.*

Elizabeth hoped no one noticed her sweep her case to bludgeon an imaginary hooligan. But the man in the trees was not imaginary. What if she was his intended victim? A shiver ran down her spine. She dropped her valise. It thumped and tumbled on the road. Quickly she stooped, took hold of the handle and began off once more, a bit faster than before.

After she had gone perhaps fifty yards, Elizabeth slowed her pace. "This is ridiculous," she muttered to herself. "Totally ridiculous, there is nothing to fear." She had allowed the miller to take a non-situation and frighten her. That man, it always was that man. How did she know that he didn't set up the whole thing? Hire someone to stand outside her window and frighten her? That would explain how he had just happened to show up at the school. That was it all along. Mr. Sonnefelt staged the whole thing.

Elizabeth stopped in the road. Her face flush with the anger at this new revelation. Turning she had every intension of marching right back and giving that man a piece of her mind, perhaps strike him once good with her bag. She would show him.

Fourteen steps back the way she had come, why she had counted she had no clue, Elizabeth stopped again. Could she be certain that Mr. Sonnefelt was indeed behind it? In her mind, she once more saw his face. It didn't fit. No, it didn't fit at all. He carried that look she couldn't quite place. It wasn't the look of a person that meant to harm or frighten her. Of course he could be hiding his real feelings. That was it, he was only acting when he came in the schoolhouse, only acting.

Once more she charged off. It was another fourteen steps, a ridiculous coincidence, when she stopped once more. Since she had arrived in Misty Creek, she had blamed the man for a great many things, and it had turned out that she had been wrong. Or was she? Maybe he had manipulated her to think she had been wrong. That was it, he had fooled her. Oh, how angry she grew. Off she stormed once again, she didn't count her steps, actually she did but forced herself to stop at twelve. She came to the cross road; she walked past the school, across the first bridge, onto the dam, and reaching the second bridge she stopped for the third time. The teacher was angry, oh yes, she was angry. And Elizabeth knew who deserved that rage, but in truth she had no proof, none whatsoever. She could see herself thundering into the mill and lashing out at the villain, but it would be his word against hers, and she remembered how that had played out before. No, she would confront the "dog," but only after she had some facts.

Mr. Sonneflt was not the only clever person in the valley. She would watch and listen. It would only be a matter of time before he slipped up. A wrong word perhaps or some indication he knew more than he claimed. Yes, if he was anything like Alexander, and she felt certain he was, then in the end his arrogance would fuel overconfidence and overconfidence would be his fall. And she would be there.

After supper when Elizabeth and the Baughman's sat in the parlor, Alberta had brought coffee and returned to her knitting. Looking into her coffee she asked, "Have either of you heard of someone called Colton Snit?"

Abner chuckled. "I wondered when you would hear that story."

"Well, I haven't really. Just some talk about a ghost that wanders the woods near the school."

"Or the far side of the valley, or up by Peabody's, or any other place that's handy," Abner said with a smile.

"Surely there is nothing to the stories. I mean there never was a Colton Snit, was there?"

Alberta did not look up from her knitting. "Those stories been floating since before we come here, and we've been here more than thirty years."

"Seems," Abner added, "that there was this trader that lived here abouts, name of Colton Snit. Nobody knows where he come from, but most are certain he never left." the man chuckled. He looked over to where Elizabeth sat. "Nothing to worry about, Lizzy. Just a story pas tell their young'uns to keep them close to home at night."

Elizabeth had to smile. "And was Mr. Snit the reason you told me not to venture out my first night?"

"Dearie," Alberta stopped knitting to look across the room toward Elizabeth, "there's enough real stuff to be a watchin'. No need to use some Halloween story."

"Mother's right. You said this country's like your Ohio, but it isn't… not really. Not far away is the wild country and things drift into this valley all the time." He drew a breath. "Chas Gant told me just the other day how he found a newborn calf tore to bits in the pasture. I s'pect it was that mangy stray dog that I've seen off and on for months, but can't be sure."

"Tell her about the wolf, Father."

"No need to frighten her, Mother."

Elizabeth caught a breath. "The wolf?"

"Now you've done it, Mother."

"Tell her or I will."

"You'll get the story all wrong again."

"Then tell it, old man."

Abner shook his head and frowned. "Well, Thomas Walker said he had seen a wolf. Of course nobody believed him. Talked about it for months." Abner shifted in his seat. "One day he comes by wagon to Peabody's. I 'spect it was two maybe three years ago. He yells, 'You been callin' me a lair for too long.' We come out and find he has this wolf he shot in the back of the wagon. I ain't seen anything like it."

Elizabeth gasped and blinked twice.

"There's been no talk of wolves since, but all the same I'd be careful wanderin'."

CHAPTER 21

ELIZABETH FROZE AS SHE STOOD ALONE FACING THE BLACKBOARD the following morning. The words *I'll be watchin* scrawled across the board's entire length took her breath away. The last word butting against the far edge may have caused the missing *G*. Her eyes swept across the words again and again. She felt the muscles in her arms quiver and the hairs on the back of her neck stood. Swaying, she placed her hand on the front of her desk to steady herself. What would her students think? Drawing a breath, Elizabeth strode to the board and with long sweeping motions quickly erased the words just before Josie and John Tomkins arrived. She turned to see the faces of the first students. They were smiling, unaware that anything was amiss.

Throughout the day, thoughts of those words printed on the board, and what they meant, crept into her mind. No matter how hard she tried to convince herself that it was nothing more than one of her students using events of the day before to frighten. Just a prank. The words did not seem to fit any of the young men and women she was beginning to know. No, it had been a warning.

The day dragged on, Elizabeth's mind jumping from the class to the image burned into her memory... *I be watchin'*. She tried her best to hide the concern that gnawed at her stomach.

At noon time, she had no appetite. She studied the lunch that Alberta had prepared, certain that the ham and cornbread would, on any other day, be delicious. Elizabeth remained distracted, as her students, one by one the finished their meal left to play outdoors. She did her best to concentrate on the muffled sounds that filtered into the room of children at play. As always Jenny was last to finish and so, for a few moments, they alone shared the classroom.

When Jenny approached the teacher's desk, it was clear Elizabeth had failed to hide her emotions completely.

"Miss Beck," the girl asked, "did you see the ghost again?"

She forced a smile as she looked at her young friend. "No, Jenny, I did not see a ghost, nor the man again."

"I'm glad," the child said with a smile. "Just thought you had."

"What made you think that?"

Jenny shrugged her shoulders. "You have been looking out the window a lot."

"I guess I have."

"Thinking about yesterday?"

"Yes, Jenny, I was thinking about yesterday."

"But you're alright?"

Elizabeth's smile grew. How kind that the child cared. She hugged Jenny. "Thanks for caring. Yes, I am fine. Now go outside, recess will be over soon." The girl turned and dashed out the door.

The remainder of the week was uneventful, well uneventful as a relative term. Elizabeth had no one spying on her or the class in any means, and she had no contact with the miller. He had waved one morning on her arrival; she pretended not to have seen. It went against her nature to deliberately ignore anyone, but this was a special case.

On Thursday afternoon after class had been dismissed, Elizabeth stopped by Peabody's Mercantile to pick up Alberta's order on her way for her weekly visit with Leah. As she entered, she noticed Ben speaking to a slender woman dressed in a brown shapeless dress. She stood nearly as tall as the reverend, her dark eyes focused on the pastor.

Smiling, Ben said, "I want to once again offer an invitation…"

"If'n you're ask'n me and my brood to come to church, you know the answer."

"I had hoped that you had reconsidered."

"Has that church changed?"

Ben's mouth moved but did not form a response.

"Thought not. Well, we ain't changed neither."

"I'm sorry," Reverend Smith stammered.

"Sorry for what? That we don't behold to your ideas, or that those ideas are wrong."

Blinking, Ben closed his mouth. Seeing Elizabeth he took a new direction. "Have you met our new teacher?" Elizabeth moved closer. "Margret, this is Miss Beck. She comes to us from Ohio."

"I'm Mrs. Simns." The woman who appeared in her thirties drew her brows down. Elizabeth did not think it possible but the woman's face grew even tauter. "I 'spected a real pastor would've known, it's only proper for a woman's husband to call her by her given name."

Once more Ben's mouth fell open as he stood there blinking.

Elizabeth stretched out her hand. The woman glanced down, ignoring the gesture while clutching her own package tightly to her chest. Drawing her eyebrows down once again, Mrs. Simns said in hard even tones, "I know your kind. You come all this way thinkin' you're doin' this valley some kind of service. Bringin' your ideas and fillin' young'ns' heads with lies. I got no need fur you or others like ya."

Elizabeth blinking with mouth open stood speechless.

Mrs. Simns looked Elizabeth up and down. "God give the job of teach'n young'ns to their ma and pa, though this man here, he don't think so. There be no need for fillin' their heads with nonsense."

Elizabeth straightened her shoulders. "I don't believe what I teach is nonsense."

The right corner of Margret Simns lip dropped a bit. "Of course not. Ya just repeating the lies ya been taught." Her hard eyes did not cause Elizabeth to flinch. "Truth will come out, on that you can be sure."

"The truth will set you free." Elizabeth looked directly into the woman's eyes.

Mrs. Simns smiled. "Then I be free a long time."

With that the hard woman stormed out of the store. With the slamming of the door the whole room felt a bit warmer.

When Elizabeth turned back toward her pastor, the man looked downward. He appeared defeated. "Ben?"

He looked up and gave a weak smile. "I try, Elizabeth, but there are those that make themselves hard to love." He shook his head.

"She didn't seem very pleasant."

"And yet she is one of God's children," he sighed. "If God can love Margret, I guess I must as well."

"Then we will both make that extra effort." She smiled.

His smile grew. "Are you bound for the parsonage?"

"Yes, as soon as I pick up Alberta's order."

The words seemed to return life to the store. "I've got her order ready to go right here, Miss Beck." She looked to see Mr. Peabody place Alberta's basket on the counter. "If Mrs. Baughman needs anything else, be glad to help."

She smiled, took the basket and nodded to Harold Peabody and to Ben as she left.

The parsonage was bursting with life as her friend welcomed her. The spotless home was filled with the scent of baking. Two loaves of bread stood cooling on the counter. Leah seemed troubled as she poured tea.

"Leah?"

She looked up and then away a moment. The smile that seemed a perpetual part of Leah's face was absent when their eyes met again.

Elizabeth reached across the table and placed her hand upon Leah's. She watched as Leah drew a deep breath. "I've been thinking about…"

"About what?"

"I keep going back to…" she hesitated. "Elizabeth, do you hate me?" Leah's voice trembled.

"Hate you." Elizabeth blinked. "Why on earth would you think I hated you?"

There were tears in Leah's eyes. "Because of all this," she said with a wave of her arm.

Now Elizabeth understood. Taking both of Leah's hands into her own, she squeezed them softly. "I will not say I do not envy what you have here Leah, your home your family, the things I know I will never have. But I do not hate you." She smiled as tears began to form. "I could never hate you." Now it was Elizabeth's turn to take a deep breath. "I may at times long for what is not, but I am grateful for what I have. I try at those times to remember the blessing that God has given. My family, mother, father, sister and even my brother who annoyed me so when we were children. I thank Him for my health, for allowing me to teach. I love the children in my class. I suppose I think of them as my own." She blushed. "And lately I thank God that He has brought me to this valley and the wonderful people I have met here." She smiled as she looked into Leah's damp eyes. "But most of all, I thank God for your friendship." Elizabeth squeezed Leah's hands. "I am pleased…by your happiness." She blinked her damp eyes.

They looked up and saw the wondering in the small faces of Micah, Rachel, and James as the children stood wedged in the kitchen doorway.

"Everything is fine children," Leah said as she shooed them away with her hand. "These are just happy tears. Go out and play." She wiped her eyes with her apron. "Too soon it will be winter and you will find yourselves trapped indoors with you noses to the glass. Now shoo."

The words seemed to settle the young Smiths, and the ladies returned to their tea. Elizabeth told Leah of the man in the woods. That was how she thought of him, The Man in the Woods. Leah seemed most alarmed, and surprised at the calmness Elizabeth showed.

But Elizabeth was flabbergasted by her friend's response when she shared her feelings that Mr. Sonnefelt was involved.

"I'm sure you are mistaken," Leah responded. "I know you have had your differences, but if you knew the man the way we do, you would realize. Well, he has nothing to do with it."

"I'm not convinced," Elizabeth told her. "It seems impossible that the man always appears at the judicious moment. It seems so scripted, if you know what I mean."

"But it is simply not the man's nature. You can ask Ben."

Elizabeth looked skeptically at Leah.

"We have known him since our arrival. I have found him a diligent, hard working man."

Just like Alexander, Elizabeth thought.

"A bit quiet, perhaps, but not sneaky. As for this man that is outside the school, you know I am not one for rumors, but…"

"If you are going to tell me about some ghost, I've heard those stories and I can assure you that this vile man is no ghost. I am surprised you would place any stock is such stories."

"I don't, but there must be something behind them."

"There is…Matthew Sonnefelt."

Leah shook her head firmly.

"Perhaps he has fooled you," the teacher said coolly. "Perhaps he has fooled everyone, but he has not fooled me." She took a sip of tea her hostess had given, then setting the cup back upon its saucer. "I am certain he is involved…and I will prove it."

By the look on the face of the preacher's wife she was certain Leah didn't believe a word. Leah drew a breath held it a moment and tightened her lips slightly. It was apparent she didn't intend to argue the point further. "I am deeply concerned," her friend said at last. "This man standing there spying on you. It sends shivers just to think of it."

"Mr. Sonnefelt does not frighten me," Elizabeth said confidently.

Leah's voice, revealing a slight tremble said, "But next time?"

The teacher brought the lids of her eyes down just a bit as she responded in an attempt to reinforce an image of bravado. "What do I care if someone stands in the woods and watches the class? Let the fool stand there. It is public property is it not? I hope the fool freezes out there, frozen to that tree. Let that be on Mr. Sonnefelt's conscience!"

The comment surprised her friend, for Leah straightened up in her chair as her eyes flew open wide. Leah begged Elizabeth to be careful. Told her that there must be more to this than she might know. The woman's eyes moved about the room as she turned her cup on the table around. "You know that other teachers left suddenly without notice."

Elizabeth watched as her friend fidgeted. "Yes, I have been told."

Leah looked directly into her eyes, her voice soft. "Maybe this man has something to do with their departures." Leah stood and moved toward the window. "Five teachers have come and gone."

"But no harm came to them."

Leah turned her way, tilted her head slightly and with straight lips said, "That we know."

Elizabeth drew her brows slightly. "That you know?"

"Well, all but Jane Olden packed up and Ben hauled them back to Thimble. They seemed well enough, but—"

"But?"

Leah drew a breath and poured another cup of tea for them. Moved the plate of cake that Elizabeth had not yet touched closer. "I cannot put my finger on it, really, but it seemed they were very glad to be leaving the valley."

"If they intended to leave, would that seem odd?"

Leah swallowed. "Perhaps not."

"And this Jane person?"

Leah shifted. "Word was she had a beau—a farmer west of here."

Elizabeth couldn't imagine going any further west.

"Martha Peabody runs the post office and told that Jane received mail from the man most times new mail arrived. One day the teacher just vanished. That was years before the teachers boarded."

"Where did she live?"

"The Andersens had a small cabin just beyond the store. Howard Peabody bought the place and tore it down when they built their house. But we found it strange that she had left all her things. I know she didn't have much, but to leave it all." Leah glanced around the room.

Elizabeth had to admit it seemed odd. However perhaps this farmer promised new and better things. "So this farmer came for her?"

"That was what Claudia Lewis said. I'm certain you have met Claudia."

Yes, Elizabeth had met Claudia.

"Claudia said a wagon came late one night, but no one else saw."

Elizabeth shook her head. She did not take much heed in what she considered "panic talk." She had known plenty of teachers that had gotten disheartened and abandoned their post. Those that did not place sufficient value on their word. She would never consider breaking her commitment, and some man standing among the trees would not drive her away. She would take the steps necessary to protect her students. Elizabeth felt certain she could take care of herself. However she did appreciate her friend's concern, even if the woman was misguided about that miller fellow.

As she prepared to leave, Leah invited her to Sunday dinner. The teacher felt it a fortunate opportunity. For Mr. Sonnefelt had an open invitation to dinner at the Baughman's, and she did not want to sit at the same table with the man. Also as of late Elizabeth had been turning down the Clarks, though she hated to see the disappointment in Jenny's eyes, but it had become harder to stifle young William's advances. Even after the confrontation in the school weeks ago, the man persisted. What a dilemma she faced? Two men she wished to avoid -- avoid for totally different reasons.

Sunday morning Elizabeth went to church with the Baughman's. As they arrived, they found Matthew Sonnefelt waiting. Not surprising, for he waited for the Baughman's each week. But the miller behaved differently. After greeting Alberta and Abner, he came to Elizabeth. Each Sunday before, he had politely said good morning or some such thing, but this time he leaned close and whispered, "I must speak with you, Miss Beck."

Strange. Elizabeth had expected something, not at church but something. "Can it wait until Monday?" she asked.

Though he spoke with a soft voice, the intensity of his eyes showed he was dead earnest. "Sooner would be better."

"I am to have dinner with the Smiths. Being the service is about to start—"

"Immediately after," he said in low tones.

"But you have your duties," she responded coolly.

"It'll take only a moment. Please trust me. It's important."

She just nodded and took her seat, as far from the man as she could, on opposite end of the same pew.

Elizabeth felt guilty that she would not remember much of Reverend Smith's sermon. Her mind wandered more than what would be considered proper, considering. Too often, she sat thinking about Mr. Sonnefelt and what he had said. She kept considering how to deal with him. She thought perhaps she would simply seem to forget. But that was deceitful, and she would not allow that to be an option. The only other course was to hear what the man had to say.

When the service had ended, Mr. Sonnefelt left the building, which was most unusual. Typically he went right to work with the other men, converting the church to a school. There was something else that seemed strange, for in the miler's absence none of the other men began the task. They mulled about as if they were waiting for something. Elizabeth just shook her head and, after shaking hands with the Smiths, went down the steps.

The air was cool, almost cold, with the hint of rain on the wind. Mr. Sonnefelt was waiting, standing a bit off to the left. He faced her way, likely expecting her to join him. She instead made conversation with Mr. Clark. Asking if he had received the note she had sent with Jenny. He indicated he had and asked if she considered the matter a threat to the school or its teacher. Elizabeth had hoped for more—what exactly she was not sure—just more. She then went over to the Baughmans and reminded them she would be dinning with the pastor and his family. There was no need, but she did it all the same. Then she went over to the Tomkins, where she deliberately spent much time discussing the progress of Josie and her brother. All the while the miller stood waiting. Elizabeth took pleasure in the fact she had taken some control of the situation with Sonnefelt, that she had not allowed a man to dictate the when and how.

Finally when no one remained to whom she could speak, Mr. Sonnefelt came to her. The man, trembling, obviously cold, for he had not taken his coat as he hurried out of the sanctuary. "If you have a minute Miss," he said in chopped words, clearly annoyed.

"Oh, I am sorry, Mr. Sonnefelt, you said you wished to speak to me," she said coyly. "I very nearly forgot."

The hard lines on the man's face showed she had not fooled the man, not for an instant.

"Perhaps we should step back inside, why I do believe you are cold," she said, sarcastically.

"No, what I wish to say had best be said here."

"Well, Mr. Sonnefelt," she interrupted, "say what you must, we are both busy people."

With that, he grabbed her arm more tightly than needed. His eyes flew open, which seemed to indicate that he was nearly as surprised as she by the action. She tore her arm free and began to turn when he spoke.

"I think I know who was spying on you Tuesday."

Of course he knew. He had hired the man. She looked hard at the miller, cruelly staring into his eyes, and though she knew he noticed, the man continued.

"It was Leon Simns."

Leon Simns—the name was familiar. Her mind went back to the woman she had met at Peabody's, Margret Simns. But there was more. Her mind wrestled with the name and then it occurred to her. "Would that be Mary Simns' father?"

"He has several children, maybe a daughter named Mary, but he keeps them close to home. I'm not sure I have met any of them," the man answered, his voice with a slight tremble. He shook visibly.

"And does Mr. Simns work for you, Mr. Sonnefelt?" she asked.

He blinked at the question. A look of puzzlement crossed his face. "No. Leon doesn't work for me, never has."

It was the answer she had expected. But somehow when she looked at the man obviously freezing in the October wind, she believed him. Elizabeth didn't want to believe him, but the man had that look, that look she had seen before. Seeing him there and remembering what she had heard from so many people of the valley, that this man could be trusted. She believed them as well. And she knew somehow that she could trust him. That she had been so very wrong about him. She quickly removed her coat and wrapped it about the man. Elizabeth noticed just how large a man he was, for her coat covered little more than one shoulder. "Sir, you will catch your death, and I alone will be at fault."

"Mr. Baker saw the man earlier Tuesday, dressed just as you had described."

"Let us go inside, surely you can tell me the rest indoors."

"There is nothing more to tell. Other than I must say he is an odd one."

"Then perhaps there is nothing more to worry about."

The man whose lips were now blue said, "That's not what I mean. Be on your watch, Miss Beck."

She blinked.

"Simns usually keeps to himself, but he doesn't cotton to visitors. One time he shot the horse out from under Mitchel Banes, so Mitchel tells it."

Elizabeth was astounded. "Shot a horse?"

"Leon claimed it was an accident. Banes was trespassing at the time."

"But," Elizabeth began, "you just cannot shoot someone's horse, let alone one that a man is riding."

"S'pect not, but trespassing's serious business."

She shook her head wondering what other kind of lawlessness existed in the valley.

"Be careful," the man repeated through his now blue lips.

She led him up the steps of the church, and as she opened the door, Elizabeth felt a chill. It was not from the cold damp wind. No, it was something very different. Elizabeth swallowed hard as they reentered the church. Nothing had changed. The room yet remained the church. Of the men that would normally help in the rearranging only Eldon, who she had met at the mill, and the pastor remained.

Benjamin noticed Matthew's trembling and rushed to them. "Matthew, what on earth?"

"The poor man," she said softly, "had urgent business to attend to, which I am afraid, took much longer than he expected."

"Matthew, you know better than to go out without a coat."

The miller nodded.

They sat him near the stove in the corner of the room. He handed Elizabeth her coat, which she promptly draped across his shoulders. "I'm sorry," she whispered. "I'm so sorry." A tear came to her eye, though Elizabeth did her best to hide it. As Sonnefelt glanced up, his eyes seemed to settle on hers and she knew he noticed.

Now the two men that had remained began the job of moving the pews. Too soon, Elizabeth believed, the miller joined them at the task. The teacher watched, for the weight of the pews was beyond her capabilities. But she noticed that they approached the chore differently than she might have anticipated. The men worked cheerfully, joking and with a good-natured teasing. The mood was contagious. Soon Elizabeth found herself chuckling as well. When they began returning the desks to their places, she assisted, carrying the chairs. Soon the space became a classroom once more.

Leah and the children had left shortly after the service's end. The Peabodys had taken them back to the parsonage in the Mercantile's wagon. So the three of them, for Eldon was bound the other direction, tightened their collars against the cold and began the hike. Their high spirits and carefree conversations made the time pass pleasantly, and Elizabeth didn't noticed the bitter weather. When they reached the Baughman's lane, Matthew bid them his goodbye and turned his way.

Elizabeth and Pastor Smith went on, quiet for a time, when she asked, "Do you consider Mr. Sonnefelt a friend?" In truth it was more a statement than a question.

The pastor smiled. "Oh yes, Matthew has been a very good friend."

"And you would trust him?"

"With my life…No, with the lives of my family."

There had been no hesitation, none whatsoever. It was a powerful statement. So powerful that it made Elizabeth pause a moment.

"He was here when we arrived three years ago. And I'm sure you noticed he can be quiet," the pastor continued. "We were the newcomers, just like you are now, and we met everyone, just like you did that on your arrival last month. Matthew was always the one in the background, just doing what needed to be done. Miss Beck, he is solid as stone, and I consider myself blessed to call him my friend." He paused a moment and then spoke carefully. "I hope what I say now will not make you angry. Leah and I have no secrets. She doesn't tell me everything, but she told me you thought Matthew was trying to frighten you, or something to that effect." He stopped, turned, and stared directly into her eyes with a look of intensity, a look she had not seen often but remembered. It was the same expression he carried when they had left Paradise. "Matthew is what he seems. He is the genuine article, and he had nothing to do with that other man."

Elizabeth had realized that fact when that man, that very cold man, told her he had never employed Mr. Simns. It wasn't so much what he said but how he said it, and the look in his eyes—deep and honest. She knew then it was the truth. Oh, she might not like the man. The man would, she was certain, upset her the whole time she remained at Misty Creek, but Matthew Sonnefelt was not a liar. Elizabeth told the pastor that she had to agree. That she had been wrong; it was hard to admit to being wrong.

"Ben, Mr. Sonnefelt said the man in the woods was Mr. Simns."

Those words brought a dark look on the pastor's face. "Leon Simns?" he asked.

"Yes, I believe that was the name."

The pastor looked away for an instant. She noticed that his pace quickened. They had reached the next crossroad and turned toward town. "Ben," she asked, "what's wrong?"

The pastor gave a quick glance her way before he responded. "Simns is a hard man. I know very little about him. He never comes to church. Been out to see him twice. I don't think I will be going back."

She was alarmed by the hard sharp tone of his voice she had never heard before. Since Elizabeth had arrived, she had gotten to know the young pastor, seen him at work, seen him with his family, seen him as he dealt with those around him, but she had never seen him this way. "Ben, what happened?" she asked as they reached the gate to the parsonage.

"Let's just say he made it very plain he did not want me to return. That he had no use for …as he put it 'my God'…and to leave him and his family alone." He looked defeated; Pastor Benjamin Smith never looked defeated. The man shrugged his shoulders, drew a deep breath, looked downward, and opened the gate and led her into the house.

Elizabeth entered to the aroma of good food, ready and waiting, the sounds of life, of children laughing, at play. A home filled with a warmth she always felt when she came, and all the questions and concerns she had felt before, seemed locked outside the door.

CHAPTER 22

CLASSES HAD FINISHED THAT FINAL THURSDAY OF OCTOBER, AND Elizabeth had left the school feeling beaten. Leaning on the rail of the bridge that crossed the nearest spillway, she looked across the water. Here, further from the trees, the breeze gave the water small wavelets, sliver reflections sparkling the afternoon's light. She felt calmer near the water.

How dreadful the day had become. Elizabeth hated the times physical discipline demanded. But rules were rules, and as much as she detested it, when a student pushed she knew she must push back. Somehow during the long hours after the confrontation she had managed to maintain control. But now tears flowed at the thought of the moment it had occurred in the late morning. Until this week Joey had been no problem, rather he was one of her brightest students. But repeated tardiness of the tall, broad lad had continued. Elizabeth had warned Joey each time, and just yesterday had she given the ultimatum.

When Joey's seat remained empty after the first bell, her stomach began to twist tighter with every minute. Each step through the day's lessons, Elizabeth couldn't help but see the empty desk and remember the demands she had made the day before, apparently ignored.

Joey arrived later than he had ever before, and when he sheepishly attempted to slip in, the knot in her stomach twisted so tight, the taste of gall filled her mouth. That tension bound with the anger of the blatant disregard for her authority propelled things in ways unstoppable. Now through the gasping sobs blended with the tears, she saw with clarity the whole event played out in her mind once again.

She did not notice the man. She did not see him standing and leaning against the rail as well some five yards to her left. The tall man, Matthew Sonnefelt.

Elizabeth felt surprised and embarrassed that anyone would see her weeping at the water's edge. After she dried her eyes, she glanced his way and saw him gazing across the water. The miller seemed lost in his thoughts as well. She turned away from him to face the water, to feel the breeze that caressed her cheek. She tried to focus on the faint scent, the wood fire smoke of some farm wife's cook stove, to listen to the sound of water slipping out the spillway far to her left, to think of anything but the man that stood nearby.

As Elizabeth stood leaning against the bridge's rail, she heard his voice.

"When we built this dam, oh, five years ago, I knew this bridge would give one of the best views of the lake."

She didn't respond.

He continued to look at the sparkling water. She only gave a quick glance his direction and wondered if she should just walk away. Elizabeth had not asked the man to join her, she wouldn't even have considered it. She drew a breath, pushed herself back slightly and she spoke in flat unemotional tone. "Then you come here often?"

Sonnefelt shook his head firmly. "Not as often as I should. I come here to think, and to talk."

Elizabeth turned her head to face the man.

"I 'spect everybody needs somebody to talk to."

Did the man expect her to confide in him? "I have no one," the words, an involuntary response, came from somewhere deep inside.

"Everyone has someone. Someone that's always close." He turned and faced her. Drawing his left lid down a bit as if examining her. "You'll find God's even here in Kansas."

She did not respond. Did this man think she did not know God was everywhere? Elizabeth prepared to walk away.

"I noticed Joey Felton came by late today."

"He has been tardy all week."

The man nodded. "'Spect he'll be late again tomorrow."

Elizabeth's mind raced. The boy wouldn't dare.

"Been to the Felton farm today."

She drew her brow wondering why the miller had gone visiting.

"Carl, the boy's father, has been sick."

"What, is the man unable to wake Joey in time for school?"

The man continued to look across the lake. "Joey's the oldest, doing his best."

Elizabeth felt confused. "His best?"

"His mother has four younger children, another on the way. Someone has to milk the cows, slop the hogs, tend the chickens, and all the rest. Can't do much before it gets light. It takes time." Sonnefelt looked her way. "I figured you needed to know."

She stared at him, her mouth moving but unable to form words.

"Joey didn't tell you. I suspected as much."

Elizabeth blinked. "But why?"

Sonnefelt faced the water once again, "The boy's thirteen, doing his best to be a man." He paused for a breath. "It's not easy to tell folks your pa is dying."

Elizabeth suddenly found herself in a vacuum, unable to fill her lungs. Her legs grew weak and only her grip on the rail kept her upright. For a person that had always relied upon language, there were no words, nothing within her mind to express the flood of swirling emotions. The boy had said nothing. He had scarcely flinched as the ruler struck his open palm. Once she regained her balanced her hands flew up to her mouth.

Sonnefelt's eyes flew open. "Miss Beck...?"

"I have made such a mistake. I didn't know."

"None of us did," he said as he took a step in her direction.

"But...but...you don't understand."

He nodded, which for reasons unknown sent her into a rage. How could the man be so consoling? This morning she dispensed her punishment without taking a moment to speak with the young man. Here this man was bobbing his head like some know-it-all fool, as if he had any idea of the events and their meaning. She felt horrified at her insensitivity, repulsed by her actions, that she failed not only Joey Felton but the entire class.

"We all make mistakes. It's part of being..."

Her glare cut him off. "What would you know?"

Sonnefelt blinked, stepped back a half step. "Maybe there is something you might do?"

"Do?" Elizabeth sneered.

He shifted a bit. "You know to make it better. Maybe…"

She threw her hands in the air. What was done could not be undone. Was she to place the ruler upon young Joey's hand and have it remove the pain she had inflected? "You think I can just offer a bit of rock candy to the boy and all will be fine?" As she glared at him, he shifted left and right as if unable to stand under the weight of her stare. "There are things that cannot be repaired, Mr. Sonnefelt!"

"I understand…"

"No, you do not. You have no idea." She fumed.

Tears began to form in the corner of her eyes. Turning away from him she bit her lip. Her mind swelled with tumbling thoughts, thoughts of her failing once again, thoughts of how she possibly did not know. Certainly she had not asked the boy his reasons, but someone in the community had to know about the Felton's trouble. Back home, that is Ohio, a situation this dire would have been on the lips of the whole community. And this valley was so like the farmland of home. She glared at the miller and would not believe his statement that no one knew. Yes, people had to know and they did not feel it necessary to tell her. Why else would Sonnefelt trudge off this very day to the Felton farm?

The rage within her spilled from her own inadequacies, wrapping itself about a community that seemed to hold her outside, and the man that stood there. In her mind it was not Sonnefelt that shared the bridge, it was Alexander Elders, tall and lanky, that had come to give his opinions. That man had done more than deride his brother, he had in a single sentence cut Elizabeth deep as well. How he had found her that May Saturday, long after she learned her fiancé had vanished, she could not know. He strode up to her as she wandered the church yard lost in her pain, feeling as dead as those whose names had been chiseled into the orderly rows of stone.

"I didn't know James had it in him," Alexander had begun with his deep husky voice, "but he finally showed us all that somewhere inside, he is a real man."

The tears came, a torrent streamed down her cheeks. Sonnefelt moved closer. She felt the touch of his hand on her shoulder. "Leave me be," she shrieked. Turning she began to walk away.

"No, Miss Beck," came a soft voice not half a step away. "I have intruded. I will go."

She watched through tear-blurred eyes as the man walked away. Sonnefelt turned from time to time, glancing back and then continuing. She grabbed the rail and steadied herself, dried her eyes, caught a short gasp of breath and wondered how she could meet someone so much like Alexander in a place like Misty Creek.

When she turned to face the miller once again, her mind screamed, look at him, he is no different than Alexander. Elizabeth drew a breath.

"What do you know, Mr. Matthew Sonnefelt?" she seethed. "You talk about understanding, but you don't have a clue. You stand so politely and say it's about being human, but you do not even have an idea of what being human means." Elizabeth's cheeks grew hot. "It is easy for you to criticize, for you are so perfect." Elizabeth hissed.

Sonnefelt blinked, hesitated a moment, seemed off balance. His hand moved slowly to the bridge rail. "I'm not perfect," he said looking away.

"That is not what I hear. Everyone in Misty Creek tells me so."

"Everyone?"

Elizabeth thought a moment. "Not everyone, but nearly."

Drawing a breath he said, "They don't know me."

"Come now, Mr. Sonefelt. You have lived here your entire life and say your neighbors do not know you."

He glanced her way. "Few have lived in Misty Creek their entire lives."

Elizabeth had forgotten the man had been born in Dakota. She blinked, tilted her head as she examined him and waited. His cheeks grew taught as he began at last. "People see what they want."

"So they do not see your glaring faults?"

"Or I've hid them well."

Elizabeth drew her brows down. "I think the Smiths and Baughmans know you well enough."

Matthew drew a breath, turned, and began to walk away.

Elizabeth wondered about the man. Did he keep secrets? Everyone did, but the things she had heard, all the positive words tied to the name of Matthew Sonnefelt, seemed to reveal the perfect man that lived among them.

"What are you afraid of, Mr. Sonnefelt?" The words froze the man in his tracks. His shoulders fell, he lowered his head, his arms fell to his side.

"That's it you know," his words came even and soft.

Elizabeth could not understand her desire to move closer to the man. "Can you not face me, Mr. Sonnefelt?"

All the pride she had seen dissolved as he shook his head firmly.

"I'm a coward," he said as he drew a breath and turned his head, looking over his shoulder to face her. "There I've said it. Matthew Sonnefelt is a coward." His voice grew stronger. "Perhaps that makes you happy." His eyes were dark below drawn brows. "God knows I'm not perfect, Miss Beck, and I never pretended to be." His words came clear and strong. "And as for judging others, that has never been my intention. If I have, then add that to my list of evils." With that he turned and walked away in slower steps than she had seen before.

"Mr. Sonnefelt," she called, but he continued and left her alone.

Elizabeth thought it would have pleased her to take Mr. Matthew Sonnefelt down a notch or two. Why then did she find herself lying in the dark, staring at the ceiling, unable to sleep? She drew a breath and closed her eyes, but each time she did, she saw the man walking away with slumped shoulders. "No matter what that man may say or even think about himself," she whispered, "he is no coward."

Elizabeth had not spoken to Alberta, or anyone, about the evening's encounter. There had been something private in that moment, as if some deep dark secret had nearly risen to the surface. She shook her head. How many times had that man forced himself into her mind? Too many to be sure. But today, only hours ago, she had witnessed another side of Mr. Sonnefelt. In her pain she had wanted to cut him, oh how she had wanted it. In that moment of self-doubt and guilt she had once again allowed her emotions to take control. Yet it had gone so differently than she had expected, and her feelings confused her.

She wondered why her feelings about Alexander, the memories of that man, influenced how she reacted to Sonnefelt. Elizabeth had no love of Alexander Elders. Far from it, he had given sufficient reasons for her to hate him. She sighed in the dark. It wasn't Christian to hate anyone, not even Alexander. She shook her head as she drew a deep breath. Why had she lashed out at Sonnefelt? True Sonnefelt was tall like Alexander, walked like Alexander, made his way in life with his hands like Alexander, but Sonnefelt was not Alexander. Perhaps it was more. Perhaps she distrusted the whole gender…the unmarried ones anyway. If a man of Jameson's caliber could act so cruelly, then what could she expect from lesser men. Nothing.

Now in the dark, she looked toward the window. The pale rectangle illuminated only by the sky filled with stars reminded her of the distance she had crossed. That distance was greater than all the railroad rails and dust strips she had endured to reach Misty Creek. That distance included the years of toil, dreams, built and shattered, and the attempt to leave that past life's rubble behind. The dim light seemed to reveal that no matter how hard she tried, she could not escape the pains of the past. They had made scars she carried. Though they might not be visible, like the surgeon's marks across her abdomen from her childhood, these scars were just as real.

A tear rolled down her cheek as these thoughts crashed down upon her. In his perfection, Sonnefelt reminded her she was damaged goods… unworthy…unlovable.

That was the real reason she had, time and again, attacked Mr. Matthew Sonnefelt. It was more than the fact he reminded her of Alexander. It was more than the fact he was very much a man. He seemed the perfect man in this perfect place…and she…

So at last she threw his perfection in his face, and saw the very last thing she had expected. Elizabeth closed her eyes and saw the tall man walking away, defeated. How ashamed she felt. That guilt mingled with thoughts of poor Joey Felton. What a burden that young man carried. Elizabeth feared the lad would be crushed beneath that load. She bit her lip knowing she had added weight to Joey's obligations.

When, at last, she had reined in her emotions, drawing a breath she considered what Sonnefelt had said, about making things right. Her reaction then had once again been too hasty. No, she could not undo the ruler's blow, but things could be done. Elizabeth would speak to Joey tomorrow, alone, when he arrived. If he arrived at all. And if he did not come, well, then, she would walk out to the Felton farm. She would not allow embarrassment of her failure to prevent her from apologizing to the boy. There was no need to make that hard working lad's life more difficult than it need be. She would do her best to make it right. Rolling onto her back she once more stared at the ceiling. Elizabeth had learned an important lesson…things were not always as they appeared.

CHAPTER 23

WHEN CLASS HAD RESUMED FOLLOWING THE MORNING RECESS, Elizabeth noticed her students glancing passed her to Joey standing just inside the doorway. When she turned he seemed uncertain for a moment, teetering on whether or not to enter. "Take your seat Mr. Felton," she said in even tones. After an instant's hesitation he moved to his desk, sat and looked down. Her heart broke for the young man, but she would speak to him later.

As the room emptied for the after lunch recess, Elizabeth asked Joey to remain.

"Now you're going to get it." Dan Jones nudged Joey with his elbow as he passed.

Elizabeth just shook her head. She stood from her desk and closed the door leaving just the two of them in the quiet empty schoolroom. Joey looked downward as he had most of the time since his arrival. Elizabeth placed her hands on the boy's shoulders. "I wish you would have told me about," she paused while she searched for the best words, "your obligations."

Without looking up Joey spoke in soft tones. "It wasn't anybody's business."

Elizabeth wondered if pride was taught or simply part of a young man's gender. But as she looked at Joey, she understood that he would not be a boy much longer. That demands would require strength, and it would take a man to carry that load. "I suppose it wasn't." Her heart broke at the thought of Mr. Felton's illness. Of how the unfairness in life gave so much pain to those just trying to get by. "I am glad you came today." She swallowed. "I need to apologize for how I acted yesterday."

Joey looked into her eyes. He blinked back the tears and wiped his face with his sleeve. "Who told?"

"Mr. Sonnefelt. Yesterday."

"He had no right!" the boy said through tight lips.

"He was only worried." Elizabeth considered all the things she wished to say to Joey. "You are such a gifted student; I hope we can come up with some plan so that you will be able to continue with your education."

The boy looked at her, blinked but did not speak.

"I know you do not need additional work, and that time will be limited, but perhaps a little one on one might help."

"After school?"

"Yes, that might be a solution, or during recess." She waited. "There is no reason to decide now. Think on it a day or so."

He nodded.

"That's all. You can go."

The boy moved to the door. "No one has to know why?" he asked.

"No one."

"Thanks, Miss Beck," he said as he slipped out the door.

The sadness of the situation took hold of her. Elizabeth returned to her desk and wanted to weep. Crying will do no one any good, especially Joey, she thought. Drawing a breath she prepared for the afternoon's classes.

Once things were settled with Joey Felton, the term progressed better than Elizabeth could have imagined. That is except for one thing, and that thing being Mr. Leon Simns. It was the first week of November, and Simns stood very near. It frightened the smaller children as soon as they noticed him standing there. Whispers raced about the room, and though she could not make out all the children said, the word ghost and Colton Snit's name caught her attention.

Elizabeth called Homer to her desk. "Who is that man, Homer?"

"That's Mr. Simns."

"Mr. Leon Simns?"

The boy nodded. "His farm is north and east of here."

Elizabeth looked to her class. "See children, it is not a ghost, Colton Snit or otherwise. It is only a man, Mr. Simns."

"That's worse," John Tomkins said with eyes wide open. "That man's just plain mean."

She wondered what John had meant, but thought it unwise to ask. "It doesn't matter. He is outside and we need not fear anyone here." She hoped her words had shown greater confidence than she felt.

The situation made her angry, so angry that this man was standing there watching, looking into the classroom, filling the young ones with fear. She controlled her first instinct. Well it wasn't the first, but she would have liked to think of it as her first. Her first was fear and to flee. But the other predisposition, the one she would have hoped to be her first, the one she resisted, was to go out and confront the man. But remembering what Ben had said and the look on Mr. Sonnefelt's face, Elizabeth felt the best course of action was to ignore the man.

It took a great deal of self-control, but she taught as if Simns was not there, or that he was no more than a squirrel or small bird that had come to observe them. Many times she had to call one student or another back to the matters at hand, when they had turned to stare out the window at the man watching them.

Simns stood there for what seemed a very long time. Then as suddenly as he had appeared, he was gone. It wasn't until he had left that Elizabeth realized the effect the man beyond the window had on her, for she felt so very relieved he had left, relieved that no one had been injured. She sat in her chair a moment, breathing quickly and feeling quite weak, worn would be the more accurate term.

The time had come for the first recess. Elizabeth did not feel comfortable allowing the children to venture outside, for she feared Simns might yet be lurking about. So from her years of experience, she engaged the children in games. The kind of games they played when rainy days kept them indoors.

By late afternoon the effects of their visitor seemed to have passed, though at dismissal she still carried a concern. Elizabeth asked that none walk alone, and if possible for one of the older students to escort a group of younger children. Homer, bless his heart, volunteered to escort Lilly Atwood and Josie and John Tomkins home. The trek being out of his way, and that the Atwood and Tomkins farms being near the Simns' place. Elizabeth had a great deal of respect for her student. She had come to count on Homer Reynolds and Jamie Watkins, two of her oldest students, in so many ways.

When the students had left and she was in the classroom all alone, Elizabeth wondered what she should do. She remained at her desk, just thinking. She half expected to hear a rap at the door and to be joined by Mr. Sonnefelt. Strange she thought, *why would I think such a thing*? It was true the last time he happened to stop by. Though she could not understand the reason, she hoped, just hoped that by chance once more he would. But the miller didn't appear.

The teacher attempted to return to her work, there was a test to grade, but Elizabeth found she couldn't. Finally she carefully gathered up the papers, placed them and her other things in her valise, checked the fire, which was about to go out, and left. She locked the door. Elizabeth had never felt the need to use the key Mr. Clark had given, but tonight things seemed different.

Standing on the steps, the teacher looked east to the mill standing across the water. She paused just a moment, wondering. Gritting her teeth Elizabeth told herself she could handle this situation. She was a teacher. It was her responsibility. She began to walk home. She had nearly reached the crossroad when it occurred to her. For though the weight of the responsibility lay upon her, the matter was beyond her ability. She could not allow the safety of her children, that's how she thought of her students, to be jeopardized by pride.

Elizabeth stood there for a moment, confused by what she should do. She could tell the Baughmans, rely on their judgment. But there had to be more. She needed to send word to Mr. Clark. The man was, after all, president of the school board. He needed to know. Why hadn't she thought to send a note along with Jenny? Perhaps it was the results of her last attempt. But now Clark would act, Elizabeth felt certain. The man had clearly shown himself a threat—or had he? All the same she would need to get word to the man, but how? Tomorrow, she would send a proper letter to the man. Leave it a Peabody's, at the post office. But no one was expecting mail. They just didn't go to Peabody's Store on a whim. It might lie there for weeks. That would not do. No, she would go directly. She would go now. It was a long walk, a very long walk, perhaps three miles, but she must. The situation just couldn't wait.

As she stood in the road contemplating, Elizabeth heard a rumble. A wagon reaching the crossroad from the south turned and came toward her. She stood there watching when who should she see but the miller, Mr. Sonnefelt, at the reins. The wagon came to a stop beside her. "Ma'am if you are in need of a lift, I can turn around and take you home."

"In truth, Mr. Sonnefelt, I need to go to Sweetwater Ranch, and was debating how I might."

The man looked down at her, then stretching his hand said, "Climb aboard, Miss."

Elizabeth had been to Sweetwater on four occasions and knew the way, but she had never made the trip on a freight wagon. It did not take long for the miller to turn around and head back to the main road and north. They were fortunate the weather was very fine, the late afternoon, pleasant though cool, but not as cold as the days earlier in the week. The clouds had cleared during the day and a bright blue sky above them gave little hint that winter would soon be here. As they rattled along, Elizabeth wondered what she should tell the man. She had expected the man's curiosity to open the conversation, but Mr. Sonnefelt did not ask. She was not certain if his not asking relieved or fed her frustration.

"Just coming back from taking a delivery to Peabody's," he said at last.

She made no comment.

"The weather's mighty fine today. Been good all week."

Finally Elizabeth could hold her tongue no longer, and she told him about Mr. Simns.

She wondered how he would react. For a moment he didn't react at all. Finally he turned to her. "Today?"

"Yes, this morning."

"And this is the reason you are going to Sweetwater?"

"Do you think it is not reason enough?" she answered.

"Yes, I do…but…" then he said no more.

They went on for a time. She regretted climbing aboard the wagon. It would have been better if she had walked. Elizabeth felt her face grow red as the man's silent presence infuriated her. Then he spoke as if he had been thinking about all she had told him and all that had happened before. "This is a serious thing Miss, a very serious thing."

"Mr. Simns? Or me going to Sweetwater to see Mr. Clark?"

Sonnefelt laughed. Laughter she felt aimed at her, which only made her more furious. "It's hard for me to see anything too serious about

William Clark, either of them for that matter. But this Simns thing, now that's a problem," he said as the smile left his lips.

Mr. Clark, Mr. Clark, he could not find anything much serious about Mr. Clark. The man was head of the school board, and he owned Sweetwater. No one, especially this, this miller, had as much wealth and power as Mr. Clark. How dare he say such a thing? "If I should not go to Mr. Clark, then who?"

"I didn't say you shouldn't go to see Mr. Clark. It's probably a good idea…well I hope it's a good idea. But that's not here or there. Sweetwater's a long way from the school…"

"If you don't want to take me, just say so," she said as she gathered her things and prepared to jump off the wagon.

He reached out and grabbed her. He had taken hold of her before, and she didn't like it. "First thing, if you want off just say so and I'll stop the wagon. No need of getting hurt. And second thing, you misunderstand. I'm not say'n it's far for us today. It is, but that don't matter. It's just that it's far from Sweetwater every day, and what happens at the school is far from Sweetwater…"

Elizabeth relaxed and he released her. "Are you saying he doesn't care what happens at the school? For heaven's sake his daughter attends."

He drew a breath of frustration. "I'm not say'n that either. Of course he cares about Jenny and the school, too, but that don't change the fact that there's distance, miles, between the school and him."

She thought a moment thought about what the man said. She wondered why she had over reacted once again. Why was it every time she was around this man she, well she did?

"Then, Mr. Sonnefelt, what would you suggest?"

"You tell William, that is William senior, about what happened today. You tell him that Simns is a threat and that threat is growing. You suggest something should be done to protect the school. Then we'll hear what he has to say," he said firmly.

She watched the man at the reins, certain he had more he wanted to say. "And then?" she asked at last.

"Then we'll deal with it!"

She was not certain what he meant, not certain in the least. But as she rode there, as they crossed the hill and saw the grand vista and the great house that was Sweetwater Ranch before them, Elizabeth felt something. What she sensed that moment was odd, or rather it seemed odd for the reason that it felt so un-odd. There came a comforts, a relief in the presence of a man she was certain she hated. A comfort she shouldn't be feeing. Yet each time she found herself thrust near him, Elizabeth felt a warm safe feeling. A feeling that though they had nothing in common, somehow they had everything in common. The feeling always left her confused.

As they approached, Josephine stood in the doorway of that grand house. The instant the wagon came to a stop, Elizabeth began to climb down, not waiting for assistance. As she turned and placed her toe on the spoke of wagon's front wheel, the teacher felt a strong hand grasp hers. The miller had slid across the seat and taken her hand in his, helping her, whether she wanted his aid or not. Elizabeth glanced up into the miller's dark eyes, quickly looking away, for she would never admit her gratitude for the man's thoughtfulness. She moved with quick steps and met Mrs. Clark and Jenny half-way to the house, while Mr. Sonnefelt moved to care for the horses.

"Miss Beck," the rancher's wife said. "Jenny told me about the man, I can't say that I am very surprised you've come."

"I would like to speak with Mr. Clark. Is he home?"

Josephine glanced toward Matthew then said, "I'm afraid he is not, but I do expect him soon."

Elizabeth then also looked back toward the wagon. "It is important I speak with him about the matter," she said as the miller walked to join them. "I'll wait."

"I can't say I know exactly when he will arrive," Josephine added. "But of course we would be glad to have you come in." Josephine began to lead the way, while Jenny took her teacher's hand as they went up the steps. When Josephine had escorted them across the wide porch and reached the broad doors, she turned and spoke again. "Mr. Sonnefelt, it was good of you to have brought Miss Beck. It is quite a distance."

Matthew nodded.

"But," Josephine went on, "it may be some time before Mr. Clark arrives. We will see that Miss Beck is returned home safely. There is really no need for you to wait."

Elizabeth looked at the man that had brought her. There was reason in what Josephine said. Surely Matthew had work waiting, she had already detained him for some time. It would be in his best interest to leave. "Perhaps you should go," she said at last.

The man's face showed no emotion—none. He tilted his head slightly as he said, "I'll be fine ma'am. It seems to me that since I'm bound for Misty Creek, it would only be wise to wait. There is no need for Mr. Clark to hitch up a wagon or such. Like I said, it's the way I need to go. If Miss Beck has no objection, I'll wait."

Elizabeth didn't understand why the response relieved her. There was no logical reason but it did. But Elizabeth noticed a slightly hardening in Josephine's eyes, as if Sonnefelt's statement didn't please her hostess. Didn't please her at all.

Matthew noticed as well. "I'll need to attend further to my horses," he said. "If you ladies will excuse me." He turned and quickly left them. Elizabeth was always surprised how swift the tall man could move.

It seemed strange, but when Sonnefelt left, two things happened, the tension that had surrounded them seemed to evaporate, a tension Elizabeth only noticed by its absence, and suddenly the teacher felt ill at ease. A strange discomfort she always felt when she visited Sweetwater. A discomfort she could never explain. The Clarks had always treated her well. They had in all ways been kind and generous. And yet whenever she was with the Clarks she always felt off balance somehow. So as Elizabeth noticed Josephine's shoulders relax a bit, the teacher fought the feelings she had, feelings of being out of place, or something to that effect. Feelings she could not quite explain—even to herself.

Elizabeth could not imagine that a home as this one could exist out here on the frontier. As she sat sipping from an English bone China cup she thought about those who lived with dirt floors. Here there were servants. There folks barely had enough to eat. Here and there, so near and yet so distant.

Mr. Clark came booming in. It seemed everything the man did was loud. He had not entered by the front door, but made his way in from the back of the large house. "What the hell is that man doing here?" he shouted before he noticed Elizabeth sitting in his home.

The language and tone caught her by surprise.

Josephine remained calm. "Mr. Sonnefelt was kind enough to bring Miss Beck. She has come to see you."

The man's face softened. "You ladies will have to pardon me. It's been a hard day. Been moving cattle all day, seein' they get some water. Lord knows there's not much." The man glared at the wall as if he could see through it, and see the man with his team.

"They tell me," Elizabeth said cautiously, "that the year has been dryer than usual."

"But there's still water in the lake!" the rancher said in a harsh voice.

Elizabeth thought a moment. The lake continued to go down. Soon it would be no more than the creek bed that wound through it. She was about to make that observation when Mr. Clark smiled and asked, "And what can I do for you today?"

"You have not been home to hear," Josephine began. "Jenny brought the news. There was a man watching the school again today."

Mr. Clark looked at his wife then to Elizabeth.

"Yes," Elizabeth continued, "the same man that had done so twice before."

"Well," Mr. Clark said obviously becoming more at ease. "If this is the third time…I'm sure it will come to nothing."

"It is Leon Simns," Elizabeth said firmly.

"Leon…Leon…now I know there is nothing to worry about." Clark chuckled beneath his breath. He's just one of those dirt farmers. Simns won't be any trouble."

"Each time he comes closer. He's frightening the children!" Elizabeth's voice grew stronger.

The man tilted his head slightly, looked down and to his right. William Clark seemed to consider her words. He did not answer but rather began to move around the room, staring out the window for several moments. "What is Jenny doing talking to that man?"

"Dear," Josephine said, "I'll call her in." She rose from her seat and went to the doorway.

Mr. Clark stood glaring through the window. Finally he turned and looking once more at the teacher said. "It's good you came to me. I'll take care of everything," he said with a smile. "There's no need to worry about that man. I'll see to it myself…personally." He then moved to a table near the fireplace, taking a cigar, placing it in his lips then, using a bit of kindling, lit it. Taking a couple of deep puffs, he asked, "Will you be staying for supper?"

The comment took her by surprise. The man that had brought her, the man that was waiting to take her home, remained outside, and would she stay for supper! She blinked at the thought, then blinked again. "I thank you for your kind invitation," she said calmly. "But I am afraid I must go."

"Sorry to hear that, Miss Beck. You always add to our meal when you are our guest." The man said with a smile.

"You will deal with this Simns matter?" she said as she began for the door.

He took her hands in his and said, "I will see to it myself."

"Thank you. As always, you have been most kind."

He nodded and as he walked her across the porch and added in a voice loud enough to be heard by anyone, "Please come back soon, you are always welcome."

Elizabeth turned and joined Matthew at the wagon. Mr. Sonnefelt helped her up to her seat. It was nearly dark when they left Sweetwater. She turned to look back. Even in the dim light, Mr. Clark appeared an imposing figure, standing on his porch, cigar in hand. She saw another man join the rancher, William Junior she felt sure. Mr. Clark seemed to get agitated, facing the other, his arms flailing about. Somehow she knew what the conversation involved.

At the sight of young William, her mind went back to her last stop at Peabody's. Alberta had sent her to the mercantile for yarn. The woman was a knitting banshee. Entering she was met by Mrs. Lewis. Now Eleanor Lewis was a big woman, tall and carrying more weight than health required. She was not known as a quiet person, sharing her opinions with all that would listen and many that did not wish to hear. It seemed that each time Elizabeth stepped into Peabody's the woman's presence seemed to fill the store.

"Well, Miss Beck, I don't know if I should be telling you this," Eleanor began, "seein' how you had spent time with young Bill Clark, but the Clarks are about to get visitors."

Elizabeth smiled politely, wondering what the Clarks future company had to do with her, or Eleanor for that matter. "I am certain that Josephine will be pleased to have someone to talk to." Elizabeth forced a smile and tried to look occupied at the display of ribbons nearby, not that she had any need for sewing supplies.

"Not just anyone, but her dearest friend from back east. You knew she came from New York."

"New Jersey," Elizabeth corrected. The puzzled look Eleanor gave couldn't have been greater if Elizabeth had said Josephine came from the moon.

But the older woman shook it off. "Well, wherever. In any case, her friend is coming all this way for a visit. A lengthy one I'm told."

"That's nice."

"Yes, yes, yes, it is ain't it? Won't come on Pastor Smith's wagon neither. No sir-eee. Mr. Clark, that is the senior, plans to send a carriage all the way to Thimble. Imagine that!"

"That was nice of him." The head of the school board did not send a carriage for her on her arrival.

"Ain't it. But that's just the half."

"Eleanor, I really have things that..."

"Yes, deary, I 'spect you do, but you'll be interested in this." Eleanor rocked back and forth with excitement, so much so that Elizabeth began to feel queasy. "She's bringing her daughter."

"So wonderful Josephine's friend does not travel alone."

"Yes, that too."

"Too?"

"Well she ain't no girl, if'n you get my meaning."

Elizabeth felt confused.

"Jennifer's a full grown lady. Elegant I hear." Eleanor was positively beaming. "She's the reason they be coming."

"Are coming?"

Eleanor's had stopped rocking, but now the large woman bounced on her toes. "Seems odd, don't you think? Them comin' so late in the year. Been smarter if they waited 'til spring. S'peck Josephine's friend'll be stranded through the winter, not that the Clarks don't have the room. I ain't seen the house myself, but Millie sez it's big enough for a couple dozen folks." The woman seemed to go on without breathing. Elizabeth tried to interrupt, but could not stop Eleanor on a roll. "All the same, it seems to me that these rich people don't got the brains God gave us ordinary folks."

Exasperated, Elizabeth said, "Eleanor, I really do…"

"I know dearie," the woman said as she tapped Elizabeth's arm. "I'm sorry for prattling so, but I must tell you that if weren't Mary the reason they coming. It's the daughter."

Elizabeth blinked. "The daughter?"

Eleanor nodded so firmly that Elizabeth worried the woman's head might leave her shoulders. "Yes, yes, Jennifer Ann or Jennifer Jane, or something like that…" Eleanor paused.

"And?" Elizabeth couldn't believe she asked.

"She coming for Bill. Same as Josephine came when poor William senior lost Lisa back when."

Why that conversation had troubled her, Elizabeth had no clue. She had no interest in William Clark Junior, no interest at all. Handsome, yes, but he came off as an arrogant boor. Perhaps the right woman…

A jolt returned her to the present. Elizabeth glanced toward Sonnefelt. He seemed focused on the dimly lit road unaware of her disconnected thoughts.

Swallowing, she asked as the wagon rumbled along down the narrow dusty way, "You have never been to Sweetwater?"

"Before today?"

"Yes, before today."

The man thought a moment as he guided the horses onward. "Never had cause."

She had been in Misty Creek for just a short while and had now been to the ranch four times, and this man who had lived here his whole life—no, he hadn't had he, not his whole life—but he hadn't ever had need, but why would he. It was obvious there was no love lost between the men and that was putting it mildly.

"Mr. Clark is concerned about the water," she said at last.

"William is always concerned about the water, everyone is," the miller said as he snapped the reins once more. "Without water the valley would be nothing more than any place else."

"But he blames you."

"Yes, he blames me. I have the mill. I have the dam."

"You control the water."

"No ma'am, God controls the water."

"Yes, that's true. But you control the lake and how much water leaves," she said calmly, fearing he would get angry. She had seen William Clark get angry about the water, angry with Matthew.

"Some see the primary purpose of the dam as power for the mill," he said calmly. "And it does. But I moved the dam downstream. Built a new one. Doubled the size of the lake. I didn't need more water, but the valley does. The farmers and the ranchers, though Mr. Clark is the only rancher left, they need the water. And if we're all careful there will be enough."

"But it's been dry."

"Yes, it's been dry."

"That's why the lake's so low."

"Yes ma'am, and it will get lower if it doesn't rain soon."

"Will we?" she asked.

The man looked at the sky. Stars began to show in the clear evening blackness. "It has always rained. Soon the snows will come. Things will be alright. Hopefully the lake will be full by May. I s'pect it's in God's hands." He snapped the reins.

Why did she believe him? Here Elizabeth sat near the man, the man she didn't like, couldn't like, wouldn't like—and she believed him. Once more she realized that even here, out in the open country, in the dark alone, she knew she was safe. She had no reason to know it, but in her heart she just did.

Things changed that night. She rested easier with the confidence that Mr. Clark would take care of the Simns matter. But that wasn't the only change. Oh, the change was subtle, a person would scarcely notice, but she no longer went out of her way to avoid Mr. Sonnefelt. There had even been a few times, though they were rare, when she thought of him by his first name—Matthew. Elizabeth knew that Sunday he would likely come to the Baughman's for dinner, and that didn't bother her. She did not look for an excuse to be away. She would not say, at least to herself, that she enjoyed the prospect, but she didn't dread it either.

Sunday at church Elizabeth shook the man's hand when they met. It didn't seem so difficult. Though she sat, as always, in the same pew, with Abner and Alberta between them, she no longer had the impulse to slide further away. Yes, something had changed. Oh, she didn't like the man, so she told herself each time she saw him, but she didn't despise him either. And at night when she was alone, in the dark, when she stared at her ceiling, Elizabeth thought about a wagon ride on a cool November night with a sky bursting with bright stars. And she wondered, really wondered, why things had changed.

CHAPTER 24

NOVEMBER MEANT SOMETHING FOR THE TEACHER IN HER. SOMEthing more than just books, tests and homework. This time of the year seemed extra special, and she loved to engage her pupils in the things that made it so. Elizabeth had begun making plans weeks before—though she had told no one, that is except Leah, whom she told everything. The school would do something special for the holidays, both Thanksgiving and Christmas.

Elizabeth had learned a great deal about her students in the nearly two months she had taught at Misty Creek, and she would use what she had learned to reveal the talent she had found among them. So for a time each day they worked on that project, a Thanksgiving program for the whole community.

Jenny could sing. She had a beautiful voice, but when that voice was blended with Josie Tomkins it was magic. Each time they practiced sent shivers down her spine—simply lovely. Homer Reynolds would read. Though he had a good strong voice he lacked confidence. "Replace confidence with preparedness," she had told him. Elizabeth hoped he would find the courage he lacked. Not that he was a coward. But to stand boldly before others took a special kind of courage. She smiled when she thought of the young man. It would be his last year.

How grateful she felt to have had the opportunity to teach him, even for one term.

Homer was not the only reader in the program Elizabeth had envisioned. She had selected, Miss Jamie Watkins, a very hard working student. Jamie had difficulties with her studies. Rather than allow the weakness lead her to failure, Jamie strove that much harder. She carried a calm strength about her, and Elizabeth considered Miss Watkins unflappable. Nothing could intimidate the girl. This was her final year as well, and that was why she had been selected, even though she was not as good a reader as Homer. But she made up that weakness with self-confidence, and Elizabeth knew Jamie would do well. The remaining children would take part in a pair of skits and sing as a group a few of the special hymns of the holiday. Elizabeth had enlisted Reverend Smith's aid as well, and had the highest expectations.

The program was scheduled for six in the evening the Wednesday before Thanksgiving. That last week things became hectic. They were studying history, ancient history as a matter of fact. Elizabeth sat at her desk telling the children about Greece and how the Persians wished to invade them, when she noticed all the students' eyes on something behind her, looking toward the doorway. Turning, she quickly realized what had their attention. He was there, Mr. Leon Simns, in her classroom.

Elizabeth saw him closer than ever before. His unshaven face, tight lips and brows, carried a stern expression—grim she thought. Dressed as before in a heavy woolen coat of dark brown and blue dungarees. His shoes, scuffed, showed their age. The man stood with his hands thrust deep into his pockets.

"Mr. Simns," she said. The man twitched at the sound of his name as his eyes opened slightly. "What can we do for you?"

He did not answer immediately, but scanned the children as he remained there in silence. Elizabeth could see the effect, see the children cower beneath the man's stare. "Class," she said at last, doing her best to keep her composure, for though Elizabeth, found herself terrified, knew she could not reveal fear, "it seems we have a visitor." The young teacher then rose from her desk, her legs nearly buckled as she steadied herself with her chair, hoping no one, especially Mr. Simns, had noticed. "Mr. Simns if you have come to observe the class, perhaps you should move to the back of the room. I am sure you can see things better there."

He looked at her. His glaring stare revealed something in his eyes, something that seemed filled with blackness, something that made Elizabeth very nearly gasp—something terrible.Yet Simns said nothing. She felt fear. A terror as she had never felt before. Fear for herself, but much more a fear for her students.

Elizabeth didn't know what to do. She wanted to ask, no demand, the man leave. She drew a breath and prepared herself. Out of the corner of her eye she saw Homer, he began to get up from his desk. With the slightest move of her hand, she signaled the lad to wait. Elizabeth swallowed hard, her hand searching her desk for something, anything to give her confidence, when through the door came a tall man.

Mr. Simns may have noticed, he should have notice, for all eyes in the room moved for just an instant to the tall man in the doorway. The look on Mr. Sonnefelt's face was calm, and it was the miller that broke the silence. "Well, Leon, I see you have come to observe the class." The tall man moved closer, stood beside Mr. Simns. "It's good you show an interest," the miller went on. "Yes, the school has done great things for the community." Mr. Simns began to turn his head, began to look toward the tall man. Simns drew his eyelids slightly and yet said nothing. "Misty Creek is very fortunate to have this fine school." Matthew went on, now moving in front of the man. "Perhaps you have some questions…or something you would like to say." Elizabeth was surprised at the miller's composure.

The room became silent. Elizabeth feared to breathe, as if the very sound of her breathing would shatter the air. Suddenly one of the girls, Martha Donnellson, just a small child, began to cry. Elizabeth's fear was replaced by a rage. Her hand still searching found a ruler. Her fingers felt it, grabbed it, lifted it, a ridiculous weapon, but she would use it.

Then with a strong yet calm voice, a voice she knew, the tall man, Matthew said, "Leon, it's time for you to leave."

The man looked directly at Sonnefelt with cold, hard eyes filled with hate. "Leave now!" Matthew said nearly shouting, the strength of his voice startled everyone, even causing Mr. Simns to flinch. Martha stopped crying. The room grew still. Elizabeth saw the miller's hands, tense hands, strong hands, large hands, clenched hands. Simns turned and began to leave. At the doorway the hard man spoke over his shoulder. "Schools be a waste—waste of time, waste of money. Goes against nature, goes against God. Teach'n' things. Teach'n' lies and such, no account stuff and such. Hear me. I'll see this place closed down." And then Simns was gone.

Martha began to cry, and she was not alone. The whole room seemed in uproar. Homer had somehow rushed to the front of the room and stood at the doorway. Elizabeth nearly collapsed now holding firmly her desk, the ruler tumbled to the floor. She watched Homer close the door while Matthew looked about the room.

"Is everyone alright?" he said. Voices filled the room as everyone spoke at once. He looked toward the teacher. "Ma'am?" he asked. There was no need to say more.

Elizabeth raised her hand to still the class, though several children yet wailed. "I think, Mr. Sonnefelt, we are all well."

He smiled a weak smile.

"We are very grateful that you happened by," Elizabeth said with a trembling voice. Looking around the room, she tried to smile, but found it difficult. She moved to stand next to the tall man though she felt unsteady on her feet. “Class,” she said, “it is nearly time for lunch. Do you think we should invite Mr. Sonnefelt to join us?”

A cheer rose up that thundered the room. “Well, sir, would you like to join us for lunch today?”

Matthew smiled and that was answer enough.

When the break for lunch had ended, Matthew Sonnefelt began to leave. Elizabeth rose and wondered why she regretted he could not stay. “Mr. Sonnefelt,” she said softly, “I am sorry we had started out on the wrong foot.”

“Ma’am, the fault was mine.”

“No, it was not. I am afraid I judged you badly.” Elizabeth looked about a moment. She could see in the faces of her students that she was not alone in wanting the tall man to stay. “Do you think Mr. Simns will return?”

He did not answer.

“Then you do.”

“Yes ma’am, I do.”

“I have never felt comfortable,” she said just to him, “with the door to my back.”

“I can understand that,” he said.

“I have spoken to Mr. Clark about it. He said he would bring it up at the school board meeting. To see what could be done.”

“But nothing.”

“I am confident.”

Matthew looked around the room. “It doesn’t look so complicated to me,” he said.

She smiled. “I am really sorry you must leave. I was hoping you could stay for a peek at tonight’s performance.”

He returned her smile—a very nice smile. “I will not be far. I would recommend that you lock the door.”

"Lock the door of the school? Sir, I have never, in my wildest thoughts, considered the need of locking the children in. This is not a prison, and I fear the children might feel that it was."

"I am sure you are right. It was only a suggestion."

Then he did something surprising. Calling Homer up, he spoke to the boy. "Mr. Reynolds, I've a task or two for you sir."

The young man looked at him intently.

"First I'd like you to keep one eye on the door for Miss Beck. The door is behind her and we would not like anyone creeping in and surprising the class again, would we? She needs someone she can trust, and I figure you're just the man for the job. Work out a signal so you can let her know." He slapped the young man on the back. He turned and began to the door, stopped and then leaning close said, "One more thing, if Mr. Simns comes back—ever—slip into the store room, out the window, lad, and fetch me at the mill." He then extended his hand to Homer, shook it, smiled at Elizabeth and left.

A week ago Elizabeth would have been upset—perhaps even that very morning she would have been upset by the man giving orders like he had. But now she understood. Mr. Sonnefelt was a man of action. It was not his nature to wait for things he thought should be done. What he had asked of Homer was both wise and clever, and more it gave her a comfort that she had not so far away—a tall someone—a someone that had stood up for her and the class. Elizabeth found herself smiling as she thought about Matthew—a tall man with a very nice smile.

Chapter 25

The day's last light of crimson and red had faded, and the air felt cold enough to snow. It was nearly six, and Elizabeth was not at all at ease. Their practice that afternoon had not gone well. The events of the morning had affected everyone. Twice young Martha had started crying again. The second time it took Elizabeth nearly twenty minutes to calm the child. It would have been best to have sent everyone home and cancelled the program. It was out of stubbornness that she had not. No, she knew that was exactly what Mr. Leon Simns wanted. Somehow they would not allow him to win, at least not this battle. After classes, Mr. Sonnefelt returned with Eldon Baker, Angus Morzinski the two men that worked with him at the mill, and Peter Wilson a farmer just across the lake. The four men worked setting up the room as the church it was on Sunday. They moved the pulpit to a corner so the raised platform could become their stage.

Each time Elizabeth had seen the men at this task, it amazed her how quickly things changed. The desks carefully carried and stacked, the floor swept down, and the pews once more in their places. And each time there was a joviality among the men. A good natured fun between those that liked and respected each other.

But the men had left hours ago, and even now only a few of the children had returned with their parents, and it was nearly six. Elizabeth had moved around the room visiting with the guests that had arrived, attempting her best not to show her anxiety. There were yet too few children for her to begin organizing things. The room felt tense, or so it seemed to her. Though none had mentioned the happenings of the morning she sensed it was on everyone's mind.

At six the Tomkins arrived as well as Homer with his father and mother. A few moments later the Atwoods and Watkins came in out of the night. Things were beginning to look up. As Elizabeth looked about the room, she saw Homer standing off in a corner and looking pale. His lips moved as he stood, his eyes blank blinking. Nerves, Elizabeth thought. She noticed it on the others as well. Twice, John Tomkins had a chance to tug on Lilly Atwood's braids and did not. It was an opportunity he would not normally ignore. The whole group mulled about, standing unsteadily speaking in hushed tones. They did not seem to be her normal boisterous pupils.

Elizabeth gathered her students and began working with them, as parents began to take their seats. By fifteen after six nearly everyone was there, that is everyone except Jenny Clark.

Jenny had such an important part. Elizabeth struggled, trying to rearrange things in her mind. If they must, they would go on without young Jenny. She could see the fear in Lilly's face. Elizabeth smiled and assured her as best she was able. Even little Martha was there. Elizabeth had given the child a hug when she entered. She told the children they would wait a few minutes more to be certain that everyone that could would arrive.

There was someone else that had not come. Someone that had told her he would be there. Someone that just a week or two before would certainly not have been missed—Mr. Sonnefelt. Elizabeth approached Leah, the Smiths were the very first to arrive.

"I had expected Mr. Sonnefelt," she said, hoping that her friend might have some idea where the man might be. "He had said he would come."

A coy smile came to the pastor's wife's lips. "If Matthew said he will be here, he will."

Elizabeth gazed toward the door, but when Leah took her hand, Elizabeth faced her friend. "You don't hate him anymore."

The teacher could see something in her friend's eyes, a joyful, playful dancing. What did Leah know that she did not? She realized. It was true. She didn't hate the man, but that was all.

"Leah, now stop that," she said more sharply than she had intended. "It is true I no longer despise that man, but I can assure you it goes no further. My feelings are…well they are neutral."

But the smile and the look did not leave her friend's face. Tilting her head ever so slightly Leah said, "Of course dear," as she patted Elizabeth's hand.

The door opened and in strode Mr.Sonnefelt. He looked lost a moment as he scanned the room. Though she did not understand why, she moved to him. It surprised her that he was dressed in exactly the clothes he had worn that morning. "I'm sorry I'm late," he said softly.

"Actually we are waiting for the Clarks. I'm afraid we will have to go on without Jenny."

"They'll be here."

"How can you be certain?"

He smiled that nice smile. "They'll be here."

Then as if on cue, the door flew open and in came the Clarks all dressed in their finest. Mr. William Clark boomed, "We're here. Let's get the show on the road." With that, everyone began taking their seats, most occupying the same places they sat on Sunday. Jenny came running to her teacher.

"I'm sorry," she said as the two of them walked quickly among the rush of parents and grandparents finding their way to the pews.

"You are here now," Elizabeth told her. "We must hurry."

Elizabeth was worried. She thought again how badly the last practice had gone. Now everything was in a different kind of turmoil as children nearly tripped over each other setting up. But then she noticed, then the children noticed, for standing at the door was a tall man. He winked and things changed. Elizabeth felt calmer and noticed that she was not alone. The children began smiling, beaming, and she knew everything would be fine.

It was more than fine. It was the best they had ever done. Jenny and Lilly's voices blended to bring the whole crowd to their feet, and melted Elizabeth's heart. The readings by Homer and Jamie went perfectly, and Elizabeth could not remember a single choir that sang finer than her students that night. Ben gave a Thanksgiving prayer, his face beaming with pride in the youth of his flock. And then it was finished, as close to perfection as anyone could imagine.

The parents came to her—mothers hugged her; fathers shook her hand. It was a night Elizabeth would not soon forget. The ending of a day, a difficult day, but in the end, a good day. Elizabeth did not eavesdrop, but overheard conversations by chance. Though the words were not spoken directly to her, they were not secret. Words shared by many different families. Words like… "We weren't going to come tonight…you know that Simns thing…but Matthew came…he told us we should…so we did."

She looked toward the far end of the room. Elizabeth saw a tall man open the door and slip out, doing his best to go unnoticed, and she finally understood that Matthew Sonnefelt was nothing like Alexander. She pressed through the crush, it took a few moments. Reaching the door, she left the church-school and stepped into the cold night air. He had nearly reached the road. "Mr. Sonnefelt," she called, "we are going to have some refreshments. Won't you stay?"

The miller turned to face her. Elizabeth could not see him clearly in the night only illuminated by the bright sparkling stars. "This, Miss Beck is your night. Yours and your kids'. I'll not steal your thunder."

"Nonsense, Mr. Sonnefelt," she responded. "It would not have been possible without you," she said as she moved in his direction. The frosty mists of their breath mingled on the cold night air.

"Miss Beck, you'll catch your death."

"Are you concerned?"

"Certainly," he said, "do you know how hard it is to get a good teacher?"

They laughed. "Please, Mr. Sonnefelt, come back in."

"I'm not dressed proper."

"You are fine. More than fine. Please."

He looked down as she came closer. When he lifted his face she saw that droplets of his breath frozen upon his mustache, bright sparkling as gems set to blaze by the night sky. Elizabeth drew a breath trying to draw in just a bit of the shared vapor. Matthew blinked, blinked again. "Only because I don't want to be responsible for you getting sick."

Elizabeth reached out and took his hand—his strong hand—his warm hand—and led him in.

Part 4
Confrontations

CHAPTER 26

HOW THINGS HAD CHANGED. ELIZABETH WOULD SAY THE CHANGE was dramatic. She smiled at the thought, straightening the room after the last day of classes for the year. The Christmas program, which the class had worked so hard to prepare, had just ended. Unlike Thanksgiving, this event occurred mid-afternoon. They rehearsed all morning, having finished their school work yesterday. Right after work that day, the men from the mill arrived to set up the room. How the teacher had come to count on Eldon, Angus, and of course Matthew. He now remained helping set things right for the coming church service.

She looked across the room as he worked, always busy it seemed. Strange she thought, how her first opinion, had been so wrong. She had found the miller a complex individual, moving in the background of nearly everything that happened in the valley. Even now she wasn't certain what to think of the man. But she had come to respect Matthew Sonnefelt. Yes, that was how she thought of Mr. Sonnefelt, a respected part of the community, an acquaintance perhaps, but nothing more.

She thought back to the time her opinion had changed, the day before Thanksgiving. That was when Elizabeth saw him first in a different light, when her eyes were opened. Yet, it was the following Sunday when things really changed. Before church she had approached Mr.

Clark once more about the Leon Simns situation. He again assured her things were under control. "Not to concern yourself," was the way Mr. Clark put it. Strange the words did not ease her mind one bit. Then she asked if, in the very least, the school room could be rearranged. He seemed to listen, but she had asked about the possibility before and had received no answer.

Elizabeth felt frustrated when she took her seat. It was Thanksgiving Sunday and the church was packed. The space not only contained more locals than she had yet met but also Josephine's guests. Eleanor's rumors had proven accurate, for the two women from New Jersey had indeed arrived. That was Elizabeth's first sight of the Evans, Evangeline and daughter Alexis, dressed in fashions Elizabeth might have anticipated in Columbus high society but seemed so out of place here on the frontier. Everyone seemed to notice, that is everyone but Alberta perhaps. She greeted the pair as if they were long lost relatives, warm and open. Elizabeth felt certain it would not have mattered to Alberta if the pair had donned potato sacks, rather than gowns, the likes Elizabeth had not seen outside the magazines her mother bought. But it was not surprising that others noticed, especially the younger women, which gave repeated glances.

The ivory dress Mrs. Evans wore may have been extravagant, but Elizabeth considered it tasteful and lovely. But Alexis's pale blue dress was stunning and seemed to set her eyes ablaze. Miss Evans, an attractive woman of twenty perhaps, had long blond hair that framed a smiling face, a slight flush on her dimpled cheeks, and dazzling eyes. She seemed to have all the men of the valley's attention, which appeared to please young William, who had also come to the service, though he rarely made an appearance at the Sunday worship. Even so, once the whispers and over the shoulder glances diminished, the service was much like any other, until the end. As Ben prepared for the final blessing, he announced that there would be a community meeting following the service and asked the congregation to remain seated.

Now Elizabeth considered herself a newcomer, and would have though nothing much about it. But as she looked around the sanctuary, she realized that what was about to occur was indeed unusual. When the pastor finished his prayer a man walked to the front—a tall man. Mr. Sonnefelt stood at the front in the open to the right of the pulpit. The room became silent.

Sonnefelt shuffled a moment, as if trying to find the words, and Elizabeth wondered what he would say. "I hope that you all had a chance to come Wednesday evening," he began. "I know most of you were here. It was quite a show our kids put on." There were several murmurs of agreement. "I didn't know we had that kind of talent, but it was more than just your kids; it was also their teacher." Again she heard several low voices. "Misty Creek is a lucky place," he began again. "The school board…especially Will Clark…done us good by finding Miss Beck." Now there was applause, imagine applauses in church. She could not be sure, but suspected that Mr. Clark was the first to clap at the mention of his name. Elizabeth smiled, she was beginning to see what Matthew was doing. "I think," he said then, "that we should also show our gratitude to our new teacher. She has worked so hard, teachin' our young'n's." The whole room erupted in rowdy applause. Elizabeth found herself blushing when they called her to stand. The applause continued for some time until the miller raised his hands. "Yes, Miss Beck, we appreciate everything you have done for this community." Someone let out a whoop and the room once more burst out with applause. Again the tall man raised his hands. "Maybe there is something Misty Creek can do for our teacher." Now the room grew silent. "You have all heard about Leon, and his visit to the school." Her breathing was the only sound Elizabeth heard in the filled room. "Well, you can see where the desk is and the door behind it. Miss Beck would prefer to be able to see the door from the front of the room. Makes sense doesn't it?"

"Then let's move the door," Dan Jones shouted. It seemed the student had no fear of speaking his mind. Elizabeth had to smile. Matthew had control of the audience.

"It really doesn't have to be that complicated," he stated.

"Let's move her desk," Dan added then. "That can't be too hard."

"Now," the miller answered, "there's an idea."

Suddenly a big man dressed in the finest suit she had seen since leaving Columbus, stood up and began walking forward, Mr. William Clark. "Now let's wait a minute. It's not as simple as just picking up the desk and hauling it to the front."

"Why? Is it nailed down?"

"No, Angus, it is not nailed down," the big man said in stiff hard tones. "But there are other things to consider. Have we forgotten that this is a church?" The room became still once again. William smiled. It was a smile that seemed to say, *Things will be the way I say.*

"Mr. Clark is right," Matthew responded. The comment caught the big man by surprise. "We can never forget that this is indeed the house of God. But that doesn't mean things cannot be rearranged a bit." Mr. Clark tried to interrupt, but the miller continued. "We can move the desk over there," he pointed to a front corner. "The chalk board can be moved to the wall there." He pointed to end wall near the east side.

"Why should we change things?" Mr. Clark shouted. "It's the way it's always been." Elizabeth saw that some heads were nodding.

"We have never had a teacher like Miss Beck before," Mr. Sonnefelt said calmly. "She hasn't asked for a thing. I say if we can, shouldn't we do this because we want to."

Cheers arose all around and it seemed that the matter was settled. Elizabeth couldn't believe it, but she wanted to shout for joy. She watched a very angry Mr. William Clark storm out of the church, the remaining Clarks and their guests not far behind.

And that was how the room changed. Yes, the change was dramatic. Elizabeth could never become accustomed to how things were accomplished. Men shed their dress coats, those that had them in any case. Tools appeared. It seemed some had come prepared. The chalk board was taken down and then re-hung. Even so, the work was not reserved for the men. For Elizabeth watched as Alberta and several women began measuring. They discussed among themselves how they would hang drapes to cover the board for Sunday Service. Elizabeth was astounded at their ingenuity. Someone brought food and so they worked through the afternoon. There was nothing found to be insurmountable. When they finished the room was, as best to be described, flipped.

That day she came to understand the man, the tall man, the usually dusty man. And as today, he was the last to leave. That day just the two of them had remained, then she came to respect the man—the man she had first thought a fool. She thanked him. Matthew told her it wasn't anything, but it was. And now nearly a month later it was the two of them finishing once again. He was indeed a remarkable man, and Elizabeth felt grateful she could consider him a friend.

But then someone else crossed her mind. Someone that had been so much more than just a friend. The smile left her face, too many memories, too much pain. She would not, could not, face it again. Once exposed to the cutting knife of absolute heartbreak was more than enough. Elizabeth swallowed as she thought about Jameson. She couldn't help it, she still loved him—and hated him. A hot tear came to her cheek. A tear that seemed to burn in the flush of anger she felt. How could he run off with Rachael? And Rachael was her best of best friends. After all Elizabeth had done? Hadn't she taught, earned what she could, given it all to him for his education? All those years, hadn't they shared a dream? But in the end, for her it was nothing—nothing but pain. Though she remained mad at the man, in her heart she would not blame him. It was not his fault, nor Rachael's. The fault was her own and no one else's. Elizabeth had been naïve. She had believed the words he had said, words like, "it did not make a difference."

It did make a difference.

It would always make a difference.

Elizabeth turned away as another tear streamed down her face. It did not come alone. She would not show tears, not now, and not to him. Beneath her breath she cursed; it was not her nature. Elizabeth cursed the lie, the lie she had been told. The lie she so desperately wanted to believe. She cursed her body, the barren vessel she was, and in that moment of incredible weakness, she cursed God—there in God's own house.

How had He allowed it? She had been but a child. He had allowed it, and she was forever changed. Nothing could ever undo it. Standing there in her own self-pity, feeling sorry for herself, was not her nature either. Elizabeth felt worthless—empty. A person of no value, not to herself or anyone.

She scanned the almost empty room. The day had neared its end, the shadows were long, and she saw him. Matthew stood across the room. He looked directly at her with those deep eyes she had come to know. She wiped her cheek. She regretted doing so, but more she regretted the tears in the first place. He didn't say a word. How many times had she expected something to fall from his lips, but he was not a man of many words. Though Matthew did not speak, she knew by the look in his eyes. She knew he had seen her in her weakness. Now she became angry at herself. Angry that she had lost control. That those hurt feelings had been allowed to surface. And she became ashamed that he noticed. He stood silent.

Matthew watched her for a moment. Elizabeth said nothing as well. At long last she forced herself to get back to straightening the room. Relieved, she heard the sound of his broom. Perhaps she was mistaken. Perhaps he had not really noticed anything at all. Perhaps it was nothing more than her imagination. But Elizabeth remembered his eyes—those calm deep brown eyes. The day seemed ruined.

"Mr. Sonnefelt," she said. Surprised she had once more used his last name. Since Thanksgiving she had only called him Matthew, but now, why not now? "I think we have things in order, shall we call it a day?"

"Yes, ma'am," came a soft reply.

The teacher met the man at the door. "I'll walk you home, Miss Beck."

Just a few minutes earlier she would have accepted his offer but not now, not at that moment. No, now that her emotions had once again been torn raw, she would do her best not crumble. But if she failed, he would not need to see. She was not some vulnerable female to be overpowered by the past. "That won't be necessary," she whispered, the words coming more softly than she had intended.

"I would be glad to."

Elizabeth saw the earnestness in his eyes -- those deep eyes. She struggled to remain firm. "I thank you Matthew," it took a bit of effort but she had said his name, "but I'll be fine. The sun is still in the sky, it is not far."

The miller nodded as if he understood that something had changed. Pulling his coat tight, for it was cold, he touched the brim of his hat, bid her good day and walked away.

Chapter 27

Elizabeth began her journey as well. It seemed to her that she had somehow wronged the man. Matthew had done nothing; he was her friend. Only Leah and the Baughmans were closer. She turned and watched him going the other direction, knowing she was wrong, and wished she had taken his offer. Yet she needed to be alone, if only for a few moments. Elizabeth could think while she walked. Yes, it would be best if she was alone.

She reached the crossroads, turned left and continued. Her feet crunch, crunch, crunched as she walked the road covered with crusted snow. She drew a deep breath, the air so pure and fresh as if the cold and snow had washed it clean. Then Elizabeth heard the sounds—the crunching sounds—footsteps upon the snow covered road, like her steps. But the sounds did not match her feet, they came at a faster tempo. It must be Matthew! Elizabeth had never been able to convince that man she could care for herself. For an instant she did not turn. The crunching came close—very close. Angry, she turned, but her rage left the instant she faced the man in the road, for it was not Matthew but Mr. Leon Simns walking swiftly toward her, less than three paces away. His dark eyes beneath drawn brows focused directly into hers. In her panic she noticed little of the tattered brown coat he always seemed to wear, or the old wool hat unable to control the gnarled windblown hair. It was the eyes, the dark sinister eyes that stole her breath.

She should have screamed. Elizabeth wanted to, but she didn't—she couldn't. Turning, she ran, certain that the man would catch her that very instant, but he didn't. She didn't slow until she had reached Baughman's lane. Looking back for an instant as she hurried on, she found that he was gone. Leon Simns was gone. It made no difference. She raced up the lane as it went up the hill to the Baughman's farmstead.

Elizabeth did her best to calm herself before entering the farm house. She did not wish to alarm her friends. Nothing had happened after all—nothing. Yet her heart raced at the thought of Simns standing so close to her. Elizabeth swallowed as she once again scanned the countryside, took a series of deep breaths, and at last climbed the porch steps and entered warm farmhouse.

She said nothing of her walk home, rather talk revolved around the school program. The Baughmans had attended and spoke on and on how impressed they had been. The three had settled in the kitchen, talking for perhaps an hour, when a loud knock thundered the back door.

"Who on earth can that be?" Alberta said. The farm wife wiped her hands on her apron as she went to the door.

Though Elizabeth couldn't see who had come, she heard a voice, a familiar voice. "Has Miss Beck arrived home?" the miller's words came quickly, one nearly atop the other.

"Yes, yes," Alberta responded. "Matthew come on in."

Elizabeth heard the stomping of big feet and the closing of the door. She stood as Alberta and Matthew entered.

"Look who's come in out of the cold," Alberta said with a smile. "Sit, sit, we've just been talking."

Only Elizabeth noticed, his eyes focused on her but a moment, then danced about the room, as a fly uncertain where it might settle. She saw concern on the miller's face.

Abner was pleased at the visitor's arrival. "Have some coffee, warm yourself."

Matthew nodded. Then spoke, "I saw Leon Simns. He was walking past the mill, on his way home I 'spect."

"Wonder what the man was doing?" Alberta said, squinting in thought. Her eyes flew open as she blurted, "And you thought. That's why. Elizabeth. Oh, my!"

There was no need for the tall man to answer.

"I thank you for your concern," Elizabeth told him, "but you can see I am perfectly fine, Mr. Sonnefelt."

"Yes, ma'am," he said as he looked into her eyes. There was something knowing in the way he looked at her. And Elizabeth found she had to turn away.

"What is this ma'am stuff, Matthew?" Alberta said crossly. "And you, you always calling the man Mr. Sonnefelt. Like he was your father's friend or something. Do I need to introduce you?" The old woman looked from one to the other. "Well, Matthew, this is Elizabeth. I call her Becky; she may not like it but it fits her. And Becky this is our neighbor Matthew; sometimes I call him Mat. Now it's done. Start actin' like you know each other."

Abner sat laughing quietly as he held his coffee.

"Yes, ma'am," the miller responded softly.

"I only let you call me ma'am 'cause I'm old enough to be your mother."

"His grandmother," Abner said, his eyes gleaming, visibly amused. Alberta gave a cross look to her husband. "Well it's true," he said, obviously not intimidated by his wife's glance.

"Don't remind me of my age, old man, or you'll do you own cookin' for a week."

Everyone laughed, including Alberta as she set a hot cup in front of Matthew.

"Now, Matthew," Abner asked, "you tellin' us all you know?"

The miller took a sip then looked over to Elizabeth. "You know Leon has been hanging around the school, and he has promised to see it closed. So when I saw him outside the mill today, I called out. He didn't answer, didn't say a thing, but he gave me that look of his, you know the one, and then ran off."

"And you thought he might have done something?" Alberta asked.

Matthew looked up directly at the dear woman. The nod he gave was barely perceptible.

Elizabeth knew there was no use in trying to hide what had happened. "Mr. Simns," she began softly, "came up behind me on the road as I was coming home."

"And you didn't tell us, Becky?" Alberta voice rose with alarm.

"It was nothing. I didn't want you to worry."

"Well, it was a good thing that Mat came by, or we wouldn't have known anything about it." Abner said, drawing his brows as he looked seriously at the teacher.

Elizabeth looked at the miller, hoping that he would give validation to her actions, but she could see he was in agreement with the others. "I am not a child," she said at last.

Alberta reached over and took her hand. "We know, dear, but I don't trust that man. He's up to no good, that's plain to see. It's just that we care for you and it worries us. You've got to tell us these things."

"I suppose I might as well," the teacher sighed. "Even if I don't," she said as she glared at the man across the table, "someone will."

Abner who had never looked more serious said, "Tell us what happened."

Elizabeth drew a deep breath and as she rotated her cup between her hands told them how she had been walking home; how she had heard the steps coming from behind. "I thought it was Mr. Sonnefelt."

"You mean Matthew," Alberta corrected.

She shook her head ever so slightly. "Matthew… But when I turned it was that man Leon Simns. He just stood there in the road."

"How close, dear?" Alberta asked.

Elizabeth could see she was deeply concerned. She swallowed as she considered how to answer. It seemed the truth —the exact truth—was best. "Very close. Not six feet away."

"Good Lord!" the farm wife exclaimed.

"Then what happened?" Abner asked, looking at her intensely.

"I ran. I don't think I have ever run so fast in my entire life. When I reached your gate, he was nowhere in sight. I think he only wanted to frighten me."

"Well, if you ask me," the older woman said, "he certainly did."

They sat quietly, no one, it seemed, could think what to say next. Finally, Abner got up. Pushing his chair back, he said, "You're gonna have to be careful."

"I am careful, Abner."

He looked at her then nodded as he moved to the back porch.

Alberta shook her head. "Seems to me that we all need to be careful."

"The man hasn't done anything yet, Mother," the farmer shouted from the porch as he left the house.

Alberta shook her head once more. "I've a bit of mending to do." Then told Elizabeth, "Why don't you get that man another cup. Seems that one's gone cold." She left the two of them sitting at the kitchen table. Elizabeth poured Matthew another cup of coffee. He thanked her. She then sat looking across the table from the tall man.

"That's all it was, wasn't it?" she asked.

"To scare you?" the miller asked.

"Don't you think?"

He looked directly at her with those deep brown eyes, eyes that showed he was considering everything before he would answer. "What do you think?" he asked at last.

The question surprised her, especially considering it was what she had asked Matthew. But before she spoke, Matthew asked another question. "When you were there in the road, what did you think then?"

Elizabeth began to tell him how angry she felt. Angry because she was certain it was he. But she raised her cup to her lips and thought a moment. Was it time for the truth, all the truth?

Elizabeth eyed the man across the table, it was the first time she really looked at the man. She had never noticed how his light brown hair seemed to tumble over the tops of his ears or the firm line of Matthew's jaw. Until this moment she had not seen the faint almost invisible scar on his left cheek that stretched upward nearly reaching the ear. No, what always drew her in we're Matthew's eyes. Chestnut brown and deeper than a well. Once again she couldn't help but stare. What had she been told years ago? That the eyes were windows, windows into a person's essence. Oh how she had resisted. How she had let past events corrupt her view of the man, to convince herself that his acts were merely a facade meant to hide a cruel agenda. Cause her to believe that within Matthew was a hard and harsh man lurking for the moment to strike. That her distrust of men, driven by past experiences, drove unjustified judgements and incorrect first opinions. And she had used those wrong first opinions force fit Matthew to others that had hurt her.

Lifting the cup to her lips, she swallowed the hot brew and decided the time had come for the whole truth. "I was angry."

"Angry at Simns?"

"No, I was angry that you didn't think I could possibly make my way home alone. That you had come after me," she said with more intensity than she had intended. Elizabeth looked at him, expecting him to say, *See I told you I should have been with you. Then Simns would not have dared show his face.* And when he did, she would be all the madder. But Matthew didn't. He didn't admonish her. He sat there quietly looking at her.

Finally, as he turned the half-filled cup between his hands, he said, "The fault is mine."

His fault. How could he take the blame? He had offered. It was her stubbornness, her pride. No, it was not Matthew's fault, and she told him so.

Elizabeth felt angry with herself. She knew that Leon Simns could be about. And though it was true that man had not done anything yet, it didn't mean he wouldn't. She considered what she had seen, and having seen the man so close, what she had thought at that moment. Wasn't that what Matthew had asked?

"When I saw Mr. Simns there, I was frightened," she said at last. Matthew looked at her intently. He seemed to consider each word she said, how she said it, as she said it. "He…he…" she began again, "had a very strange look about him. You know in his eyes."

"Like when he came to the school?"

"Yes, but different. I can't say exactly what I mean. It was something…something…" She shook her head and noticed she was trembling. She felt the touch of his hands on hers, across the table he had reached, and there was a warmth and a strength. It seemed to move from his hands to hers, and then up her arm. It moved with a calming warmth that seemed to fill her. She looked across at the man, the tall man, the strong man, and she felt something. She pulled her hands away, and that feeling disappeared as suddenly as it had come. Elizabeth thought the whole thing would make her feel uncomfortable. But as it had always been, being near that man, well, it felt natural somehow, and that troubled her.

Finally changing the subject slightly she said, "I really didn't want Baughman's to know."

"To know about Simns…on the road…today?" he asked.

"Yes, and the other times as well," she said softly.

"It's a small place. Word gets around."

"Yes, and a great deal faster than I would like."

Lifting his cup he said, "It's not all bad."

"Doesn't anyone understand I'm not a child? I can take care of myself. I have come half way across the continent alone after all."

"Is it wrong that people care?"

"It's more than that. For heaven's sake they are not my parents." She was surprised what she had allowed to slip. It was just -- well it was just -- when that man was near she seemed to say the wrong things.

Matthew put his cup down softly. "They're the closest thing you've got here."

How did he do that? How did he so calmly reach to the very heart of the matter? Elizabeth could not respond to his comment, but in truth was there anything she need say? She had come to love the Baughmans. They had taken her not only into their home but into their lives, and they were not the only ones. She had become more than just the teacher of children; she had become part of the community. Wasn't it the community that changed the school room? Hadn't the community, over and over again, wrapped its arms around her? No, she was not some outsider from across the Mississippi, some spinster woman that came but did not belong.

Elizabeth was becoming one of them. For each of those that now lived in the valley had come from someplace else. Yes, some had been here longer than others, but in each household were the first generation. The ones that had come to stake out a life in a new place. They were not so different than she. Each had reasons for leaving what they had known, to strike out, and if it be God's will, to endure. Here in Misty Creek they did more than just endure. A dusty valley with a small creek was turned into, how did Ben put it, "the pearl", and that was what it was, and whether she liked it or not she was becoming a part of the community.

Elizabeth looked at him with damp eyes. Matthew held out his right hand, palm up. She looked down at that callused, big hand. A hand she had felt before. A hand that had helped her to her feet when she had stumbled in the dark. A hand that when raised could quiet a room. A hand when clenched that could convince a man to leave the school. She wanted to place her hand in his hand, to once more feel its warmth, to draw on its strength, but she did not. Elizabeth stared at that hand and the tears threatened to come. She did not know how long she could hold back the tears of past hurts, tears of what could never be, so she fled the room without another word.

She raced past Alberta. The woman barely had time to look up from her work. Elizabeth rushed to the stairs and ran to her room. There alone, there behind the closed door she wept. Angry with herself. Why had she allowed those memories come to the surface? Why today?

Lying face down upon her bed, Elizabeth heard footsteps as she sobbed. A gentle knock on the door. "Becky, dear," came the soft voice of the dear woman she had passed downstairs, "are you alright?"

She did not answer immediately.

"Matthew left, dear. Is there something the matter?"

Yes, there was something the matter. Something she had to deal with alone—always alone.

"Can I come in, dear?"

Could she come in? Why, it was her house. Alberta had every right to go into any room she wished at any time. Elizabeth swallowed hard. She bit her lip and controlled her sobs. "I'll be alright," she said at last. "I just need some time alone."

"Are you sure?" Alberta asked. "Sometimes we only think we need to be alone, when what we really need is someone to talk to."

The woman was right. Most times Elizabeth had found Mrs. Baughman so very wise. But though perhaps she should talk to someone, this was not something she wished to discuss with Alberta. "Please," she pleaded. "I need to be alone."

"Very well dear. I'll call when supper's ready."

"Thank you, Alberta." Elizabeth called out as she slid off the bed and moved to the window. Pushing the curtain aside, she could see the ice that formed lacey patterns covering the glass. With the warmth of her hand she melted a small spot, just large enough to look through. Matthew was already far away. She watched as he went down the lane, turned onto the road, and was gone.

She had been so wrong about the man. Matthew Sonnefelt was a good, honest man, a decent, hard working man. He was someone she could trust—really trust. Elizabeth felt so grateful that he was her friend, but that would be all he could be. She drew a breath. It would be enough for her, but she wondered if it would be enough for him. Never once did she give him any kind of indication that she sought something more. Elizabeth moved away from the glass. Surely he would find someone, soon perhaps. A good man like him would meet a good woman to share his life. "Yes," she whispered, "it would be best." Yet strangely, it made her uneasy to think of Matthew marrying. "This is ridiculous," she told herself.

So as Elizabeth thought these things, as she pondered her own life, she knew she must be strong. She would rely upon herself. It didn't mean she had no friends. It didn't mean she didn't need friends. It just meant, when the lights went out, she would be alone, and Elizabeth was alright with that. Yes, she could be fine. She would be fine. And so Elizabeth began to repair the wall, the thick stone wall around her heart. It had cracked that day, a small fissure had allowed some of the pain to leave, and a bit of compassion to enter—but no more. No, she was tough. She could be hard, as hard as she needed to be.

She went back to the window, as if she could once more see Matthew. But he was gone, long gone, and that was fine. It was better than fine, it was for the best, for her best, but more the best for him.

CHAPTER 28

THE SIXTH OF JANUARY WAS THE FIRST DAY OF SCHOOL OF THE year, the first time in five years that school was held in that month. The Christmas break had seemed long. Perhaps because it was her first Christmas away from home. Even the mail, as slow as it was, had stopped. The snows had prevented the trips to Thimble, and she felt completely cut off. Oh, she had her friends; the Baughmans had done so much, and she especially loved her visits at the Smith's. Leah had become like a sister, even closer it seemed. They could talk of anything, and often did. She had told Leah of that day when Leon Simns had followed her. She had told Leah about Matthew, about the comfort and warmth the man gave, and how she had drawn away. Leah seemed to understand—she listened, and Elizabeth knew she heard, really heard what she told her.

There were times when Elizabeth expected her friend to give advice. Not that she would have taken it. Not that she even really wished to hear it, but she expected it all the same. But Leah did not, and that made her love the woman more. Though Leah was her dearest and closest friend, it was not just for her she came to visit. Ben was home more, and if she considered Leah a sister of the heart Ben was a new brother. The cowboy preacher, had been her first friend of the valley, and how he could make them all laugh as he told stories of his treks across the wilderness. But the winter made travel very difficult, nearly impossible. There were no wagons going to the rail head now, and he rode out to the settlements only when the weather was fit, which lately it wasn't. And then there were the children, Micah, Rachel and James, the closest things to angels, Elizabeth was sure, though their mother saw them differently. Oh yes, she loved her visits with the Smiths and went there at least twice a week.

But today school would start once again, and in truth she couldn't wait. Elizabeth had arrived at the schoolhouse early. Cleaned the erasers herself. Usually she had one of the younger boys take them outdoors and beat them together, a white cloud filling the air. But today it was different, it was the first day back after Christmas. The air was so cold it felt brittle, as if she might shatter it with the clump, clump, clump of the dark gray felts slamming against one another. She worried about the children, some came so far. Many of those that came the furthest rode in wagons or on horseback. Elizabeth wondered how many would come.

Most did come, and it took some time and all her experience to once more regain control of the class. However it was not unexpected and she managed to rein them in before first recess. As the children ran and played in the snow, now nearly knee deep, she watched Josie Tomkins. She remembered that first time she had met the young lady, and the friend named Mary she had brought along. Elizabeth felt sorry for Mary and the others whose parents simply did not approve of "outside meddiln'" as they put it.

She knew of six families that would not allow their children to attend school. Most were farm families that lived the furthest from the school. They kept to themselves. Only one of the families even came to church. She had spoken twice to Mrs. Harper, introducing herself as the teacher, trying her best not to force her private opinion on the woman. Mrs. Harper was civil. That was not the first word that came to the teacher's mind when she thought of Jeremiah Harper. A short hard man that refused to say a single word to her. Elizabeth had learned later that he considered it improper for a married man to speak to a single woman. Later still, she learned, he considered it improper for a woman of her age not to be married. But in conversations with Mrs. Harper, the farm wife asked about news from outside the valley. She had watched the woman with her four small children. It was plain she loved them dearly, and Elizabeth would not interfere.

Yet in her heart she hoped that somehow things would change. It troubled her that members of the community considered the school and the teacher, for that matter, evil. She drew a breath allowing it to escape in a quick huff of vapor that floated a moment and vanished in the frigid air. Elizabeth shook her head. She could not control what others thought. Doing her best, that was the only solution. Teach to prepare her students for the changing world, and allow time to show the truth.

The first day went well, and she intended to walk over to the mill. Elizabeth had a small project she wished to have done, a bookshelf. For the mill was not merely a grist mill, but also the site of a water driven sawmill. Late November rains and the snows of December had nearly refilled the lake. The mill was operating once again and everyone knew the lake would be full long before spring. Even Mr. Clark had ceased his complaints, at least for the time being.

The snow on the road had been packed down, so the walking easy. It seemed no warmer than the early morning jaunt that had brought her to the school. Yet bundled, she did not find the afternoon uncomfortable. Elizabeth stomped her feet as she entered the mill. *Strange,* she thought, *how seldom she had come.* The mill stood so near to the school and yet she had only set foot in the building perhaps four times. The air little warmer inside than the January afternoon's chill. Elizabeth would guess the temperature hovered just over freezing. Angus and Eldon were busy at work. A great wooden shaft turned the stone as she watched. All manner of machinery seemed in motion, as if the great building was alive.

She asked where she might find Mr. Sonnefelt, and was directed to an adjoining room, his office.

She stood in the open doorway as a bit of warmth spilling from a black wood stove in the room's corner flowed over her while she waited for Matthew to notice. With a pencil tucked behind his right ear and papers strewn across his desk, Matthew stared at a column of ciphers, which he was comparing to documents he gathered here and there. Finally she rapped on the doorway.

He looked up, smiled, rose from his seat, and moved around his cluttered desk. "Miss Beck, what can I do for you?"

"Miss Beck? You had better not let Alberta hear you call me that, she will certainly correct you."

His smile grew. "But she might forgive this instance," he said, "for I suspect you have come on business."

"And that makes it different?"

Sitting down on his desk, right on top of the papers, Matthew tilted his head ever so slightly and asked, "Doesn't it?"

She had to smile at his relaxed attitude. "I suppose," she said at last. "And yes, I have come on business."

He motioned her to a chair and she sat. The room seemed warm, the potbelly stove in the corner evidently raging. The miller noticed, for he said, "It's the only heat in the building. So it gets hot in here while the rest of the place…well doesn't."

"Do you spend most of your time here?" she asked.

"Oh no," he answered. "The truth of the matter is I don't spend enough time at my desk, which is why it is now covered with a month's worth of…" he looked down at the papers all around him, "…of this stuff." He laughed.

Matthew's laugh was pleasant. Elizabeth had never heard him laugh before. It was not like the full body laugh Ben had. It was not exactly like anyone's she had heard before. It was just a pleasant, unassuming kind of laugh, and hearing it made her smile all the more. She told him that she wanted a bookcase for the school, and asked if he could build one.

He assured her that it would be no problem. They discussed the dimensions and type of wood.

Elizabeth asked, "Is it were possible to match the desks? Oh, I would not think it would be required, but it would be nice."

"I was thinking the exact thing." He smiled. "It won't be a problem at all." Matthew looked at her with those deep eyes, eyes she would have thought might make her uncomfortable, but his gaze did just the opposite.

"Would you like a tour of the mill?"

"If you have a moment."

Sonnefelt looked down at the papers strewn about him. "It will do me good to step away from this for a bit."

He began by showing the room in which they found themselves. "I am sure you have figured out this is my office." He chuckled. Other than his desk, the room seemed very organized. Matthew then led her the way she had come, to the mill room, the main room. "This is where most of the work is done," he began. "We have two sets of stones for grinding. The shaft," he pointed to the vertical wood beam that turned, "spins the lower stone. The upper stone is stationary."

"So the grain is ground between them."

"Yes, and see how the grain is dribbled down the hole at the center of the stone. As it grinds it moves to the outside of the lower stone."

"Centrifugal force."

Sonnefelt smiled. "Yes, and the angle cuts in the stone as well. The fineness is controlled by how close we hold the stones. We check the meal as it comes out for texture." He took a handful of cornmeal and held it in the palms of both hands. Sonnefelt nodded toward the workmen. "Looks good Eldon."

"How do you know it's right?" she asked.

"The boss, he knows," Eldon responded while Sonnefelt held the meal closer for Elizabeth to see.

"Been doing it for a while. Comes natural," Matthew added with a smile that seemed to fill his face.

Elizabeth didn't think it came natural at all, that this milling business was much more complex than she had imagined.

He tossed the meal in the box with the rest, slapped his hands together and wiped them on the legs of his trousers. No wonder the man was always dusty. He spoke of how grinding different grains required different stones, but she didn't catch all the details as she looked about in awe. She felt a slight tremble as all the machinery moved, driven by the water and the sweat of skilled hands.

"The meal goes up by that elevator."

"Elevator?"

"Yeah, that's what it's called. There are buckets, or small hoppers, attached to a chain that moves through those box tubes, I guess you might call them. The elevator takes the meal upstairs."

"Upstairs?"

"Yes," Matthew glanced upward. "This is the milling floor. The one above is the processing floor."

Elizabeth looked back to the box containing the cornmeal. "So that isn't the finished product."

"Come," he said with outstretched hand. "I'll show you."

Elizabeth glanced at the large hand encased in its leather glove but did not take it. "Lead the way, Matthew."

He led her up wide steps made of thick boards. The climb was easy, but she caught her toe on the top step. A strong hand caught Elizabeth by the elbow preventing her tumble. The foolishness she felt was quickly replaced by a strange sensation that seemed to flow from the man's hand and set her skin to tingling. When she looked into his eyes, she blinked, swallowed, and wondered if she was blushing. She expected Matthew to comment, but the man said nothing, just stared in her eyes. Elizabeth swallowed again and took a firm grasp on the handrail. He released her.

It took her a few moments to regain her composure as they stood in a room filled with flat belts driving wheels of different sizes. The shafts above their head whirred. She heard little of what he said of this machine or that, her mind swirling with the memory of his touch only an instant ago.

"Above are the storage bins." These were the first words that registered. "We keep the grain there as well as the meal to be processed and bagged."

She drew a breath. "Taken there by the chain hoppers, that thing, the elevator."

"Yes, the elevator," he beamed that she had remembered.

They left the processing floor down the same steps had nearly caused her to fall. Elizabeth led the way, placing each foot carefully on the treads while maintaining firm grip on the handrail. She felt grateful that Matthew did not reach to take her arm, and yet strangely wished he had.

A narrow stair took them down from the milling floor to the lowest floor, to a large darker room below grade, with its walls of stone and great column of wood supporting the floor above.

"That heavy shaft is the wheel shaft," he explained, pointing to a large wooden shaft that turned on two gigantic bearings. "You can see the main gear, that large wood one that drives everything." She observed a slowly turning large wooden gear driving a smaller gear, which in turn drove another large gear and a second smaller gear which spun a pair of bevel gears, she believed he called them that drove the millstones. It all looked so, so, industrious, for lack of a better term.

It was the very mass of the equipment that took her by surprise. Elizabeth had looked across the water at the large building so many times and had no idea, not even a slightest clue, of what the building contained. Though she did not understand exactly how things worked, Elizabeth found herself impressed.

He then led her back to the mill room where Angus and Eldon were filling bags of cornmeal. "If the weather shapes up a bit, we need to send a wagon load out next week," Matthew told her.

"I thought you couldn't send wagons to Thimble in the winter."

"Not to the rail head, Ma'am," Eldon answered. "But to the settlements, Paradise, Hancock's Bluff, Marshall, and Kerockville."

Matthew explained how each delivery could be done on a single day, weather permitting. The loads would be light and two wagons would go together. When the two went east, they would cross the saddle and follow the road to the crossroads. There, one would go north the other south, and would meet again for the return. "Getting back and forth in a day reduces the chance of being caught in bad weather," he continued. "In any case, the driver can hole-up at the settlements if things go south."

Even so, the thought of men sitting so many hours on a wagon in the winter, even if it were good weather, sent shivers down Elizabeth's spine. "We take turns," the miller explained then, "so no one goes out each trip."

"It is dangerous business, isn't it?" she asked.

"It can be, miss," Eldon said then with straight lips and a grim look in his eye. "But we got word last week those folk have a need."

Elizabeth shook her head. "Don't the folks in those settlements have wagons?" she asked. "If their families were in trouble wouldn't they send wagons here?"

The answer Eldon gave concerned her greatly. "There sickness in the settlements. It's not only cornmeal we be takin' but other things they really need, like all the blankets we can spare."

Angus added, "Even if they had men strong and well enough to make the trip, we couldn't let them come. We won't go to the settlements themselves, but leave the supplies where they can get them."

Elizabeth shook her head once again. "You men must be careful," she said as she looked at the three of them.

"Oh we will, miss," Eldon said with a smile. "We got plenty of reason to be extra careful. I got five young'n's that'll need their pa, and Angus has got six with another on the way. Don't you worry your head none. We know what we're doin'. We'll be alright."

Elizabeth really wanted to believe them, but she saw concern in Matthew's eyes.

Elizabeth drew a breath in the silent moment that followed. "I want to thank you Matthew for your valuable time," she said with a smile. "And I am grateful that you will be able to make the bookshelf for the school."

The man tilted his head returned her smile. "I was pleased to show you around."

As she turned to leave, he followed her to the door. It was late in the day and soon the light would fade. "Give me a minute to grab my coat and I'll walk with you. That is, if you don't mind the company."

Chapter 29

She wanted to refuse. Elizabeth did not want to lead the man on, give any reason for him to think, well to think, that she would allow him to court her. But her heart felt a yearning for things that could not be. Jameson's departure had taught her the foolishness of her hopes. Dreams of husband and home were for others. That had been a painful lesson to learn, there was no need to venture into that territory again. Yet her heart ached in a mix of past's pain and what she felt were the present's impossibilities.

While Elizabeth considered the dilemma she faced, the man waited patiently. The look in his eyes revealed that Matthew perceived there were reasons for her hesitation. The man looked at her with those eyes, those deep brown eyes that seemed to see into her very soul.

"Ma'am," he said at last, "let me walk with you, just neighborly. It won't mean anything. I'd just feel better knowing you were not out there in the dark alone."

"But you will have to come back alone," she responded quickly.

"That's so. But I won't have to worry about how the trip is goin' because I'll be there," he grinned. She had to laugh. There was no logic to the answer, and he knew it. She nodded and soon the two of them were side by side crossing the dam and the two bridges, making their way toward the Baughman's.

They walked for a time. "Mr. Sonnefelt…I mean Matthew," she began tentatively. "I feel I must tell you something."

The man looked her way but said nothing.

She drew a breath, swallowed and trudged on. "But I do not know how…"

Softly he spoke with a calm voice. "You don't want me to think, how do they say it, you're available or something of that sort."

He had done it again. How did he do it? It was as if he could reach into her head and see her thoughts. "Something like that," she answered.

Matthew nodded, showing he understood. Indicating she need say nothing more, but somehow it seemed to her that he also indicated that nothing had changed. "I understand," he said at last.

How could he understand? Deep inside, her temper began to rise. The man had no idea what she had gone through or what she felt. Wasn't his statement, those two words—I understand—a bit presumptuous?

He tilted his head slightly, his eyes opened a bit. Elizabeth saw confusion in the man's face, a question perhaps. Seeing that confusion, seeing that unspoken question—What have I done now?—she realized she had leaped to a place she should not have gone. The man had spoken only out of politeness.

She turned and began walking once more.

"Ma'am, I mean Miss Beck, I mean Elizabeth…I didn't expect a fine lady like you, coming from the east and all, would have any interest in a simple man like myself. I'm sorry that I put your mind to fears. It's just I thought you might need a friend."

She stopped suddenly. So suddenly that Matthew had taken two full strides before he too came to a halt. Turning, he faced her. Elizabeth looked at the man—the tall man. She wondered again what kind of man he truly was. She had been told Matthew was what he seemed, and yet somehow, she felt he was so much more. Simple, by no means. He was perhaps the most complex man she had ever met.

"Matthew," she said softly, "I wish things were different. For if things could be, I would very much hope you would choose to be more than the very dear friend you have become. You are a special man, Matthew Sonnefelt, rare indeed."

He stretched out his gloved hand. She looked at it a moment. Elizabeth wanted so much to grasp it, to feel the strength he had, but she did not. "We can only be friends."

He nodded as he continued to offer his hand. At last she took it. Her hand felt so small, lost, yet not, in his. They walked on in silence, as if each had so much on their mind and found themselves unable to speak.

"Matthew," she asked as they reached the Baughman's lane. Elizabeth liked the sound of his name; it fit him somehow. "Why haven't you married?" Surprised at her boldness, she wondered what had possessed her to ask such a personal question.

"Can't honestly say," the man told her without changing his stride. "I 'spect I haven't met the right woman."

She waited a few steps then said. "I'm certain you will."

"I don't know," he said with a smile. "I'm quite particular."

She chuckled. "Are you now?"

"Oh yes, ma'am, I am."

"Here I thought it was because you were just a bit odd." She wondered if she had taken it too far.

But he laughed as he said, "More than just a bit, I'm afraid."

They both laughed. Why was it each time she was near this man she felt—well at ease—comfortable? Elizabeth forced her mind not to consider that question, not at that moment, but rather to enjoy the winter walk with a friend.

CHAPTER 30

THE DAY'S BITTER WINTER WIND PUSHED ELIZABETH ALONG AS she made her way homeward. She drew her scarf up a bit, pulling it tight. Her mind was filled with thoughts of her students. That they braved the cold each morning and afternoon always left her concerned. Elizabeth drew a breath, with the releasing, the vapor seemed torn away by the wind at her back. Perhaps the temperature would rise by Monday morning, for the week's classes were behind them. Friday's twilight surrounded her as she shuffled along in the ankle deep snow.

In the road a noble coal black steed approached, a spirited animal ridden by a spirited man. William Clark Junior looked down on her from his perch. The horse with wild wide open eyes, neck arched, snorted, displeased his rider's pull on the reins halted the homeward journey. The black horse moved restlessly in the road, longing, Elizabeth felt certain, for its warm stall at Sweetwater Ranch.

William glared at Elizabeth with tight lips and drawn brows while his horse continued to rock and sway. "Bound for Baughmans?"

"Where else would I be going?"

The horse turned completely around before William gained full control at last. "It's hard telling where an independent woman like you might be going."

She unhappy by the young man's statement. "Now if you will allow me to pass…"

"Allow you to pass. That's rich." He pulled his hat down against the wind. "Here and I have come all this way to find you."

Elizabeth blinked. Since the Evans had come to the valley, she had seen little of the young rancher other than at church. For though he had not spoken to her, she had watched him with Alexis Evans, always dressed exquisitely, on his arm. "And why, William, have you come seeking me?"

The black stallion rocked impatiently once again, and William yanked back upon the reins which caused the steed to paw the snow covered road. "I've come to see if you have changed your mind."

Elizabeth tilted her head, confused. "Changed my mind?"

His face grew stern as he shook his head. "Yes, changed your mind about my courting you." The curt words came through tight lips.

"That's an odd question," she responded. "And what of Miss Evans?"

"What of her?"

"It seems that the two of you are an item."

He looked away as he spoke. "I'm not here to talk about Alexis." He looked down at her again. "I'm giving you one last chance."

Chance! What did this man think that he was some sort of grand opportunity that any woman would wish? She squinted her eyes. "No William, I have not changed my mind. And now if you will have that nag step aside, I am cold and wish to be on my way."

"Exactly what kind of fool are you?" he hissed. "I know there is no man in Ohio. Never was." The horse shifted responding to the raised voice of his rider. "Perhaps you feel content watching other people's children. But at the end of the day you will be all alone. A spinster growing old." The black tugged at the bit, lurched left a half-step before William regained domination. Then, with drawn brows and straight lips, he added, "Or is it that you find yourself fond of that useless miller man?"

Now Elizabeth no longer felt the cold. Her anger sent her heart to pounding. How dare this man speak to her in this manner? "Call me a fool if you wish, but my life is none of your business." Then in a most uncharacteristic manner, she struck the black stallion's hind quarters with her valise, sending steed and rider down the road and soon out of sight. "Who's the fool now? You ride a horse you cannot control." She muttered after him, and continued the walk home.

In the dark, as she lay in her bed, William's words played time and again in her mind. She had not mentioned the confrontation with the Baughmans. Elizabeth could not be certain she would even tell Leah. The whole event meant nothing…but it did! The cruelty of the young rancher upset her most of all, that and his angry ramblings. Each time she tried to push the image of the man seated upon a black horse aside, the words *A spinster growing old* echoed in her head. Was that her future? Was it what she wanted? No! Elizabeth swallowed as tears began to form. She turned her head and saw the pale rectangle of her curtained window across the room. It seemed so cold, so empty. Would her future be so…empty? She trembled blinking back the tears fed by a heartless man and lost hopes.

The evening's meeting added to her conviction of the value she placed upon most men of her generation. Insensitive, self-seeking, and cruel seemed reasonable description of young William and so many others. By the man's actions she wondered how much truth existed in the rumors that had flown through the valley. Shortly after Mrs. Evans and her daughter, Alexis, had arrived, tongues began flying. And by all appearances the words seemed justified. For though the beauty from New Jersey was seen seldom beyond the rather broad lands of Sweetwater Ranch, when she appeared, William Junior was at her side. Each time Elizabeth had seen the pair, they seemed to enjoy one another's company. She drew a breath at the thought. Truth was the couple had added to her heartache. Alexis coming from the east filling the place at William's side, a space Elizabeth had rebuffed, gnawed at her. For though her mind said she had no interest in the man, her heart was continually reminded of its emptiness.

She turned away from the window to face blackness of the other wall. She wondered. If the rumors had any value, why would William approach her on the road? What was his real relationship with Alexis? Of course they had only known one another for two months.

Why the image of Matthew covered in dust, as always, with a smile that seemed to reach those deep thoughtful eyes, Elizabeth couldn't imagine. She drew a breath and held it as in her mind she remembered the sound of the miller's laugh. For just the briefest of instants she compared Matthew and William Junior. Even after all these months, she could not say she knew much about Matthew, but Elizabeth knew one thing, that no matter what anyone said, particularly young William Clark, Matthew was not useless. Elizabeth was not certain if anyone in the valley knew the true value of Matthew Sonnefelt, but she had seen over and over again the times the miller had shown his worth. The image of Matthew smiling as he sat upon his paper strewn desk pushed William completely from her mind, and then sleep finally came.

CHAPTER 31

IT WAS THREE WEEKS LATER, MID-MORNING ON A DEEPLY OVER-cast day, as Elizabeth sat at her desk, that the door began to open, slowly, silently. In November, she and Homer Reynolds had agreed upon a hand sign, just as Matthew had suggested. Homer was to indicate if someone, particularly Mr. Simns, was entering the school. Now that Elizabeth faced the door, she saw the first indication and placed her left hand, drawn into a fist, thumb up on her desktop. Homer's eyes flew open. Elizabeth sent her attention darting toward the door and then back to the young man. Homer rose and moved swiftly across the room, reaching the storeroom door, just as Leon Simns entered.

Elizabeth could not know if the man noticed Homer's departure. Calming herself, she placed all her attention on the scruffy looking man, standing at the back of the classroom. Simns seemed surprised that she had seen him, surprised perhaps that the room now faced the other direction. Elizabeth took the initiative.

"Mr. Simns, have you come to observe the class once more? We were just discussing Magellan's voyage. You might find it interesting."

The man grunted as he gathered his composure. Squinting his eyes a bit, he looked across the room, directly into her face, and she feared for her students. Elizabeth began to lose her patience with the man, as she glared back, attempting to control her temper. Too often she had allowed her anger to get the best of her. She would not allow it to do so now. Drawing a breath, holding it a moment, and carefully allowing the air to slide out, Elizabeth did her best to calm the tremble caused by the rage that grew within.

The tension began to permeate the entire room. Josie and some of the students had turned to look at the man who had crept into the room, while others stared forward at their teacher with faces gone pale. Elizabeth could see the fear in the young children's eyes. Only Jenny seemed to radiate a confidence in her teacher, and Elizabeth felt her own confidence growing.

"As we were discussing," Elizabeth began again, pretending nothing in the least was unusual about Simns' presence, "Magellan sailed from Spain crossed the Atlantic, and followed the coast of South America until at last he reached what we call Cape Horn, at the southern tip of the continent." Elizabeth was surprised she had kept the tremble out of her voice as her legs shook. She moved to the world map which hung along the front wall. The teacher allowed her finger to move along the route, best that she could guess in any case, yet all the while keeping close eye on unshaven farmer standing near the door.

She noticed Matthew just outside the window. She drew another breath trying not to stare as Matthew's hands moved, some sort of hand signs. Elizabeth gave the slightest nod, so slight she hoped only the miller would notice. Matthew vanished. Leon jumped in surprise when the door burst open and in strode a tall man. Matthew slapped the man on the back and walked right past.

"Have you come on business, too?" he said as he turned to face Leon, standing directly in front of the man. "Good morning, Miss Beck," the miller said without turning. "I'm sorry I'm late. I had intended to get here before classes began."

"That is quite alright, Mr. Sonnefelt."

Before Elizabeth could say another word, for she was not certain what the Matthew had planned, he continued. "You had said there was something not quite right about that bookshelf."

Elizabeth moved up the center aisle toward the two men. "Yes. The truth is, it was not quite as large as I had hoped," she said as she neared the center of the room. Her concern for the safety of her students propelled her toward the men, but. Elizabeth had no idea what Simns intended. Matthew, appearing to disregard the man, turned to face the side wall and the bookcase in question while standing between Leon and the class. "I had wondered," the teacher began again, "if perhaps you might be able to make another."

The miller put his finger to his chin as he tilted his head slightly to the right, looking as if he was considering the request. "It will take a couple of weeks, but I don't see a problem."

By this time, Elizabeth had closed to perhaps six feet of where Matthew stood. She drew a breath, wondering what she would do next. "Two or three weeks will be fine Mr. Sonnefelt," she said trying her best to maintain a steadiness in her voice.

Slowly Matthew turned to face the other man standing less than an arm's reach away. Elizabeth took a half step to her right so she could see past Matthew. She watched as Simns slipped his right hand beneath his coat. With furrowed brows and dark eyes, Leon glared at the miller that stood before him. The room grew silent. Elizabeth was certain she would always remember the look in man's eyes, a cold dark look—an angry hateful look.

The skin on Matthew's face grew taut, his brows lowered, his lips thin and straight. "What brings you here today, Leon?" Simns gave no response. It seemed a very strange, dangerous standoff, and as she watched, Elizabeth was afraid even to breathe, as she wondered what she could do to protect her children. She wanted to scream, not out of fear but out of rage, to shout at that man, to command that he leave.

But instead she carefully controlled her voice and her words. "Yes, Mr. Simns," she asked, "what brings you to school today?"

At last Simns spoke, without taking his eyes off the man that stood before him, she could not say that the farmer even blinked. "I've come to see the school and what yer teachin'."

"I think you have seen enough," Matthew said.

"I just come to watch. Ain't no harm in that. It's a free country," the man said, letting the words slither out between his teeth.

"You've seen," the miller responded coolly. "Now it's time to leave."

"I ain't leavin' till I have my say," the man said in a stronger voice.

Only a few seconds passed, yet it seemed an eternity. Elizabeth watched as the miller's arm grew tense, his hands clenched and then released, yet very much in the ready. "Say your piece and be gone," Sonnefelt said in loud, clear, even tones.

"This school," the smaller man said then, "is a filthy corruption of this building. This is s'posed to be God's house, ain't it? Here it is, filln' these youngsters head's with lies."

"Just because there are things you do not know, Leon, doesn't make them untrue," Matthew interrupted.

"It's all lies, I tell ya, and God'll judge ya all. Condemn ya all ta hell!"

Elizabeth could not contain herself any longer. "Mr. Simns, I will ask you to watch your tongue! There are children present."

"And a lady," Matthew reinforced.

"A lady…hell…that woman," he said as he pointed toward Elizabeth, "ain't no better than a whore."

"That's enough!" Matthew shouted. "You've had your say, now get out." The miller's face had grown red, his fists tightly clenched. Simns' hand moved a bit beneath his coat. Elizabeth feared what the man had hidden there.

"I didn't call the teacher a whore. I just said—"

"We all heard what you said!" the miller shouted. "Now get out!"

Elizabeth could see the tall man rising up on his toes ever so slightly, and she saw something new in the eyes of the other—fear. But as Elizabeth watched, she worried what Simns would do next. "You don't send your kids to school, and that's your choice. Nobody's trying to force you to. But the parents of these children have chosen to send them, and you're interfering with their education." Matthew's voice strong and clear.

"Lies, all lies. That's all that's teached here!" the man spat.

Then suddenly things changed. Simns smiled a strange smile. He slowly drew his hand from beneath his dirty brown coat, Elizabeth relieved to see it empty. As Simns turned the flap of his coat moved just enough for Elizabeth to catch a glimpse of a large hunting knife sheathed on his belt. The sight sent shivers down her spine. Leon Simns stood in the doorway and shouted without looking back, "God's justice will prevail, and damn any that stand in His way!" Leaving the door open, he was gone.

When Matthew strode to close the door, Elizabeth felt her legs grow weak. Drawing a breath, she wondered how long she had held the last one. She steadied herself by grasping Jenny's desk. The ordeal was over. Matthew turned, his face pale and smiled a weak smile. Elizabeth found she was unable to return it with a smile of her own. She turned at the sound of the sobs coming from the front of the classroom. Rushing forward Elizabeth wrapped her arms around Martha and Abigail and found herself surrounded by all her students. "Where is Homer?" she asked at last.

"He was to stay at the mill," Matthew said as he leaned against one of the rear desks. "I told Eldon to keep him there, even if he had to tie the boy down."

Elizabeth smiled with weak trembling lips. "I will be surprised if that was not necessary." Though her heart yet raced, she did her best to calm the class. "Mr. Sonnefelt, we are very grateful that you arrived so quickly."

"You can thank that young man you sent."

"Yes," she said as she gave the little girls another hug. "We must be certain we thank Homer. Yes, we must."

They accomplished little school work during the remaining part of that day or for several days that followed. Everyone seemed on edge, that is those students that came back to school. She knew the parents were concerned about Leon Simns' visit and had written notes, which the children took home that very day. Many families did not send their children to school for the remainder of the week. There were even two, the Monroes and Lears, that would not allow their children to return at all. This upset Elizabeth all the more, for it seemed Leon Simns was having his way. But what could she do? She had visited her former students on two occasions, hoping to convince worried parents, but in truth she could not guarantee the children's safety.

However those of the community might wish to place that responsibility on her shoulders, she was a teacher not the sheriff. Elizabeth grew angry that none would confront Mr. Simns directly, at least none that she knew. Well, that was not entirely true. Hadn't Matthew confronted the man, twice for that matter? And she would not be at all surprised if the miller had spoken to him on other occasions. Elizabeth had brought up the situation to Mr. Clark. Being so persistent in the problem, the man did his best to avoid her entirely, particularly at church, where she spoke to him each week.

Each time Clark gave the same response, the situation was being dealt with. Mr. Simns would be no problem. Elizabeth felt that Mr. Clark and a few of the others, considered the seriousness of the matter in the least exaggerated, perhaps even fabricated. They might have some grounds for that opinion, if the whole series of events had not been witnessed by their own children, not to mention Mr. Sonnefelt, whose name she mentioned continually. But Mr. Clark had very little respect for the miller, and Matthew's action following Thanksgiving had not improved his opinion one bit.

However, with the passing of time, Elizabeth began to put some stock in what the rancher had told her, for she had not seen Mr. Simns since that terrible morning. So as the weeks passed things became more normal, though Elizabeth always kept one eye on the door.

Chapter 32

Winter passed and spring came. The days grew longer and the snow left. Enduring the winter had been difficult on everyone, but the season's change filled Elizabeth with a new optimism. Spring had that effect on her and all she met. For a time she did not think of Jameson, well not every day in any case.

The lake had filled and more, as water flowed freely through the spillways. Elizabeth began to notice the scent of new life on the breeze. The orchards bloomed, and all around the spring wildflowers could be seen. Violets and small white flowers, she did not recognize, carpeted the woodlands. It was on one of those delightful warm sunny bright spring afternoons, she went with Lilly Atwood, Martha and Joe Donnellson as they walked home. For they were the closest neighbors to the Tomkins. Josie Tomkins and her brother John had missed most of a week's school, which was very unusual, and she intended to stop by for a visit.

They followed the path which the children walked each day along the creek bank, for to take the road would increase the distance to the farms by more than a mile. All the children that lived north of the lake and on the east side of the creek went by that route, a path well-traveled, going along orchards, fields yet bare, and woods. It was a delightful walk as the children chattered and skipped in the afternoon sun.

"Did you hear the news about Billy Clark?" Martha said as she looked up at her teacher.

"Mr. Clark," Elizabeth corrected.

"No, not old Mr. Clark, but Billy."

"She means William Junior, Miss Beck," Joe clarified.

Elizabeth wondered what news the children had heard. "I don't listen to gossip," she told them, "and you should not either."

Martha shook her head. "It's not gossip if it's true."

"How would you know it's true, Martha?"

Joe picked up a stick and heaved into the woods on their right. "Everyone's talking about Billy finally gettin' married."

Elizabeth stopped. She had heard nothing of young William's nuptials.

"Miss Beck, is something wrong?"

"No, nothing Lilly. I had not heard," she said trying to hold her voice steady. "And unless you heard it from one of the Clarks, it is still gossip." She strode forward.

"It's true all the same," Joe said as he picked up a small stone, rolled it over between his fingers, and then dropped it on the path.

Elizabeth drew a breath. Why did the news of young William's engagement trouble her? She had no interest in the young rancher. It was only natural that someone as eligible as he wed. For no logical reason, her mind flashed to that Saturday last May, how her life changed directions so completely. Yes, others would marry, but she, never. Elizabeth swallowed, realizing she had heard little of the children's chatter.

"Here's the path to our farm." Martha stood proud of the dirt strip that led between the trees on their right as if it were the gate to the Taj Mahal.

Elizabeth smiled. "Then home you go. We will see you Monday morning."

The Donnelsons said their goodbyes and dashed down the trail and out of sight.

"Well, Lilly, it is just the two of us."

Lilly smiled, took her teacher's hand, and led her on. After they had gone about three hundred yards, by Elizabeth's guess, Lilly pointed down a path. "That way is my house." The pathway, unlike the Donnelson's, began with a small gate in a pasture fence leading to a foot-worn trail across open fields to the farmstead in the distance. Smoke rose from the chimney of the white farmhouse, yet far off it seemed.

Elizabeth gave the child a hug.

"Maybe I should show you how to get to the Tomkin's house."

Elizabeth brushed a strand of hair out of Lilly's eyes. "I will find the way."

"You go on and take the second path. Don't take the first one, that one goes to Mary's."

"Mary Simns?"

Lilly nodded. "Remember take the second one."

Elizabeth smiled. "I will."

"I'll go with you, I don't want you to get lost."

"I won't. I'll just go on and take the second path." She was touched by her student's concern, but the instructions seemed simple enough. "You had best get home. I am certain your mother is waiting."

Lilly nodded and said good-bye, and Elizabeth found herself all alone.

A short time later, Elizabeth knocked on the back door of the Tomkins' home. The common use of the back door was another part of living in the country Elizabeth had learned. A pale, thin woman, standing slightly shorter than she, dressed in a faded green dress, cautiously opened the door.

Mrs. Florence Tomkins smiled when she recognized the teacher. "Miss Beck, come in, come in."

Elizabeth moved through the back porch and into the kitchen, with Florence chatting. "It's so good ya come. I ain't baked today, so I got nothing ta offer 'sep coffee."

"I'm sorry, I should have brought something." Alberta always had something warm and fresh. Elizabeth felt certain her friend would have insisted she bring fresh bread, or cookies, or whatever else had recently come from the oven, if she had known that Elizabeth intended to go visiting.

"No, no," Florence said as she pointed to a chair at the table. "You have no need. Your coming's treat enough." The woman smiled as she leaned upon the back of a chair across the table from Elizabeth.

She watched as the farm wife drew a breath. "You're not well. Please sit down."

Florence waved the comment aside. "True I been under the weather, but I be on the mend." She took a deep breath. "Thank goodness for John. That boy's worked so hard, his pa been gone and all."

Elizabeth's eyes opened wider. "Mr. Tomkins is gone?"

"Went to MacBain. You know, a couple counties away." The woman pointed over her left shoulder. "Left Monday." Florence settled into the chair and looked toward the window. "S'posed to be back any day." The woman returned her eyes to Elizabeth. "You come about the young'ns."

Elizabeth nodded.

"I weren't feelin' so good, so Johnny, he done the chores. Sorry but it takes all his time. It's my fault."

"Your fault?"

Florence nodded. "Bein' too weak to do the work I ought."

"But Mrs. Tomkins, you're sick."

The woman shook her head. "Don't catch the fever often. Most times it slows me a mite, but this time I got to where I couldn't get up from my bed." The woman took a deep breath. "Like I said, my Johnny he done good, but he weren't gona let Josie go ta school by her lonesome."

"I can understand that, especially with this Mr. Simns business."

"The Simns are neighbors, Miss Beck. I cain't say nothing bad about them folks."

Elizabeth bit her lip.

"People depend on their neighbors, you cun understand that."

Elizabeth nodded.

"But Leon and his misses, they ain't like others, that they ain't." Florence drew another breath and rose. "Got coffee on, I promised ya a cup." Florence pushed hard on the table trying to get to her feet.

"Allow me."

But the farm wife drew her brows. "My coffee, my kitchen. You just sit a mite." Once upright Florence moved toward the stove, "You come a visitin'," she smiled back at Elizabeth, "don't get much company." She stood at the stove a moment. Taking two cups from the cupboard setting them clumsily before Elizabeth, Florence returned to the stove. The pot rattled as she grasped the handle, it shook in her hand. As soon as she had poured the pot was returned with a clang to the stove top.

Josie peeked in the doorway. "It is you, Miss Beck."

Elizabeth stretched out an arm and the young child ran to her embrace. "I've missed you."

"I wanted to go, really I did, but John said I couldn't."

"He is worried for you."

"I'm not a baby you know. I wouldn't get lost."

Elizabeth smiled. "Of course not. But John is responsible for you and your mother while you father is away."

"Daddy went to see the banker."

Elizabeth looked over toward Florence.

"It's true. Been having a hard time." The farm wife slid the non-chipped cup closer to Elizabeth. "Run, child. Me and Miss Beck, we're a visitin'"

"Yes, mama." The girl moved with sagging shoulders to the back door.

"Josie," Elizabeth called out. "I will stop to say good bye before I leave."

The child glanced over her shoulder, smiled, and vanished.

"She's a smart, sweet child. You should be proud."

"I am, truly I am," Florence drew a breath. The woman glanced toward the door. "Life's hard enough, no need a burdenin' youngin's. The last couple years been lean, leaner than usual." She looked down to her cup. "But springs comin'. Though I 'spect Claud would hope we get another snow or two before it dries off proper." Once again Elizabeth reached across the table and touched Florence's hands. "Been powerful dry."

"But water is so near."

"It's not here, Miss Beck." Florence's eyes glistened.

"Surely there can be away to bring some water."

"Them's the things dreams are made of." Florence glanced toward the window. "Sometimes I wonder if this country were meant to be farmed. They say rain follows the plow, but sometimes I wonder." She drew a breath as she turned to face Elizabeth. "Mr. Clark made an offer on the place."

"Surely you won't sell?"

"If Claud cain't get the bankers to see things his way, we got no choice." A tear rolled down the woman's cheek.

Elizabeth shared in the sadness. How she forgot. Being in the valley's center where everything fed by the lake was green and lush, but how different things were here on the fringe. Elizabeth found herself unable to speak as they sat in silence.

Voices drifted in, the sounds of shouting. "Florence, I'm home, woman."

The farm wife jumped to her feet, nearly toppling with the effort. "Claud, my Claud." Her face lit up. She abandoned Elizabeth without a word and moved unsteadily out the back. The teacher followed, fearful that she would have to pick Florence off the floor, but the woman surprised her, gathering new strength with each step and she soon stood wrapped in her husband's arms.

"We got it, Florence. The bank's gonna give us another chance."

"Praise the Lord!"

He held her tight. "Yes, praise the Lord." He pushed her back just a bit. "You been sick, woman?"

"Been, but I ain't no more," she said as happy tears flowed down her cheeks. "You be home, Claud." she buried her face in his chest. John and Josie ran about the couple, dancing at their father's return.

Elizabeth turned and moved away. She would not intrude.

"Claud," she heard. "Miss Beck come for a visit. Weren't that nice of her?"

The farmer strode her way with hand outstretched. "You'll stay for supper?"

"You and your wife are so kind, but I must be going."

He tilted his head. "You sure? You'd be more than welcome."

Elizabeth smiled. "Thank you, but I have a long walk."

"Take you back myself."

"No, you have just come home, Mr. Tomkins. Stay, share the good news with your family. It is such a fine day, I will enjoy the walk." She crouched down and Josie ran into her arms again. "Soon you will be back at school."

"Tomorrow."

"No, tomorrow is Saturday."

"I forgot," blushing, the child looked downward.

Elizabeth, with a finger beneath her chin, raised Josie's face and gazed into the child's clear blue eyes. "But Monday I hope you will come."

"She'll be there, Miss Beck, yes she will." Color had returned to Florence's face.

Elizabeth smiled. The despair of only moments ago had been set aside, at least for the time being and that was enough. She drew a deep breath and knew soon two of her special students would return to their studies.

CHAPTER 33

WHEN THE YOUNG TEACHER BEGAN THE JOURNEY HOME, SHE FELT light on her feet, knowing Florence would soon be well. Even here in the valley, life could be hard. Yet the birds sang all around her, and the sun shone in a clear blue sky. It was spring—life was good. The path rounded a bend, and Elizabeth found herself between the rapidly flowing creek and the woods. She studied the forest floor as she walked, engrossed with the ground, covered with its thick green and sprinkled with white and purple. Closing her eyes, she drew in the earthy scent of the leaves that carpeted the forest floor, blended with the delicate aroma of the thousands of violets that surrounded. A snapping twig broke into her thoughts of spring's beauty. Stepping out of the wood, a man stood very near. She gasped at the sight of Leon Simns leering at her from the shadows, with a wild look in his eyes and a smirk on his lips.

Elizabeth would have walked right past the man in his dirty red flannel shirt and tattered coverall, except for his smile. The strange expression on his face, with lips that drew upward more on his right than the left, caused her to stop. She saw something most peculiar in that smile, something very wrong and felt afraid—very afraid. Elizabeth turned and ran as she had never done before. He quickly caught her, with a sudden tug on her dress that sent her reeling. Two stumbling steps later she felt his arms wrap about her waist and his hot breath on the back of her neck.

She twisted to face him. "Let me go," she screamed.

Shaking his head slightly, his unblinking eyes terrified her. "I give 'nough warning. You had your chances, but no, you stayed."

She struggled against his grip, feeling his fingers tighten on her wrists. "Let me go," she pleaded.

"Yesterday maybe, but not today. This ends now. I'll not have anyone corrupting the valley. You come here to destroy the good that we have. You brung the evil we left behind." He sneered.

Elizabeth sensed his grip weaken on her right arm. With a quick jerk she pulled that hand free. She flailed at him, trying to escape the man. As she lurched and swung at the man, scratching his cheek, she felt her left hand slide. Just a bit more. Just a bit more, she hoped. But a hard hand across her face broke the moment.

"You're a feisty one, I'll give you that," Simns chuckled through his dark stained teeth "But it ain't gonna do ya no good. Not today."

He pulled her from the path, dragging her into the wood. Elizabeth screamed. Simns struck her; he struck her hard, and she screamed again.

"Ain't nobody gonna hear ya…nobody."

Perhaps things happened fast, but it seemed to her everything moved slowly. She struggled with all her strength. Elizabeth scratched, she bit, and the man hit her again and again. Simns tore at her clothing, ripping her dress, and there was nothing she could do. She felt the coarse skin of his filthy hands that pawed at her as she breathed the stench of his breath. Elizabeth turned away unable to look into the stubble covered dirty man's face. His head covered with matted dark hair that clung to his forehead. He was all over her. And suddenly he wasn't. Simns wasn't over her. Wasn't holding her down. Wasn't pulling her dress to shreds. Someone else had come. Someone had grabbed that vile man and tossed him aside—a tall man—a strong man.

Matthew Sonnefelt stood between her and Simns. He didn't look her direction, his eyes focused on the other.

"Run, Elizabeth, run and don't look back," he ordered. "Go to the Donnellson's."

Elizabeth jumped to her feet in an instant, but after running only a few steps she stopped and turned.

She was not the only one that found their feet beneath them, for Simns stood defiantly facing the miller with rage in his eyes, and a large knife in his hand. The knife she had seen beneath his coat that cold winter day. He came at Matthew. The miller with a quick move grabbed the man and held him, but Simns squirmed and broke free. Matthew glanced her way and saw her standing there. That terrible moment when he shouted. "Go…go…you must go…" That terrible moment when he did not see. That instant Leon Simns lunged for him.

It seemed as if time itself nearly stopped. Elizabeth willed Matthew to be fast enough, but he was not. Simns drove the blade deep into the miller's chest. Elizabeth screamed with all her might. Matthew, brave strong Matthew, pushed the man aside, and yet the battle continued. Again the man slashed, this time striking Matthew's leg. Again Elizabeth screamed, yet heard nothing, knew nothing, except the pain visible on Matthew's face.

The two men rolled about on the ground, so intertwined it was difficult for Elizabeth to tell which parts belonged to which man. The knife swung about, its task incomplete, swept passed Matthew's ear. Again they tumbled, Matthew on top an instant, then Simns. Over and over the awful contest continued and Elizabeth felt powerless, frozen, unable to look away.

Suddenly she saw the knife had somehow found its way to the miller's hand. How Matthew had taken it away from Simns, she had no idea. But no matter how surprised Elizabeth might have been, Simns's eyes flew open out of shock and fear. The smaller man rolled quickly aside, broke free, and dashed headlong into the woods. It was over.

For an instant Elizabeth just stood there, looking down at Matthew bleeding before her. She rushed to him, pleading forgiveness, crying as she knelt beside her wounded friend. Elizabeth tore her dress into strips. Using Leon's knife, she cut away Matthew's legging and bound the makeshift bandage. Next she tore open the shirt and was horrified at the sight. Elizabeth placed a wad of cloth torn from her garment over the wound in his chest.

"Matthew," she said as she moved his hand over the rag, "hold this. Can you hold this?"

The man blinked, his mouth moving but said nothing.

"I'm going for help. Just hold on."

He coughed, his head swayed as she pressed his hand down upon the fabric now dyed red with his blood. Matthew nodded, drew a raspy breath, his glassy eyes closed and opened again. His gaze seemed far away, disconnected, but his hand remained firm. He reached for her with his free hand, and Elizabeeth grasped it with both of hers. Stunned that the strength and warmth she had always found there was missing.

Releasing his hand she turn and left him.

Part 5
The Promise

CHAPTER 34

ELIZABETH RAN. OH, HOW SHE RAN. FEAR DROVE HER. NOT FEAR for her own safety but fear for Matthew. As she raced on, it became hard to clear her head, to remove what she had witnessed. Elizabeth knew she must stay focused on getting help and quickly. A short distance down the path she turned the direction Martha and her brother took what seemed a lifetime ago. She found a gap in the fence wide enough for her to pass but not large enough for cattle. Onward she sprinted, gasping for air, her legs throbbed. Times she nearly tumbled forward, her feet unable to keep up the pace yet she pressed on.

How far she ran she did not know, but each step a reminder of how far away Matthew was from the help he needed. Time was what mattered, and with each minute her fear grew. When at last she reached the farmstead a dog barked, but she did not slow. Elizabeth burst into the house using what little breath she had left shouted for help. Mrs. Donnellson's eye's wide open at the sight of the teacher.

"Good Lord!" the woman said as she rushed to Elizabeth.

Elizabeth panted, trying to gather enough air to explain the need for someone to help Matthew. Young Joe Donnellson left in a flash. In moments the whole kitchen seemed filled. Questions were asked. Elizabeth tried to be coherent. She was not certain she was. A door. Why were they taking off a door? Then the men, Mr. Jacob Donnellson, his two oldest sons, and his hired man, left. Elizabeth found herself sitting now in one of the kitchen chairs at the table…crying. Martha stood in the corner with horror in her eyes.

"Now, now, missy," Teresa Donnellson said, "the men will soon have him here. It's gonna' be alright."

Elizabeth looked up into the caring face of the farmer's wife while she continued to sob.

"But let's get you cleaned up a bit," the farm wife continued.

Elizabeth stared at her hands, covered with blood. Her clothes in rags. She hadn't given it a single thought to herself. Teresa set Martha to pumping, while she helped the teacher to her feet. How weak she felt. Her legs like rubber. As Elizabeth stood unsteadily, her thoughts focused on a man, a tall man, a brave man, lying in the woods, dying there because she had failed him. If only she had done what he had asked? If she had run, then he would not be lying as he was—in his own blood. But no, she had not gone. She stayed, and now he might die because of her.

It took time and some scrubbing to clean the blood that had dried. It took time and patience to untangle and remove what remained of her dress. Teresa brought a dress, certainly one of her own. It appeared the best dress the farm woman owned. In the hazy fog of Elizabeth's mind she could not accept, even in loan, the garment. She protested, but the woman was resolute, and the teacher had learned to accept the generosity of these people that had so little, yet would gladly share all they had.

They waited in the kitchen. Elizabeth declined the coffee and food Teresa offered. She sat there in a fog. The wait seemed an eternity. She sat there unable to take her eyes off the door.

Elizabeth rose to her feet. "I should have gone with them. They will never find him."

"Now don't you fear none, they'll find him sure. You told them plenty, my boys got tracks all over them woods, know 'em better than the skin on their hands. Besides, look at you, you be in no shape to go a traipsin' about." Teresa glanced toward the door. "I 'spect they be stompin' in any time now."

In her muddled mind Elizabeth heard the dog bark. It seemed a neighbor's dog, far, far away. She blinked and the sound became clearer—nearer. The men came in, Matthew tied with blankets to the door they carried. They strode right past her as she stood in the kitchen. Matthew looked so pale.

"They use the closet door, it's narrower." Teresa explained. "Done it before, when Bart, got rolled by a bull years ago." She drew a breath. "Bart was busted up pretty bad."

Elizabeth looked toward the woman and felt so afraid. Teresa, her eyes dark, sharp, and stern, said, "Bart pulled through." And added with a weak smile, "The miller's a strong man, missy."

Yes, Matthew was a strong man. He had shown strength over and over again. She had seen him handle those large heavy sacks, unload crates, and all manner of things. Yes, he was strong. But Matthew had strength in other ways too. He was strong in ways she hadn't seen at first. Strong in character, strong in his commitments, and most of all strong in friendship. A person someone could always count upon.

Joe remained in the room with them. "Pa says it's bad…real bad," the boy said softly.

Elizabeth collapsed to the floor, the fog quickly moving in, sights and sound filled her head, things happening around her, but also thoughts of that struggle, her mind filled with Matthew and Simns there in the woods. Simns with his knife, the look on the man's face as he lunged. Elizabeth once more saw the knife in Matthew's shaking hand. Simns' face changed, there was surprise, but there was also fear.

There lying on the Donnellson's floor she scarcely noticed the light touch on her cheek, or the gentle hands cradleing her head. Just as the fog completely faded to black she heard Teresa's voice near. "Joey you'd best find the preacher." And Elizabeth was gone—gone to the darkness—lost to the fear.

Chapter 35

How long had it been? Elizabeth had no idea. The day had ended, the night did its best to surround her. She lay in a bed, whose, she did not know. A lamp burned on a table across the room. It seemed far away. A dream. It surely was a very bad dream but a dream none the less. Then as she stirred Elizabeth heard a voice nearby. "You gave us quite a fright, missy."

"Where am I?" she asked.

"Don't fret none, missy, you're safe and sound."

"And Matthew?"

The room grew silent for a moment. "He's still with us, Pastor Smith is sittin' with him." Things grew quiet as Elizabeth waited. At last Teresa spoke, spoke solemnly in the dark. "If prayers can work, and I think they can, and if the good Lord is listnin', and I know he is—then that man has a chance. But that's all it is missy, a chance."

"It's all my fault."

"It ain't nothing of the kind!"

"But you don't understand. It's because of me he's dying." Elizabeth trying her best to keep from sobbing.

Sharp words came in the dark. "No, missy it ain't your doin'."

"He told me to run and I didn't. He saw me. I was standing there. He looked away and…and…"

Elizabeth sat up in the bed, filled with the guilt she felt. Teresa slid beside her, wrapping her arm around the young teacher, holding her, rocking her. "Now, now, don't you go blamin' yourself. Sometimes things just happen. That Leon Simns, he's a mean one, and he's the one to blame. The whole valley's out lookin' for the man. I 'spect they'll find him."

"What will they do?" she asked.

"I 'spect that depends on whether the good Lord takes our miller or not," Teresa said with a touch of anger in her voice.

Finally Elizabeth whispered. "Matthew didn't deserve what happened."

"I guess no decent body does, missy. And Matthew is as decent as any I've met," came Teresa's soft voice. "He's rest'n'. The bleedin's stopped…and like I said people are pray'n for him. Not just Pastor Smith but everybody. As long as there's life, missy, there's hope."

"Can I see him?"

"It's the middle of the night, missy. He's sleep'n' there's nothin' to see. You need your rest too. Wait till morning."

"Please."

Finally Teresa relented. Helping Elizabeth they went downstairs as quietly as they could. The door was open just a bit. "Pastor," Teresa called softly. Ben met them at the door. "Missy here would like to see him. I told her he was sleep'n'…but…"

In the light from the lamp Teresa held, Elizabeth could see the tired face of her friend. Ben smiled. "Of course," he said as he led her into the room, which was illuminated by a single candle that burned on the dresser. In the dimness Elizabeth moved to the bedside.

Down on her knees, Elizabeth felt the warm touch of Ben's hand upon her shoulder. Elizabeth heard Matthew's labored breathing, the sounds of life. She touched him. Cold he seemed, too cold. It took everything she had to steady the tremble in her voice. "Is there a chance…a real chance?" she asked.

"Yes, Elizabeth…there is a chance."

Elizabeth wanted to know more. To know for certain that the man that had saved her would live. But, there in the dark, she understood no one could make that kind of promise. For only God knew for certain whether Matthew Sonnefelt would live or die. So as she lay her hand on the cold fingers of the miller, as she kneeled there in the dark with Pastor Smith's hand on her shoulder, she prayed. Elizabeth prayed that God would save a tall man, a very decent man, a brave man. And she prayed that the God and master of the universe would forgive her.

CHAPTER 36

SOFT WORDS CAME TO HER, SO SOFT THAT SHE ALONE HEARD Ben's gentle voice say, "You've come to love him, our miller." It was not a question. She looked up over her shoulder to the face of the man that had been more than her pastor. The cowboy preacher was smiling, and she realized he was right.

She had built a wall around her heart. Each day she had added to its fortifications. But there in the dark, hearing the words, Elizabeth knew it was true. And there, kneeling beside a bed as she gently stroked the cold hands of Matthew, that fact came to her. Yes, she loved the man. She didn't want to. She had done all she could not to—but she did.

Elizabeth looked at the man she feared would die. Why had he come? How did he know to come? Those questions filled her mind. Elizabeth swallowed as she watched him, a bitter taste filled her mouth. She didn't know what she should do, what she could do, to save him. Matthew had saved her.

How angry she was at him that first night. It seemed so long ago, though only a few months had passed. But now she realized something she had not seen, not then, not until this very moment. Slowly Elizabeth rose to her feet. Slowly she left the bedside. Ben followed her to the door. "How long have you known?"

Ben smiled. "For a time."

"But…?"

He put his arms around her and held her with his strong arms. "Really, it's alright to love. It's part of God's plan."

"But…?" she asked again.

"Elizabeth,it will be alright."

"You know?"

He drew a breath, "Don't be angry with Leah, she told me."

She was not angry, in truth she felt relieved. "Then you know it can never be," Elizabeth said softly into his shoulder.

"You cannot seal yourself off from love. Oh, you can try, but in the end, in the very end, love will break down any walls you have built to keep it out."

"But Matthew, he deserves better."

Ben pushed her away just far enough to look her into the eyes. "Don't you think that it's up to Matthew to decide?"

She looked up at him through damp eyes.

"He loves you, you know?" Ben said calmly.

"How? When? Why?"

Ben chuckled. "I will let him tell you those things."

"But he's…he's…"

"Yes," the pastor interrupted. "He's badly injured. But perhaps God has plans for him yet. Now you must rest. You have been through an ordeal of your own."

Ben walked her upstairs to her room. There at the door he bid her goodnight. She could wisdom in his eyes. A wisdom she had seen before. Elizabeth once more thanked him, and in that room, in the bed the kind farmers had provided, she thought as she stared into the darkness. She thought about times past, about bitter memories, and their pain. She thought about why she had come. She had been running from that pain. She thought about how that pain had found her. She had not left it behind. She thought about the anger she had felt. How she had allowed that anger to lash out at Matthew. And she thought about Matthew Sonnefelt, a tall man, a strong man, a brave man—the man she loved. There in the dark she prayed like she had never prayed before, prayed as tears flowed, prayed for a man downstairs. And though she would have thought it impossible, at last sleep found her, a deep sleep, a sleep filled with pleasant dreams, a sleep that separated her, for a time, from the terrors she had faced and was facing.

When she awoke it was another a beautiful spring day. School was closed indefinitely, or until she could return. Though Elizabeth protested, Ben insisted she take at least a few days off.

"You need some time to get back on your feet," he explained. She at last succumbed to his advice. There had been no change with Matthew. Ben maintained it was not a bad sign. He left the Donnellson's once Elizabeth had eaten. She would sit the vigil for a time, and he would go home to his family. "I'll be back later. I know I leave my friend in the best of hands." He smiled and walked off. *Misty creek was indeed fortunate*, she thought, *to have that man.*

That was how those first days went. Elizabeth sat at Matthew's bedside, rarely leaving even for short moments. The pastor arrived near the end of each day, and sat up with his friend most of the night. Ben brought news from the valley each day. He told how every man had searched for Simns.

"I told them that God would not allow vigilante justice. He's to be captured alive, if possible and taken to Thimble or Baxter for trial. There'll be no lynching in this valley."

The thought caused Elizabeth to tremble. "Has anyone seen the man?"

"Not yet, Eldon and Angst have kept the Simns place on watch, haven't seen hide or hare of the man.

"Who's running the mill?"

Ben looked down. "No one. Likely it will not start up again until—"

"Until Matthew's back in charge."

The pastor nodded.

They had remained silent a moment. Ben looked toward her with a twinkle in his eyes. "Why, even Mr. Clark and his men have joined the search."

Elizabeth opened her eyes wide. "Mr. Clark?"

"Yes, Mr. William Clark."

"But that man has no love for Matthew." She wondered if the rancher would give Simns a reward for the attack.

Ben smiled. "No, but Matthew wasn't the only one attacked, and he is the—"

"President of the school board." Elizabeth shook her head. She tried to imagine William Clark riding here and there in his fine suit in search for Leon. She couldn't quite picture it, or young William's black stallion bounding across the prairie in some direction the young man had not really intended.

"I expect they will find him." Ben's words shook her from her thoughts.

But as the days passed, no word of Leon Simns came. Angst and Eldon reported that they had only seen Mrs. Simns and the children, but life on the farm just went on. Folks began to think he had gone – though none knew where. The not knowing hung like a dark cloud over everyone in the valley.

The days passed slowly. The Donnellsons were such kind caring people. Teresa, dear Teresa, watched when she could. That with minding her own family, cooking and cleaning, it was more than Elizabeth could expect.

Martha and Joe would come in and spend time in Matthew's room as well. Elizabeth did so enjoy the time the young Donnellsons spent with her. Oh, they tried to be quiet, but they were young, so full of life, and they brought that life with them. It reminded her, of a need the community had. A need she had come to fill. A need she felt now neglected. Elizabeth had time to think of such things, of the school, of her place in it, of the children's future, and how she tried to help them achieve it.

Then while she sat alone, in the room watching, waiting, hoping, on the third day following the attack, Elizabeth Beck driven by love and fear prayed like she had never prayed before.

Why Lord, why? Why is Matthew dying? Why do you take any man I love away from me? Why? When you tore Jameson out of my life I came to this place. Finding a new love was the last thing I had on my mind, but… she drew a gasping breath. *He's a good man, Lord,* she closed her eyes tighter. *He doesn't deserve to die. It's all my fault.*

Ben says that you love us…that we are your children, but all my life I have been taught that you are a vengeful God, dealing your justice on sinners. Elizabeth squeezed her hands together tightly. *What have I done?* She drew a breath releasing it slowly, opening her eyes. *Over the years a chasm has grown between us. I have pushed you to the fringes because I blamed You for all my pain and disappointments. Forgive me Lord, but please do not take Matthew, this valley needs him. I would do anything, if only…if only You would bring him back to us…all of us.*

She drew a breath and wondered what she could do. She wondered how high a price she would willingly pay. Elizabeth thought about love, real love, selfless love, about love's price. But what sacrifice would be enough? *What can I do, Lord?* She drew a ragged breath. What price would she pay? Elizabeth stood from the chair and moved to the window. She pushed the curtain aside, filling her lungs with the freshness of the spring air while tears began to flow. *Save him Lord, she pleaded, save Matthew and I…* But what? Her mind went to Jameson, about how she had felt about him, how she intended to tie her life to his, how content she would have been as Jameson's wife. But the reason the man had left her standing, well, the reason hadn't changed. It was just the way things were—just life. No, it wasn't fair, and she knew that Matthew deserved more than she had to give. Because she loved him so much, she would not to saddle Matthew with that unfairness. Matthew deserved to live. And living he deserved to be happy, and she knew the price she would pay.

I will never marry. I promise.

Late morning when Teresa had forced her to leave the bedside, Elizabeth moved onto the back step. Above the sun shone in a bright blue cloudless sky, the day seemed full of promise. New life seemed to be bursting out everywhere she looked. The grass was green on the hills and she could see fields where the land had been opened for the spring planting. The sounds of Joe and Martha at play blended with the low bellow of Donnelson's cow. Surely Dolly was impatiently waiting for her feed. Elizabeth drew a breath as she thought about life all around. She felt grateful that young William Clark had been wrong. He had told her that day how the Donnellsons would be leaving. Now six months later, she saw no indications that it was the case. Even here at the fringe of the valley life seemed vibrant.

Joe came to her bouncing with excitement. "Did you know," the boy said, "that we are getting water this summer?"

"Water?" she asked.

Martha joined them. "Joey means the canal."

"Yeah, we're getting water, from the lake." Joe's voice was strong and clear.

Elizabeth considered Mr. Clark's comments about farmers, and she remembered how he had looked at Matthew. It was about water. She knew that. But if more water was to be directed to the farmers, then less would pass through to the rancher. She understood that this turn of events would not please the big man, nor his son.

As she stood with the young Donnellsons at her side, Elizabeth heard a shout from the house. She turned as fear welled up deep in her heart. "Missy! Missy!" came Teresa's voice. "Where are you?"

CHAPTER 37

ELIZABETH FEARED THE WORST.

"He's awake! Matthew's awake!"

Elizabeth would not remember how she got there. The steps she took. The doors she passed, but she found herself at his bedside. Matthew seemed agitated, upset, calling out. "Beth, Beth, where are you?"

No one called her Beth, no one but her father. It was the name he always called her. Others called her Elizabeth, Miss Beck, or like Alberta, Becky. She drew the chair close to him, reached out and took hold of his hand as it flailed about. "I'm here Matthew. I'm here."

At the sound of Elizabeth's voice he calmed. The tall man's voice seemed so weak, his words so far away, and though she touched his lips biding him save his strength, he spoke.

"Are you alright? Simns didn't hurt you did he?" He coughed a bit, gasping for his breath.

"No, Matthew, he did not hurt me. I'm fine." She let the words out carefully as she held back the tears welling in her eyes.

"Beth, I'm so sorry," he said as he turned to face her. His brown eyes darted about as if searching for something.

Matthew's eyes focused on her left cheek. "He did hurt you."

Elizabeth hadn't thought about the marks left by Simn's blows. She looked into his eyes. "That mark is all he did, it will be gone soon. It is nothing…really. You have no need to be sorry," she said as the tears began to flow. "I've done this to you. It's all my fault," she whispered. "Can you forgive me?"

Even in the dim light she could see the look of confusion on the man's face. "Your fault?" he asked, his voice seemed stronger.

"Yes," she cried. "If I had only gone like you asked, then—"

Elizabeth felt his hand clasp hers. Even now there was strength in that hand. A smile formed upon his pallid face. "No," he said calmly. "None of this is your fault."

Elizabeth bent her head downward as she wept. "Please forgive me."

"Always, Beth, always."

She looked at him, into the face of the tall man, and she believed him, really believed him. Elizabeth held his hand, that strong hand that had reached her in the darkness. It felt good to hold; it had a bit of warmth. The man was alive. They shared no other words, and he drifted once more to sleep, a restful sleep. Yes, things were going to get better, and Elizabeth would not forget the promise she had made.

In the evening Ben returned, delighted by the news. Matthew had awoken the second time some hours before. He had even taken a bit of the soup Teresa had made for him. Elizabeth met the pastor in the hall, the first time she had left the bedside since the morning's miracle. "Ben," she said carefully. "I need a promise from you."

He turned his head slightly. With a furrowed brow, he eyed her with concern.

"You are not to tell Matthew how I feel."

"That you love him?" Ben asked.

"Yes."

He led her outside where they could speak privately. "May I ask why?"

Elizabeth looked away. The sun hung, as an orange ball, low over the western horizon. Far off she could hear the song of a robin singing the day's end. She felt her heart break. "Please," she said. "I have my reasons."

"And you won't tell him?" Ben asked.

She shook her head.

"And you won't tell me why?"

Again she shook her head firmly, looking away, afraid to match eyes with her friend.

"This is wrong Elizabeth, very wrong."

"Please," she begged.

"It goes against my better judgment," he said calmly, "but I will respect your wishes."

She saw a stern look on his face, but his hard eyes and stiff lips melted as she looked directly at her very special friend. "Thank you, Ben."

"And what if he guesses? What, Elizabeth, if he figures it out on his own?"

"He mustn't!" The words came out sharp as she tapped into the strength of her decision. "He just mustn't!"

Ben shook his head. "I'll go in and see him now. Come when you are ready." He left her there standing in a lot beside the barn, alone. Elizabeth fell on her knees, and she prayed. She thanked God that He had brought back Matthew. Yes, there was yet risk ahead, but she was now confident God would see him through. And she told her God that she would be true to her promise. The promise she had made. A promise she would never forget.

She went for a walk as the day came to its end. It was full dark when Ben found her returning to the porch. His face showed concern; she was not certain who had troubled him now. "You haven't eaten since breakfast, not one bite. Don't lie, Miss Beck, Teresa has told me."

She wouldn't deny it.

"This course you have chosen is wrong," he said sternly. "I don't know why you have chosen it, but it's wrong."

Elizabeth spoke, her words came flat with no emotion. "But it is the path I have chosen. You must accept that I feel it is best."

"And what about Matthew?"

"It is for Matthew."

"I can't believe that. I just can't."

"But it is. Truly it is."

The hard look in the man's eyes softened. Ben drew a deep breath and spoke softly, more gently. "I care about you and Matthew," he said, "and I have watched the two of you. If ever there were two people meant for each other—"

Elizabeth put a finger to his mouth, stopping words she knew he was about to say. Words she did not want to hear. "When Matthew is well, I am leaving."

"Leaving!" The tone of his words rising, shock clearly in his voice. "Leaving, Elizabeth? You must reconsider. What about Matthew? What about the children?"

"They have had other teachers."

"What about Leah and the Baughmans?"

Strange she had not thought about Leah, dear Leah. For a moment she paused. "Leah will understand."

Elizabeth turned and began to walk away from her pastor. "Maybe she will. God knows I don't. But Matthew, will he understand?"

"Someday, Ben. Someday I hope he will understand."

"You won't give him a chance, a real chance. You'll walk away, and not give him a chance."

How she managed to hold back her tears, she did not know, as she said coldly, "It's for the best. He deserves to be happy."

"And you?" the pastor asked, his strong voice booming.

She did not answer but walked down the steps and into the darkness. Elizabeth felt the need to be alone. Firm in her convictions. No, this was not time for tears. But Elizabeth heard footsteps coming up behind her. She did not turn. And a voice, a booming voice, a voice she knew, came out of the night. "Before you decide what's best for that man, maybe you should know his story."

Elizabeth froze; the words had struck her, struck her hard. She turned.

"I only know bits and pieces, but before you just walk away, maybe you should consider just who that man in there is, and where he's come from, and everything in between." Ben's words came with an edge.

She didn't answer.

"That man has been on his own since he was ten," Ben said softly. "Don't just walk away Elizabeth, please just don't walk away. He needs you and more, you need him."

They faced each other in the dark. Elizabeth didn't know what to say, how to react, what to feel. She saw the silhouette of the cowboy preacher and wondered why she had come to this place—why? What purpose? What reason?

"Matthew needs you," came a soft voice, a caring voice, Ben's voice.

Her mind seemed to explode with thousands of thoughts. Thoughts of how the walls around her heart had been breached and the love she had locked there flowed toward Matthew. Thoughts of how her damaged body made her worthless. Thoughts of a promise made in the dark.

"He needs more than I can give," she blurted.

He moved forward with open arms as if he would gather her in as a child frightened by a storm, a storm she faced. But Elizabeth drew back.

"He deserves better…much better," she said in even tones.

Ben stood there scarcely an arm's reach away, but he just stood there, and she cried. "I promised. Don't you understand I made a promise?"

"To whom?"

"To God! I made a promise."

"You promised God you would leave?" the pastor asked softly.

"No!" she shouted. "I promised God I would never marry—never—if only He would let Matthew live."

She looked at him through tear blurred eyes. Ben's head bend as he looked downward. Elizabeth spoke scarecly more than a whisper. "I know what I must do."

He raised his head and there in the dark he said calmly, softly, "God does not hold you to that promise, a promise you made out of desperation and fear."

"But I do!"

Ben, the man that had met her at the station, her first friend in this place, did not speak for a moment. Then he at last said, "Promise me, we will speak of this again. Not now, but soon."

"It will do no good."

"Promise me."

She took a deep breath and calmly spoke the words he wished to hear. "I promise."

"Then come," he said. "Let's go back to the house."

"I need to be alone, Benjamin."

He nodded and turned, leaving her there in the dark—alone. And Elizabeth felt certain of the course she must take. There beneath the night sky, a sky filled with the brilliance of stars, stars she thought were only visible on the prairie—a sky filled with diamonds. To her left she saw a shooting star, a bright light that streaked across the dark sky. Elizabeth would have thought the meteor a sign that she had made the right choice, but there in the dark alone, it seemed to open more questions than provide answers.

Elizabeth stood there for a long time. She lingered until the early spring air grew cold, until the night's dampness settled upon the grass and her as well. Then chilled, she heard the voice of Teresa call. Elizabeth answered and returned to the house.

Chapter 38

Later, in the dark of the room she had been given, as she lay staring at the ceiling, Elizabeth could not sleep. She would have thought the relief brought by Matthew's improvement would have made sleep come easily. But too many things swirled in her mind, of things said and things left unsaid, of things done and things that had not, of a prayer and a promise. And mixed in with all these thoughts was another. The thought of a boy, only ten. How many classes had she taught had contained ten year olds? *None,* she thought, *could have survived on their own—none.* What was the cause? What had happened? There were so many possibilities, none that seemed pleasant.

Elizabeth rose from that bed and sat in a chair near the window. She gazed out into the darkness. A crescent moon hung yet low on the horizon. She sat there for hours and found no answers. When at last she felt certain sleep would come, she crawled quietly back to the bed, but sleep did not come, not that night. The first light of the new day found her with a mind filled to bursting. She rose, dressed, and made her way to the kitchen. Teresa was busy, the woman was always busy. The farm wife took one look at her and offered her a cup of coffee.

As Elizabeth sat there sipping, she made conversation, even though her mind raced on other things. They talked about the weather, it might rain, about the children, about the school. Ben heard them, or perhaps smelled the coffee, for he joined them. He informed them that the patient had slept quietly through the night. Matthew was most assuredly on the mend. Those words should have given Elizabeth greater comfort. She just did not understand how she felt. Oh, she was glad the miller seemed better, part of her was giddy, and yet another part felt so confused. It was clear Ben saw it on her face as he glanced her way repeatedly.

"The swelling on your face has gone down a great deal," he said at last.

Elizabeth had not thought about herself, about the bruises or the swelling where Simns had struck her. At his words, she raised a hand and gently touched the tender areas of her cheek. It stung at the touch but not nearly as severely as before. Elizabeth tried a weak smile.

"You think, Miss Beck," the pastor said over his coffee, "you might soon open the school."

Taking but a second, she said, "Yes, I think it would be a good idea."

The comment seemed to delight Mrs. Donnellson. "Yes missy, that would be good, good for the children and good for you."

"But I want to help take care of Mr. Sonnefelt."

"Of course, missy, but you need something else to think about," Teresa said as she dried her hands on her apron.

"Yes, I would agree." Reverend Smith added. "Shall we say tomorrow, or the day after?"

It seemed so sudden. Elizabeth's head swam from lack of sleep, so much had happened -- happened so quickly. She had felt comfortable with the thought of returning to the classroom, but not so soon.

He took a sip of the coffee Teresa had put before him. "I don't think we need to worry about Leon Simns. He seems to have vanished. No one has seen a trace of the man since—"

"Since that day."

Ben nodded. "It would be best," he said softly, "if you could bring some sort of normalcy to your life. It would also help the children as they come to terms with all that has happened."

Children, come to terms, of course. Why hadn't she thought of that? Their teacher had been attacked. Their friend nearly murdered. Things like that did not happen in their world. "But how will we get the word out?" she asked sheepishly.

"You leave that to me," Ben said with a smile.

Elizabeth returned a weak smile.

"Perhaps this afternoon you might come and see Leah. She has so missed you, and hangs on every word of news I bring home."

Elizabeth's smile grew. "Yes, I think I will and stop by the Baughman's too."

"That will be an excellent thing," he said with his booming voice. "But ladies I must take my leave. The worst here I believe has past, and I leave my friend in very capable hands."

"Pastor, you must stay for breakfast."

"Mrs. Donnellson, I have tread upon your hospitality too long. And I so wish to share breakfast with my own brood. So if you forgive me I will be off." He rose and moved toward the door gently placing his hand upon Elizabeth's shoulder as he passed, grabbed his hat off a hook at the door side, said his goodbye and was gone.

Mrs. Donnellson rose from her seat and began to clear the table. "The valley's lucky to have that man," she said softly. "And the man in the other room was luck too." She looked up into Elizabeth's eyes. "You saved him."

The teacher didn't believe what she had heard. "I didn't save Matthew."

"You did as sure as your sitting at my table," the farmwife said without hesitation. "If you weren't there, the man would not be in my bedroom. No, we would have been building a box rather than tend the man."

"That's not true," Elizabeth protested. "It was my fault he was injured in the first place."

"Pshaaw…that's little more than nonsense. You can't say what would have happened if things had been different. A man with a knife is a dangerous thing, missy. Who knows what might have been. 'It do ya no good thinkin' ya might', that's what my ma used to say. I'll just tell you what I know. If'n you had come here straight away, the men folk would have gone, just as they were. They wouldn't have known what they'd needed. They wouldn't taken blankets or anythin' else. But you bound that man up. He would have bled ta death for sure if'n no one had. And I know what I'm a say'n. My first husband, God rest his soul, got hisself tore apart by a tree he was fellin'. Hurt no more than that man in that other room. But I found him too late." Teresa turned and faced the window. "Even today I can see him there. Things like that you don't forget."

Elizabeth was shocked by Teresa's words. "I'm sorry. I had no idea."

The farmer's wife turned and with a trembling smile and eyes visibly wet spoke. "It's not somethin' I talk about much. It was a long time ago. I was younger than you then, scarcely more than a bride. Our first winter and our last." She resumed her work. "It was hard to get over, but I had to do somethin'. Lucky for me Jacob was available. Me in the motherly way and no man." She wiped her hands on her apron and looked once more at the teacher. "Don't get me wrong, missy, Jacob is a good man, and maybe now with a bit of luck things will go better."

"The children told me that you were to get water soon."

"It's what this land's been needin'. We can thank that man over there." She pointed toward Matthew. "It's his doin'. We owe that man," she said as she turned away. "He wouldn't like me to tell, asked us to tell nobody. But he's the only reason we're still here." She pulled back a chair and sat across the table from the teacher. "We'd lost this farm in October. It was done and we knew it, all the work, the sweat and the blood, even the bones of my man on the hill over yonder…for nothing."

Her voice trailed off. "It was Matthew that gave us a few dollars. It was all it took, and Jacob going all the way to Bendon to pay it. Bought the place back he did, at the tax sale. You should have heard Clark. He had his hooks in the place; thought it was his already." Her voice grew stern. "He got no call to be angry. It's not his blood in the dirt here, no sir, missy, it's not." She became quiet for a moment and Elizabeth watched the woman she had come to know these past few days. "Matthew Sonnefelt is just that kind of man. He understands about the cost. About sweat and blood, about goin' hungry when times are hard. Yes missy, he knows. And he cares."

Elizabeth thought about what the farm wife had said. Thought about all that had happened since that spring day, a day that seemed so very long ago, a day she went to check on her students, a day when this ordeal began. She thought about the burden this farm family had undertaken. Made a place for Matthew, certainly too weak to be moved, and made space for her as well. Elizabeth felt she had taken advantage of the situation. "Teresa," she said, "you and your family have been so kind and I…well…I am afraid have taken advantage. I should—"

"Pshaw…missy, you've done more than your fair share. You've helped me around the house, and you've been an extra pair of eyes when we needed to keep that man under watch. Been glad to have you here. Sometimes a woman gets lonely. Sounds strange don't it, with children and men underfoot. But there are times I miss havin' a woman to talk to. So don't fret, you'll be back at your life soon enough, teachin' and such."

Elizabeth couldn't help but smile.

As Teresa worked preparing breakfast, Elizabeth listened. "You don't know how grateful folks are to have a teacher here in the valley. You've made a difference here. Yes, missy, you have."

"I haven't done so much," she protested.

"Yes, you have. My Joey, he doesn't like learnin'. I'm sure you've noticed."

"He is quite bright."

"I didn't say he weren't. Just that he don't like school. It was hard for me to get him to go, and times he just cut out. But he hasn't, not once this year. I don't know what ya did, but it has to be good."

Elizabeth wanted to change the conversation. She never felt comfortable about praise, especially praise she thought she did not deserve. "Have they found Mr. Simns?" she asked.

"I haven't heard. Seems, we would be about the first to know if they had. They're out lookin'. It's just a matter of time I'm sure." Teresa glanced out the window. "The men folk be in soon," she said. "Maybe you should check on our patient."

Elizabeth soon found herself in the darkened room. The first light of the morning was just peeking in the window. Strange, as she moved to the chair at the bedside, she wondered what day it was. For even in the dimly lit room she saw the multi day growth of stubble on Matthew's cheeks, a sign of the time that had passed. She counted down the days and realized it was Sunday. How could it be? Elizabeth watched the blankets rise and fall. Saw the faint quiver of the hairs of his mustache with each breath. She noticed how the early morning light cast shadows, painting every contour of his face in light and dark.

Now that Matthew had eaten and been alert from time to time, their next concern was infection. If only there were a doctor, but the nearest was in Thimble, and he never came out this far. She supposed they were on their own. The Donnellsons had done their best to clean the wounds that terrible afternoon, and she had helped changing dressings. So far, so good.

She studied at the man lying in the dimness. The firm jaw line, the curve of his lashes, and the curl of hair that touched the top of his left ear. Elizabeth wanted to memorize each detail of the tall man she had come to love. Elizabeth wondered how she would face the days and perhaps weeks ahead. It was easier before. She forced the thought out of her head as she noticed Matthew waking.

"Have you been here all night?" the man asked groggily.

"No," she whispered. "I've just arrived. Ben has watched through the night."

"I feel I have put an awful burden on everyone," Matthew said with a weak voice.

"Don't be silly, we're all just worried, but you're getting better," she said confidently. "Before you know it, you will be on your feet and bossing people about again."

"I didn't realize that I did."

She smiled. "Don't worry about that either."

"And you," he asked. "When will you be back to teaching?

"Perhaps tomorrow," she said in a voice scarcely more than a whisper.

"They haven't caught him, have they?"

He didn't need to explain who the 'who' was, she knew. "No."

After his eyes swept across her face, Matthew drew a breath. "Does it hurt much?"

She swallowed, resisting the instinct to touch her bruised cheek. "No Matthew, not much."

Matthew's jaw set, his lips a tight line.

"It's not that serious Matthew. Really."

Even in the dim room she could see the intensity in his eyes. "Be careful, Beth."

There, he had called her Beth again. Matthew had never called her Beth before that afternoon, but now it was rare if he called her anything else. Elizabeth nodded her head slightly. "Rest a bit. I will bring some breakfast soon." She watched as his eye lids blinked twice and a moment later seemed to be sleeping once more. As bad as he was, yet he worried about others. Elizabeth shook her head as she leaned back in the chair, and drifted into a sleep that had avoided her all night.

CHAPTER 39

SHE HAD SLEPT LESS THAN AN HOUR WHEN THE ACTIVITY OF THE busy farm house returned her to the here and now. Elizabeth would remain behind as the family attended church. She was grateful for the chance to allow her new friends the freedom to continue their lives. The house grew still with their absence. Matthew had fallen asleep again. It seemed he slept a great deal, and her mind began to race. What if Simns was watching? What if he was waiting for an opportunity to finish what he had started? These were among the thoughts that swirled around in her head.

She spent the time wandering around the house, fearing if she sat for more than a moment she would fall asleep. Elizabeth would look in on Matthew, walk to the kitchen or parlor, look in on Matthew again, and make quick trip to her room, go down and check on the man again. It made for a long morning. Any sound, no matter how trivial, made her jump, and the house made many sounds. Once when looking out of a window upstairs, she thought she saw something move. Scarcely allowing herself to breathe, she waited to see if it was indeed a person. Only after several minutes did Elizabeth convince herself that it was no more than her imagination.

At last exhausted, she collapsed in a chair near Matthew's bed. Though she tried, really tried to remain alert; she fell into a deep sleep.

Elizabeth did not know what had awakened her, for she awoke, gradually as if something was leading her away from her dreams, gently, softly. When her eyes opened, she saw Matthew was awake as well, lying in his bed watching her. The man smiled when she began to move.

"How are you?" she asked.

He blinked slowly, glanced away an instant. "I'm fine."

She didn't believe him, at least not entirely. Elizabeth felt his brow, pleased there was no fever.

"The Donnelsons have gone to church."

"And you did not go with them?"

"Who was to watch over you, sir?"

He shrugged his shoulders.

"You may think there is no need, but you are still a very ill man."

"Even if I needed watching as you said, you feel it is your responsibility?"

Elizabeth looked deep into the man's eyes. "The Donnelsons have been so kind. I thought—"

"You thought you would give them a break."

"Something like that."

"Once again, Beth, you show your courage."

"Courage?"

"You, an unmarried woman, dare to spend hours in this house alone with a man."

She chuckled. "And you feel I should fear you, Mr. Sonnefelt?"

"Don't you?"

She shook her head slightly. "You are in no condition to cause anyone harm."

"You might be surprised," he said as he rolled up on one shoulder.

She placed her hand on his. "Careful, Matthew."

He took a labored breath and collapsed upon his back. "You may not be afraid of me today, but there was a time."

Her mind raced through dozens of memories. Matthew had made her angry, so very angry. He had startled her at the school that first night, but she never feared the man. Why? But she did not wish to share this revelation with him now, not now. "I suppose that is true," she said at last. "But you do not fear anyone or anything."

He looked away. "Everyone has their fears, Beth, everyone."

Once again Elizabeth's mind saw a boy on his own in the world. It might sound courageous, but Matthew was but a child unprotected and alone. She felt a tremble. "Yes. Everyone has their fears."

They sat in silence for a moment. "Matthew, you seem educated, or informed in the least. Where did you go to school?"

He looked away again. "I didn't have much schooling. Left after fourth grade."

"But—"

"It gave me enough, a foundation. I guess I taught myself," he said as he turned to face her.

"Yourself?"

"I like to read, and Gerrit taught me my cyphers."

"Gerrit?"

"Gerrit Sonnefelt."

"Your father?"

"I loved him dearly, but he wasn't my father, if blood be the measure." He drew a deep breath, his eyelids fluttered.

Elizabeth longed to ask about his boyhood but considered it an inopportune time. "You need to rest, Matthew."

He nodded and soon had drifted off to sleep.

Later, nearly mid-afternoon, Elizabeth set out for the Smith's. She would have preferred walking but found herself riding on a farm wagon with Joe Donnellson at the reins. Martha had joined them and the three were talking about everything and anything that happened to pass their minds. The weather, the Bobolink they heard, about clouds, and puppies—just chatter, delightful happy chatter.

"Miss Beck, we can't stay long," Joe said as he looked at the darkening sky. Clouds were building; rain was on its way. "It's a long ride back, and we don't want to be caught in a storm."

Elizabeth smiled, a long ride, perhaps two miles. How long a trip had she made, coming all the way from Ohio, and that bone jarring ride from Thimble. No, *that* was a long ride.

Leah and the children stood at the door even before the wagon had come to a stop. Oh, what a delight it was to see her friend. Soon they were talking in the parlor, and the children, except for the youngest, played outdoors.

Elizabeth could see that Leah was concerned by her appearance. "Ben told me that you had been injured, but Elizabeth—"

"I am fine, really." Elizabeth slid her hand over her left cheek. "The swelling is down."

"But the bruises. Poor. Poor dear," Leah wrapped her arms around her friend. "Ben told me but…"

"Seeing…"

"Yes."

"It is not nearly as bad as it looks," Elizabeth said with a smile.

Later as they sat with their coffee, Leah asked, "Are you really leaving?"

Elizabeth had expected the question. She wanted so desperately to come, to explain all the reasons to her closest friend. But, "I feel I must," were the only words that she could force from her lips.

"But the children."

"I'll finish out the term, only a few weeks remain any case," Elizabeth answered slowly. "In truth, I had not decided if I would return next term. No one has approached me on the matter."

"Ben has told me that the school board is very pleased with your work here," Leah said nodding her head. "He expected the members to tell you so themselves."

"The entire board? Pleased?" Elizabeth prodded.

"It would not be proper for me to say any specifics," Leah said then glanced away. There was a silence, an uncommon silence, at last the pastor's wife spoke once more. "You have every right to be angry with me," she said as she looked downward. "I know what you told me was in confidence. I told no one but Ben, and even he doesn't know the details."

Elizabeth moved closer to her friend. She held Leah's hand and smiled. "It was right for you to tell Ben. He's your husband. I understood that. You should keep no secrets, not from him."

Leah wrapped her arms around Elizabeth. Elizabeth watched as a single tear slid down Leah's right cheek. "I wish you wouldn't go."

"It is for the best," Elizabeth whispered in her ear.

Leah looked up with wet eyes. "Is it? Really?"

Elizabeth drew back a bit, her eyes focused on something far away. "I must do what I must do."

"Ben says it is because you have feelings for Matthew."

"It is more, I fear Matthew has feelings for me," she answered softly.

The room grew still, so still. "I can understand how you feel."

"Can you?" Elizabeth spoke sharply.

A hurt surprised look crossed Leah's face. "No, I suppose I can't," she said very softly as again she looked downward. She then looked directly into Elizabeth's eyes. "But you have given up hope, all hope, and that's not right at all."

Elizabeth prepared to respond when Leah began once more. "It's a terrible thing you have had to bear. A terrible thing that has happened. No, you may not be able to change what has happened, but you should not allow it to imprison you."

Imprison her -- imprison her -- what on earth did her friend mean? She was free to go where she chose. There were no bars holding her! No, she was free or was she? Elizabeth thought about that word, imprison. She thought about how she had felt, hurt, yes, deeply hurt, oh yes! How had she reacted? The wall she had placed about her feelings, her heart, a strong wall, a thick wall. She thought about how that wall had been shattered. She had not meant to let anyone in to that place once reserved for Jameson. No, she had placed barriers—strong hard barriers. Why? Because she would not be hurt again. No, Elizabeth was not held in a prison of metal barred windows, but she had imprisoned herself from any hope. Hope that someone, anyone, might provide the love for which everyone yearns. A love she had convinced herself she did not deserve.

"Ben told me about the promise," Leah said at last softly. "Don't be too angry with him. It's just that we have come to care for you so much. He's worried about you Elizabeth. So worried you will cut yourself off from everyone and anyone that gets too close."

She had listened to her friend, yet nothing had changed. Elizabeth felt herself a person of her word. She believed that it was important to be true. It was a matter of character. She felt Leah lay her head on her shoulder and Elizabeth drew a deep breath. What could she say? She had made a promise, and not just to anyone but to God. It was set. It was done and there was no undoing.

Leah spoke words that were barely audible, "Don't you think God would release you from that promise?"

Elizabeth didn't know, hadn't considered the possibility. In her mind that choice was not up to God. She had made the promise. She would stand by it, a covenant, like in the Bible.

"Perhaps," Leah said carefully, "you should ask Him what you should do, rather than tell him what you will do."

The comment surprised Elizabeth, shocked her greatly. She wasn't telling God anything. Was she? She became angry. If anyone could have understood, she felt certain it would be Leah. But no, telling God—what nerve.

"I must be going," she began. "Joe said we couldn't stay long, rain on the way. I must get the children home." She rose abruptly taking her friend by surprise.

"Please don't leave angry," Leah pleaded.

Elizabeth turned and looked at her friend. Leah had become the dearest person in her life. Elizabeth forced a smile. "I'll think about what you have said. Really." She gave the pastor's wife a hug and calling the children they were soon on their way.

CHAPTER 40

THE AIR WAS CHANGING; THE WIND THAT SEEMED TO ALWAYS BLOW was stronger and noticeably cooler. Joe kept looking upward, watching the dark clouds that now filled the sky. He continued to urge the horses on. Soon they heard thunder, loud booms that caused their ribs to tremble. Perhaps Elizabeth should have been more forceful when she suggested they wait out the storm at the Baughman's. Perhaps they should have remained at the Smith's, for that matter. But they hadn't. Rain pelted them even before they had crossed the dam. They were very wet by the time they reached the crossroads, yet Joe drove the horses onward. Not that it took much convincing for the beasts were just as anxious to be safely in their stalls as the young man was to get them there.

Jacob stood at the barn door waving them to drive directly into the structure, which Joe accomplished with expertise beyond his years.

"We were worried," the farmer said in a voice that could be scarcely heard above the large raindrops pounding the roof, above and the booms, which followed the brilliant flashes. "Weather began to change just after you left."

"We should have stayed at the Smith's," Miss Beck apologized.

"You'd a been there till morning, I'd 'spect," Jacob shouted. "Joey, see they get safe to the house."

"Pa, I'll help with the horses," the boy protested.

"I'll see they're dried down, fed, and put away." The farmer looked seriously at the boy. "You see to the women."

The boy nodded, and a few moments later they were running to the house, across the porch, and in the back door. Teresa standing at the stove shook her head angrily. Elizabeth wondered if the boy desired to remain in the barn out his obligation to his father and the animals or to avoid facing his mother's wrath. Elizabeth watched as the mother brought towels to dry her children and guest. Then said, "Joseph…I thought you knew better."

"The storm came up on us, sudden like. We only stayed a couple of minutes. Headed back most right away." Joe said looking up to his mother's angry eyes beneath furrowed brows.

Martha nodded. "'Spect it's true. You haven't been gone long. But you put such a fright in your mama." With that, she wrapped her arms around her children, held them tight enough they protested in muffled tones. "And you, missy, you'd best get out of those wet clothes as quick as your able. I'll get the fire hot and we'll have some tea. Then you can tell me the news. If'n you were there long enough to get any," she said with a sharp eye on her son.

The teacher moved quickly toward her room, but before she rushed upstairs she peeked into Matthew's. Elizabeth didn't notice the miller was awake and prepared to turn away when she heard. "How're Leah and the kids?"

She crept into the room, concerned about the water dripping from her clothing onto the clean floor. "They're fine. How are you feeling?"

"Better, I think. Had a bit of soup. Hoped to have some real food, but I won't argue."

"That will be a change," she teased.

"I didn't realize I was so difficult to get along with."

She stepped closer. "But you are. Most cantankerous I would say."

"This is revealing," he said a bit more forcefully. "So I am argumentative, bossy and cranky too."

"Only when you don't get your way," she ribbed.

"Which is quite often I must say."

"Less often than you think."

"You make me out to be no more than a spoiled child."

"Aren't you?" she said as she turned and left him.

"And now you run off and leave me?" he called out.

"Only because you are simply impossible." Elizabeth giggled as she ran up the stairs. As she reached her room, Elizabeth realized that bantering with the man had been—enjoyable. How had he done that? How was it that each time she was near him she lost all her sense? She grew stern as she undressed, shaking from the cold, or at least she thought the tremble fueled by the cold. Drying and dressing herself, she continued to tremble. The house was not cold. Elizabeth could not say she was chilled, yet her limbs shook ever so slightly. She gathered her wet things to be cleaned, angry with herself that she had allowed her control to slip away, and stormed down the stairs.

When Elizabeth returned to the room of the wounded miller, she was colder—not in temperature but in temperament. Matthew noticed.

"Am I such a difficult patient?" he asked at last.

Difficult, difficult, on the contrary he had been little trouble. "You were easier to tend when you were sleeping," she said her tone flat with no emotion. Elizabeth knew he noticed the change, for he grew quiet. She came to his bedside. Looking down on him she could not prevent the smile that came to her lips. "No, Matthew, you have not been difficult. And I wish to apologize if I implied you were."

"But I am cranky, bossy, and want my own way," he stated.

A tear came to Elizabeth's eye. A tear she hoped he would not notice in the dimly lit room.

"No, Matthew, you are not any of those things." She stood there a moment, feeling so confused, trying her best to keep her emotions in control. "I'll see if we cannot find some real food you will be able to eat." Elizabeth said as she turned and left. When she reached the door, she dashed upstairs, back to her room, for she was unable to hold her emotions in check a moment longer.

Chapter 41

Elizabeth had been in and out of Matthew's room several times as the hours passed. The storm made it unlikely Ben would arrive to sit out the night. And in truth, as much as the miller had improved, the nightly vigil no longer seemed necessary. All the same Elizabeth and Teresa spent a great deal of time with Matthew. He had eaten soup again, and had dozed off. Elizabeth was preparing to leave the room when he woke.

She had reached the door when Matthew's voice came to her in the darkness. "You're leaving us."

How did he do that? How did he know? How was it, Matthew always seemed to perceive things so clearly and then speak so directly? In just a few words he had gone to the very center of the matter. Elizabeth hesitated before she answered.

"It is time I return home," she said and then plunged forward before he could speak so very certain of what he meant. "I have been a burden on these dear people too long. I'm sure that Martha and Ann are tired of sleeping on the floor and would be grateful for their room." Elizabeth wondered if she had been successful in sidestepping the statement he had made. "You, on the other hand, are in no condition to go home.

We're just so glad that you are progressing. I would be leaving tonight, except for the storm, so I will—"

"That's not what I mean." Matthew interrupted her.

"I will, tomorrow…I mean, I will go home tomorrow. Back to the Baughman's." She wanted to turn, to leave him there. To go away and not to face the man. But from the doorway, looking back at him, she just couldn't walk away. So standing there, with only a single step away from avoiding the words she felt certain she had not the courage to say, Elizabeth paused a moment as she held the door, took a deep breath and at last spoke. "The term is nearly finished. Leaving was always part of the plan." She had done her best to keep the quiver out of her voice. Elizabeth was not certain she had succeeded.

"And next term?"

"The board will need to find someone…to teach."

"And the children?"

She felt herself fading, growing weaker. "The children have had other teachers."

"But they have never had someone, a teacher, they love."

Her lip trembled as she heard those words. "I'm certain you exaggerate, I am just their teacher—"

"And nothing more?"

He had stolen her words. Taken them before she could allow them to leave her lips.

"And to you they are only students. Nothing more?"

Elizabeth turned away from him and leaned her forehead on the edge of the door. She drew a breath, then another, unable to speak.

"Beth," he said softly, "is it always so difficult?"

She allowed the silence to answer.

"It is because they are more than just students?" he whispered.

She swallowed as she looked back at the man, the tall man -- the very perceptive man.

"Beth," he whispered, "you have come to care for them. You love them, and they love you."

"But that doesn't change anything," she said with a trembling voice. A voice that came out so weak she doubted he had heard, but as Elizabeth looked over, looking through her tear-dimmed eyes, even in the half-light she could see he had heard.

"Then you will be returning home?"

Home. Strange she hadn't thought of it as home. Perhaps it had been only a few months, but the Baughman's house had become her home. Oh, she missed her family. She missed Columbus and Ohio in general, but at that moment, at that particular instant, it was a faraway place. A place where many of those she loved and missed did live, but it—how could she feel that way—was not home.

Her legs grew weak. Elizabeth felt uncertain she could stand much longer. Wanting only to walk out the door, stumble up to her room, seal the door, that would be that. But instead she returned to the chair at Matthew's bedside. Sitting there she took the man's hand; it felt good in hers, too good. Elizabeth tried to smile. She failed. And looking down at that man, that tall man, that ill man, Elizabeth at last spoke.

"I never intended to stay here, Matthew. Never. I thought perhaps one term, maybe two, and then return east. East is where I belong. I am not hard enough for this country."

Matthew began to speak, but she put her finger to his lips.

"Yes, I have come to love the children, and more. The people that call the valley their home, but I must leave. Please understand. The longer I stay the more difficult it will be to leave. I am not Eloise, there at the bluff, tough as steel, hard as stone, and you would not wish me to become so."

"No," he whispered, his voice very weak, so weak that she feared once more for him.

His hand felt warm. Why hadn't she noticed? Elizabeth touched his brow. The man had a fever. She left quickly and found Teresa. The leg had become infected. Together they worked at cleaning the wound again. Matthew flinched in the pain but said nothing.

"It's not bad yet," the farmwife said. "It's good you noticed, missy. By the time we changed the dressing tomorrow it would have been too late. It was to be expected, but I thought he might just get lucky. That salve ought to pull the poison out. It's all we can do for now." Teresa looked gravely serious at Elizabeth. "Best you get some rest. I'll take the first watch."

Elizabeth couldn't leave Matthew, the man they had returned from the brink and yet might lose. She loved the man, his fast strides, his gentle hand, and those deep brown eyes. She had a desperate need to do whatever she could, and if she could do nothing else, to sit, to watch, to pray. "No, Teresa," she protested, "you have done too much, I'll sit with him."

Mrs. Donnellson looked at the teacher, opened her mouth as if to order the teacher out, thought an instant, shook her head, and moved to the doorway. "Any change—anything at all—you fetch me. Ya hear?"

Elizabeth nodded.

It was another long night. Though Elizabeth did her best to remain alert she dozed twice. She woke with a start, angry with herself, and began to mumble quietly, criticizing her failure. As she turned up the wick to brighten the room, she noticed Matthew awake. "Did I wake you?"

He gave a weak smile. "No, I was watching you sleep."

"You should have woken me."

"Why?"

Elizabeth grew exasperated. Had the man been well, she would have told him a thing or two. As she considered how best to answer the man he spoke again. "You looked so tired."

"But I'm to watch you, sir, not the other way around." Elizabeth lightly touched his brow, surprised to find it only slightly warm. "You seem to be improving." She drew back the blankets and examined the leg for redness. The leg seemed slightly less swollen and not as hot to the touch. "Well, I am quite pleased," she said. "It seems Teresa has work a bit of a miracle."

"It would be best to reserve your judgment for morning," the miller said frankly.

Elizabeth checked the timepiece in her locket. "Sir, it is morning."

"Are we back to that?" he asked.

"Back to what?" Elizabeth asked impatiently.

"Ma'am and sir."

She couldn't help but smile. "It seems fitting, don't you think. After all, sir, you have a lady in your room alone with you," she responded coyly.

"Do you not feel safe, ma'am?"

Strange, but she'd never felt safer. "I do not think you are in any condition to be a threat."

He smiled at her as she once more sat down in the chair beside him. "As I said before, you might be surprised."

She feigned alarm. "Are you not a gentleman, sir?"

Matthew chuckled. "That I am, dear lady. That I am."

"You should rest, Matthew, you need your strength," she said with as stern a voice as she could muster.

"It's all I've done for four days. I believe I'm completely slept out."

"All the same," she began, but found she could not go on. Elizabeth looked at Matthew. The man she had intended to hate. The man she felt certain was a fool. The man that had rescued her time and time again, and turned her face away.

"You should go to your room, Beth. It's plain to see you are exhausted," Matthew said as he reached for her hand.

"Who is the patient here?" Elizabeth responded as she took his hand in hers.

"Teresa shall have two if you don't get some rest," his voice came stronger.

"I'll fetch her. It is plain you would prefer her company to mine in any case," she said as she placed his hand on the bed, rose and moved to the doorway.

But she stopped there at the doorway, there just before leaving the room, for she heard him say, "No Beth, I prefer no one's company above yours." She did not look back as she raced to find the farmer's wife.

Teresa came to the door when Elizabeth gently tapped. There was a look of concern on the farmwife's face, but Elizabeth assured her things were well. Together they made their way back to Matthew.

"I hear you have driven the school teacher away," Teresa said acting cross. "And after all she has done for you."

"You know me, Teresa, a total ingrate," he said gruffly.

Teresa chuckled. "That you are, Mr. Sonnefelt. The most ungrateful man I've ever had the pleasure to meet."

"Teresa," he said then, "will you send that poor thing to bed before she falls over."

"You're right. I told her so hours ago. But no, we don't do it we don't. Sit up with him I will. All night I will. Well it's long past the night's middle so off to bed with ya, scoot!"

Elizabeth did as she was told. Though she would have thought her mind's racing would have prevented it, she soon drifted off to sleep. It was full light when the sounds of the house grew loud enough to wake her. Dressing quickly Elizabeth went downstairs, checked on Matthew, who bid her good morning. He was yet feverish, though not nearly as hot as the night before. Teresa came in and together they changed the dressings on leg and chest. The wounds left Elizabeth with great concern, and once again she wished for a doctor.

Chapter 42

All the while they worked Teresa spoke about the storm, shingles had blown off the barn roof, about the children, Joey had locked Martha in the outhouse, and about anything that passed through her mind. Later when they had finished, she drew Elizabeth aside.

"I'm a worried about him, missy. We'd been lucky 'til now. The infection seems better than last night, but we got to watch it close." She then changed the subject and asked. "Will you be teachin' today?"

Elizabeth wanted to remain and did not answer.

"It be best if'n you did."

At last Elizabeth nodded.

"Be a muddy walk," the farmwife told her. "I'll have Joey hitch up the wagon and the three of ya can ride."

She couldn't focus on teaching when she arrived at school, but soon, very soon she was able to put her concerns aside. It was the children, always the children. Each one so different, some were the best of students, quiet, studious. Others were, well, just a bit rambunctious, full of life, hard to keep on track. But Elizabeth loved them all. Yes, teaching was the best thing for her now. She would not say the day went quickly, but it passed more quickly than the days she had endured before. Elizabeth would return to the Baughman's, if Matthew seemed well enough, but first she would see for herself.

Matthew's condition had not significantly improved, but Teresa was most positive. "It's not gett'n' worse…that's my fear. I s'pect the next day or so will tell."

"I'll sit with him for a while."

Teresa just looked at her then nodded.

Elizabeth sat in the chair watching the very ill man, watching the covers rise and fall with each breath. She fell asleep. The sound of another in the room woke her just in time to see Teresa leave. As Elizabeth got up quietly and moved toward the door, she heard the man stir. She looked back at him, so pale, so drawn.

"I'm sorry," she said, "I didn't mean to wake you."

Matthew gave a weak smile. "How was school?"

She smiled. "The day went fine." Elizabeth drew a breath. "Surely you did not miss me?"

He did not answer.

She stood there for but a moment and moved back to the chair. "Matthew," she asked, "you once told me you had traveled, where is your family?"

When the man turned away, Elizabeth regretted asking. The room became so still, only the sounds that drifted in as others worked. The faint sound of the oven door opening and closing, and unrecognizable words, spoken by familiar muffled voices, which seemed a world away.

"I think they're still in Dakota Territory," Matthew said at last.

She didn't know if she should continue to ask questions that had haunted her since the conversation under the stars with Ben. At last she pushed on.

"Have you contacted them?"

He shook his head.

"Tell me, Matthew…tell me your story."

"There's nothing to tell."

"I would like to know."

"It's not pretty," he said with a hard edge to his words. "Not pretty at all."

"Perhaps later when you're feeling better," she said as she began to leave again.

But as she reached the open door she heard him begin. "I have four brothers and two sisters. At least I did. I'm the one in the middle."

She turned and he continued. "I was ten that year. There was a drought, and well, food was tight real tight…" He told her that during the winter of that year the entire family faced starvation. That another farmer needed someone to help, and paid his parents fifty dollars for a boy. Matthew had volunteered to save his family, and he had only seen them once since. The Lyndsecks had been mean and hard, cruel to the boy. Demanding more than he could give, giving less than he needed. Yet he knew he could not leave them. He could not runaway and certainly could not go home, for the Lyndsecks would demand their money back. Nearly two years he had slaved for them. Nearly two years of beatings, two years of slop they dared to call food. And then he left.

He had lived in their barn, the winters so cold. When Matthew left he went south. It had to be warmer in the south. He was still in a boy's body, but he had become so much more. He met many people along the way. Most were good, decent folk, others cruel as the Lyndsecks. For more than three years he traveled. Down to Texas, he followed the Rio Grande upstream into New Mexico territory and then moved eastward. Somehow, by chance, he ended up in Misty Creek.

Here in this valley, he met a man that changed his life—Gerart Sonnefelt. Matthew worked at the mill for the man, but more the Sonnefelts took him in, a stranger, dirty, tired, and alone, and they made him their son. No, it wasn't legal—if papers are what it takes—but in every way Matthew was their son, and they became his parents.

Gerart and Ellen's children had grown and moved away. That generation had no interest in the mill. So Mr. Sonnefelt taught his new son, and that new son learned everything he could. It came to the point few knew Matthew was the boy that had just drifted into the valley; he was just Gerart and Ellen's son. Matthew told Elizabeth they had saved him, that he loved them, and took care of them until they died. Now the mill was his, but this mill wasn't the same one. No, he had built a new dam downstream, built a new mill. The lake on Misty Creek had grown to nearly twice its size. The water served not only him but all the farms of the valley and Mr. Clark as well, though the rancher was a hard to please. Because of the lake, there was water for everyone. He had learned from Gerart Sonnefelt that water gave the valley life.

Elizabeth sat quietly and listened, the story nearly broke her heart. She had watched Matthew as he had told his story. The man showed no emotion—nothing. The tale just facts to him. When Matthew had finished, his eyes searched hers as if wondering if she understood. Elizabeth understood. Though she had never had to endure the trials of her friend, she could understand. She felt Matthew must be a strong man, for weaker would have been destroyed.

She asked him, "Do you hate them?"

"The Bible teaches we are to hate no one," he said with flat tones as he looked into her eyes.

"But that does not answer my question. For we are but mortal, and have our failings. It is true we are taught we should not hate. But do you hate them?"

Matthew looked away, turning his head he seemed to stare at the ceiling. "The Lyndsecks?"

It was not her intention to ask about the Lyndsecks. Of course he would hate those that had so abused him.

"No, I do not hate the Lyndsecks," he said without emotion. "I have forgiven them long ago."

The comment shouldn't have caught her so off guard, but it did.

"They are what they are. They did what they did. It is past. I pity them. Does that seem odd that I would pity that family as hard and cruel as they were? They do not know anything else, only hardness and cruelty. I could not allow that to shape me, to become like them. No, I learned that from the Sonnefelts as well."

Then Elizabeth swallowed and asked what she had asked before. "Do you hate your parents?"

Matthew's eyes searched hers. A look of confusion came across his face. "Why would I hate my parents?"

"They sold you off," she said barely able to hold back the sobs.

A determination returned to his expression, a determination she had seen before. "You misunderstand," he said, "they did not sell me off against my will. I went willingly. My contribution to the benefit of those I loved most. I considered myself old enough to know what I faced, and to face it head on."

"But you were wrong."

"Yes, I was wrong. But that was not my father's fault, nor my mother's. It was just the way it had to be. My older brothers were needed to help on the farm, and I would not dream of sending my kid brothers away. No, it naturally fell on me…and I took it."

Life could have made Matthew hard. How many scars did the man have? Yes, his flesh bore marks of a hard life, and soon the wounds he had now received would also leave their tracks, but what about those scars—those invisible scars of years of neglect and abuse. Elizabeth shuddered at the thought.

"Have you ever contacted your family?"

Again he looked away. "For years I was afraid that if I did the Lyndsecks would place demands on them." He looked again to her with damp eyes. "I couldn't. I just couldn't." He paused. "Imagine them taking Michael or Tim. How could they survive?"

She looked at the man, the tall man, the wounded man, and Elizabeth felt pity for all he had faced alone. "Your parents must wonder," she whispered.

"Yes," his voice soft and far away.

"Perhaps I could write them for you?"

He blinked. "Perhaps."

Matthew looked so tired. Elizabeth feared she had drawn too much from him. "You need to get some rest."

The man did not answer but after a time his eyes closed and he seemed to fall asleep. But when she moved to the door he stirred. Elizabeth looked back, and Matthew spoke in low tones. "I ask that you tell no one, for no one knows those things I have told you."

Elizabeth wanted to ask why she should not share his story with others, but instead responded, "If that is your wish."

"It is," he said, scarcely more than a whisper. "It is."

Elizabeth stood there at the doorway a moment watching. He seemed to be a peace, so she left him.

CHAPTER 43

ELIZABETH SPENT THE DAYS THAT FOLLOWED TEACHING, AND THEN when classes were finished she returned to the Donnellson's. She did not walk alone, for Mr. Simns' whereabouts, though the men of the valley continued to seek him, remained unknown. The growing consensus of those that lived in the valley was that the man had fled, leaving his family behind. Margret Simns, his wife, gave the searchers no assistance of any kind. Which left some to wonder if she was hiding her husband. None of the valley's children were allowed to venture far from home alone. The first week school resumed, many of the fathers would be waiting outside the building at day's end, to see their children, especially their daughters, home.

Jeremiah Donnellson, Martha and Joe's oldest brother, came for them each day. Elizabeth rode with the Donnellson brood for her daily visits. She, being gone nearly a day at a time, began to notice the improvement. Matthew was recovering. On Friday, after she had helped Teresa change the dressings on his yet swollen leg, Elizabeth and Matthew spoke of general things, of school and the weather. The miller seemed much stronger. Elizabeth smiled and told him she must leave, but would see him the following day.

Matthew nodded. But as she reached the door he asked, "Am I the reason you are leaving?"

"You know I must return to the Baughman's," she told him softly.

"No, the valley."

Again Elizabeth found herself confounded that he was so perceptive. She drew a breath, held it a moment as she considered a response. The young teacher thought herself a truthful person, but when she answered Matthew, she lied.

"No, Matthew, it has nothing to do with you." Again Elizabeth drew a breath. Fearful she would betray herself, she added, "I must leave. We will talk more tomorrow." Then moving swiftly out of the room, Elizabeth steadied herself on quivering legs, trying to regain her composure in the hallway.

She remained quiet when Jeremiah took her home. He was a fine young man, seventeen or eighteen if she were to guess, broad and tall, though not as tall as Ben or Matthew. The son of a farmer and destined to be a farmer in his own right. Gossip, though she gave such talk little heed, throughout the valley said that he would soon marry Rose Avery, and buy the Hampstead farm at the south end of the valley.

Elizabeth never asked his plans while riding along, instead she considered how life seemed to go onward. Children were born, they grew, married, and then one day had children of their own. These thoughts fueled her melancholy mood. For she understood too well that she was not to be part of that cycle. So as they went along, when she glanced over to the young man, she couldn't help but see him as a father. Strange, Elizabeth thought to herself, he was little more than a boy.

The teacher thanked him when she got off the wagon at the gate of the Baughman lane, and apologized for the inconvenience.

"It weren't outa' the way at all," Jeremiah Donnellson said as he smiled. "I'm bound to the Avery farm up the road. Got me an errand ta run."

She waved as young man left with a snap of the reins, going it seemed with an apparent urgency. She smiled as she watched the wagon hurry down the lane and out of sight.

The following week Matthew improved a great deal. There was talk that he would soon be fit to go home. Not that the Donnellsons were in anyway pressuring him to leave. By the contrary, they did their best to postpone the transition. However by Thursday, though he could put no weight on his left leg, the miller was hobbling around the house at will. Then Teresa shared with Elizabeth a concern she had kept to herself. For the farm wife feared the need to remove Matthew's leg.

"It was close," she told Elizabeth. "So close to having the need. I dreaded the thought and lay awake many a night a feared it would come to it." Theresa drew a breath. "But we, and he too for that matter, were lucky. Yes missy, we were all very lucky."

That thought had not crossed Elizabeth's mind, not once during all those days and long nights. Yes, she feared for his life but she never contemplated the need to amputate. Good Lord, she thought to herself, how would we have found the strength?

At the end of that week, on a Saturday afternoon, Elizabeth had come alone. Enough time had passed that she had dared to walk the open road. Sitting on the front porch with only Matthew, he asked, "You told me you would speak further of your departure," he said as he looked across the fields.

Elizabeth had hoped he had forgotten. She knew he hadn't, but hoped all the same. "Must we?" she asked weakly.

He turned and looked at her, the man sitting there, the tall man -- the true man, and Elizabeth could not face him. Then Matthew once again said something that shocked her, "No."

She drew a breath and faced the man. "Matthew, you are my dear friend, my true friend," Elizabeth responded as she tried her best to rein the emotions that attempted to take her away. "You have shown once more how good a friend you are that you would not demand some reason. It is not fair that I should go leave this valley forever and not offer you some explanation."

His eyes focused on hers with a softness. "Beth you need tell me no more. It is enough for friends to trust, even at the time of parting. Soon you will be returning to your home. I would hope that you would think fondly of us from time to time."

She took his hand in hers. It felt so right. "I will never forget this place and the friends I have made here."

"You have changed this valley," he said softly.

She grasped his hand firmly, and said with all the strength she could muster, "No, Matthew, you have changed this valley, made it a special place. You have touched the lives of all the people that live here, and you have touched mine as well. I have just passed through, been here but a short while, and yet Misty Creek will always be part of me."

Matthew's trembling lip curled slightly. "Will you be leaving soon?"

"Yes," she said, "the week after next."

"Back to Ohio?"

"To Columbus."

Elizabeth watched as he drew a deep breath.

"I'll make certain that Ben takes you to Thimble and sees you safe on your train."

"Thank you, Matthew. That will be kind."

Neither spoke, the evening song of a robin drifted on the breeze along with the scent of freshly worked earth. The songbird's song blended with the muffled voices beyond the walls. Elizabeth swallowed as she felt the warmth of Matthew's hand and the breaking of her heart. His eyes, those deep dark eyes, seemed focused on the cloudless azure sky. Even now as they shared a touch, she knew a distance grew. She blinked, drew another breath and forced her resolve to strengthen.

Elizabeth slowly placed Matthew's hand upon the man's leg. He looked her way and yet said nothing. But even in that silence something passed between them. Something jumped the chasm. He blinked twice and she looked away, fearing what she might see and fearing her own strength.

As Elizabeth rose, the love she felt for Matthew was more than she ever imagined. The feeling deeper than it had been with Jameson. She blinked back a tear as she turned, filled with the desire to wrap her arms around the boy so abused and alone that had somehow grown into a tall man – a fine man. Guilt racked her as she considered how wrongly she had labeled Matthew on her arrival. Since she came Elizabeth had learned so much about the miller, a man so different than he appeared.

Her eyes went across the open country. The late afternoon light played long shadows in the field, light and dark the rows of plowed soil that stretched far before her. The day would soon end, as would this chapter of her life. Why had she come to Misty Creek? To escape the pain of abandonment. Yes, she was fleeing the hurt and brokenness. Seeking some place where she could exist—but not really live. Elizabeth felt she could find comfort in an emotional isolation. Leah called it her prison; perhaps it was. But the pain remained. Each day she dwelt upon past hurts, plucking at the wound, while she continued to build a wall around her. A wall she would let none through. At least no man.

Elizabeth had developed the opinion that no man was worth the pain. And she felt the more masculine they were the less value, they carried. Men like Alexander and William Clark Junior showed strengths many would admire, but they were strengths without compassion and sensitivity. The things that had drawn her to Jameson—kindness. But even kind, sensitive Jameson had failed her, another "black mark" on the gender. If cruelty could reside in gentle Jameson, what hope could she find in others?

But Matthew had taught her much about love, real love. In those lessons, he taught her about sacrifice. So no matter how much her heart yearned, Elizabeth would not be selfish. The man she loved so desperately deserved more than she could give. He deserved a whole woman, not this empty vessel. She left him then. She left him there. She left him knowing that she loved him, and leaving the valley would the most difficult thing she would ever do.

CHAPTER 44

THE WEEKS PASSED QUICKLY. APRIL FLOWED INTO MAY AND ALL the able bodies were needed on the area farms. So, as in the rural schools Elizabeth had taught before, the term came to its end. Ida Edwards, Jamie Watkins and Homer Reynolds would be graduating. It filled her heart with pride at the thought of those young scholars. As her eyes fell on Ida, yet a girl, so soon to become a woman, a tear came to Elizabeth's eye, for Miss Edwards was bound for teacher's college in Wichita. And she would never forget Homer brave lad that he was.

The term's end meant they would no longer be students in the white clapboard church-school of Misty Creek. But there were five others whose education would likely end. Elizabeth understood that life here on the frontier or in any rural community did not place the highest regard for more than basic education. She did not agree, but it was the way of things.

But completion of the term, the first full term in years, came with much fanfare. Elizabeth had every confidence in the cowboy pastor who would officiate the service. She smiled each time she hung that label on the man, and blushed at the thought he might learn that she secretly called him so. The whole valley, it seemed, came and the church-school was filled to capacity. But of all that came that day, the one she was most pleased to see was Matthew. The miller arrived early, which was his nature, hobbling in on his own power on the crutch Eldon had fashioned for him, which in itself was a triumph She watched Matthew as he seated himself in the back row, which also fit his personality.

Though she was so very busy in the final preparations, Elizabeth pushed through the crowd to speak with him. "Matthew," she said with a smile, "it is good you have come."

He returned her smile with one of his own. He had a nice smile. "I wouldn't miss it."

"You are looking well."

He tilted his head. Not speaking for an instant, he blinked then said, "As do you."

He glanced away and shifted in his seat. Elizabeth placed her hand on his an instant, the warmth she had felt before began to flow through her fingers, filling her hand. She yanked her hand away. She swallowed, blinking. "Matthew…." But the sound of Mr. Clark's thundering voice caught her attention. She glanced the big man's direction.

"Seems you're needed." Matthew's words broke into her thoughts.

"Yes, it seems," she whispered.

He smiled. "We can talk later."

She nodded, turned, and walked away on trembling legs.

Elizabeth tracked down the president of the school board. "Mr. Clark, sir you have not yet signed the diplomas."

"No worries, Miss Beck, I haven't forgotten."

"Perhaps if you follow me to my desk, we can see to it this moment."

"But…"

"There are only three. It will take but a moment."

He looked away.

"It will mean so much to the graduates if you did."

Clark's eyes seemed far away looking in Matthew's direction. "They are not official without your name."

"Farmers and that man," he muttered under his breath.

"Without your name they are nothing but paper."

He blinked. "Yes, of course," Mr. Clark faced her with what seemed a painted on smile. "Lead on."

With Clark's signatures on the diplomas, another task was completed and Elizabeth could attend to the many things that demanded her attention. She found Leah and Ben just outside the doors, doing their best to keep the excited students reined in as they waited. Josie Tomkins seemed especially anxious standing off to the edge of the group of fidgeting young people, chatting among themselves.

"Josie," Elizabeth said as she crouched down to look her young friend in the eyes, "are you all right?"

Josie's nod did not show confidence.

She wrapped her arm around the child, moving a strand of hair from her face. "It's just like we practiced."

"I know but there's—"

"There are a lot of people."

Josie nodded firmly.

"But they have all come for you…for all of you." Elizabeth looked into Josie's eyes. "They are so happy for you and the others."

"Kinda' like a party?"

Elizabeth smiled. "Yes, like a party. And you children are the guests of honor."

Josie squeezed her teacher.

"Just like we practiced," Elizabeth repeated.

The child nodded firmly.

Elizabeth felt Martha Donnellson tug upon her sleeve. "Teacher, is it true?"

"Is what true, Martha?"

"That you're leaving?"

Her heart skipped a beat. "We will talk at the end of the assembly," she told the child with damp eyes. She saw questions in the eyes of others that gathered around. "Now everyone, let's get lined up."

Finally, when the last preparations from weeks of work was completed, Miss Elizabeth Beck, teacher of Misty Creek school, led her students up the center aisle to their seats that faced all assembled. For the briefest instant as she examined the glowing faces of this group she had taught, the students she had come to know, these young people she loved, a lump formed in her throat while a tear flowed down her left cheek. Elizabeth brushed the stray drop away with the ruffle of her sleeve hoping none noticed. Drawing a breath the young teacher turned and addressed the gathering.

"The school board, students, and I wish to welcome you to our end-of-year celebration, awards ceremony and of course graduation…." And so the event began.

When the simple ceremony had finished, a meal awaited them on the church lawn. Elizabeth asked her students to remain. Together they watched the adults file out of the building.

"Will you all sit please," she smiled at the familiar faces. "I want to tell you all just how proud I am. Each of you have achieved so much, I could not ask more. Ida, Jamie, and Homer the first three to graduate from this building. You will not be the last. I know that you will go on and reach even greater heights. As for the rest of you, your journey has not ended." Elizabeth drew a breath trying to control her emotions. "You have heard the rumors." She paused a moment to scan the faces of her students that filled the first two pews. "You know how I feel about rumors." Several heads nodded as all eyes focused upon her. "Now that the school year is officially completed, now I must tell you the talk you may have heard of my departure is true." Tears welled in her eyes as she looked into the young faces that seemed to go blank. "God leads us all on this grand adventure we call life. We have shared, this year, in that adventure," her voice cracked. "It is my hope that you will remember your teacher, for I will never forget you." Elizabeth blinked back her tears, swallowed, looked up an instant, then gave a weak smile. "Now your families are waiting, don't you think we should join them?" Her students rushed to her, surrounding, each reaching to touch her, as Elizabeth's tears flowed.

She remained in the church-school alone after hugging each of her students. Elizabeth drew a breath as her eyes moved about the room. Trying to hold back her tears, her mind filled with sounds and sights of the term threatened to undo her.

"They sent me to find you." The booming voice of Ben seemed to fill the entire space.

She tried to smile. "I'm sorry, Ben. It seems that I became lost in my memories." She expected him to remind her of a yet unfilled promised conversation.

"Do you need a few minutes?"

Elizabeth blinked, drew a breath. "No, Ben, I have taken too much time."

Ben swept his arm toward the door. "Shall we go?"

She had to chuckle. "Yes, the term has officially finished."

Chapter 45

Each parent came to Elizabeth, one by one, pleading she return. They spoke words like, "You're the best teacher we have ever had," or "My Susie has never done so well…" and other words of praise. Elizabeth could not find even a moment to herself, but that was understandable. But as she scanned about the crowd of faces of those who had become familiar, she could not find him. At last she asked Leah, "Where is Matthew?"

"He said he was tired and went home." Her friend's reply disappointed her.

Later when all had left, except the Smiths, Elizabeth smiled as she sat upon the steps of the school, feeling exhausted. But that happiness was mixed with other emotions. The teacher felt joy at the achievement of a completed term, the moment of pride when she sent those to try their own wings in the world. It was wonderful to share that time with such dear friends. But the day was bittersweet, for she would leave the valley with no intention of returning, returning to Misty Creek—returning to Matthew Sonnefelt.

Had Elizabeth been bolder, she would have allowed the Smiths to leave her there at the church-school and gone over to the mill to see him. But that was not a boldness Elizabeth possessed, and perhaps it was best she did not. For who could say she had the strength to leave? So Elizabeth rode the buckboard with the Smiths, they bore her to the Baughman's farm, to the place that had been her home, to the people she loved as family. As the sun began to set and the reality of her departure came crashing down upon her, those thoughts brought a very dark sadness that Albner and Alberta noticed. Though they observed her mood, the farmer and his wife remained cheerful, bless their hearts, and did not delve into matters they understood well enough.

Elizabeth did not see Matthew the days that followed. He did not come to church that last Sunday she was to be at Misty Creek. She feared to seek him out, afraid she would say words, words she longed to say, words she knew she should not say, words that would change everything, but the promise. That promise held the center of her mind those days. Though Leah had done her very best to assure Elizabeth that God would not bind her to those words. Yet Elizabeth felt it was best for the man, the tall man, the good man—the man she loved more than life itself, that she leave him free to find a joy she knew she could never give him.

On a Tuesday morning in early May, before the sun had fully broken the horizon, Elizabeth found herself at Peabody's Store. As that evening in September, the room, that was in so many ways a social center of the community, was packed. And as that evening, Mr. Clark made certain he was in charge. The big man, in his fancy suit, ordered folks about, and some actually following his instructions.

"Miss Beck." His strong voice rattled the windows. "We're real sorry to see you leave. As president of the school board, I, I mean we," he spoke with a grand flourish of his right hand, "ask that you reconsider your decision and return to us in September."

A blend of other voices could be heard.

"You have made us proud of our school, and we're real grateful." The man went on and on about the successful term, the valley's growth, and great many things including, at last, the weather. Whatever that had to do with the school or Elizabeth for that matter, she did not know. But she nodded in what seemed to be the right places and at long last Mr. Clark seemed to just run out of words. "Yes, Miss Beck, you have, you have…." And his speech was over.

Angst Morzinski, Harold Peabody, and Thomas Watkins, the remainder of the school board approached. Mr. Watkins took her hand. "I'd wish you'd come back to us."

"Please, Miss Beck," Angst added.

She swallowed as she looked at three of those that had become friends. But before she answered Mr. Peabody leaned in. "You have changed this place, Miss Beck. I 'spect you miss your family, but you're loved here too. The valley could be your home. Won't you please at least consider coming back to us?"

She looked into their pleading faces, drew a breath. "I will think about it, but know that I do not expect to change my mind. This valley is a wonderful place, filled with wonderful people. I am so pleased to have had this opportunity to live here."

"You done more than live here," Harold Peabody interrupted. "You're one of us now."

She turned away. Elizabeth wanted to bury her face with her hands, but blinking her tears aside, she did her best to remain strong. She swallowed and faced her friends.

"And you all have a special place in my heart," her words stumbled passed trembling lips. Though Elizabeth's mind was set upon what she must do, her heart yearned for an excuse, any reason to return to that place, to those people, and to Matthew.

Everyone, it seemed had come to see her off, everyone but Matthew. It was best, she told herself, as Mr. William Clark escorted her to the waiting freight wagon. Yet while she climbed to the seat, she searched through the faces for a tall man—a man on crutches—but he was not there.

The morning air held a dampness as they set out, seated upon the hard planks that made up the seat of the freight wagon, which was loaded with smooth white bags of cornmeal. Elizabeth turned back and waved with tears in her eyes as they crossed Misty Creek, leaving the town and its people behind. Neither spoke as they began the long journey. Ben's silence was out of character. Yet Elizabeth would not, could not, bring herself to speak. They approached the valley's edge with the hills known as the saddle before them, she saw a man in the distance at the roadside. Shading her eyes, Elizabeth made out a tall man, a true man, a man that leaned upon a crutch. How had Matthew come so far?

When they reached him, Ben pulled hard on the reins bringing the team to a stop. Elizabeth sat frozen, not knowing what she should do.

Ben locked the brake. "We'll ma'am, it seems the man has come to see you off," he said as he climbed down, strode to her side of the wagon, and offered his hand. But Elizabeth just sat, staring down at the man. The man that had saved her life. The man she loved. Her heart pleaded with her mind. Her heart screamed that she should leap from the wagon and throw her arms around him. And for the briefest of instants her heart took control. For the briefest of instants she firmed her grip, began to tighten the muscles of her legs, to lift out of the seat. For the briefest of instants she began to move, to climb down. But her mind regained its control, and she did not. Elizabeth sat on that wagon's seat while a very perplexed Benjamin Smith stood with arm outstretched.

"Mr. Sonnefelt," Elizabeth said, trying her best to calm the quiver in her voice. "You have wandered quite far this morning."

"Aye, ma'am."

Elizabeth felt hot tears building and was certain any moment she would begin to weep. "You're looking fit, Matthew."

He did not answer.

They remained staring at each other, he at the road's edge, she on the wagon's seat. "Safe journey," he said at last.

"I wish you much happiness, Matthew," Elizabeth said as the first tears began to form.

The miller touched the brim of his hat, as he had so many times before, turned, and began to hobble away. Ben, standing beside the team, glanced back and forth between the teacher and the miller, watching the scene unfold. He looked positively forlorn, which only added to her sadness.

At long last her pastor climbed back, released the brake, and took the reins. "You must believe that a person can bargain with God," the pastor said with a shaking head as they clattered along.

I don't understand what you mean," she responded through her tears.

"You think your misery is a price God demands for that man's life, as if you could force God to act for good or bad!"

"I made a promise!" she said, her voice trembling.

"No, on that you are mistaken! You struck a bargain. If this, then that. You cannot bargain with the Almighty!" he said, his voice booming.

"It is what it is. It is finished. There's nothing more to be done."

He pulled back on the reins and the wagon once more came to a stop.

She could see fire in his eyes. "Please, Ben, do not be so cross."

The pastor turned away and then said in a softer tone, "I see you making the biggest mistake of your life and blaming God, or using Him for your excuse." He looked back toward her. "Don't you see? Can't you see? It's because Leah and I love you. We care."

Yes, Elizabeth understood their intentions. Leah was her dear friend. They had bonded as sisters and surely Ben was as much brother as Albert at home.

He threw his arm around her as she wept. "Dear Elizabeth, do you love him that much?"

She nodded and cried all the more.

"Don't you think he should know? Shouldn't you tell him?"

She shook her head violently.

"What are you afraid of, dear Elizabeth?" the pastor said at last. "He's not like most men. He's not like any other man. Don't you think the choice should be his?"

"No," she wailed. "He may say something now, but in the end he will hate me. He will, and I just couldn't bear it. I couldn't bear the thought of that man I so love, hating me."

He snapped the reins and they began the journey again. When they reached the saddle, the very top, Elizabeth looked back for the last time, looked back at Misty Creek. And far off, a dark speck along the road, she saw him, and knew it was him, and knew deep in her heart Matthew was watching, and her heart broke, shattered once again for the love of a man -- a good man -- a tall man…

Elizabeth Beck's departure from the valley known as *Misty Creek* is not the end of her story. Her travels back to Columbus, Ohio only begins the next part of her life. In *Elizabeth's Journey*, she faces a time of growth and realization in unexpected ways.

Elizabeth's Journey, the follow-up novel to *Misty Creek.*

ACKNOWLEDGEMENTS

FIRST, I MUST SAY THANK YOU TO MY BELOVED JACKIE. YOUR faith in me has never faltered, and it was you that inspired *Misty Creek*, a story I wrote just for you. You remain the leader of my cheering section and I am unable to properly say how much you have done for this man of modest talents. Thank you!!!

Secondly, *Misty Creek* would not be in its present form without the unmeasurable aid I received from Kristina McBride Purnhagen, my editor and member of *Write Sisters Novel Consulting*. Your patience and careful coaching has helped me move from draft to draft...revise to revise. And in the process have become a friend I trust. Thank you.

Thirdly, all my writing friends far and near, especially those of the PAWW (Plymouth Indiana Writer's Workshop). How often I have leaned upon you all and have never been found wanting. Thank you.

Fourth, I wish to thank the amazing staff of Palmetto Publishing Group. You have given form to the dream *Misty Creek* has been for more than seven years. You have guided with all your questions, but listened to my words and together we have built a book...my book. Thank you all.

And I would be amiss if I did not thank the God that gave me these talents in the first place....

About the Author

John W. Vander Velden is graduate of Purdue University a retired farmer living with his wife and their small dog in northern Indiana. An avid reader and life long story teller, he approaches life with open eyes, hearing ears, and a heart willing to feel, striving to put to words the world he observes, in ways that reach deep within others. He has attended Antioch Writer's Workshop and is a member of Plymouth Area Writer's Workshop. John publishes weekly on his literary blog titled, *Ramblings… Essays and Such….*

Reach John by e-mail: jvandervelden86@gmail.com
Or follow the John W. Vander Velden Author's page on Facebook.

Made in the USA
Lexington, KY
02 February 2018